INVITATION TO TERROR

His roar shook the window. And for the first time ever, Gabriela was afraid of him.

"Damn you!" the monster-Marcus seethed, grabbing her shoulders with clawing fingers, jerking her like a sawdust prop mannequin. "Leave me be!"

"I won't," Gabriela cried. "I can't. I won't leave you, Marcus—not until you tell me what's going on."

To her surprise, he laughed then—a biting, bitter chuckle, baring locked, gleaming teeth. "So that is the game, then? You want to know 'what's going on?' "

The last, he spouted as if she'd begun a joke, but only he knew the finishing line. As he threw his head back and enjoyed the cruel jest, Marcus hauled her across the apartment, starting and stopping their journey in raging rushes of movement.

"Marcus." Gabriela winced, squirming in his increasingly constricting grip, "Marcus, you're hurting me—"

He laughed. "Too late for hurt now, sweeting." But when he stopped to tighten his hold on her, his mirth again descended into a beast's twisted glower. " 'Tis too goddamned late!"

They reached the opposite wall of the room, just four feet from the double doors Gabriela had entered through. Marcus flung back a wide Persian drape to reveal a second door to the apartment: smaller, more narrow, strangely suspicious. . . .

Utterly eerie.

"Come, you little fool," snarled her captor, as he kicked the door back into a narrow, unrelenting blackness. "Come with me to hell."

ROMANCE FROM JANELLE TAYLOR

ANYTHING FOR LOVE   (0-8217-4992-7, $5.99)

DESTINY MINE   (0-8217-5185-9, $5.99)

CHASE THE WIND   (0-8217-4740-1, $5.99)

MIDNIGHT SECRETS   (0-8217-5280-4, $5.99)

MOONBEAMS AND MAGIC   (0-8217-0184-4, $5.99)

SWEET SAVAGE HEART   (0-8217-5276-6, $5.99)

REDEMPTION

Annee Cartier

Pinnacle Books
Kensington Publishing Corp.
http://www.pinnaclebooks.com

PINNACLE BOOKS are published by

Kensington Publishing Corp.
850 Third Avenue
New York, NY 10022

First Printing: February, 1997
10 9 8 7 6 5 4 3 2 1

Printed in the United States of America

For Davis Gaines . . .
A special performer,
A special person.
Thank you for igniting life to Marcus
with the gift of your incredible talent!

AND

Special, Unequivocal Thanks
to the angel who believed in this book
beyond the call of duty:
Madeline Baker,
The gods smiled when they imagined you!

Big, BIG hugs of mucho gratitude to
the gang who put up with my "Marcus Obsession":
Dena Hawkins
Gail Link
Linda McLaughlin
You should all be nominated for sainthood. I love you.

One

Marcus found her. At last, after a bloody hour of pacing the catwalks and searching the chaos of sets, costumes, curtains, animals, and humanity below, he found her.

Now that he had, he did not veer his sights from her. She joined the mayhem by way of the greenroom door, flanked by two other actresses who shared her confident look of a successful preliminary rehearsal. Marcus nay blinked as he watched their bustled and beflounced forms trek across Drury Lane's stage. He nay blinked, and he nay breathed.

He felt the heat surge through his senses, centering behind his temples—as he expected it would, as he hoped it would not. Slow yet intense, the fire momentarily scorched away his vision, heralding the need and pain wracking him. As if he needed a reminder.

The resulting glow in his eyes would give him away like a lightning flare if she tilted her gaze an inch toward him, but Marcus cared naught. He stood there, as paralyzed as he'd been last night and the two months of nights before that, and watched her. And watched her.

And he remembered why he had given up on this insanity called feeling nearly three hundred years ago.

Loneliness was hell.

People weren't supposed to feel lonely with a hundred other people around. Gabriela Rozina ordered herself to

accept that rationality as she stopped at the center of
Drury's stage, in the midst of preparations for the show's
first all-cast rehearsal.

Yet as scenery whizzed by, stagehands shouted, the ballet
girls giggled, and Act Two's flock of lambs bleated on their
way to fulfill their cue, an uncontrollable, *un*rational emptiness surrounded her . . . an aloneness so complete she
might as well have stood on that wooden plane in solitary
blackness.

Circling to face the rows of unoccupied seats—the
"house," as management neatly classified it—didn't ease
her ache. And that, Gaby commiserated, tied her most con-
fusing knot. For the last two months, this sight hadn't given
her insides even a quiver, where once a glimpse of Drury's
magnificence set off flurries of joyous anticipation.

Yes, for two strange, sad months . . . ever since that afternoon she'd gone to Buckingham Palace. Ever since that
day she'd stood in the rain with a hundred other actors
and actresses, sharing their silent pleas for the arrival of
the notices signed by Victoria's own hand. . . .

The queen answered their supplications. At four o'clock
that day, the word became official: the Prince's Grand
Theatre Troupe would be transformed from ambition to
reality within a year. The finest works of English theater
would be rehearsed, then taken to every corner of the
globe welcoming them—performed only by a meticulously
selected company gleaned from the finest stages throughout the British Isles.

Imagine it, Gabriela had gasped along with the hopefuls
around her. A royally sanctioned company, cheered by
throngs in houses across the globe. . . .

It wasn't just the opportunity of a lifetime.

It was the chance to call the whole world *family.*

Affirmation. Approval. *Acceptance.* At last.

In short, it was the fulfillment of Gabriela's dreams. And
more.

Her heartbeat doubled as she simply thought about the Prince's Troupe again. But Gaby hurriedly ordered herself back under control. She could *not* fall into the trap of deluding herself. Shattered expectations were no longer her specialty. Not to mention that she'd not aimed her hopes at such a spectacular goal before . . . oh heaven's gates, could she earn the rank as one of Her Majesty's "meticulously selected" few? She didn't have all the experience. She didn't have all the credits.

But she had all the passion. And she cherished every ounce of the precious dream in her soul, where it mattered.

Somehow, Augustus Harris had seen that. Yes, *the* Augustus Harris, London's youngest and most innovative producer . . . and he'd decided she deserved a chance because of it. Far from a pumpkin-coach-and-glass-slipper chance, but it had landed her *here*, beneath the gas lights of London's most famous theater, rehearsing the first part "Augustus Druriolanus" himself cast her to.

There were times—many times—when Gabriela still couldn't believe the blessing. As Augustus's new protégée, she'd catapulted from "nothing" to "promising" in three months. *She* still felt the same, but a few daring journalists even began their raves in this week's papers, extolling Augustus's "fresh flower in the dying London theater garden."

So why now, of all times, did she feel like a sapped daisy, ready to be pressed and forgotten in a book? Why did this loneliness return each night, its gawky claws imprisoning her spirit, shredding the crumb of confidence in her soul?

Even at the age of seven, when only a chipped chapel bench comprised her stage and a dozen other orphans her audience, the anticipation of performing had stirred music through her blood. Each "show" orchestrated her heart in a chorus of fulfillment. She'd ached with the need to pour out her soul before a crowd, then accept the offering back brimming with their laughter, tears, and applause. Could there be any sweeter ecstasy on earth, any greater way to quell the emptiness that had yawned so deep and black since the day a five-year-old Gabriela had dropped tear-soaked daisies atop the fresh graves of her parents?

Just like the emptiness clinging to her now.

She tried to concentrate on warming up. While humming a series of vocal exercises, Gabriela read through her script again, taking note of pages with the underlines denoting her dialogue or prompts.

In truth, she labored unnecessarily. She'd memorized the scenes weeks ago. Augustus had, of course, reserved the female leads of the next three productions for the French diva gracing Drury with an extended visit, but the parts he assigned Gabriela were nonetheless a far cry from chorus girl. From the first rehearsal on, Gaby vowed to prove herself worthy of the honor.

Now she prayed she could satisfy that commitment.

"Ready for first cue?" a throaty voice asked at her shoulder.

Gabriela turned to meet the confident smile curling Donna's lush lips. Her roommate's name stood proxy for the actress's full stage title—"Donna, as in *Prima* Donna," she constantly reminded the tabloid writers—and Gabriela didn't think she knew a person who filled the flamboyant requirements of the persona more.

"I'll never be ready," Gaby tried to banter back, her nerves racing faster as Act One's ballroom backdrop unfurled from the flies over the stage.

"Oh, dove," her friend drawled, "none of us is ever ready." Donna looked ready to expound on that theory when her well-tapered eyebrows leapt by an inch, directing Gaby's sights to a figure approaching down the right aisle. "But Luuud," the woman amended on a sultry undertone, "at least you've got *that* on your side."

A bevy of squeals from the ballet coincided with Donna's appreciation of the top-hatted, leather-gloved blade striding closer on patent leather boots. Yet unlike her swooning castmates, Gabriela's tension climbed with every step those boots took. The sight of Alfonso Renard transformed her empty stomach into an acidic churn of dread.

Why, she lamented, tonight of all nights, did the man have to appear at a rehearsal he had nothing to do with? Why did he have to dissolve what poise she *had* garnered by forcing her to battle his lascivious paws? For being, in his own words, one of the city's "most up-and-coming producers," the lecher had an astounding amount of free time to take advantage of Augustus's hospitality—and actresses.

"Oh, he's good," Donna crooned, eyeing Renard's "bashful" wave at the dancers. "Modest, but manly. Sort of . . . Lancelot crossed with a bit o' the Black Irish."

Gabriela said nothing during another round of giggles and sighs. "Black?" she finally snorted. *"There's* an apt description at last."

She underlined the sentiment by jerking her script open and burying her face so far between the pages, the text blurred. If the dancers wanted the viper's attention, let them have it.

Her heart sagged when she heard Renard stride right by the giggling contingent. Her spirit plummeted to her toes when the rustle of his coat ceased at the edge of the stage . . . directly in front of her.

"Miss Rozina?" came that distinct, slick-as-oil voice. "Don't tell me you weren't even going to say hello."

Was it her imagination, or did the man's line evoke stagewide silence faster than Augustus's throatiest bellow? When she heard the ballet captain's gossipy whispers even from across the stage, Gaby knew the infuriating answer to that.

Slowly, she lowered the script and forced herself to meet the black, rapacious stare waiting at the stage's edge.

"Good evening, Mr. Renard." She managed the reply only by locking her back teeth.

A mock scowl fell across Renard's sharp features. "Come, come. It's just Alfonso, remember?"

She gripped her script tighter, certain her knuckles turned as white as the paper. "Alfonso."

His satisfied grin replaced the frown. The ballet loosed another collective sigh. Gabriela struggled to take a decent breath of air. It wasn't easy—especially when he reached beneath his overcoat to produce an eye-popping bouquet of red tulips and roses.

Then even the blasted lambs fell into silence.

"I've brought you a gift," her visitor murmured into the expectant pause.

Gabriela released a long, heavy breath. The man's smirk didn't falter.

"Mr. Renard—"

"Alfonso."

"Stop it!" He hadn't crossed the line of her patience—he'd demolished it. Finally willing to brave the titters from the orchestra, Gaby stomped down the stage's temporary steps and hissed, "I have made it perfectly clear that I will not accept your gifts!"

Renard's only response: a perfectly remorseless shrug. "Oh, little Gaby. I apologized for the pearls, did I not?"

"After I threw them in your face."

The man had the grace to color. "That's water in another tide now, isn't it? Now, these blooms . . . think nothing of them but what they mean—"

"Another lure into your bed?"

He chuckled. "You're witty today, dear. They are but a tiny reminder of my admiration. A fleeting token of my wishes—"

"I don't want them."

"For your good luck."

Gabriela's snag of breath preceded everyone else's by

just seconds. *Devil take him*. He'd done it now, and his impeccable, cocky grin showed it. To wish a performer "good luck" anywhere near the theater, let alone three steps from the bloody stage, boded certain failure to the performance.

To undo the damage, for the entire cast's sake, she'd have to take his wretched flowers. And the knowing kiss he trailed on the back of her hand when she reached for them. And the possessive, almost brutal rake of his eyes over her body as she turned the blooms over to a stage boy.

"There, now." He leaned and whispered it into her ear as the final dagger in the ordeal. "That wasn't so bad, was it?"

Gabriela willed herself to breathe, though it meant suffering Renard's opulent cologne. For only then did she gain the strength to reply in a voice dripping with acid-laced honey: "If you must know, sir, it was as pleasant as letting a maggot kiss me. And if you dare such an underhanded stunt on me again, I promise I'll dispense of your roses, and their thorns, in an area due much farther south of your pretty face."

She only made one mistake with the proclamation: firing the words so near him. Alfonso coiled a furious hand around her elbow before Gaby could step away. But even if the man ripped her arm out of its socket, she willed her gaze to remain steady, her posture proud.

"You used to welcome my face," he finally growled.

"And you used to be a kind and considerate friend."

"Friend?" He spat and laughed the word at once. His endless black glare bore into her, teeming with the force of his acrimony. "You little fool, Gabriela. Don't you know me yet? I have no need for *friends*. I'm not a milksop who wastes my money or manners on enterprises that won't pay me well in the end. That's why I'm going to be bigger than your precious Augustus someday. I'll produce the biggest plays London has known, with the biggest ticket take, as well."

"That's splendid." Though her throat quivered with the effort, the retort flowed with a cool disdain even Victoria would applaud. "I do, however, apologize that I won't be in London to see this conquest."

Gaby should have expected his answering tremor of fury. And the bruise he twisted tighter into her arm. Nevertheless, she notched her chin higher, clenching back the wince of pain clawing in her throat.

Then, strangely, Renard laughed—a low, mocking snort. "The lady won't be here," he repeated. "I see. So we're still entertaining our pipe dream of stardom with the Prince's Grand Theatre Troupe?"

It was the one slur she couldn't deflect with a shield of composure. The one barb able to penetrate her soul and deflate it into a mass of raw vulnerability. "What do you know of dreams?" Gaby rasped. "What do you know of beliefs or hope?"

Renard laughed again. The sound ripped Gabriela deeper than any audition dismissal she'd ever been dealt.

"I only know that most dreams don't come true," he sneered. "So why you pine away to join that company, royally sanctioned or not, is beyond me."

"And it is beyond me why every performer, producer, and stagehand in Town is *not* vying to win a place with the Prince's Troupe."

Gaby couldn't help it. As her mind's eye succumbed to the vision, her limbs gave up their battle against Renard. Yes, the vision . . . the adventures and images she'd dreamed so many times, she often wondered if she'd been born with them.

"Don't you see?" she said then. "Don't you realize the feat they plan to accomplish? Only the finest English works will be showcased, from Shakespeare and Marlowe to opera and musicals. And the entire world will be waiting . . .

the entire world will remember the performers who take these works to them. It's a chance to inspire thousands, perhaps millions, across the globe."

"But you can be an inspiration right where you are." Renard's soft protest blew into her ear again. "You inspire *me,*" he continued in a coarse murmur. "Can't you think of it, dear Gaby, even now? My brilliant scripts and staging, complimenting your hot-blooded Italian delivery—"

"My hot *what?*" She shoved from him with a stiff lurch. Something akin to nausea quirked her stomach. "Wh-what does my blood have to with anything?"

The man actually tossed another chuckle at her. "You little vixen," Renard teased. "As if you didn't know. Gabriela, you'll seduce all of England on my stage . . . all that Italian passion, inspired by the private lessons you'll receive in my arms. We'll be unstoppable together. Just think of it!"

But Gabriela thought of nothing but the bile roaring up her throat, the need to find a hot bath and scorch away the shame his words encrusted over her. She yearned to flush back the outrage and hate she thought she'd tucked away into one rarely visited cubicle of memory. . . .

Aye, that's right; her seventh birthday tomorrow, Parson Reeves. That will make two years she's been here at the orphanage with us. Such a delightful child. What's that? Oh aye, you be right again, that does makes it harder to discourage her dreams. And she always dresses so pretty when the families come, looking to adopt. But it's that tainted blood of hers. Parson. It's so . . . obvious. *That thick Italian hair. Those eerie Italian eyes. The girl can see straight to my soul with those eyes, I'm certain of it. It's too bad. Just too bad.*

Gabriela gained her freedom from Renard's talons with one desperate, despising shove. Then she ran. She ran from the loneliness and the fear, and she didn't stop.

* * *

Marcus had known something was wrong. He suspected from the instant Gabriela turned to the house and just . . . well, just *looked* at it tonight. Usually, it was as if Christmas morning occurred for her each night beneath those lights, the gold flecks in her almond eyes as luminous as the gas glow surrounding her. He knew that expression well. He'd memorized the sight.

But the popinjay with the flowers didn't see anything. Even now, when she bolted from the man as if he had sprouted leprosy, he just lifted a calm brow at the ballet chits who still swooned at him. Finally the clod began to stroll after her, as if retrieving a recalcitrant puppy, not an angel he was blessed to have on loan from heaven. Marcus decided the man was daft, dangerous or as dead as—

He grappled to cut the thought short. No use. His brain finished with relentless surety: *as dead I am.*

He spun and raced back along the catwalk, as if the words were wasps giving chase—for an instant, wishing they were. He would verily welcome the stinging onslaught, if he could feel it. He would invite the pain, if it replaced the sensations she'd so exquisitely forced upon him in the last two months. All this wanting and dreaming, this confusion and frustration—

What the *hell* was wrong with him? He had never encountered trouble distancing himself from any mortal, physically or mentally, since he had made the mistake of trusting a doe-eyed Hungarian farm girl in the early seventeenth century, and found himself stalked by the whole of her crucifix-bearing village.

After that, it had been no grand feat to discern the obvious: losing control would mean losing his life.

Losing control made him into this beast to begin with.

The reminder fortified him at the right moment. Reaching the end of the catwalk, Marcus faced the choice of the secret walkway over the dressing rooms, to his right, or the ledge over the now-empty greenroom, to his left. A half dozen strides would land him over the dressing room Gabriela Rozina assuredly locked herself into at this very moment.

Marcus turned toward the greenroom.

He dropped onto the dark ledge with a weary but grateful sigh. He usually visited the greenroom later in the evening, as the cast filtered in to relax after rehearsals or performances. He greedily eavesdropped on their rowdy regalements, for the simple assurance that he could still laugh at a joke or feel compassion at a tragedy.

Then Gabriela had come, and shown him he could feel far more than that. Before she had even entered the room on that fateful night—was it only a day over eight weeks ago?—his preternatural psyche whirled into chaos, rejoicing in the kinship he immediately sensed in her lonely soul, but warring against the life she provoked him to feel again . . . the hope she dared him to believe in. A hope he had nay needed or wanted in a long, long time. . . .

"No," he gritted, shoving the memory away.

God's teeth. Coming here had been a bad idea, after all. He shoved up from the ledge, preparing to head back along the catwalks, toward home.

His legs buckled on his first step. His heartbeat slammed a sudden timpani roll in his chest.

Ah, God. He was in trouble this time. Just like that first night, but a hundredfold more intense, he felt her—he felt her coming nearer, fast. He smelled her; her warm, smoky stage scents blended with pearl powder and female essence, the way he had breathed her in so many times, when he allowed his mind to wander in fantasy. Only now she wasn't fantasy. . . .

She dashed into the greenroom, but didn't turn up the dimmed lamp. She whipped an angry circle around the faded couch, marking each step with a vibrant huff. She stopped on another sharp breath and clawed errant tendrils of thick, dark auburn hair from her flushed face. A vein beat wildly in her neck.

Marcus barely contained his agonized growl.

He wanted her. Sweet Jesu, he wanted her. Her body, perfectly formed for his. Her spirit, searching for the answers his could give. Her life, her dreams, such lights in the darkness of his.

And her blood . . .

He opened his mouth, struggling for the right words, for once wishing that a mortal—*this* mortal—was under his unearthly power, and he could just close his eyes and will her to his side. *But I shall not do it,* his soul shouted to her. *I cannot! Damn you, damn you, Gabriela—*

"Gabriela!"

The command jolted the lamp's glass chimney. And her.

"Gabriela . . ." Marcus repeated in a whisper, his voice an echo of the odd trepidation he felt in her as she tugged at the pleated lace in her skirt.

She dropped her hand an instant before the popinjay appeared in the doorway. In that moment, full comprehension slammed Marcus—she was nay nervous, she was afraid. The scent of her fear reached him between her sweet talc and the intruder's cologned stench.

But a man needed no superhuman senses to decipher her widened eyes or the darts of her tongue over her lips. *This* bastard still nay seemed to see her anxiety—or care.

"We aren't finished yet," the popinjay growled.

"The devil we aren't," she retorted. Then trying again, softer, "Alfonso, just . . . just leave me alone. We're two different people, with different ideas—"

"No. No, *not* different." The clod stepped forward, arms coiled across his chest. "Gabriela, don't you see? We're so much alike, it's frightening. Why don't you just admit it? Why don't you just give in to what you want?"

She stopped tugging at her skirt. Her hands curled into

tight white fists. "You don't know a thing about what I want."

Renard cocked a knowing smirk. "Oh, really?"

"Stop it! Can't you just stop it? I know I *don't* want you, your plays, or your version of stardom. Not at your filthy price."

Silence. Then, slowly and mockingly, "Then what do you want, Gabriela?"

Another pause brewed, simmering with her tension. She turned and looked away again, looked *up*, as if pleading to a higher power. She nearly found Marcus, instead, still fallen to the catwalk beyond his ledge. But like second nature, the ability to move like mist came to him again; he slid back into the shadows with less noise than a puff of fog.

She looked back down. And answered the clod with three words that echoed in Marcus's soul with the terrifying ring of memory, from when he had uttered them himself lifetimes ago. . . .

"I want more."

Another heartbeat of silence thumped by.

Then the popinjay exploded in laughter.

Marcus tried to emulate her incredible show of will. He tried to clench back the lust to swoop down on the sadistic boor and rip that vile head from that vain body. But like a fool struggling in quicksand, the more he fought, the more he fed the ugly force. He was lost. He was thirsty, so thirsty.

He was damned.

"Gabriela," he grated as he spun and stumbled away. Too far gone with the madness to waste his sight on the inky shadows of the catwalks, he groped his way to the stairs, the blessed stairs that would take him back to darkness. "Oh Gabriela, I would kill the bastard for you!"

And for me. I would kill him for me, and I should love doing it.

Gabriela—Gabriela, what are you doing to me?

Did it only seem eternity until he reached the bottom of the stairwell and clawed his way to end of the dank, subterranean passage? Did his own breathing rage in his ears like the pantings of a beast too long starved? Were those his hands before his eyes, fumbling to turn the copper key in the lock of the huge oak door, slipping because they dripped with his saliva?

God . . . God, was this the hell his existence had come to?

He finally managed the lock and burst through the portal with a groan. He folded to the stone floor in a mass of gasps and emotion and icy sweat. For long minutes, he remained that way, attempting to soak in the calming effect of the black, damp air in the deep-buried chamber.

The calmness never came. But a measure of strength returned. With it, Marcus pushed to his feet and staggered to the small rise of packed dirt dominating the dark room.

And the open coffin waiting on top of the mound.

As he tumbled inside and lay back against the cool satin, his looming fatigue battled savage despair. "Gabriela," he whispered once more, knowing his mind, even in its exhaustion, called out to her, too. And knowing, despite the hyperhuman power he could summon to any muscle in his undead body, that she'd no more hear or respond to his thoughts than she would a wisp of wind.

Only one feat could make that possible. And he'd never subject her to that debasement . . . that depraved act . . . that repulsive confirmation of the sick creature he was. *Never.*

The injustice of it all reignited him in fury. Marcus clawed out at that tormenting sensation with a snarl, lifted a fist to it with a roar.

Only desperate echoes answered from the black world beneath London. Inviolable dark surrounded him once more.

"Damn you," he said to her then. *"Damn you,* Gabriela. I won't let you do this to me. I cannot. *I cannot."*

Gabriela . . . ah God, Gabriela . . . I shall not let you turn me into a monster!

Two

"I won't let him do it to me again."

Gabriela underlined her declaration with a jab of carmine to her chin. But upon surveying her handiwork in the dressing room mirror, she found Haresfoot and Rouge's advice, from their "acclaimed" *Practical Guide to the Art of Making-Up,* utterly useless. The color worked no miracle on her pale and glowering face.

Donna didn't lift her mood by sliding into the other chair before the glass, already the picture of glamorous serenity an hour before the opening night curtain's scheduled rise.

"Now, dove," her friend cooed, absently toying with an errant copper curl. "I don't understand your frostbite toward the man at all. Renard doesn't pick his teeth or his nose, dresses better than Prince Eddie, then showers *you* with gifts befitting a princess—"

"With his personal price tag attached to each," Gaby shot back.

Donna threw her head back on a husky laugh. "So?"

"So, despite what the better portion of London thinks about the women of our 'trade,' I am *not* on the market."

She emphasized the retort with such a stab of frustration, her camel's hair eye brush slipped and slid down her cheek. While Donna's chuckles sprinkled the air, Gaby sighed and redoused the area in pearl powder. "One laughs at *farce,* my friend," she said then, "not tragedy. Not *this* tragedy." She straightened, laid the cosmetics down and confronted her own determined gaze in the mirror. "Bloody blast, Donna. We are *not* interchangeable commodities, to be written into any producer's portfolio at whim—"

"The hell we aren't."

Gabriela's gaze shot to the side—where her friend's heavy-lashed observations met her in the mirror. A faint smile loosened the red bow of Donna's lips.

"Gaby," she queried softly, "what do you think you're doing here?"

A tenuous pause fell—ended when Gaby jerked her chin back up. "I'm doing my job. Improving my craft, in the best way I can."

"Fine. You can call it that. You can even call it art, or magic . . . but under any title, it's all still an illusion."

At that, Donna looped a long-nailed finger back at the mirror. "That illusion, my friend, is what London pays to see. It's what the producers will pay *us* well to see." Another worldly-wise chuckle. "How do you think we got a nearly free lease on a two-bedroom Mayfair flat? Where do you think my fur parka came from? My ruby earrings?"

"Stop." Gabriela bounded out of her chair in a rustle of well-crinolined costume. "I don't want to hear any more."

A soft tsking began behind her—the metronome of Donna's aggravation. "Oh, dove. I know I haven't been *that* discreet with my little . . . assignations. And you cannot be *that* sound a sleeper."

"I'm not." Gaby turned to where her opening scene costume hung, tried to busy herself straightening the fringe of forest green beads along the sleeves. The turn of this whole conversation unnerved her. Despite Donna's affectionate nickname, Gabriela was not a mindless dove;

she knew what happened when a man and a woman kissed in a certain way . . . then touched in certain places. . . .

Those caresses led to feeling certain things. Sometimes, when heaven smiled upon the destined lovers, magical things. But those feelings led to doing certain other things. Actions that caused irrevocable results. Results like a baby. A baby who grew into a child; a child who could be beautiful and bright, cared for and cherished—

Or orphaned. Or abandoned. Despite the best intentions of all, sentenced to an existence marked only by days of loneliness and nights of tears. . . .

"Look." She laughed in an effort to banish the dark memories. "I know about your amusements, Donna. And I don't mind them." She faced the mirror again. "But that's your life, not mine." A sigh escaped her on a traitorous quaver. "It . . . it won't ever be mine."

One of Donna's perfect brows arched. "You don't ever want steady work, beautiful clothes, and exciting companionship?"

"Oh, I *will* succeed." The statement didn't wobble a note this time. "But I want a success different from yours." Then the mirror transformed into a glassy garden, full of fertile soil for the seeds of her expanding, exhilarating visions. "Oh Donna," Gaby said on a fervid murmur, "I dream different dreams . . ."

"Ah, yes," the other woman drawled. "How could I forget? The Prince's Grand Theatre Troupe. Your 'opportunity of a lifetime'; isn't that how you phrased it to my understudy yesterday?"

Gabriela waited a long, telling moment before slowly turning back to her friend.

"I will obtain an audition with that company, Donna." She leveled each word the same way she meted out her gaze—with unfaltering conviction. "And I'll astound them . . . somehow. I have to. I don't care what stories Renard is telling the rest of the cast; I don't care if they

all think me the next candidate for the freak show. I will
do it—no matter what it takes."

"Now, dove." Donna tsked again. "I didn't say you
wouldn't. But Alfonso Renard . . . Gaby, the man is a *thor-
oughbred*. And he wants to make you his star. He wants to
do it now!"

"I already told you. I don't want to be his star."

With the flashing grace of a tigress, Donna jumped from
her chair now. Curling hands to her gold satin-skirted hips,
she gave Gabriela a stare-down of equally feral fervency.
"Then by Saint Genesius, Gabriela, what do you want?"

Gaby opened her mouth, but pressed it shut again. The
answer both flooded and eluded her at the same time. But
she smiled at the bittersweet incongruity, because she
sensed—no, she *knew* that somehow, the disparities formed
a truth; they molded into the unshakable belief that something incredible awaited her, in a place even more wondrous and beautiful than Drury's glory. And that, just
perhaps, a magical someone awaited her there. . . .

And from that soul-deep conviction, her answer came
at last. She gave it in a voice clear and strong, and filled
with the power of unbreakable dreams.

"I want the world, Donna. And I'll have the world . . .
but I'll have it with my soul intact."

"I refuse to put up with any more of this nonsense,
Gabriela."

Renard's ultimatum echoed effortlessly through Drury's
empty house. Aye, even up to the fifth tier box Marcus
confined himself to in hopes of rendering himself deaf to
the now-nightly confrontations—and the fury these epi-
sodes summoned inside him again . . . this violent appetite
he was so bloody sure he had quelled two and a half centuries back. . . .

But nay. As he rose and leapt from the box down to the

passage over the dressing rooms, he actually had to concentrate on controlling his ire. He had to think about his
steps along the way, steps that used to be gracefully silent.
He forced the raging acid in his throat to erupt a hiss, not
a snarl.

Amazing, he thought with a wry grunt. Three months
ago, he could nay remember how to growl, let alone snarl.

His body tensed as he stopped over the space Gabriela
shared with that Donna creature. He found himself shaking with the desire to bury killing claws into the shoulders
of the hulk who loomed over her now, instead.

"You are not being asked to put up with anything,"
Gabriela told the bastard then. Marcus's muscles constricted harder. The strain in her voice stood out as clearly
as the fatigue lines around her mouth. "As a matter of
fact, *sir,* I should have had you barred from backstage long
ago," she continued, "but out of deference to your friendship with Augustus, I have been more than tolerant. My
tolerance, however, has reached its limit. So good night."

She started for the door, clearly to show him out or quit
the room herself. But in one savage sweep, the hulk yanked
her elbow and flattened her against the wall.

"It's not going to be that easy," he leveled. "Not tonight,
Miss Rozina."

Marcus lurched forward, but stopped when Gabriela
fought back with twists worthy of the most vicious snake
in India. "Let—me—go."

"Not until I get some answers. Not until you tell me how
much longer these after-hours stunts will continue."

"Rehearsals," she snapped. "For the last bloody time, I've
been staying after performances to *rehearse.* "

"For three weeks straight?"

"Yes!"

Renard released a weighted huff. "Gabriela, you've gone
over the line."

"And you, Mr. Renard, don't draw my lines."

"Damn it, your castmates agree with me!"

Reflexively, her eyes widened. Mercilessly, the bastard seized the opening of her surprise. He leaned harder against her, lowering his voice to a soft but severe cadence. "Now why does that surprise you, darling? Nobody sees you any more. You hardly wave your hand past the green-room every night. They don't just call you the cast eccentric any more. You're now the cast lunatic."

Marcus yearned to roar a bravo at the glare she raised in response, a copper and gold sensation of defiance. "Because I'm bettering myself and my craft? Because I'm pursuing my dreams?" Another silent cheer to the derisive laugh she shot at the bastard. "They're rehearsals for my audition piece, not seances. You know rehearsals, Alfonso? Practicing until one gets the thing perfect? It's a concept you might want to try sometime."

Renard's grip visibly tightened on her. "And you might want to try looking at this Prince's Grand Troupe as the garbage it is, and resign yourself to the role you were meant to play."

"In your bed?"

"For a start."

"I'll be dead first."

"Be careful what you wish for, darling."

Marcus started forward again. It was nay the whoreson's threat as much as the undercurrent of tone—the malevolence so strong it slashed through senses, ripping a violent, protective instinct through Marcus's mind, clouding his vision red. He shook his head just enough to clear his sight, so he could aim his attack on the bastard correctly—

But his gaze refocused in time to watch Gabriela beat him to the task. Her knee cut a swift jerk up between the man's legs. Renard's gut-deep moan filled the dressing room. Gabriela stepped out of the lout's way as he crumpled to the floor, snapping her skirts out of his path.

Finally, she cleared her throat and raised her chin, yet

pointed an unfaltering stare back down at the groaning heap.

"Well," she said on a satisfied breath, "I am truly happy we cleared that up, Mr. Renard. But ah, yes"— she flicked a three-inch swath of skirt back at him—"one further item. Please be notified that if you refer to my work as 'garbage' again, you'd better pray you've bedded half of London, because you won't be able to again."

And without looking back, she reached for a script on the dressing table, a lace shawl hanging over the dressing screen. "I pray you have a good evening, Mr. Renard," she commented with so much respect, the Shah of Persia might have sat clutching his groin at her feet. "I am now very late for my *rehearsal*. Good night."

Marcus raced her to the main stage via the catwalks, wondering when the overhead paths had become so frustratingly complex. A faint remembrance came of that night, seemingly so long ago, when he condemned her and himself and sworn off the sight of her forever. But he was like an opium addict who knew bloody well what he did, yet could nay control his self-destruction. The need to see her, to watch her in all her furious glory and life, had become an unthinking obsession.

He could only liken the feeling to distant memories of mortal lust. As he found a dim but open-viewed corner formed by Catwalk Five and the House Curtain, his heartbeat pounded a cannon rhythm; he clenched his thighs against the agonizing, joyous arousal at their juncture.

But the sensation, as wondrous and exhilarating as it struck, was temporary.

When Gabriela appeared, his senses overflowed beyond desire. His mind detonated beyond thought. His body detached from his awareness and soared beyond his control. A tight, agonized groan escaped his throat, despite his effort at restraint.

Dear God. This woman would burn him alive long ere he saw the sun again.

"Someday," Gabriela spat as she stalked out onto the stage from the greenroom, "I'm going to burn Alfonso Renard alive."

The angered beat of her stomps reverberated in the wings, and her bloodstream. She forced herself to halt at the House Curtain line and take several breaths, hoping the action would somehow cleanse the grime clogging her senses, scrape her skin clean where Alfonso's touch lingered in all its foul glory.

She froze when a pain-filled moan echoed around her.

For ten more seconds—tormenting eternities each one—Gabriela didn't breathe. Then she spun toward the open greenroom door and demanded, "Who's there?"

Only a shaft of hazy yellow gaslight spilled from the portal . . . just as it had last night *and* the night before, when this same heart-pounding sensation had also washed over her. The same feeling she'd attempted to describe to Donna three weeks ago, as if an "extra sense" waited just beyond her reach, filled with sights, sounds, scents, and perceptions she'd never experienced before.

Only the feeling never possessed a voice before . . . a voice that groaned. Over all these nights, she'd never been tempted to assign the feeling anything close to an identity, thinking if she called out again, something . . . somebody . . . might answer back from the darkness.

She wouldn't call the sensation fear. She'd never be afraid here, beneath the lights and standing on the floorboards that served, for all intents and purposes, as home. No, this awareness stemmed from something else. . . .

"Oh, yes," she wryly agreed with herself. "An awareness three notes short of Bedlam."

She laughed at that, and the sound drifted into the

blackness shrouding the seats beyond the tenth row. No groan echoed back this time. But invisible fingers seemed to reach out and pull at her, encircling her waist . . . and, for the first time in months, finally filling the empty core of her with a strange but stirring warmth. . . .

Oh, this warmth . . .

This warmth!

Gabriela heard herself laugh again. Her eyes slid shut. Her head rocked back. Her whole body reveled in the magnificent, miraculous heat, flaring farther inside her, reaching straight for her soul. Flowing flames. Fantastical fires. Liquid lightning . . .

What in the world was happening to her?

She slammed her eyes open and whirled back toward the greenroom. When her foot slipped out from beneath her, her apprehension erupted on a panicked shriek. Yet common sense took over with relieving speed; she regained her posture and emitted a mild oath, instead.

"Bloody leaking roof." Gaby examined her twisted ankle. "Somebody's going to kill themselves on one of these puddles."

She regretted the remark instantly. With her words came the repetition of another observation, like a demon haunting her mind: *Be careful what you wish for, darling.* . . .

"Stop it," she commanded her rampaging imagination. "Stop it and get to work. Phantom voices and misplaced rain puddles are no excuse for the sorry state of this audition piece, Miss Rozina."

With determined haste, she pulled the script from beneath her arm and smacked it open. Then she cleared her throat and read from the top of the page in a strong, sure voice. *"Hamlet, Act Three.* All right, Denmark, here I come."

And, beginning to recite the three-hundred-year-old dialogue, she climbed into the heart and soul of a maid named Ophelia . . . sort of. Oh, blast it, she tried. But every line came as clumsy as a elephant's minuet; every inflection she tried ended with a violent shake of her head and a muttered beratement against either her childish pitch or her forced delivery.

Finally, eyes feeling like they contained half the sand of the Sahara, she declared the rehearsal yet another fruitless effort. With a frustrated sigh, Gabriela made the trek back to her dressing room.

Once there, she turned the lamp halfway up and sank heavily into the corner chair. She wished Donna were here. But a glance at the table clock placed her friend deep beneath the covers of her satin-blanketed bed . . . or about to climb there with somebody else. The thought, which normally brought a squirming discomfort in Gaby's chest, caused a different, but even more intimidating reaction tonight.

The feeling insisted on calling itself loneliness.

"No," she dictated to her thoughts again, setting her chin as if the force were a physical assailant.

She looked to the clock again. There on the table, in the shadow of the soft-ticking hands, she gratefully discovered the weapon to keep her solitude at bay. Her leather journal invited her attention. She'd neglected her entries in the past week, as the news of Harris's "latest theatrical success" had spread across London, turning her life into an unstopping frenzy. Now the book came as her ideal confidante in this silent hour.

Gabriela found the next blank page in the journal, shook the ink loose in her pen, and settled deeper into the chair. This would take a while. She had much to share regarding the last few whirlwind days.

But ten minutes later, the page still loomed white and blank. She tried to summon words—and words came—but the ink scrolling them across her mind came with slow, evil surety, carving in each syllable like the steady glide of some heathen torture master's blade. . . .

See it all for the garbage it is, Gabriela, and resign yourself to your true role.

He wants to make you a star, Gaby. Steady work and beautiful clothes.

Your true role, by my side . . . your true role, in my bed.

"No." Her fist trembled around the pen. "I know where I belong. I know what I want! Why don't any of you believe it?"

Why was she the only one who believed?

And why, so suddenly, did it hurt so much to believe alone?

She sucked in a breath, struggling to reclose the lock on her emotions, but in that moment, it didn't matter. She didn't care. She didn't want to fight; she didn't want to believe anymore. She was tired and discouraged and lonely . . . *yes, so lonely.*

The lock sprang open. The tears came. She let the pen and the journal slide to the floor, curling in on herself as the pain stormed the barricades of her heart.

Gabriela had no idea how high she'd fortified those ramparts, until she gave herself permission to let them down. Her sobs filled the room, but stopping the release was as impossible as damming the Atlantic. It felt horrible. It felt wonderful. She wanted to die.

"Nay. Nay, you do not want to die."

Her cries caught in her throat. The voice, she thought . . . *that* voice. The same ghostly, but silken tone behind the moan over the stage . . . she was certain of it!

Dear God. Alfonso was right. I'm insane. Raving starkers. The Prince's Grand Troupe will never want me now.

The thought made her cry harder.

"God and the angels," the ghost muttered. "I pray you to cease, sweeting. Or 'twill be but moments before you drown in your tears."

"So what if I do?" she choked.

The ghost, believe it or not, also had a laugh. His

chuckle rumbled over her like a distant thunderstorm, powerful but musical. "I should have to haul you out of the puddle, you nit. And I am nay partial to saltwater."

"So let me drown."

"I could nay do that."

"The devil you couldn't!"

"Do not shout. 'Tis not good for your voice."

"Stop it!" she shrieked. She balled fists at her temples, yearning to beat this insanity out of her. "Stop it, just stop it! You're not real! I'm not insane! And it's not all garbage, it's my dream! I'm not . . . insane . . . I'm not!"

"Oh, sweeting." Now the voice returned to its near-groan. Gabriela pulled tighter in on herself, trying to ward off the aching seduction of that voice, so rife with grief, as if experiencing this sorrow right along with her. Dear Lord, he sounded so *real.*

"Gabriela," the dream called again, "do not cry. You are more sane than the bloody lot of them. I shall kill them all if they say naught."

"But you're not real. You're just—"

Raw shock sucked the rest of the outcry off her lips. Somewhere between one sob and the next, a hand brushed her tear-soaked hair off her neck . . . brushed it back across her scalp, cradling and soothing, warming and caressing.

A real hand. A gentle, powerful, wonderful and very real hand.

Her heart stopped. Her head snapped up.

Lightning struck her world.

She'd yearned for him so many times—invoking him in the realm of her fantasies, where the world at last under-stood her, and the world was nothing but him. Yet those daydreamed concoctions didn't do justice to the man fill-ing her vision now. Thunder-black hair slashed against his strong forehead and his straight-cut jaw; the dark cascade rained to just inside the collar of his white shirt. And oh, that *shirt*—or more appropriately, the V of dark chest muscle the material folded back to reveal, down to where a rugged black vest took over, blending into rust-colored breaches and black laced-up boots that outlined each hard inch of his thighs and legs so well, Gaby felt herself blushing at the masculine glory of him.

But the power of the lightning came from his eyes. Dear God, the force of his stare, almost *glowing* at her, in a color she could only label . . . silver. Every thought she'd ever had, every dream she'd yearned to fill, every desire she'd ever known . . . he held them there, in his eyes, in his soul.

"Oh, my God," Gabriela rasped. Her fingers flew to her tremoring lips. "Oh, my God."

Three

Words spun in Marcus's head—so many things he wanted to say, so many sensations begging for release. Nothing broke past his motionless lips.

Mayhap that was for the better. Mayhap he could disappear while she still sat in her shocked daze, relegating himself to the realm of simple hallucination in her mind's eye, permanently correcting this disaster his stupidity created in the first place.

Bloody hell, how *had* this happened? Three weeks ago, he had avowed never to look at her again. And tonight, merely the sight of her unhinged his fatal groan over the stage. Just the sound of her weeping froze every nerve in his body like January icicles. So he had come to her; he had come as swiftly as every extrahuman muscle in his body could manage. . . .

To face the biggest terror he had ever known. The terror of staying with her. The terror of ever leaving again. The dread of shattering this moment in any way at all—this miracle of sitting here as the sole object of her shivering stare, beholding him as if he were a god and not the sickening opposite.

No! his soul snarled at that hope . . . at her. *Do not look. I am a monster. I want your blood as bad as I want your exquisite soul. Run from me. Run and end this ordeal before we are both annihilated.*

Gabriela nay moved.

Damn her.

Ah, God, damn her for the beautiful stare she unleashed upon him, those rich copper depths not just mirroring, but *absorbing* the unhuman silver beacon of his. Damn her for the joyous tears slipping down her cheeks, for the fervent tremble of her lips. Damn her for her unknowing, unrelenting sensuality as she rose from the chair and slid a trusting step toward him.

No! He flinched back from her outstretching hand. *Do not trust me. Do not look at me!*

"Who . . . who are you?" she whispered.

I am a freak. Get back. I shall love you. I shall kill you.

"Are you real? Or am I just dreaming again? Please . . . oh, please tell me I'm not dreaming."

Oh, God.

You are nay going anywhere now, Marcus Danewell. Her words held him like velvet-covered chains; her outstretched fingers slung invisible ropes around his gut.

"Dreaming," Marcus echoed on a gruff, awkward laugh. "If it were only that simple."

Her lips parted on a tearful sigh. Marcus's fists clenched in fury and remorse. Apparently, no matter how violent his effort at control, her mind had fallen prey to the psychic influence of his. She could nay be experiencing this battle of exhilaration and terror on her own.

But then she reached to take his hand.

A wolf's snarl escaped him, pure instinct, before he could check the reaction. They both jerked back, breathing hard.

Marcus wrapped his hand around the knuckles her fingers had brushed. He wanted to hold the heat of her there forever. He wanted to push her energy through his skin and make it flow through his body, his heart. He wanted her life pulsing inside him.

He wanted to be inside her.

The thought slammed him back, firing a strangely *mortal*

weakness into every muscle and bone. He stumbled from her, plowing into the door frame and giving in to another humiliating growl.

"No!" she cried. "Please, don't go! I won't do it again; I promise!"

Another laugh escaped him. Marcus braced a hand against the wall, clawing at the wood, watching splinters embed under his fingernails as he fought the self-loathing beneath his reply. "No," he concurred in a harsh breath. "We shall *not* do that again."

"All right. Fine." The comeback vibrated with the anger he'd hoped to incite. And a breathtaking sizzle of rebellion. They had dubbed him a rebel in his time, too, he recalled . . . all those Whitehall wenches so thinly hiding beneath their pious pearls and "virgin's" lace, coyly dropping the suggestive words between weather remarks and whispers about Drake's latest daring in the name of his sovereign.

All but Raquelle. Raquelle, all satin and skin and blatant, coyless sex, who had brought his end—and his beginning. The end of his life. The beginning of his hell.

But she is not Raquelle, a voice in his heart easily asserted. Too easily. *She—is—not—Raquelle.*

"I have to go," he heard himself say. He forced himself out into the hall while commanding himself to believe the statement. If one woman had seduced him into this existence, another had only one disaster left to lead him to.

"No. Please, I've only just found you!"

"Let me be, Gabriela." His voice sounded animalistic even to his own ears, grating and hungry.

He heard her astonished catch of breath just behind him. "You . . . you know my name. How do you—"

" 'Tis not important. Let me go."

"The devil it's not important. How did you know I was here? Where did you come from? Why—"

"Damn you!" He spun back upon her. His lungs heaved

with heat; his blood turned to flames. "Damn you, go away and leave me be!"

He appeared Satan's cousin. Her eyes told him so, reflecting his imposing height, bared snarl, and burning stare. Judas Iscariot, he silently swore. Any self-respecting chit would be daintily unconscious on the carpet by now.

Gabriela Rozina barely flinched.

She just stood there, mussed and gorgeous, her hands clenching and unclenching as if she prepared to go to fisticuffs with him right there in the hall. In the dim silence, her rapid breaths filled the air. Then he heard her heartbeat, hammering blood to those straining fingers. Then came the whole chorus of her, the beautiful, irresistible symphony of her, daring to defy him like this. Daring to not only brave his wrath, but throw it right back at him.

"I have to go," he forced out again. He dragged his gaze over her once more, needing this last heaven of a moment to take into eternal memory with him. "Please," he rasped, "don't follow me."

She didn't move either way. Nor, for a tight silence, did she speak.

In a low and shaking murmur, her words finally came. "Bastard. You malicious, terrible bastard. You come to me like this, saying you understand, saying you care—"

Her throat caught on the last word. She shook her head. "Damn *you*. I don't even know your name."

"Gabriela . . ."

"Nor do I want to know it. Go, then. Go."

The word came out of him with nary a thought, let alone a chance at restraint. "Marc," he said softly.

"Marc?"

"My name. If you need anything—*anything*—just call for Marc."

"Marc." Unbelievably, a small smile wobbled across her lips. "Marc. That's nice."

"Now . . ." He pretended to adjust the lamp in the wall sconce, instead disguising the moment it took to focus a mild hypnosis over her. Amazing, how swiftly the powers returned; how easily he could summon them for his own self-serving purpose. "Now go home, Gabriela."

Nay, not self-serving, his brain growled back at his heart. *Self-preserving! For her own good, damn it—and yours.*

She blinked slowly at him. Then again. Then murmured with all the tender trust of a three-year-old, "All right."

He smiled, then, too. He imagined kissing her, right on her high, smooth forehead, running his mouth along her soft hairline. Then he willed the image to oblivion.

"Good night, Marc," she said.

"Goodbye, Gabriela."

For a long while after the stage door slammed behind her, he stood there, motionless. A thousand times, he commanded himself to cast out the warmth from his blood and his soul. *Her* warmth. Two thousand times, he ordered up an exorcism of the life he had slowly, unknowingly allowed himself to revel in the last months.

He began the impossible task of forgetting . . . forgetting Gabriela forever.

Hours passed. The lamp's oil burned down and died. Darkness, only the quiet and fleeting tenebrosity that permeated the world in the night's last tenacious hour before dawn, descended.

Gabriela's warmth still clung to every inch of him. Her life still filled his nostrils, his sights, his mind.

Let her go, a voice ordered, seemingly from thin air. But his conscious did that when it said things he nay wanted to hear.

You could have only hurt her, the voice continued, despite Marcus's protest of squeezed eyes and fisted hands. *And she could have hurt you. Irreversibly. Do you nay learn? Do you nay remember the last time you were so hard and hot and obsessed over a woman, you thought with all the control of a bonfire—*

"She is not Raquelle."

Bloody hell she is not. She is a woman. She thinks and moves and schemes just like the bitch, even if she nay drinks the next gullible fool for breakfast.

"She is not Raquelle!"

She would ruin you.

"Go to hell!"

Without thinking, without caring, he stormed down the hall. For the first time in a long time, he felt pricks of the approaching sunrise, and he welcomed the hot needles in his skin. He contemplated just giving up, just giving in— just choosing, at last, the relief of eternal death over the torment of eternal loneliness.

But he would not. He was too much a damned coward even for that. For all the drinking and swordplay and bedded wenches he'd crammed into his depraved mortal existence, Marcus was, deep in his rotten gut, passionately afraid to die.

And so he'd descend to hell once more.

The exhausted weight of his body pulled him back down the hall, toward the locked door at the end. Curiosity about what lay beyond the mysterious portal had long ago waned among Drury's ever-changing tenants, their histrionic tales of the theater's famed "ghost" replaced by the more stylish excuse of a never-used broom closet. In this sole matter, Marcus appreciated the intervention of style. He just wanted to get out of here. He just wanted to forget.

He just had to take the steps past Gabriela's dressing room first.

With a determined curse, he quickened his stride as he approached the portal. He steeled his gaze straight ahead. He would not look, he vowed in a repeating mental litany. *He would not look.*

But she'd left the lamp in the room turned up just a fraction.

Like distant recollections of autumn sunsets, the view

beckoned to him with magical force. All the elements of her world lay motionless and yet vibrant in the deep umber light: the gleam of her crystal hairbrush on the dressing table, the twinkling beads on her costume hanging on the screen, the frayed copy of *Hamlet* she'd been working from earlier.

And a dark leather book on the floor, shushing softly on the floor boards as his boot bumped it.

No, Marcus amended as he stooped and flipped the pages open, not a book, but . . .

"Gabriela," his stunned lips emitted. He hauled the volume up with both hands, drinking in the scrolling, curled words on the pages as if they were written in water from the spring of life. Knowing he should hurl the damn, dangerous book away. Clinging to it harder with each passing moment.

"Oh, Gabriela," he grated, slumping against the door frame, eagerly and painfully soaking in each entry of her heart, each revelation of her life. "Gabriela, I didn't ask for this. I didn't ask for *you*. I won't survive you!"

But how, his soul roared back in the dim and consuming silence, would he exist any other way again?

Lightning.

A hundred times the next morning, Gabriela berated herself for the ridiculous comparison—and for the even more irrational jolt through her nerves whenever the memory of *him* struck. A long morning bath didn't help. Neither did indulging in breakfast for once, nor allowing herself a perusal through the current issues of *Theatre* and the *Contemporary Review*. No, the rememberances hit without timing or care; the haunting visions of stormy black hair and rain-smooth grace stealing over her and paralyzing her just like—

Just like the lightning she'd seen in the eyes of a beautiful stranger named Marc.

Now, as she reentered her dressing room by the gray light of the rainy afternoon, that silvered sensation overtook her with double the force. She didn't move to turn up the lamp. At this moment, the room appeared just as it should: draped in soft shadow, unnatural and unreal . . . just as she remembered it from last night. Just as she remembered the magical scene which had transpired here. . . .

But magical or not, the encounter *had* been real. Hadn't it? And if it had, what strange being had it transformed her into? One minute, she'd burned with the most intense anger she'd known, matching Marc snarl for snarl. The next, she found herself trapped in a whirlpool of light, emanating from the splendor of his eyes . . . wanting only to please him. Like some puppet-headed maid transfixed by a wizard from a penny novel, she left the theater in a mindless haze, leaving behind her cloak, her manuscript, her reticule, and her journal.

Oddly, the misplacement of the latter filled her with the most anxiety. She'd kept the journal updated with every thought, feeling, and experience she'd had this year . . . even the intimate longings that came alive when she lay awake nights, trying not to listen to Donna and her flatmate's "visitors" just beyond the wall at her back. . . .

The image jolted Gaby from her trance and into a brisk stride across the room. As quickly as possible, she had to retrieve that book—and the deep secrets the pages kept safe for her.

She stopped at the big chair she'd curled into last night. She'd been waging battle against a blank page in the journal before the tears had come, and *he* had appeared. She'd let the book slip to the floor, just to her right. . . .

But a search around the chair, the table, and soon the rest of the room turned up everything except her reticule and one leather-bound journal. Three makeup brushes, two bootlacing hooks, and a handful of hair pins richer, Gaby slammed hands to hips and threw an exasperated scowl about the chamber.

"Saint Genesius." She used Donna's mildest oath in a mutter. "That'll teach you not to gawk at silver-eyed strangers again, Gaby."

What kind of spell *had* that sad, mysterious man worked upon her?

For an equally enigmatic reason, she didn't want to know the answer to that.

She huffed away the question and its accompanying trepidation, then turned a determined stride down the hall, toward the main stage. "Louis!" she called on her way. "Louis, it's Gaby. I need your help."

Just invoking the stage manager's name helped usher a calming flow into her heart. If anyone could help her locate the elusive journal, the grizzled but good-hearted hulk was the man for the job.

"Louis," she shouted again, pushing open the stage door, "there's something I need you to—"

A chaos of hammering drowned the rest of her sentence. She would have started again, but her mouth dropped open in astonishment.

The scene resembled the area she knew as the main stage—vaguely. Only now, props and sets were white-draped ghosts, the stage floorboards flooded by a sea of musty tarps. That sea sprouted several mountainous ladders and one carpenter's cart of an island. At least ten dirty-bibbed workmen whistled as they lumbered around her, their tunes bouncing in time to their big strides.

She navigated her way through the chaos, locating Drury's stage manager pacing a hole into the tarps downstage right. "Louis." She tugged on his sleeve. "What's going on?"

The man's head, topped by its own tumult of brown,

ropy hair, jerked up. A glare narrowed on her, textured
too much like burlap to soothe her disquiet. "What are
you doing here?" the manager snapped.

"I left my things here last night. But I can't find my
journ—"

"Haven't seen it. Gaby, you're in the way here."

She hurried behind him as he stomped to the opposite
wings. "In the way of what? Who are all these men? What's
going on?"

The man turned so fast, Gabriela came inches from en-
tangling herself in the watch chain looped across his girth.
"What the bloody hell does it look like is going on?" Louis
retorted. "We're fixing the damn roof."

Gabriela barely checked her jaw from dropping in her
second amazed gape. "But we've all been having trouble
with those rain puddles for months."

"Yes, yes, I know. Listen, I have to have this done by
tonight."

"You said we'd just have to put down rags until the show
broke a profit. Don't tell me business has been that good."

"Gaby, I don't have time to explain."

"But I told you about this repeatedly, and you—"

"Well, somebody decided to listen!"

His growl erupted with an extra dose of vehemence due
to the approach of a workman bearing several bills to be
signed. Louis swore at the figures, but signed the papers
with short, harsh pen strokes.

"By the devil's own mother," he muttered halfway
through the third invoice. "I've only met the lunatic once,
but it's like he has eyes and ears everywhere."

"Who?" Gabriela asked, but only partly from curiosity.
Mostly, she wanted to know who to thank for this miracle.

"Marcus 'I Want it Done by Tonight' Danewell, that's
who." The watch chain jiggled as Louis pocketed his pen.
"Calls himself a silent owner of this place, but he causes
more chaos than six of Augustus could. Thinks he can

leave a note on my desk like a bloody royal decree, and the roof will patch itself overnight, good as new. I swear to you, Gaby, I'd leave this place, if . . ."

But Louis's stormings faded to a low drizzle beneath the thunder storm his first sentence stirred. Gabriela turned and clung to a ladder for support as the words crashed, then resounded in her head: *Marcus. Marcus Danewell.*

Marcus "Marc" *Danewell.*

Like regaining perspective after a triple pirouette, comprehension came between one blink and the next. Gabriela laughed, yet the sound held no mirth, and she shook her head, finally whispering, "It can't possibly be."

Yet it could. It very much could be. As a matter of fact, it made too much sense. She recalled the moment her gaze had first locked with Marc's. She remembered the quicksilver sensation through her veins; she remembered thinking he'd been watching her with that surreal intensity for hours. As if he was perfectly at home in this building, and she was the strange new creature recently arrived into his private forest.

A new question haunted her then: how many times before *that* had he watched her . . . had he studied her every move?

Plenty, Gabriela suspected. Enough to know the backstage rain puddles had caused her a number of precarious slips . . . then wield his power as silent theater owner to order the problem rectified within a day.

Theater owner.

Why hadn't he told her?

That was a silly question. There were a multitude of things Marcus Danewell had never told a soul about himself. She'd stake her own soul on the fact.

A cacophony of whacks resounded through the theater; the workers' hammers began pounding at the roof. Gaby's heartbeat thundered loudly enough to join the din. She searched the expanse of the theater and each box on both five-tiered sides, wondering if he watched her even now. Wondering if he even took notes. . . .

A mixture of heat and cold pushed her away from the ladder. Icy fear dueled with searing anger along the corridors of her nerves. Gabriela marched through the greenroom, but didn't turn back to her dressing room. No, she angled the opposite direction, through the back door and into the street, welcoming the rush of April wind on her cheeks and through her hair. She hoped the cold blasted away the skirmish raging inside her—but knew she might as well wish for the Thames to stop flowing.

She didn't stop to look for her journal again.

Because she knew exactly who had it.

Eight hours later, just after the last orchestra member shouted goodbye from the back door and the theater fell into a dim silence, Gabriela stomped to the middle of the stage. She threw back her head to make her voice carry to the highest rafter, and shouted as loud as she could.

"Marcus! Marcus Danewell! I want to see you *right now!*"

Four

Silence.

And she'd really expected something else?

He's not there, a voice taunted from inside—the same demon that delighted in tugging at her insecurities before auditions . . . and long ago, had heckled her each visitors' day at the orphanage.

A voice she fought now with shaking, clenched fists.

He told you to go away once, the voice jeered on. *He meant it. You didn't listen. He's not there.*

"No!" she snapped, securing her stance tighter. Blast it, she knew what she felt—despite the blanket of blackness answering her desperate, searching gaze. Unignorable, these hot-cold fingers of sensation, waging harsher battle over her nerves than they'd dared this morning. Unavoidable, this cacophony of her heartbeat, pounding like triple timpani with each second passing farther into the night. But worst of all, she couldn't shed this breath-catching awareness . . . this superreal sensation that he still watched her, followed her . . . haunted her.

Gabriela moved to the edge of the stage. She stopped when her toes jutted out into the dark—trying not to liken the view to the unreadable abyss of her senses.

"Coward!" she accused into the chasm. "Backing down from the challenge, now that I've figured out a little more than I should? Hiding in your precious shadows, Mr. Thea-

ter Owner, enjoying the drama of the hopeless actress, going slowly insane?"

At that, she backed from the edge. She shook her head
in time to her stiff, but proud steps. "Well, I hope you like
tonight's repertoire, Marcus. It's the last you'll get. I don't
play to cowards." She pivoted toward the wings. "Or
thieves."

As she marched across the stage, she refused to let the
dry heat behind her eyes liquify. She refused to let her
shoulders sag or her step falter. She'd give in to her humiliation only upon escape from those all-seeing silver
eyes.

Wherever the bloody hell they were.

Two steps from the stage left wings, she gasped and
skidded to a halt as two black-clad, black-booted legs
stepped into her path. Her journal and reticule hit the
floorboards between those boots with a forceful thwack,
tossed there with a deceivingly effortless toss from a
strong, long-fingered hand.

Gabriela's stare connected that hand to an arm, the arm
to a endlessly broad shoulder, encased in billowy black silk.
Her sight continued up the cords of a dark neck, to the
almost spiritual power of Marcus's face.

If it were possible, that otherworldly force radiated with
even more potent impact tonight. He looked hewn of gold-
swept granite under the gaslights, his hair swept off his
high forehead like onyx turned to velvet.

But most of all, he looked furious.

Marcus glared at the purse and the journal, then back
to her. "I am not a thief."

Gaby didn't pick up the items Not yet. Instead, she
nudged one foot forward, her reticule on one side, his
boot on the other.

Her stare rose to issue the same challenge to his eyes.
"You took them without my permission. You stole them."

"I borrowed them."

"Borrowed?" An incredulous laugh sliced up her throat. "Oh, this is indeed a new way to play the scene."

"Gabriela . . ."

"You mean to tell me you decided to *borrow* my reticule—"

"Aye," came the sure comeback. "I do."

"Planning a big evening out and didn't have one of your own?"

"Gabriela." This time, locked lips vented the syllables.

"And my journal," she persisted nevertheless. "The worst of it, Marcus, is my journal. Did you stop to think you were taking the record of my deepest thoughts and feelings? Did you consider *asking* before you violated my privacy . . . my life?"

He issued no reply for a moment. Then, with the slightest motion, his boot pressed against her foot—beckoning her reluctant gaze up to his again.

"If I had asked," he queried softly, "what would your answer have been?"

Gaby swallowed her telling silence behind compressed lips.

"I rest my case." He dropped his gaze. But not before Gabriela glimpsed the flash of silver light beneath his dark lashes—his surrender to a moment of such intense and unguarded pain, his eyes looked as if they. . . .

Glowed?

She shook her head, ordering her imagination free of such hallucinations. Blast it, *he'd* wronged *her*, not the other way around! She snatched her pity back from him, hastily shoved it down to the well in which she kept such dangerous emotions trapped, angry that Marcus Danewell stole from her yet again—especially this time, seizing such a vitally important component of her Ophelia's emotional success.

"Well?" She locked judging arms across her chest, proud of the equally unyielding tone she delivered.

Marcus didn't look up. "Well . . . what?"

She slid her foot away from his. Suddenly, her voice didn't come so strongly. "Well . . ." She faltered, and blamed him for it. "Well, did . . . did you read it?"

He considered her question for what felt like hours. Finally, he looked up again as he leaned toward her, very slowly, like a great beast used to watching every step for fear it would crush something. He took a long, nearly silent breath before answering.

"Aye."

Damn him.

Damn him for saying the word with such meaning, for looking so penitent, yet proud as he did. Again, as if *he'd* experienced every fear and feeling, every triumph and sorrow she'd expressed on those pages.

"Bastard," she spat.

"That will nay procure you an apology." Marcus leaned yet closer. Towering. Mesmerizing. A fine wine in human form, dominating her senses whether she liked it or not. "I am not sorry I did it."

"Yes," she snorted. "I know."

"Your words are beautiful."

"Stop it."

"I memorized them."

"You think that's going to redeem you?"

The briefest shadow crossed his face. The briefest, *blackest* shadow.

"Sweeting, nothing can redeem me."

Then the night held its breath around them.

He meant it, Gabriela realized, watching the shadow return and become such dark and hard imperturbability he might be one of the prop statues. Her anger inverted to amazement, then back again.

"Why?" she rasped then. "Why are you doing this to me?"

His taut silence told her everything—and nothing. Their

gazes locked once more. And once more, Gabriela stared into a silver storm roiling with every tear she'd cried, every laugh she'd loosed, every emotion she'd known.

Dear God. This man moved her. And terrified her.

"This . . . this isn't just about the journal, is it?" she forced herself to continue. "It's about what happened last night, when we first saw each other."

Marcus raised his hand as if to touch her; instead, he curled long fingers into a self-damning ball. "I nay meant to frighten you."

"That's just it. You *didn't* frighten me. For a moment, I was startled . . . but then I looked into your eyes, and I felt only that I'd known you for a very long time. But now I realize it's because *you* knew *me.* You'd been watching me, every night—"

"Nay." He slammed a fist to his thigh, punched out a frustrated growl. "I mean . . . God, Gabriela, I meant you no ill!"

"Then I'm right." Her voice wavered. She didn't know it until now, but a part of her had held on to some strange hope, desperately willing him to repudiate her—fervently wishing any other expression on his face but the confirming grimace curling his lips. "Dear God," Gaby repeated in a rasp. "I'm right."

"Gabriela . . ."

"How long? How long has this been going on, Marcus? Do . . . do you follow me everywhere? To my *dressing room?* Do you follow me home?"

"Gabriela, nay—"

"Stop it." She clutched a fistful of skirt, advancing upon him. "Stop lying to me! God, I *am* a fool. It all makes sense now. How else could you know everything about me? How else can you look at me and make me feel like you look *inside* me? How else can I feel this way every time I look back . . . losing myself in your eyes; losing myself in your . . . oh God, it's *not fair*—"

A dry sob cut her short. Marcus's nostrils flared on an audible intake of breath. Gabriela tried to breathe . . . she tried to understand, no matter how the confusion and fear drained her strength.

Her hands fell to her sides, palms open, entreating. "What . . . what the blast are you doing to me? Damn you, just tell me what you want from me. Tell me why you're doing this!"

She still held her breath. Marcus's face didn't change. Except. . . .

Except for the slight parting of his lips, revealing his locked teeth beneath—big, beautiful, straight and perfect teeth, but for the slightly extended tips on opposing sides of his front pair.

"Because . . ." those lips said then, the word a sibilance of raw need, pure ache, utter worship. "Because you are the most beautiful thing I've seen in my miserable existence."

God's wounds.

He might as well strip naked and stand there before her, Marcus concluded. He would be eminently more comfortable, and equally as exposed.

Yet even with the tremors of the confession still rocking his body, his mind struggled to believe he had said it. From the look of Gabriela's wide, blinking stare, so did she.

So much for the pretty-worded popincock who carnalized half of Whitehall behind Good Bess's back. Admit it, Danewell. You are old. Very old. And you are nay near worthy enough for an angel like Gabriela Rozina.

He let out a long, weary sigh—and nothing else. He nay trusted his mutinous mouth to release safe words anymore.

Slowly, he turned . . . then plodded heavy steps toward the door leading to safe, wretched darkness.

"Where the bloody hell do you think you're going now?" she called at him.

He stopped. Not voluntarily. Marcus swore under his breath, commanding his feet forward. Instead, his boots grated against the floorboards as he pivoted and faced her again.

Sweet God.

She'd aroused him before. But always from the heights of the spiritual realm he would never achieve again, or on the stage far below and far away—either way, a reaction he quelled with the understanding he would never find fulfillment.

Yet now . . . blast and balls, now she stood there visually sparring with him, just as confused as he was . . . and close, so beautifully, achingly close. Again, she squared off at him in that let's-cuff-it-out-right-now pose, bracing tapered fingers to a waist he could span with his hands—but a man could nay gauge that sort of thing properly anymore, no thanks to the barbaric underpinnings they currently called "style." Still, the corset contraption thrust other things into perfect view. Swell of creamy breasts . . . soft lines of graceful hips . . .

Damn her. *Damn her.*

Powered only by that fury, he managed to bite out a retort. "I shall go where I bloody well please, if it concerns you—which it nay does. But suffice it to say I will nay tamper with your precious sanity again. Goodnight, sweeting."

"No!"

He gritted back an obscenity he had not heard for at least a century. And swung his gaze back toward her.

She still stood there as proud as an empress, though now she shifted her hands to intertwine in front of her, forming a V that centered his sight—and his thoughts—straight at the crux of her. . . .

Ah, God!

He forced his sight to her face.

Yet when his scrutiny arrived there, he almost laughed. Gabriela's glower had faltered into an uncertain scowl. She clearly did not enjoy the ambivalence.

"Believe it or not, Mr. Danewell, my sanity was in trouble long before you came along." Then, in a swift mumble, "And I do, in fact, care where you go."

"Well, do *not*," Marcus countered.

Her chin dropped again. "Why not?"

"Just . . . do not. Do not care, Gabriela. Do not *begin* to care. I . . . you . . . we are two worlds crossing at the wrong time. God's wounds, that should nay have crossed at all."

"I don't happen to agree."

At that, he *did* laugh, a short, hard grunt. "You are hardly qualified to render such a verdict."

For exactly two heartbeats, she said nothing. But during that silence, Marcus felt every moment of her two deep inhalations, every muscle coiling tighter into her two white-knuckled fists. . . .

The calm before the storm.

"How dare you." The third heartbeat finally exploded with her tempest. "How *dare* you," she reiterated. "I am *most* qualified to render that verdict!"

She dug those fists into her skirts, grabbing the material up into rhythmic, writhing twists as she closed the space between them like an avenging ghost of Denmark in her own right. "You're not the one whose thoughts and dreams were last night's bedtime reading, sir! You're not the one most exposed here, most vulnerable!"

As she tightened the distance further, finally stopping but half a step away, Marcus swung his gaze down. *Oh, sweeting,* his heart cried out to her accusation, *if you only knew.*

"I think," she finally said, an exhalation struggling for composure again, "that if anyone has the license to *care* here, it is I."

Marcus did not answer. With his head still bent, he

watched her hands uncurl, then her fingers start a shaking, vain attempt to smooth the creases she had just imparted to her dress. But when Gabriela noticed that *he* noticed her action, she dropped her arms and spun away.

"And . . . and what I really need to care about here is this bloody script," she rushed on. "But you already know that, don't you?"

At that, he dared one careful, gentle word. "Aye." Then, after a pause about as comfortable as disrobing for a first-time lover, he could not repress the rest of his thought. . . .

He could not resist caring for her in return.

"Your rehearsals . . ." he ventured softly, "you wrote many times of them . . . many times, of your vexation with them."

Now, Gabriela chose her moment of circumspect silence. But when she turned back toward him on slow, suddenly unsure steps, the stamp of pain on her face turned into a mallet of confirmation on Marcus's heart.

And he recognized the aching urge to hold her. The hunger to hold her, and *taste* her, and kiss away that mortal frustration from her senses. . . .

But another force routed him to the job. An amazing, instantaneous power, igniting her features into a beaming, cheek-breaking smile. "Marcus!" she cried, giving him the wondrous experience of hearing his name spill off her lips in joy. As he stood there, numb and dumbfounded from the wonder of the miracle, she grabbed both his hands with all the mischief of a lass contemplating her first May Day kiss.

"Marcus," she exclaimed again, "*you* can help me! *You're* just what I need: a partner to help me run the lines!"

He turned even number. But he willed his hands to jerk free from her, despite their instant retreat against his chest, their subsequent recoil into shaking, white-backed fists. "N-nay," he blurted, swerving away in mortified shame. "Nay, sweeting, I cannot."

"Of course you can. Of course you *will*. Come on, grump. Stay and make yourself useful for once."

"I am not a grump," he growled. *Whatever the blast that is.*

"The bloody saints you aren't," she returned. "But I need help with these lines. Marcus . . . I need *you.*"

Her last words tumbled out so swift and so soft, they would be inaudible to a mortal man. But Marcus heard. Oh aye, he stood there and he listened and he soaked in every word . . . and then the nervous breath she drew in after . . . and the intensifying pounding of her heart as she awaited his decision. So swift and urgent a heartbeat, he suddenly realized, that the tempo could claim only one dance master.

Fear.

Disbelief took over his actions. In one sweep of motion, Marcus whirled back to her, curled a finger under her chin, and commanded her sight to his. Still, he nay expected her to meet his challenge so directly—enabling him to secure an instant link with her psyche. And her soul.

And for once, he delved his mind into the deepest core of hers without hesitation.

Aye, he rapidly discovered, she *was* afraid. Very afraid.

But, came the next shocking revelation, she was not afraid he would stay.

She was terrified he would leave.

Marcus swallowed. Then swallowed again, as the glimmer of a tear swelled in her right eye. A tear she tried to fight back, but lost; the heavy drop defied her with a slow descent across her smooth cheek.

Ah, God. He knew tears like that. He had battled back tens of thousands like it. Tears of rejection. And certainly, of anger. Of frustration . . . and utter aloneness.

Of all the pain he had known himself over the last nearly three hundred years.

And now, terror gripped Marcus, too.

God's blood. What the hell have you started, Danewell?

"Gabriela." Though he whispered it, raw torment permeated his voice. He slid his finger from her chin to her cheek, tenderly retracing the path left by her tear, trying not to meet her gaze again . . . hopelessly losing himself in that dark copper beauty.

"Oh, Gabriela." The more hard-edged mutter helped him regain a measure of control. But not enough to hold him back from saying, "You were working on *Hamlet*, weren't you?"

Five

Gabriela broke into a watery grin.

She couldn't help herself. She also had a devastating urge to hug him, but she quelched the temptation with the memory of his reaction when she'd only touched his hand last night. Never mind the response of her own senses from just imagining such a scene: of pressing herself close to him, of feeling his broad strength next to her, of perhaps discovering, at last, the secret of the inescapable power he had over her. . . .

How that fathomless force could grow more intense, she didn't understand, but the next moment, Marcus induced her to defy her own pledge of decorum. Gabriela swayed closer to him as his features changed again . . . his eyelids lowering, his fingers rising to roam her cheek . . . his firm lips parting farther, as if the picture in her mind became the fantasy in his, too.

Dear God. A woman could lose herself in that look.

All of herself.

Every dream you ever had. Every hope you carried through those black, solitary nights. You could lose them all. . . .

Again as if he read her soul more clearly than the acts in a program, Marcus yanked himself back. Yet he did glance up to her again—and in that moment, her heart slammed to another stop. Somewhere in an unnameable part of her mind, Gaby swore she heard, in the most fervent whisper: *I do not want you. Sweet God, Gabriela, I could never hurt you!*

But before she could work her jaw around a stammering reaction, Marcus found her script atop a prop boulder and started to thumb the worn out pages. So blithely, as if he'd heard—or said—nothing.

"So . . ." He braced his bent knee to the boulder and the script to his knee. "My mate Augustus is actually staging the great *Hamlet,* is he?"

It took several moments for Gaby to realize he lent a *voice* to the words this time. "What? Oh . . . oh, yes. We begin rehearsals in three weeks, but I wanted to prepare more thoroughly. This production is particularly important to me."

He turned another page, noting her marked lines and cues there. "Ophelia is that tightly intwined to your soul, then?"

She frowned. "I beg your pardon?"

" 'Tis a play close to your affections. You just said so. And you do stay so late, laboring on your lines. Surely, it is because you liken yourself to the poor Ophelia."

"I do *not!*" An incredulous sputter exploded off her lips. "Great saints, Marcus, whatever gave you . . . this is just the role Augustus assigned to me! I'm going to learn it and perform it as best as I can, but . . . well . . ." she huffed again, throwing him a glance flooded with the perturbation he'd incited, "Ophelia was a lovesick sagmop who drove herself insane because of a *man.*"

He lowered the script and slanted a stare back at her. A vast, ceaseless stare, unfaltering as polished pewter. "And you have never wanted to go insane because of love?"

Gaby only fired back another sardonic snort.

And that maddening man on the boulder only continued his unblinking, unnerving scrutiny.

He kept staring even as he redeposited the script atop the boulder and paced toward her. "Are you telling me

your heart has never been broken, Gabriela Rozina? That
you've not lost so much or grieved so deeply that you
wanted to die, too?"

Dear God, her soul cried back. *More times than you'll ever
know. More times than you* want *to know.*

But his eyes told her he already knew that.

His eyes told her he wanted to know more.

A *more* she'd never give anyone.

Gabriela dropped her head. She jerked up her skirts,
attempting to sidestep the approaching scoundrel, but
Marcus moved three steps ahead, slicing each escape route
short. He *always* seemed to move three steps ahead. . . .

"Look," she said from clenched teeth as they squared
off for the fourth time, "I said the *production* was important
to me, not the role. And I never said it was 'close to my
affections.' "

"Ahhh," came his knowing reply. "Yes, how could I have
forgotten? You have that honor reserved for the Prince's
Grand Theatre Troupe."

She didn't question how he knew that. Between the teasing she weathered from the rest of the cast and the self-
reminders she railed during her after-hours sessions, the
man didn't need Pasteur's genius to deduce where her
aspirations lie.

Instead, Gabriela dared another gaze up at him. But this
time, she met his examination with pride—perhaps a little
defiance. All right . . . a lot of defiance.

"Yes," she finally stated. "Making the Troupe is my ultimate dream. There's nothing wrong with that."

Marcus held up both hands, palms out. "Nothing at all."

His lips remained a solemn line, but now, his eyes
smiled. The combination befuddled her. Gaby didn't know
whether to embrace him for his understanding, or slap
him for his insolence.

"You're serious, aren't you?" she said in lieu of either
choice. "You truly think I can do this?"

She didn't know what response to expect at that. Yet the next moment, this strange and mysterious man took her beyond befuddled and into speechless shock. He did it by sliding his hands into hers, lifting them to his lips as gingerly as crystal roses, then bestowing the barest brush of a kiss along her knuckles, so reverently, so slowly. . . .

She didn't even feel his breath on her skin . . . yet she felt like fainting. She'd never fainted before, but certainly this sensation counted as the prelude to such—tingled fuzz replacing her brain, languid warmth flowing instead of her blood . . . the increasing drumbeat of her heart echoing in every cell of her body. . . .

Marcus's murmur threw that dangerous rhythm off just in time. "I think," he told her, "that you can do anything, dream anything, and become anything you want."

Now she felt like crying. Gaby squeezed his hands to test if this moment was real—unable to hold back her joy from bursting on a misty laugh when nothing changed except an odd drop of his left eyebrow.

"It . . . this is . . . I mean, you are . . ." she tried to explain in response to his puzzled expression. "It's just that you're the first to ever believe in me."

"Nay," Marcus countered. "*You* were the first."

"Me?" She shook her head. "But I'm not important."

"Is that what Alfonso told you?"

Gaby jerked her hands away and spun from him. She should have known. Blast, but she should have realized . . . he knew everything else about her life, didn't he?

Even so, that didn't excuse his underhanded method of approaching the subject. Or rather, sneaking it in from the shadows—waiting to strip her senses to a defenseless nothing, then slithering the question around her so easily, so gently, like a noose before the hangman cinched the knot.

"Alfonso is none of your business," she retorted. "And I will thank you to leave the subject alone."

"He is a clod. You know that, do you not?"

She snapped back around. His voice loomed directly behind her—and so did he, suddenly standing so close, she shook from the stunned tremors her spine composed in answer.

But *how* had he gotten there?

She stifled a strange urge to run and take refuge in the nearest church. Dear Lord. The man snuck his large body around the same way he slipped in his blasted questions: with disconcerting, almost . . . deadly silence.

The thought provided the agitation she needed for her caustic comeback. "Thank you for the insight, but I've discovered Mr. Renard's filthy fortitude very easily on my own. And I'll dispatch the wretch just as simply."

To her surprise, a chuckle underlined Marcus's response. "Oh, I nay doubt that."

"And what's that supposed to mean?"

He spread out open hands again. "That is, most verily, rather obvious. 'Tis no secret you hot-blooded Italian misses have a talent for dispatching wretch—"

A sharp slap cut his charge short. But it was the crack of her descending wrist slamming into his steeled grip, *not* the stinging ring Gaby craved, assuring the slap of her hand against his face. She struggled against his hold. Marcus held on with amazing, yet effortless power.

"Let me go," she seethed.

"Nay." He didn't just state it. He drawled the word with infuriating calm, taunted her with tone as exquisite as a well-placed caress.

"How . . . dare . . . you. How dare you!"

"I do dare, madam. And it seems I succeed at it, as well."

And oh, how he was right. Damn him. *Damn* him.

Gabriela drew in a furious breath. She glared up at him. His gaze answered her scowl with smooth silver serenity.

"You . . . you baited me with that on purpose," she charged.

"Aye. I did."

"Why?" Her voice cracked with the approach of tears. Gaby gulped hard, forcing them back. *Not now,* she raged. *No! Not now! Don't let him in. Don't let him see the pain!* "I thought you cared about me, Marcus."

"Sweet Gabriela." To her astonishment, his own voice shook as he urged her chin back up. "I do care. Do you not fathom it is why I long to know . . . why do you bear shame of what you are? Why are you afraid?"

With a strength she didn't know she had, she wrested free of him. Her mind reeled. Her heart thundered. Dear God. He'd hit the target of her soul with fatal accuracy, and she didn't know whether to cry or die.

"Gabriela?"

"Because it's not good enough!" She burned beyond tears now. Her sobs came dry and fast. "Don't you see? *I* will never be good enough!"

A potent silence preceded his solemn response. "So you pretend to be someone else."

"If I have to." Her fingertips lost blood as she curled them around her sleeve ends and pulled. Hard. "Now I'll thank you to close the subject. Permanently."

"We have nay discussed Renard yet," he objected.

"Yes, we have."

"Gabriela—"

"The matter is closed!"

"Damn it, now why do *you* not see? The man is dangerous! You are in mortal jeopardy!"

He raised his arms, hands shaking, muscles straining with his vehemence. And Gaby, shameful wretch that she was, swallowed back her urge to set free a sudden laugh. *Mortal jeopardy? Oh, Marcus. Dear, determined Marcus. Where did you grow up? In the Age of Chivalry?*

When her valiant knight saw his dramatics hadn't made a scratch in *her* armor, he dropped his arms with a frustrated snort. "Blast and hell," he grated. "You said you trusted me."

"Yes," she replied softly. "I know." *And I meant it.*

"I only want to prove myself worthy of that gift, Gabriela."

"I know that, too. So stop glowering. Your intention is not a sin."

To her shock, that last word rendered the same effect as a knife through his middle. Gabriela watched in growing amazement—and remorse—as Marcus's face twisted in something between a sob and a grimace. Pain beyond words. Sorrow beyond tears.

Two minutes ago, she'd thought of nothing but running from him.

Now, she longed to run *to* him. And hold him . . . and banish that terrible agony from his face, forever.

"Not a sin," he repeated, emitting a harsh laugh. "Oh, dear nymph, in thy orisons be all my sins remembered."

He looked to the blackness of the theater as he pronounced the last words with musical intimacy, as if truly speaking to someone out there in the dark. And standing there, simply watching him, Gabriela knew she'd treasure this instant as one of *her* most precious memories. With his dark hair falling over his high forehead, his stance high and proud and strong, his jaw a searching uplift of a right angle beneath his firmly set lips, he appeared to gaze beyond even this building's paltry walls, windows, and confines.

He looked as if he gazed along the very depths and dangers of time.

Gaby slipped so deeply into a contemplation of *that* thought that several moments passed before she comprehended Marcus's expectant turn toward her. And the similar incline of his raised eyebrows.

"Wh-what?" she stammered.

"Act Three, Scene One," he leveled with sudden, not

to mention strange, efficiency. " 'Nymph, in thy orisons be all my sins remembered.' 'Tis your cue, young lady. You told me you stayed to rehearse, didn't you?"

"Well, yes." He *was* right. The line *was* her cue. And he *was* Drury's silent owner, signifying his devotion to the arts beyond mere lip service. . . .

But none of it dimmed the impact of this addition to Marcus's ever-lengthening string of surprises—by far the biggest eye-opener so far. Gaby hadn't considered this factor when she blurted her hasty plea for him to stay. She'd only watched him trudge toward the wings with the certainty that he carried a piece of her soul with him—and scrambled for the swiftest excuse to bring him back. The entreaty for his help with her lines came easily, logically.

It never occurred to her that he'd be good at the job.

No, not good, she revised over the next two hours, "magnificent" fit the bill more adequately. Breathtaking. Beautiful. He countered her Ophelia with a Hamlet so real, she wondered if the Danes had lost a prince sometime in the last thirty or so years. His deliveries bettered even the Lyceum's Breezy Bill Terrace, fluent to the point of poetic, speaking each word as if the ghost of Shakespeare possessed him—entrancing her so completely, Gabriela fell into continual lapses of awed silence, her own lines forgotten to the conviction in his face, the desperation in his tone, the eloquence of his body.

Now she gaped her way through the fiftieth of those pauses, staring at his wide-legged pose just downstage of the prop boulder. His presence still held the tension of Hamlet's last line, from his dark scowl down to the calf muscles straining at his boots. Not that Gaby cared about *any* of his muscles. . . .

"Gabriela?"

His prompt jerked her sights back up. The scowl had transformed to his expectant, and increasingly impatient, stare.

"I . . . I'm sorry," she stumbled. "That was my cue again, wasn't it?"

As she expected, he cocked that stare to one side as he wrapped his hands around opposite shoulders. If tendencies of the evening continued, a lengthy sigh would follow now, succeeded by the what-am-I-going-to-do-with-you shake of his head that, Gaby rapidly discovered, shot the strangest arrow of aching heat between her breasts. . . .

To her surprise—and odd, sudden disappointment—he just smiled, instead. "Perhaps we should stop there."

"No."

Gaby hated herself for the desperate plea, but couldn't dam the tide of fear his action flooded through her. On that same disconcerting surge of alarm, she rushed at him.

"Sweeting, it's late." Marcus easily halted her charge with his hands at her elbows. Yet his smile matched the gentle assurance of his voice.

"No. No, it's not." But a traitorous yawn selected that moment to surface. Gaby ignored Marcus's corresponding chuckle. *"Please*, Marcus," she persisted. "We still have so much to work on."

To her further disconcertment, his touch remained light, almost fearful, around her elbows. Tension edged the corners of his lips. *Hold me*, her heart implored. *This is so crazy, but I need you to hold me. I need your strength and your weakness and your insane beauty around me.*

"You . . . you are progressing well with the material now," he stated instead. "Just remember to keep your head lifted at the end of the monologue—"

"No."

He answered her brisk syllable with a glower, left eyebrow dropping lower than right. "What?"

"I said no. I'm sorry, but I don't remember a thing of what I learned tonight." *A statement not terribly far from the truth.*

She balanced her shaking tone with a light laugh, her

instinct screaming orders not to frighten him away with her desperation. "I . . . I really need much more rehearsal. With a master. Someone who knows this play like the back of his hand."

I need you, Marcus.

"Gabriela . . ." His hold suddenly clamped around her, hard. Then released her, swiftly. "Nay."

Then he stepped completely away.

Gaby attempted to go after him. But he swept his hand between them, his outstretched fingers fluid, yet commanding, a directive as powerful as shouted words. Despite every screaming protest of her mind, her body obeyed.

She aimed her most vehement scowl at him. No effect. His eyes . . . his beautiful eyes just continued their steady torment, holding her in place like threads of shimmering steel. Gaby ordered herself to look away. Yet that silver magic wrapped around her senses like the hangman's noose . . . tighter, tighter.

Too late, her brain recognized the assault of that lethargic fog again—the same haze that descended before she'd stumbled home last night, taking over her will, controlling her actions. Her senses struggled to banish the murk. They waged the battle in vain.

"Don't!" she managed to rasp, even as that invisible force pushed her farther from him.

"Don't?" It sounded as if he stood in China, not four steps across the stage.

"Don't . . . don't do this to me." Shakespeare's grave, she didn't sound much better. More like she'd just practiced drinking, not drama. "You . . . *you*, Marcus, you're doing this. I . . . I don't know how—but *stop*."

A long pause preceded his reply. A pause in which a myriad of strange, horrible emotions washed through her—Lord, almost as if another person stepped into her body, then leapt back out. Confusion. Despair. Sadness. Longing. *Lust?* Then confusion again.

"Go home, Gabriela."

"No."

"*Aye.*"

"Say you'll come back tomorrow night."

"Gabriela—"

"Say it."

He sighed. At least she thought he did. The sound echoed in her head more than her ears, a breath full of weight and longing—as if he were an old man waiting to die, not a vibrant, magnificent dream come to life.

"I'll think about it," he finally murmured. "Damn you, I'll think about it."

He had only said the words to make her leave. God's blood, Marcus raged, what else could he have done? The woman gave persistence a new meaning, standing there swaying like a feather fan under his hypnosis, but blurting commands as if she held Queen Bess's own scepter. Then she refused *his* directions while persisting with her adorable, impossible supplications.

The muck of the whole thing was, he really did think about her pleas.

Nay. Nay, he corrected himself over the next fourteen nights, he thought nothing through at all.

No other excuse justified why he returned to meet Gabriela every one of those nights, addicted to her like opium, drawn to her like a star to the moon. He cursed himself with each step up the secret stairway, only to take all the doubt back when he moved close enough to feel her presence again . . . her excitement, her dreams, her drive, her life. . . .

And her smile. Gabriela's unabashed, unpretentious smile, showering him with warmth each evening when she met him under the golden stage lights. Her smile—meant for his eyes only. He didn't have to delve an inch into her psyche to determine *that.* The magic of their deepening connection shone in every inch of that smile. It glimmered in every fleck of her happy gaze, resonated in every step she moved at his stage directions, manifested in every intent nod she rewarded his suggestions and even demands to better her performance.

Not that she didn't snap back a few demands of her own occasionally. Well, more than occasionally. But between their rows and their discrepancies, her obstinance and his overbearance, Gabriela began to grasp the essence of a woman named Ophelia—first in tentative dialogue changes here and there, then in growing breakthroughs of emotion and spirit.

The result was a performance guaranteed to be an absurd success. Marcus knew it—but most importantly, he saw that Gabriela knew it.

Especially when each of her triumphant smiles thanked him for it.

Excuses? he pondered one evening as she rearranged props for their rehearsal. Why the bloody hell did he keep floundering for excuses?

He had all the excuse he needed in Gabriela's sweet smile.

Right now, however, her soft huffs invaded his attention. Marcus looked upstage to the sight of her bustled little bottom, as she bent to the task of pulling a three-dimensional prop tree to center stage.

For a moment, he only managed a puzzled gape. Then he halted her foolery by moving behind her and bracing a hand on the limb over her shoulder.

"May I take the presumption of asking what the hell this is for?" he asked.

She straightened and turned. Only then did Marcus realize he should have planned his positioning more intelligently. Now she stood pinned in the valley created by his arm and body—so close, so tempting. He only had to lower his hand and pull, and she'd be caught in his embrace, too.

He grew hard just thinking about it . . . and he'd worn only a pair of his old loose knit hose tonight. If she took a step closer, she'd feel every inch of his longing, every pulse of his desire. She'd finally know how much he wanted her, needed her.

For a moment, however, she looked as if she already knew. And for another perilous moment, Marcus thought she might feel the same torturous ache—unless he'd slept through some decade, and a woman's high flush, moistened lips, and shallow breath now stood for an entirely contrary reaction.

"I . . ." she finally got out. "The tree . . . it's for . . . I've got to die tonight."

That not only tamped his arousal, but hailed a storm of nerve-freezing sensations—consisting mostly of terror. *I've got to die tonight.* Ah God, what provoked such a comment? Had she found out about him somehow? Gotten curious during the day, during the hours of his deepest sleep, and broken into the subterranean vault? Nay, he reasoned, he'd have noticed the damage to the door locks.

Then what?

Perhaps that whirling mind of hers merely suspected his truth. That would nay surprise him. The blasted newspapers screamed with that *Varney the Vampire* serial, enough to give her more than a few misgivings about a teacher who only came to her in the dead of night, complexion fading or glowing depending on his feeding schedule, always refusing bites of the fruit or bread she brought. . . .

"What on God's earth are you talking about?" he managed to retort with convincing incredulity. Perhaps, Marcus hoped, if he maintained a guileless charade, she would toss off her suspicions as imagination and everything would return to normal. Or as normal as things could be.

But her expression didn't falter. Marcus braced himself

for another comment hinting at subjects like wooden stakes and silver crucifixes. Or mayhap a take-no-prisoners accusation, more true to Gabriela's form.

He did *not* expect her to duck beneath his arm and begin an almost casual saunter downstage. "Oh, Marcus," she called. "Stop teasing. You do remember that Ophelia falls out of a tree, into the stream, and dies? I want to start work on the scene tonight. Come on."

At that, Marcus contemplated *anything* but following her carefree lead. Dropping to his knees in gratitude fit the picture more accurately, even if heaven would nay hear his prayers again.

"Of course I remember." He yanked the tree forward with a cheerful spurt of unguarded—and unnatural—strength. Thankfully, Gabriela busied herself at a side table, slicing an apple and some cheese. "But the scene nay gets played out on stage," he added. "Gertrude laments the matter in retrospect."

"Not in Augustus Harris's version." She punctuated the assertion by sucking stray apple juice off her thumb with a pleased smack. "This is modern theater. Nothing sells tickets faster than characters loving, lying, fighting, riding, or dying on stage. Augustus has guaranteed his *Hamlet* contains generous portions of all. So he attracts 'good society' by presenting a classic, but collects from the masses with the spectacle, 'the show.' "

She stopped with knife halfway through the cheese. "Why am I telling you all this? You not only know it, but you stand to make a shiny shilling from it. Surely *you're* happy about the revision."

Marcus couldn't quell a sardonic grunt. "Be careful what you assume."

She frowned. "What do you mean?"

He leaned back against the tree's trunk and regarded her steadily. For once, he knew exactly of what he spoke. "I did not invest in Drury Lane to make a 'shiny shilling,'

Gabriela. Shine will one day fade. But truth and integrity are constant beauty. I am concerned that the theater stays true to that beauty, and the artists who made it that way. It seems that nobody will listen to me unless I own a piece of their weekly salary."

"That's probably true," she replied. "Unfortunate, but true. Yet Augustus *has* stayed true to Shakespeare's text. He's only inserted extra imagery."

The comment filled him with an unexpected rise of indignation. Before he could quell the anger, Marcus shoved violently from the tree. "Don't you think if Shakespeare wanted to show Ophelia's death, he'd have written in the blasted scene?" he bit out. "Perhaps the man had a reason, a bloody good one, for leaving the *imagery* out!"

Gabriela only answered by popping a cube of apple into her mouth. She watched him as she chewed contentedly, a look Marcus usually found adorable. But tonight, he turned from her. Her opinion was painfully clear: she thought him eccentric, just like the rest of these "modern" geniuses who butchered beauty for the sake of next week's ticket box take.

But Gabriela was *nay* like the rest. Marcus wanted her to know, needed her to understand. . . .

"Perhaps," she said lightly behind him, "When Shakespeare wrote the play, he didn't dream this kind of production would be possible."

"Oh, he knew."

At that, Marcus lifted his sights to the rafters, to the backdrops rolled there, a collection of at least a dozen new worlds waiting to be unfurled to an audience's imagination. The setting sent his own vision traveling back, lost for a precious moment to those days of laughter and music, of daring new dreams. . . .

"He imagined all this, and more," he continued softly. "God, how people laughed at him for those ideas. But he never gave a care. I do not think Will Shakespeare knew the meaning of fear. One day, he even marched right into Whitehall, and—"

"*Will* Shakespeare?"

Her startled question brought his thoughts crashing back to the present. And his heartbeat froze in his chest.

Marcus whirled back to her. Without stopping, without thinking, he met her gaze.

A disastrous mistake. Her face had maintained that half-amused mien, until the truth came flying from every corner of his own shocked stare.

Then her smile dropped. Her face paled.

Just before her hand, still holding the knife, sliced through her apple and into her palm.

"Oh!" she cried. "I'm such an idiot!"

At the sight of her first wincing grimace, Marcus rushed forward. With his senses so stupidly uncloaked the moment before, he felt every jolt of the knife's slide into her skin. He knew only her pain, and only that he longed to stop it.

That all changed when he smelled her blood.

He slid to a stop three feet from her. A hungering moan went barely controlled in his throat. Sweet . . . ah God, she smelled so sweet and heady; her life force filling his nostrils, flinging open his senses, arousing every cell in his body. He grew hard again; an unbearable ache thrumming in time to the primal beat of his own blood. It ordered him to join that throbbing flow with hers, to take her, to take her *now*.

Christ. Sweet Christ, help me!

"Marcus, would you help me? The cut's not deep, but I'm awkward with only one hand."

Unbelievably, his feet carried him forward in two jerking shuffles. The journey felt more like a hike over the Alps. When he reached her, Marcus forced himself to breathe, dictated himself to find his sanity again, and cling to it. He commanded his sights downward to avoid her scrutiny—God's teeth, what his gaze must look like when the rest of him quivered like this—but the action only aligned his view with her injured hand. Her beautiful hand. And her beautiful blood, a bright red ribbon across silken white skin. Her life . . . her spirit . . . her soul.

Take her. Take her. Take her!

"Thank goodness I wrapped the cheese in this cloth." Her murmur tickled his ear, intimate with awkward humor, innocent of the hidden battle he raged. "Bet the poor thing didn't know it would be doing double duty as a tourniquet."

She laughed and held out the cloth. Marcus inhaled excruciating breaths, and continued to stare at her hand.

"Marcus?" came her faint, concerned prompt. "Marcus, you need to wrap the cloth around my hand. Like this . . . oh!"

Her outcry came between his panther-swift lunge and his bearish, violent tug, bringing her hand to a breath's space from his lips.

"Gabriela," he whispered, closing his eyes, savoring her scent. His mouth watered. So close. Her essence teased him, so sweet. *I want you . . . Jesu, how I need you.*

But then she spoke. "Marcus?" And there was no mistaking the lilt of fear in her voice. Marcus released her, hating himself with a vehemence bordering on nausea.

Until her psyche burst over his with the power of a lightning flash—and he realized she wasn't afraid *of* him.

She was afraid *for* him.

Dear God. Dear God, Gabriela, you darling, trusting fool.

"Marcus." Again as if through a fog, he heard her short, nervous laugh. "Come, now," she chided. "It's just a little blood. A little accident like this can't affect you so deeply . . ."

Just try me. God, don't try me. Please go away . . . go away!

But the light of her voice would nay let him escape. Her presence beamed brighter into his darkness, seeking him even in the corners of his black despair. Her voice repeated his name, dragging him farther out of his night each time . . . finally compelling his gaze up and into the copper sun spectrum of her own.

But that euphoric dawn lasted only a moment. As he dreaded—as he expected—Gabriela took in his features, and a horrified gasp eclipsed her smile.

"Marcus," she whispered. "Wh-what's wrong? Your . . . your eyes . . . and . . . and you're shaking . . ."

"I know," he stammered. "I know. Please Gabriela, just—" *Just go. Leave me to my ugliness. Leave me to my hell!*

"Tell me," she urged instead, her voice shaking. "Tell me what's wrong."

The sound snapped his head back up. Amazement pummeled the air from his gut as the gas glow reflected off a lone, salty droplet skidding aimlessly down her cheek.

Ah, God.

Her tears. Her blood. Her body. It was all more than he could bear. Marcus felt a growl form deep in his throat, and the will fled him to swallow the sound. No more strength. No more sanity. Now he shook as badly as she, fighting his need, battling his lust.

He emitted the growl as he turned his head, capturing the inside of her wrist against his lips . . . and gently grazing her soft, warm skin. He nuzzled aside her lace cuff with his nose, and suckled halfway to her elbow. Oh, Jesu. She smelled so good. She would taste even better.

"Oh, Marcus," she rasped with more tears, forcing him to blink his way back to reality on a damn near impossible breath.

"I know," he replied, gently rolling her clothes into place. "I know, sweeting. I . . . I'm sorry."

"I'm not."

The two syllables narrated a moment of magic. For in that moment, Gabriela replaced her wrist with her lips.

Ah, *God.* She moved so shyly, so *honestly* . . . and that

brave innocence proved his undoing. Marcus drowned as her warmth flowed into him, tasting of apples and woman and life. Her trusting arms wrapped around him, full of hope and passion.

It was the first time he'd been kissed in over two hundred years. But Gabriela, his bold, beloved Gabriela, was worth every second of the wait.

Nevertheless, Marcus swiftly set about making up for lost time.

Six

Gabriela had never been more terrified in her life. Not even on the day Lord and Lady Rothschild had come to the orphanage for a second interview with her, and she'd taken the kitchen bleach to her hair. Surely, she'd thought, if she *looked* the part of a good little English ten-year-old, they could teach her the rest. . . .

But the need in her now burned far deeper than chlorine. Her heart's hunger for acceptance had gone so much longer without nourishment. And these new achings of her body . . . she whimpered against Marcus's mouth with a yearning she'd never dreamed she'd know, never *wanted* to know, until now. Until this man. Until Marcus, who knew her soul with the power of his eyes, awakened her body with the touch of his hand.

And so she kissed him, desperately showing what she couldn't say in words. She embraced him, despite the stiff, almost angry response of his own limbs. His arms froze at her sides, hands tightening into shaking fists, and the thighs she pressed against felt more like stone pillars. But she delved on, wanting to show him—needing to love him.

She knew the precise moment he got the message. Marcus's surrendering groan precipitated her heart's exuberant leap. His hands flattened, releasing their coiled energy into restless roams across her back, pulling her closer with commanding intensity. His lips not only answered the

questing foray of hers, but seized control in a dominating
sweep, molding her mouth to his in masterful strokes,
teaching her the ages-old colloquy of man and woman,
soft and hard, desire and surrender.

When he prodded her lips apart with his own, she
yielded. When his tongue sought hers, she responded. And
when she heard his voice in her head this time, she set
her senses free, reaching out to him in answer.

Yes . . . I want you, too. Take me, Marcus. Make me complete.

On an explosion of breath, he tore back from her. His
wide stare raked over her like she'd just turned into a
ghost—but Gabriela knew the truth in the brief flounder
of an instant his eyes strayed to hers.

"You heard me," she gasped. "You . . . you really heard
me, didn't you?"

He twisted away. "Gabriela, please—"

"Answer me! Marcus . . . who are you? How did you . . .
what did we just . . ."

His shoulders shuddered. "It was wrong."

"No," Gabriela protested in a whisper. "It was beautiful."

He froze again, fingers curling with that wordless, endless fury. Gabriela rushed to hold him, to make those stiff
arms wrap her in his strength and passion again. . . .

But she blinked on the way. And he was gone.

You're a fool, Danewell.

Marcus stopped counting how many times his mind bellowed the condemnation—especially after he ignored it
enough to order his private box made ready for the next
evening's performance. Now, the phrase showed no mercy.
The dooming words thundered louder in his ears than the
standing ovation of the audience below.

And he sat in the darkness of the box's back row, agreeing with every echoing syllable. *You're a fool . . . you're a fool. . . .*

The agony grew unbearable when Gabriela reappeared to take her bows.

His heart strained against his ribs as the footlights illumed her once more, still dressed in that forest nymph costume from the last act of the play, its flowing layers so perfectly celebrating her siren's body, her angel's beauty. He moaned as the ache robbed him of breath, but his grief was engulfed by the crowd's roaring approval. As she moved forward, the crescendo rose; a few "bravissimis" even embellished the din.

Marcus gripped the handles of his chair, weathering an agonizing swell of pride. London loved her already.

Gabriela barely noticed.

Oh, she smiled and waved as she accepted a bouquet of flowers. She even bowed again, and blew a demure kiss to the source of the "bravissimi" in the second tier. To this crowd, she exemplified the portrait of grace, beauty and happiness.

To Marcus, she might as well have been a wooden cutout for a child's toy theater. He felt the locking of her teeth beneath her pleasant smile. He felt the tension of her hands as they curled around the flowers.

He felt her heart aching as she looked up to his box.

Dear God . . . she somehow knew he sat here. She stared and then stared some more, wordlessly telling him how deep her pain went. Assuring him she was far from ready to let him forget it.

Surely enough, the moment the last house lamp was turned down and the last stagehand slammed out the back door, her determined footfalls clattered across the stage. She shook even the catwalk beneath Marcus's feet, where he stood listening to her, over the stage right wings. He dared not actually watch her. The chance ran too great that she would sense him doing so. But he could nay move, either. She effectively cut off his only route home as long as she stood there, fists on hips, waiting for the slightest abnormal noise or motion in the building she knew so well.

"Marcus."

She did not yell it this time. Nay, despite his effort to resemble the wall in his stillness, she spoke as if he stood right next to her. Then he felt her mind reaching out to him, purposely seeking him. . . .

Marcus's legs nearly buckled in the battle to keep her out. *By God's wounds.* How was this unreal connection of theirs possible?

It was not. He knew the rules. Fate had given him nearly three hundred interminable years to memorize them. Before anything like this became remotely possible, a vampire had to initiate a mortal: take in their blood once, sometimes twice, then reach inside their mind, literally touch their soul.

But what if . . . what if Gabriela had already given him her soul?

He did *not* want to know the answer to that.

"Marcus," she called again. Her voice rose in uneven pitches. Her hands fell to her sides, began tugging at her skirt in steady-tempoed tension. "Damn you, I know you're here. Answer me!"

I cannot.

"Please don't do this to me. You . . . you *can't* do this to me." He heard desperation. And fear. And loneliness.

Gabriela . . . His heart broke as sharply as her voice. *I never meant to hurt you. I never meant—*

"Is that it, then?" she whispered. "You won't even talk to me anymore? You won't even let me explain?"

But it's not your fault!

"No."

He started at that. She issued the word as a suddenly

hard—and determined—ultimatum. Her fists latched back to her hips.

"No," Gabriela called again, stronger yet. "I refuse to believe it. I refuse to yield my white flag to you, Mr. Danewell."

If she startled him before, she utterly baffled him now. She offered no further explanation of her statement but the view of her back as she pivoted toward the opposite wings, then marched on as if taking the field at Waterloo. Then she disappeared.

Marcus opened his senses in as wide a crack as he dared, straining to hear what the bloody hell she was up to.

Before he realized what she was *up* to.

He barely checked back a maddened growl at the sense of her coming close again—taking a vertical path this time. And aye, a moment later, he sighted her scrambling up the same rickety wall ladder the stagehands used to get to the catwalks, with one critical difference: Gabriela's hands barely caught the rungs, so tightly was she bound in that moronic corset, while she wrestled her legs past a number of underlayers surpassing ridiculous.

The devil only knew how she guessed to look for him up here. No matter, really, because the chit would kill herself doing it.

As she pushed off the ladder and onto the catwalk, Marcus could not decide whether to let either relief or rage assist him in this conundrum. He debated the issue as Gabriela pulled herself upright—but both sensations lost out to alarm as he observed her entirely too shaky execution of the act. She started down the narrow wooden plank at an equally unsure totter, her face draining three shades of color even while it maintained a determined scowl.

"Blast you, Danewell," she muttered through clenched teeth. "Heights have never been at the top of my talent bill."

Now she told him.

Gabriela. You impossible, beautiful fool. Just keep walking . . . keep walking, and for God's sake, don't look down.

She kept walking. While she looked down.

And, in a dizzy stumble, blundered straight into a stray scenery rope in her path.

All too clearly, Marcus watched the line snap around her ankle—then watched the confused thud of her other foot, trying to compensate. Then watched every second of her scrabbling struggle, her hands flailing for purchase against a thirty-foot fall to the stage.

He did *not* remember the two hand rails and three prop clouds he demolished while charging to make sure she fell into him, instead.

For a moment, in raw horror, he wondered if his feat knew success. He swallowed a chestful of relief when he looked to her ashen face against the crook of his arm, her eyes still blinking dazedly. She waved one hand about, trying to balance herself. When her fingers collided against his face, he turned and kissed them fervently—angrily.

"Marcus?" she murmured. "It *is* you. Wh-what happened?"

"You almost killed yourself." His growl emanated from the deepest part of his gut; the pit where raw fear lived. "God's teeth, Gabriela. That was the most ludicrous, damfool stunt I've ev—"

"Wait a minute." As she dropped her hand to his shoulder, it became a fist. As she tilted her head to meet his glare, an indignant copper fire flashed to life in her own. "Don't try to hang this bad review on me. You're the oaf responsible for my 'damfool stunt'! Put me down. Just put me down and let me go, Marcus. I don't know why I even bothered. You're clearly very happy being a cowardly bastard. I should have remembered that."

She struggled in his grip during the dissertation, but now Marcus cut his tolerance short with renewed fury in his hold. "What the devil's eye is that supposed to mean?"

"You ran from me in the beginning. You tried to run that second night. You only stayed after I begged for your help with my work. Your *gaze* runs when I look at you, Marcus." She punctuated that with a bitter laugh. "Need I go further? You're happy when you're running, so put me down and I'll let you do just that."

He should have called her game. He should have dropped her on her well-bustled little bottom, given her his retreating back and let her toss slurs at him until she turned blue.

But an undeniable instinct said she wasn't playing games. That same impulse flooded him with the vehement need to prove her wrong.

With a growl, Marcus flattened her to him as he spun around. He ignored her stunned cry as he stalked toward Drury's pitch black wings, a singular destination in mind.

Darkness, more darkness.

Gabriela didn't liken the texture just to the labyrinth of halls and stairwells Marcus carried her along. She felt him attempting to throw that numbing black fog over her senses again, this time a grim anger turning the cloud into more a massive thunderhead. But, as ridiculous as the notion seemed, she concentrated her consciousness on fighting back—and she sensed he didn't try *that* hard to force the haze upon her. She sensed his thoughts focusing elsewhere, on one pinpointed purpose. . . .

As if his mind fled from thinking of other things.

At last, after stomping up an endless, dim stairway, he stopped and kicked a door open. The chamber he carried her into didn't provide much more light.

Until he set her down on a velvet couch and swung aside two wide window shutters.

Gabriela broke their taut silence with an awed gasp. She recognized they now faced the back of the thea-

ter—lamps glowed on Drury Lane proper far below as
proof—but she preferred the more breathtaking land-
marks across London's nightscape as markers. Far out and
straight ahead, she identified the distinct oval of Finsbury
Circus. Inward, her sights took in the soaring dome of St.
Paul's. To the right, the currents of the Thames, half-
shrouded in a silver mist, and above the river, London
Bridge's stately lights. Everywhere else, street lamps comprised a maze of mystical night glow. Stars seemed to
stretch below them as well as above.

The added light helped Gabriela see the luxury of this
apartment, as well. Two wide Renaissance chairs matched
the dark indigo shade of the couch she occupied. A massive oak dining table filled the wall between the two windows, buttressed by a pair of chairs with intricately
embroidered cushions. Tasseled tapestries swagged the far
wall, replacing the mirror that should have backed the oak
sideboard. Atop that, a large Italian washing set and a well-
stocked wine rack kept each other company.

Elegance. Majesty. Beauty for the sake of being beautiful.
Magic.

"This . . . it's beautiful," she at last breathed. She
looked up to Marcus. As much as she resisted noticing, *he*
was beautiful. A small, but potent smile flickered over his
lips at her praise; long, dark lashes dropped to hide an
undeniable spark of pleasure in his eyes.

"Many thanks," he murmured. He lit one more candle
and took it along in an ornate silver holder as he crossed
to the wine rack. His free hand closed around what looked
like a very old vintage, the liquid echoing the candle's
light with a shimmering amber glow.

"I didn't know this apartment was up here." She issued
the comment to rid herself of nerves as much as curiosity.
Marcus moved and acted differently in this heavenly hideaway, and she didn't know what to think of that yet. Despite
his simple open-necked white shirt and unassuming brown

breeches, he walked with an owner's stride at last. She watched his hands uncork the wine with deft confidence. Again, she felt as if he peeled away the layers of another, surprising part of himself to her.

"Nobody knows this is up here," he qualified to her statement. Then, very softly, "You are the first I have ever brought."

He followed that with one of his long, dare-me-to-stop stares. Gold candlelight and silver soul light combined there, burning their way across the room at her. Still angry with her. But still adoring her.

And still touching her.

Gabriela laughed nervously and glanced away. "Well, I'm certain Augustus will be happy to hear that."

"Not unless you wish him to think you even more a loon."

She shot an amazed stare at him. "Not even Augustus knows about this?"

"Especially not Augustus." He answered as if informing her one and one obviously made two. Gaby's scowl must have proclaimed her next befuddled question, because he went on to explain, "I simply claimed the top and bottom of the theater as mine. I gave Augustus a liberal hand over the rest. And of course, I did all the interior design and construction of the apartment myself."

"Oh, of course," Gaby countered in sardonic astonishment. She circled another glance around. But yes . . . now that she looked, she saw Marcus everywhere in the apartment. She admired scrolled friezes carved with a mastered masculine touch, intricate paintings along the mantel depicting the lyrics of a romantic hunting tale. . . .

And an element she hadn't caught in her initial discovery . . . a half-draped doorway to her right, opening onto a room with the biggest bed she'd ever seen.

"My God." She couldn't help herself. She vaulted off

the couch and whipped the drape aside. "Who did you get that from? Queen Elizabeth?"

She thought she heard his sharp catch of breath behind her, but her head picked that moment to try its luck at a dervish dance again. Gabriela stumbled to the bed's nearest post, latching onto it with a weak moan.

Almost immediately, Marcus dashed behind her, his broad torso pressing against her, his strong arms slowing the dervish. He eased her down to the bed's wide counterpane, made of cloud-soft white down.

"You got up too quickly, aye?" he rebuked in a rough murmur. "Little fool." The knuckles of a cool hand brushed her brow. "Drink this," he prodded. "It will help smooth your nerves."

That same hand pressed a silver goblet of wine into hers. But even after she gained a secure hold on the chalice with both hands, Marcus didn't let go. He assisted her with several long sips of the rich and fruity bouquet. And Gabriela didn't resist, simply for the pleasure of feeling his strong fingers over hers.

"Better?" he finally asked, depositing the half-downed glass on a dark wood nightstand. His other hand rose to skim stray auburn curls from her cheek.

Gaby silently, slowly nodded. She leaned her cheek into his broad, hard hand. "That . . . that feels good," she whispered.

And it was the truth. While the wine mellowed her tattered nerves, Marcus's touch swirled magic through her blood. Silken warmth enveloped her. A slow, aching need rose inside her, like nothing she'd ever felt before. A need to hold this man, to touch him. . . .

"Gabriela . . ." He began the word as a protest, but ended in a guttural grate. He tried to lower his hand. She wouldn't let him. Instead, she took his hand in both of hers, urged him closer.

"You feel good," she amended. Oh, how *that* was the

truth. God had made this man with such infinite care—
even his hands were so hard, so carved. Gabriela ran her
marveling touch over his knuckles and palm, through the
valley created by his thumb and forefinger, over his wide
wrist, up his broad forearm.

"And I trow you are feeling much better." Marcus ex-
tricated himself with gentle haste. With equal tension, he
rose from the bed. Though he turned and held out a hand
to assist her up, too, his gaze fled, fast and unfocusing, to
the Italian-carpeted floor. He breathed as if he'd just swum
the Channel to France and back. "I'll escort you back
now."

She gave his hand a cursory glance. Then folded her
arms in her lap. "I don't think so."

That prompted his eyes up. Ready for him, Gabriela responded with a resolute scrutiny of her own.

Marcus's hand curled into a fist. His lips twisted over
locked teeth. Gabriela almost laughed. She'd give her
signed copy of Henry Irving's *Macbeth* to hear the oath he
wrestled back.

"Damn it, Gabriela," he finally growled. "If I must be
rude—"

"Go right ahead." She rearranged her skirts with dainty
tugs. "It won't change a thing. We have a few things to
discuss, Mr. Danewell—namely, why you feel you can appear and disappear from my life on your whims. And I'm
not going anywhere until that is accomplished."

He planted that fist, and the other, to wide-braced hips.
"I owe you no explanations."

"You owe me quite a number of explanations." She
crossed her knees and shifted her folded hands to cap
them, her form so flawless, *The Habits of Good Society* would
surely use her as its next model for demureness. "But tonight, I am only interested in a few."

"I want you to leave."

"And I said no."

"Then I *order* you to leave."

"No."

In an unexpected, almost violent rush, he hauled her up by the waist. Gabriela's breath exploded from her in a stunned whoosh. Her ears rang. Still, as he snapped her head within inches of his, she swore she heard a . . . *canine* snarl resonate from his throat.

Marcus didn't give her time to wonder about the occurrence. "You—are—leaving," he charged. His grip clamped harder. His eyes roiled with dark gray thunder.

But despite all the ways he clearly tried, he didn't frighten her. Her throbbing, escalating heartbeat—*that* terrified her. The swelling hammer of her pulse, powered by the old fear and the new hurt, drowned every breath until Gaby had to reclaim air in aching gulps.

But she wouldn't cry. Blast him, he would *not* make her cry.

"Damn it to hell," Marcus spat. "Why are you being so difficult about this?"

Too late. Her cheeks burned with wet, salty heat. Gabriela fired a hot, hateful glare up at him. "Why did my kiss repulse you so much?"

His left brow plummeted. His gaze arrowed in on her. "*What?*"

Gaby notched her chin higher. "You . . . you heard me."

"Aye," he answered, slower and softer. "But . . . Gabriela . . . what the . . . why do you think—"

"Answer me, damn you!" She freed herself from him in a shaking backstep. She wished he'd just drive the knife of his rejection home and get this torture over with. "I'm not leaving until you do."

Marcus stepped to her again, reaching for her hands. Gabriela whipped them away, trying to move back again too. But he trapped her against the bedpost, his height and power looming so close, too close.

"What makes you think your kiss repulsed me?"

Each word hung eternally between them before falling and drenching her senses, like moonlit snowflakes melting into crystalline rain. Beyond her control, Gabriela's soul drank eagerly of those precious drops, absorbing them even in all their feigned meaning and misleading tenderness. She closed her eyes and cursed herself for this unrequited weakness, hated herself for the fresh rush of tears down her cheeks . . . and over Marcus's hands, finally gaining access to her warm, wet skin.

She swallowed hard. Twisted her head away. "Don't," she implored. "Please don't keep making me believe you care. Just tell me the truth this time, Marcus. I want to hear it from your own lips, then I'll be gone."

"God's blood," he muttered to that. It came as no surprise that he followed the oath with a grunt of dark laughter. "How you arrive at these conclusions, woman, pales my compreh—"

"Don't!" Gaby swung a fist into his chest and a glare into his face. "Damn you, just stop it! I've been dismissed enough times in my life that I know how to accept it, all right? But I will not be lied to about *why*. Not by you, Marcus!"

"Gabriela." He caught her fist and held on. Tight. "By all that is in me, I am not dismissing you."

"Liar!"

"I do not lie. But there are things I cannot tell you . . . things you nay want to know—"

"Tell me."

His jaw locked. "I cannot."

"Tell me!"

This time, she didn't dare imagine the expletive he bit back. More than clearly, his taut glower translated the furious intent of his following bellow. "Why?" Marcus exploded at her, grabbing her other wrist and hauling her against his heaving chest. "Why the hell do you push me like this, Gabriela?"

The answer erupted out of *her* before thought or reason
or fear could throw themselves in the way.

"Because," she sobbed. "Because, blast it . . . I'm falling
in love with you!"

Seven

They both stopped breathing.

They both released gasps.

Gabriela stared at Marcus through aching tears, enduring the inevitable barrage of beratements and excuses on her brain. *Oh, Gabriela Angelica. What have you done now? What have you said now? Nothing you've thought about, that's for certain. You're still dizzy from the catwalks. Or fuzzy from the wine. Or hopelessly furious with this bastard.*

Or hopelessly in love with this bastard.

No inner argument retaliated to that.

Which only squeezed more painful tears from her heart. And released a wave of realization so strong she took back her rage, and redirected it inward.

He'd made things clear from the beginning, hadn't he? He'd all but commanded her not to need him, declaring his very world off limits, let alone his heart. But she hadn't listened. One more time, Gabriela had gambled her soul on the conviction that if she believed hard enough, wanted strongly enough, and worked diligently enough, someone in this world would open the gates of their trust and love in return.

And oh, how she wanted *this* man to be that someone. She just had to be an extra good girl this time. And she had been good, hadn't she? Surely God would see that, and finally give her the miracle she'd prayed so long for.

But Marcus's face told her differently. Marcus's taut, strained face, clenched to the point of immobility save for his nostrils as he dragged in harsh breaths and his eyes, searing across her features with intensity hotter than a limelight. . . .

Yes, Marcus's face said all she needed to know.

She'd gone and blurted the completely wrong thing.

She couldn't bear his unremitting stare any longer. "I'm sorry," she rasped as she pushed away, aiming the words at herself as well as him. "I'm so sorry."

But he didn't let her back away more than a step.

Her gaze leaped back to his. And her lips emitted a gasp of amazement. A nearly luminous sheen all but drenched the torch heat in his eyes, yet branded her as deeply—*more* deeply—with that piercing silver glint. He continued to breathe hard, in and out, that rhythm corresponding to the kneadings of his lips over his teeth. As if he were very hungry.

As if he were very hungry for her.

Gabriela still pondered where she'd gotten that nonsensical notion when Marcus hauled her a step closer, and then some. And then some . . . until his big body pressed against every inch of her and his mesmeric eyes glowed just inches from hers.

"Say it again," he commanded, in the barest guttural grate.

It took a stunned, searching moment to retrieve her voice. "Say wh-what again?"

"You know what." His hold tightened. A shiver awakened every nerve ending she possessed. His chest expanded and dropped against hers, as if forcing himself to maintain their proximity. But then he repeated, nearly implored, "Say it to me again, Gabriela."

"You want to hear me say I'm *sorry* again?"

To her surprise, the hint of a laugh skipped across his

lips. "Nay. The other." Then, in a whisper along her cheek and her neck, "The *other.*"

"Oh." Realization, warm and incredible, surged against the strange shiver. The sensations collided and consumed at the same time his lips captured the bottom of her ear. "Oh, *Marcus,*" she gasped, all too willing to follow the guidance of his hands, sliding her arms around his neck. "Marcus. . . ."

"Say it."

"I love you."

"Again."

"I love you."

"Yes. . . ."

He trailed the word out in a slow, fervent hiss around her ear, down her nape, then into her hair as he swiftly searched for coifing pins there and tugged them loose. When her waist-length tresses tumbled free, Marcus caught them in his shaking fists, lifted them to his slightly parted lips and kissed each dark auburn curl as if the strands were the petals of Saint Elizabeth's roses. Speechless wonder rendering her incapable of anything else, Gabriela watched him through a watery mist.

Finally, he coiled swaths of hair around both hands until the tension gently pulled her head back. Gabriela yielded, offering her face up to him . . . her heart open to him.

He didn't squander a moment of the invitation. Marcus plunged his lips over hers with bold, conquering strokes. He parted her mouth with unadultered masculine possession. His kiss assaulted and savored. His touch cherished her and excited her.

And wanted her.

And somewhere deep in Gabriela's consciousness, an answering voice of need shouted out to him—a voice she never imagined herself capable of, a hope she'd dismissed as incinerated by the flames of disillusion, using her girlhood as kindling. No, she'd never even dared to dream of this reeling splendor, this unabating joy . . . all because of one man, one soul, one heart.

But she'd known that from the beginning, hadn't she? Hadn't she realized, in that moment her heart first stopped and her eyes first locked with Marcus's silver stare. . . .

Her heart had never been destroyed. Merely waiting.

Waiting for her destiny.

Thank you, God, she said with the tears in her eyes and the love in her heart. *Thank you . . . thank you for this, at last.*

But as her last few words flew heavenward, Marcus broke off their kiss. Before his startled gaze speared her, Gabriela knew he'd heard her prayer. But that only made her smile.

Yes, she told him with that same inner voice, kissing him softly. *Yes, I was thanking God for you.*

I love you, Marcus. Oh, how I love you.

No silent answer echoed in her mind. But his deep moan proclaimed what a thousand love-sonneted words couldn't. The sound reverberated through Gabriela, awakening a corresponding part of her own spirit. The part matching spark to his ember . . . singing aria to his polyphony . . . fitting woman to his man.

They kissed again. Tenderly, then deeply. Mouths fusing. Hands claiming. Hearts twining. Marcus stroked her everywhere, as if memorizing her form, and Gabriela rejoiced in his impassioned assault, arching and sighing against him as proof. Her own hands raced along his shoulders, down his chest and back again, reveling in this new, hard tactility called male.

They finally dragged their lips apart, breaths mingling at the same rhythm, heavy and fast, excited and expectant. Gabriela opened her eyes, yearning to see her new emotions made into something even more magic by their reflection in Marcus's gaze.

That captivating silver world didn't await her. Instead,

she traced fingers over facial angles that had actually tightened the last few minutes—and over the eyes that trembled in his effort to remain closed to her.

As if his bloody obstinance would deter her. Without hesitation, Gaby followed her fingers' paths with her lips. She nipped Marcus's strong chin and straight jaw, suckled the end of his nose, brushed feathery trails over his forehead and finally adored each set of his black eyelashes with soft, deep kisses.

She didn't miss his shaking catch of breath as she bestowed those last two touches. She didn't ignore the amazed tremors chasing down her own limbs, as well. Her lips came away from his eyelids tingling with a warmth she'd never experienced before . . . as if she'd just kissed two burning stars. Considering the man those eyes belonged to, Gaby didn't cast away that theory as impossible.

She wanted more.

She leaned up and kissed him again, lingering in the creases between his eyelids and brows. The mesmeric warmth flowed from him again, filling her mouth, too. Gabriela smiled.

Marcus moaned. A shudder consumed him, devouring its way up toes then knees, thighs then torso. "Gabriela," he pleaded hoarsely. "I pray you, sweeting—"

"Sssshh." She drew him into her arms, burying her fingers into the thick waves of his hair. "Marcus, whatever it was . . ." she murmured, "whatever you did . . ."

"Nay . . ."

"Thank you."

"Gabriela . . ."

"You're beautiful."

He expelled another moan into the crook of her neck. "Nay! Gabriela, you must—"

"Love you. That's all I must do. I love you."

"Dear God."

His lips croaked helpless surrender as they raked from

her throat to her mouth. Yet Marcus claimed her differently this time. Very differently. His mouth plundered as if he couldn't get enough of her; a drowning man sucking his last moments of life. New tears squeezed out Gabriela's eyes as she gave him what he wanted—what he needed— opening her lips to his hunger, her senses to his passion. As she did, the astonishing occurred: he kissed her deeper, harder. His desire became the very tidal wave that would claim the breath he clung to.

She felt his hands form into desperate claws at her back, grazing the row of tiny buttons along her spine. His arms trembled in frustration. His thighs clenched against hers, a hardness at their juncture making Gaby achingly aware of the pooling wetness between her own.

She didn't need to see his eyes to know what he wanted now. Because she wanted that ultimate union, too.

And for the first time in her life, she knew why Ophelia flung herself from that blasted tree for Hamlet.

Gabriela tore away from their kiss, her lips seeking Marcus's ear. "Love me," she implored when she found it. "Make love to me, Marcus."

His body only clenched tighter. His arms quivered as he lowered them from her. His throat vibrated with the effort to hold back an agonized half-growl, half-sob—in vain.

The sound spoke louder to the primeval feminine instincts inside her . . . needs lain dormant for much, much too long. Those impulses guided her hand lower, sliding past Marcus's waist and along the solid swell between his thighs.

"Gabriellll—!"

But she stole the final note from him in a bold, open kiss. As she did, her other hand yanked on the back of his head, pulling his lips upon hers. His responding groan fulfilled her more than the loudest roar of applause. Gabriela never dreamed she'd know such joy, such passion. She never imagined she'd kiss a man like this, caress a man like this, or whisper the very increments of intimacy she'd hushed from Donna a month ago.

But she'd never imagined Marcus.

She never imagined wanting him so badly. Yes, all of him, around her . . . inside her. And if that meant taking the seed of his babe, too, she'd thank heaven again. Things would be different. She'd *make* them different. Marcus's child would never know a day of heartache or loneliness. Not with all the love she'd shower on the beautiful being. Not with the way she adored their extraordinary father.

With that thought, she clasped Marcus's arousal tighter. His tremor bespoke the effect she rendered. Her lips curled in a pleased smile against his before she raised both hands to his face, cupping his jaw and kissing him deeper, deeper yet, pressing herself again to the ever-hardening ridge of him. Marcus answered in action, sliding his hands to her bottom, teaching her hips the same undulating rhythm set by their thrusting tongues.

And the conflagration consumed them. Up and down. In and out. Heat, raw and raging, sparking and flaring, scorching away the rest of the world. They breathed desire. They drank of need. Past the point of any control. Past the point of no return.

On a surge of impassioned triumph, Gabriela felt Marcus's hands at her back again, fumbling at her dress buttons. After frustrated minutes, when only one button loop surrendered its prize, he tore the material away in one savage jerk.

"I'm sorry," he rasped, even as his shaking touch roamed her bare shoulders.

Gabriela smiled. "I'm not."

And the next moment, she showed him so. She dug fingers into his shirt front and ripped until a broad ribbon of dark torso lay naked to her eager touch.

"My God." His amazed gasp preceded his renewed assault of ardor. Before she found her breath for a squeal of astonishment, Gabriela found herself swooped off the floor and onto the bed. The plush counterpane and blankets billowed as Marcus plummeted with her, fleecy folds curling around them as seductively as Highland clouds flirting with morning birds.

Nothing permeated that downy heaven for several minutes but the joining of two frantic heartbeats—and the rasps of more rending fabric. He took two rips to dispatch her dimity bustle. Three for her foulard petticoat; five jerks and an exasperated oath to wrench her corset free. Gabriela accidentally tore his breeches, pulling the flap the wrong way in her valiant haste to set his desire free.

Yet when she did, his shuddering moan took the place of her embarrassment. The length of him fell into her grasp, overflowing the span of her fingers, taking her breath away. Gabriela began a wondrous exploration over his long, velvet erection, her exhilaration tripling when his head fell back in mute ecstasy. His hair gleamed ebony and gold in the lamp glow, features such a flawless study of tight anticipation, she expected Michelangelo to materialize any moment for the privilege of carving him.

And she knew the time was right.

She gazed up at the beauty of her midnight lover, despite his continued obstinance not to look back. She glided her hand to the taut muscles of his torso.

"Love me, Marcus," she whispered. "Love me now."

He said nothing in return—in words. But his touch . . . his silken, sensual fingers; sliding, stroking, worshiping her body as he guided her hips to an intimate position around his. Everywhere he touched, he left the same magical warmth she'd gleaned from his eyes. Gabriela trembled and tingled, her senses a chaos of physical need, her soul a rapture of awakening love.

At last Marcus pressed over her, his whole body quivering with tension, a taut-muscled slingshot ready to snap. His hands moved to either side of her face as he kissed her deeply, then he burrowed his straining forehead into the hollow of her neck.

The tip of his sex parted the first folds of her womanhood.

"Gabriela," he grated. "Ah, *God*—"

"Don't stop," she urged, kissing his neck, twining her fingers in the damp waves of hair at his nape.

"I don't want . . . to hurt you."

"You'd never hurt me." Knowing intimacy warmed her voice. "You told me so yourself. Remember?"

"Sometimes . . ." He slid in farther. A strained huff escaped him. "Sometimes I do things I don't . . . I can't . . . control."

"Good." Instinctual femininity replaced the gentle tone. Gabriela lowered her hands to the curves of his straining buttocks, and squeezed.

He moaned. Rock-hard heat prodded farther into the core of her. Gabriela relished her victory, arching into him, opening wider for him. That coaxed him another half inch. He moaned again, deeper. His legs quaked. His rapid breaths warmed the coverlet next to her face.

Clearly, the man had made up his mind to be slow and gentle.

Gabriela wanted him intense and complete.

So she gave him no choice in the matter. Following instinct older than Antigone, she thrust her hips up to meet his, gathering his body fully into her own.

They both gasped.

Gabriela steeled herself for the pain. If she'd learned anything at the orphanage besides table manners and bread making, it was that loving also meant hurting, especially for a woman. And yes, the brief tearing of her flesh came—but not before the joyous completion. Not before the profound knowledge of oneness with this man, her love, her heart.

The feeling surpassed happiness. Exceeded the expression of tears. Her throat constricted on waves of transcending intensity, barely allowing her sparse gasps, let alone spoken words.

Yet words existed. Spilling from deep inside her, sibilant and sensual, translating themselves into heartbeats that spoke directly to the powerful presence above her, around her, inside her.

Marcus . . .

Gabriela. My sweet. Dear God, Gabriela . . .

It's wonderful.

I've not hurt you?

For a moment. It's gone. There's only you now . . . only you. I've waited so long for you . . .

I know. I don't know how I know that, but I know.

Forever. 'Tis been forever. You feel so good . . . ah God, don't stroke my thighs like that—

You don't like it?

I love it. Too much. Sweet heaven, I'll lose control . . .

Good.

And Gabriela set about making him do just that.

She did *not* expect him to take her on the wondrous journey with him.

No, she didn't imagine the breath-stealing strokes his hips answered to her instinctual thrusts. Not once, even in the fathoms of her fantasies, did she dream of the magic his hands rendered to her body, discovering her, exposing her.

And never, *never* did she dream of the force he'd unleash in her responding, awakening body. The feeling built to such a crescendo that only her impassioned cries filled her ears. And when she opened her eyes to let her lover see his effect on her, only a hot silver glow filled her gaze, bathing the whole room in a hypnotizing, otherworldly light. . . .

Marcus!

Close your eyes!

Marcus, what's happening? What is it?

Only the power you have over me. Do you not feel it? Close your eyes, open your senses . . . and feel me.

I feel your heartbeat . . .

Our *heartbeat.*

Your body . . .

Our *body.*

Your desire . . .

Oh, aye. Oh, aye. *Oh . . .*

"Gabriela!"

His outcry shattered the silver silence with primitive passion. The last syllable of her name continued on his lips like an animal's roar of possession, raw and dominating, volume rippling in time to the pulse of his release inside her. Gabriela accepted his dominion with complete acquiescence, lips curving in a joyous smile as a corner of her mind secretly added finishing lines to this mystical, magical night.

My love . . . our love.

She awoke to more silver light. But now the luminescence came from the early morning haze filtering through the gauzy white bed curtains. Gabriela fingered aside the drape to look through the open doorway into the apartment's living room, where the same light bathed oak and velvet and tapestries in hushed gray stillness.

A stillness intensified by Marcus's absence.

Gaby's heart felt that fact before her eyes confirmed it. Yet while vacant in person, her dark lover filled the room in essence. Yes . . . Marcus was everywhere still, living on in the images her mind recreated as she ran adoring fingers over the sheets and counterpane around her.

She envisioned him as he'd finally withdrawn from her and fell to the pillows, satiated and smiling. She relived the magic of his tender kisses throughout the next hour—

then the renewed desire that stirred in them both. With a secret smile, she remembered the reckless abandon of their second coupling . . . the heaven Marcus pulled her to, higher than the first time, then his guidance to the most ultimate paradise of all, a release throbbing in the deepest part of her, inciting a groaning explosion from him seconds later.

Her memories reluctantly returned to the more temporal realm of the morning. Still, Gabriela entertained the yearning to just burrow back under the covers and fall into a sleep made of passion-filled dreams. Damn the interview she had today with the *Chronicle*. Forget the emergency costume fitting and the extra rehearsal so tonight's understudy could finally get Act Two right.

Marcus, Marcus . . . I only want you, Marcus.

Where *was* he?

Only his empty pillow stretched across the other side of the bed as answer. At first, Gabriela brushed her knuckles across the white expanse, as if by caressing the few black wavy hairs he'd left behind, she'd somehow conjure the whole man. When the motion only yielded sharper longing in her heart and deeper want in her body, she gathered the whole pillow to her, breathing in his musky, manly scent.

Her eyes popped wide as her sight cleared the top of the pillow.

Gabriela tossed the feather-filled cushion away before scrambling across the covers and jerking back the curtain at the foot of the bed. As if remembering to do so at the last moment, she hastily wiped at her eyes. Surely she *imagined* the exquisite sight before her. Maybe she really did need more sleep. A lot more.

They didn't make day gowns this beautiful . . . did they? Yet she reached up to the garment hanging on the dressmaker's dummy and ran fingers along a velvet polonaise that felt luxuriously real enough. She recognized quite real

satin neck trim and marveled at an eight-layered under-
skirt of breathtakingly real ecru lace. A velvet and silk hat
rested atop the dummy at an elegant angle, its flowers
matching the lush lavender of the polonaise, its chin ribbon and bows corresponding to the gown's creamy lace.
To the side, lace-trimmed gloves rested next to a full toi-
lette of equally frilled underthings. Completing the ensemble: a double-bowed pair of slippers straight out of
Cinderella.

Gabriela laughed at that analogy. "Oh, Cinderella," she
whispered. "You could only hope to have *my* Prince
Charming."

Confirmation of that statement came in the form of a
small card she noticed then, tucked into the intimate V
where the gown would accent her breasts. Warmth suf-
fused her as she grabbed for the envelope and ripped out
the card inside.

Only two words awaited her gaze, penned in a script so
formal, it appeared medieval. Yet the careful calligraphy
made the words more precious, filled her heart with that
much more love for the man who told her, simply and
solemnly:

Thank you.

"Marcus," she breathed. "Oh, Marcus, thank *you.*"

She pressed the card against her heart for long minutes,
hoping that somehow the man's handwriting wielded as
much power as his gaze . . . and his loving. In that silent
pause, she reflected on everything she'd come to love
about Marcus Danewell. The kinship of his lonely, seeking
spirit. The wordless understanding they shared, manifest-
ing in the magical communication between their souls.
And, of course, their mutual love of the theater; her unending discovery of his natural talent, his unbreaking belief in hers.

The stumble over *that* thought effectively halted her reverie—and snapped her eyes back open. Dear God. What

the bloody blazes was she doing here, lifeless as an owl in the middle of the morning, when priorities lay waiting to be attended? Priorities Marcus not only encouraged her to meet, but *expected* her to maintain. On the back of his note, he'd even penned a reminder about the morning interview and directions on how to get out of the apartment.

And now more than ever, she longed to not only meet, but exceed his expectations.

Now more than ever, Gabriela finally believed in dreams coming true.

That realization almost coaxed another laugh. To think she once feared Marcus would strip away her dreams. Instead, he'd stepped right into them . . . changed them into incredible reality.

For instance, the Prince's Grand Troupe didn't loom as a terrifying icon any more. As she dressed, Gaby admitted she'd come to consider the selection process as challenging, not insurmountable.

And Alfonso's intimidations? She thought on the poor man's ramblings now, and found herself smiling at amusing stories, not crying from haunting threats.

That brought another joyous realization. With Marcus by her side, the world was filled with many smiles now. With Marcus in her heart, self-doubt had become self-assurance.

With Marcus in her life, what could possibly go wrong?

The answer to *that* filled her heart as perfectly as the bliss of indulging in a girlish twirl in her new clothes. The day gown fit to the inch—but no great surprise inundated her at how well Marcus knew her measurements.

Gaby only wished she had a mirror to truly revel in the finery. Yet a thorough search of the apartment's doors, closets and even spacious bathing room didn't yield even a hand-held looking glass.

No matter, she decided. She'd wear the gown again when she saw Marcus after the performance tonight, and let the intensity of the glints in his gaze be her true gauge of success.

She'd let her own gaze do a little assessing, too, . . . such as the look she'd level before telling him just how much she loved him. Then she'd *show* him just how much she loved him. . . .

A perfect night. A perfect man. A perfect life.

She could hardly wait.

Eight

Marcus could hardly wait.

And now more than ever, he hated himself for that fact.

He hated standing here and shaking in this cold, damp chamber, abhorred the knowledge that as London prepared for its Saturday evening enjoyments a hundred feet above, he barely breathed while anticipating the arrival of St. Thomas Hospital's latest corpse.

His dinner.

A humorless grunt resonated in his throat as he slumped over his coffin, weak with hunger. So he had wheeled a fine turn at becoming Hamlet to his Ophelia, after all. Just as Will Shakespeare's sweet prince fell to the blade of Laertes, so his body's cry for blood had slashed into the sublime moments he had known just after awakening tonight.

He could nay remember the last time he had slept so peacefully, or recalled such paradises of dreams . . . or actually smiled at a previous night's memories. For a long while, he had simply lain in his coffin, for once grateful for the blackness that allowed sovereignty over his mental mementos of an angel named Gabriela. He relived every caress of her flowing hair and smoke-soft skin; he savored the blessing of her kisses, the healing of her touch . . .

Then the hunger took control, seizing on his body's satiated vulnerability. He composed himself long enough to stumble out of "bed," scrawl a note to Joseph at the hospital's morgue and summon his favorite street urchin to deliver it. All the while, his mind and soul churned with one name, one vision:

Gabriela. *Gabriela.*

Beautiful Gabriela, giving her body to him. Precious Gabriela, entrusting her heart to him.

Innocent, unknowing Gabriela, falling in love with a beast.

"Oh, sweet Jesu," he groaned, struggling for gasps of self-loathing. His lungs only cooperated with a pair of shallow wheezes. "Sweet Jesu, what have I done?"

But even in his debility, the answer to that resonated with terrifying clarity. Marcus knew exactly what he had done.

Last night, he had fallen in love with Gabriela in return.

Nay . . . now that he thought on it, he had fallen in love with her a long time ago. He just never allowed the acknowledgment to bear fruition, his subconscious chopping short the buds of a tree he nay dared to eat from.

But then he had heard Gabriela weeping that night—ah God, that fateful night—and his senses fell prey to the same beautiful spell she cast over the rest of him. He had comforted her even as he felt her tears water the tree, coaxing the branches of his soul into bloom. And she nourished the tree in return with her smiles and laughter, tempting him more each day with the forbidden fruit of her love.

Selfishly, Marcus had finally devoured the bounty. Senselessly, he ignored the laws of decency, of man and maybe even of God. Stupidly, he had taken a heart he had no right to claim.

That final confession slammed his mind to the next wrenching conclusion.

He had to give that heart back. No matter what. No matter if he would prefer handing over his own arms and legs, instead. But he felt dismembered already, knowing the torment that lay ahead . . . knowing the pain he would have to pound into Gabriela's stubborn skull in order to transform the loving amber flecks in her eyes to shards of hate. Knowing the lies he would have to hurl, accepting the bastard he would have to be.

Knowing that after she walked away from him tonight, he would never see her again.

He tried to hearten himself with the assurance that her hurt would heal. Her world would continue, her years would know more loves and laughter, sorrows and hardships, then at last, the peace of a mortal end. In time, she would find oblivion in the comforting cycles of life . . . and death.

And Marcus would not.

Then again, perhaps he was dying now. Surely the agony ripping across his chest equaled no less. From that chasm deep within him, a long, low animal's moan erupted, echoing off the chamber walls to inflict his pain back at him fourfold. Marcus threw his head back and acquiesced to the torture, feeling every pitch of that broken wolf's howl, every note of that outcry from a condemned creature of the night.

"Gabriela," he rasped. "Gabriela . . . I love you." *I'll always love you. Forever . . .*

As he slid to the ground, folding in on himself, the grate of an opening stone door resounded through the chamber. A chilled wind hit his hunched back, smelling of rain and rumbling with thunder. A man's shuffling footsteps and grunts of exertion followed. The steps scuffed to a stop a moment later.

"Guvnah?" came a coarse, yet strangely musical voice. "Hey, guv, ye in here?"

"Aye." Marcus barely managed the word. He didn't bother to rise or offer his exact location.

Joseph nay cared, anyway. As long as the hospital's nighttime morgue keeper received his generous compensation for these twice-weekly deliveries, Joseph remained a staunch guardian of the stranger—and his vile secret—living in darkness beneath Drury Lane. Even ten years ago, when Marcus had finally trusted the man to bring his "packages" directly to the subterranean vault, Joseph simply indulged a swift glance at the coffin and then said, "Don't give any answers and I won't ask any questions."

Since then, only Marcus asked the questions. Even tonight, with the stamina of both mind and body cut in half, he forced his thoughts to wade through mental marshland and dictate the necessary words to his lips.

"You have brought a . . . recent arrival?" His jaw shook around each syllable. Sweet God, he hated this. He asked about a human body like a fishwife haggling over a plucked duck at market. He hated this and he hated himself for not ending it.

Joseph, on the other hand, might as well have been on a Sunday picnic in Hyde. The man whistled a bawdy version of "Good Luck to the Girl Who Loves a Sailor" as he moved toward Marcus's left and plunked his burden down on the stone slab in the chamber's alcove.

"Can't get more recent than this," he interrupted himself long enough to boast. "Fetched ye a blighter straight off the hospital's back porch. Never even made it inside before he passed on, so I didn't have to waste time on his papers. Not that I'd get anywhere with 'em, anyhow. Just another gutter duck; couldn't remember his own bleedin' name. Anyhow, he's still warm. I think ye'll be pleased."

"And . . . he has no family?"

An exasperated sigh blended with the first drips of rain down a distant drainpipe. "No. No one."

" 'Tis *crucial*, Joseph," Marcus growled. "I cannot take someone's father or brother or—"

Or lover, his mind added with nearly instinctual swiftness. For the first time in his life, mortal years included, he comprehended what a precious word the term could be. Or what a soul-robbing loss.

"Like I told ye, guv," Joseph interjected, "he's another John Doe." The man emitted a phlegmy, uncomfortable cough. "I got a gander at him meself before he passed completely on. And the blighter's eyes . . . well, he cashed out o' life a while ago, if ye catch my flounder."

"Aye," Marcus replied in a relieved murmur. "Aye, I do." He folded his arms, enduring renewed shivers brought on by a fresh wave of hunger as he realized fulfillment lay so close now. "M-many thanks, Joseph," he stammered. "Your recompense will be delivered to the hospital tomorrow eve."

"Ahhh, thank *you*, guv." The mortal made his way back to the door with a lighter step, his burden now deposited. "Always a pleasure."

Marcus only answered with another grunt. *Joseph, you ignorant, opportunistic fool. This is anything but a pleasure.*

"Health and strength to ye, guv. Good evenin'."

Not a dot of mockery punctuated the man's remark, but as the door slid shut behind Joseph on its weight and pulley-powered track, Marcus ruminated if Joseph was truly serious about his remark. *Health and strength.* Good God. Surely by now, a morgue keeper, of all people, had developed a fairly accurate guess about Marcus's true state of "health." As for strength . . .

He couldn't help loosing a feeble chuckle at that. Perhaps, this once, Joseph didn't issue *that* tiding in vain. Not only did Marcus's body draw on dangerously dwindling reserves now, but the coming hours would demand all the strength he could get. And he owed Gabriela the dignity of saying goodbye to a man who at least looked and sounded normal.

Gabriela wished the curtain call would just end.

As instantly as her mind courted the thought, she begged forgiveness for it. Though never officially thou-

shalt-notted on Moses' tablets, surely somebody somewhere considered it sacrilege to wish oneself finished with
a five-minute Drury Lane standing ovation complete with
armloads of roses and vocal outcries even from the private
boxes.

All the private boxes—except Marcus's.

Therein lay the seed of her transgressing impatience.
Though she couldn't actually see the box—the footlights
blinded her to all but the first two rows—her heart confirmed Marcus's absence more assuredly than if a spotlight
blared upon the unoccupied space. She still didn't understand the amazing mental connection they shared, nor did
she think it vital to, but she knew their physical union had
strengthened the psychic bond so powerfully that her emptiness without him equaled her fulfillment in his arms and
by his side.

That made the emptiness bloody nearly unbearable.

Gaby dipped two last curtsies more resemblant of chopping Chinese bows and nearly tripped over her skirts twice
as she hastened off stage. Surely theater business detained
Marcus from attending tonight's show, but she swore she
felt him awaiting her in the upstairs apartment now. . . .

At that, she curled a clandestine smile. Now that the
waiting was nearly over, she almost thanked Marcus for it.
The prolonged anticipation spiraled her nerve endings to
new crests of awareness, inspired her body to an increased
and intimate sense of readiness. Yes, every second of this
interminable separation would be well worth the agony
once she stepped into Marcus's arms again . . . once she
surrendered to his dominating kiss . . . once they became
a single heart and being again.

"I'm coming, Marcus," she whispered into her flowers,
oblivious of the backstage revelries as she hurried down
the hall to change clothes. "Not long now, my love."

Three steps from her dressing room, her arms dropped
with the same cold startlement sluicing her spine and legs.

The bouquets plunged into an unceremonious heap at her feet. Cloying cologne doused their scent.

Cologne emanating from the slick-dressed blade waiting in a casual slouch against the wall.

"Mr. Renard," she stated, hoping her tone conveyed the same ice invading her blood. "Good evening."

Thin lips quirked at her in a mockery of a smile. "Darling," came that too-familiar drawl, "I thought we'd agreed on just 'Alfonso.' "

"Mr. Renard," she repeated, "I really do not have time this evening—"

"You haven't had time many of these evenings." Alfonso countered her tension with equally deliberate torpidity, stretching her nerves along with his words on a verbal torture rack. He finally shoved from the wall, slid in front of her, and snaked a hand around her nape. "And I've missed you so, little Gaby."

"Don't." She jerked back from him as far as a passing costume rack allowed.

"Don't what?" His well-oiled smile curled again. "Don't miss you?" A soft chuckle. "Impossible. I'm afraid you're a fever, darling. You've gotten into my blood and you won't leave."

A scarf selected that moment to slip and snag in one of the rack's wheels. As the dresser fumbled with the detainment on one side, the forest of costumes closed Gaby and Alfonso in on the other.

The snake wasted no time seizing advantage of the situation. "Don't say you haven't missed *me,*" Alfonso crooned, reaching for her again. "Don't say you haven't been lonely, rehearsing night after night in this barn by yourself. Gabriela,"—when she refused to look up, he jerked her chin up with both his hands—*"when* are you going to cease this late-night nonsense?"

Despite his painful hold on her jaw, Gabriela almost laughed her reply. *Late-night nonsense?* If the fool only knew the paradox he spewed. In the velvet magic of London's midnights, she'd discovered a new dimension of life grounded in anything but nonsense.

She wondered what Alfonso would say if she stepped back right now, stared him in the eye and pronounced, *I'm never going to cease, Alfonso, because I'm never going to stop loving Marcus Danewell. Heaven has blessed me with a person you can never hope to become—a man you will never be.*

She yearned to shout the declaration into his sharp-edged face, but thinking the words gave her the strength not to voice them. This wasn't the right time. What she and Marcus had still gleamed like a newly formed diamond: the creation perfect, but unpolished; therefore, at a precious and vulnerable stage. One day, with Marcus's fortitude more deeply ingrained as part of her, too, she would confront Alfonso with the truth.

Tonight, she counted it victory enough to step away from him with the same silent serenity a director used on an unwanted actor. As the costume cart wheeled on again, she continued toward her dressing room with the inner command to ignore, then forget him.

But two feet from the room's threshold, Gaby found her way blocked once more by cologne-reeking torso.

Still dictating control to her composure, she tried to step around to the left. Alfonso braced an arm to the portal at the level of her breasts. She didn't attempt the right side. God only knew how far he'd extend the blockade effort there.

She drew in a long, even breath. Then steadily stated, "Let me pass."

Alfonso only clicked his tongue—as if *she* held them both up here with *her* childish antics. "But you haven't answered my question."

Gaby's head pounded. Locking her teeth against the frustration didn't help matters. "It doesn't warrant an answer. You know I won't give up until the Prince's Theatre Troupe comes to call."

Impatience bested her. She tried to pass on the right. Alfonso shifted an arm *and* a leg into her path. "And you think your handful of good reviews will bring them running?"

The agitation drummed harder. Gaby tugged repeated handfuls of her costume's silk skirt. The costume mistress would kill her for the wrinkles. *And Marcus would give up and go home if she didn't get to him soon.*

"I don't think it's of your business," she snapped. "Now, *let me pass.*"

Instead, she found herself forced back against the unforgiving oak portal, both of Alfonso's hands clamped around her shoulders. His fingers dug into her skin. He loomed over her with quiet, almost frightening calm.

"I think it *is* my business, dear." Poison laced his wine-smooth utterance. "Perhaps you'd be interested to know they've already selected over half the principals for the Prince's Grand Theatre Troupe."

The last four words, he spat with extra venom. His toxin met its mark. Gabriela jerked her sights up, barely noticing his satisfied gleam at her consternation—and too stunned to care.

But with comforting alacrity, suspicion jumped in. "And how do you come by this intriguing little *bruit,* Mr. Renard?" she parried. "I'm not inclined to believe some tidbit whispered during a tryst with your latest willing chorus girl."

Alfonso flashed an indulgent chuckle. "Quick, darling. But wrong. I dined with Davis Webber last night. Very nice fellow. He's quite excited about the ensemble they've gathered."

Her stomach plummeted. Davis Webber . . . the creative and casting director for the Prince's Troupe. She didn't think Alfonso *knew* the man, much less dined with him. Then again, Alfonso seemed to know everyone. . . .

"I still don't believe you," she blurted. "Why didn't I see any notices in the paper?"

"You know Davis." A shrug, as sincere as Alfonso's shrugs came. "He wants to announce the entire cast at the same time. Make a production out of the production, so to speak. It's all a secret until then."

Lost to bewildered ponderings, Gaby didn't say anything. Apparently, that translated into an unspoken invitation for Alfonso to press closer, his hands softening at her shoulders, finally drifting to her collarbone.

"But sweet Gaby," he murmured, "that doesn't mean *we* have to wait."

"What?" she replied distractedly. "What are you talking about?"

"Darling, you're through with this Prince's Theatre Troupe foolery now. And *my* stage still awaits . . ."

She'd endured the words fifty times before. But as the man's fingers drifted lower over her bodice, a frisson of alarmed instinct pierced the muddle of her mind.

"I'm not through with anything." Gabriela channeled her frustration into shoving from his arms and dashing into her dressing room at last. "Except you and your manipulations!"

"Gabriela, stop being a fool!"

"Go away!"

She slammed the door and twisted the key in the lock. Alfonso's inevitable poundings of fist and foot came right after, but the clamor diminished to a dull background behind the din of questions onslaughting her mind.

How could she believe the wretch? But how did she dare not? And if his assertion held an iota of truth, what did the news import for her chance at the remaining Prince's Troupe positions? Short of reading Davis Webber's mind, how did she know if she'd even turned the man's head yet . . . if her letters of interest had ever crossed his desk . . . or if even now, she'd do better likening the dream to a pile of incinerated ashes?

The dream.

Gaby started. For a moment, she wondered why her mind jogged back to those words and repeated them with such fixated purpose. Then a comprehending smile took hold of her lips and her heart. "The dream," she murmured, nodding. *The* dream. Not *her* dream, as she'd always known it, but *the* dream . . . in other words, a vision to which she no longer claimed exclusive ownership.

And she realized her soul's declarations to Marcus last night had lacked one important addition:

My dream . . . your dream . . . our dream.

She dashed to the dressing table with a soft but excited laugh. She couldn't give up on her goal now if she wanted to. She imagined merely attempting to tell Marcus such a thing. Her mind's eye saw the flash of his gaze at her, burning with only one indisputable message: *you're giving up only when I give up.*

And Marcus Danewell, Gaby seriously suspected, did not know how to give up.

Alfonso's poundings escalated. Funny; the beats timed perfectly to the faster meter of her heartbeat, now calling out for Marcus with an urgency beyond physical or emotional completion.

Now her soul needed him, too. Her spirit yearned for the affirmation of his embrace, the boldness of his kisses, the silver magic in his eyes that transformed her into an angel, capable of doing anything and going anywhere her fantasies led.

Her soul needed to know he still believed in the dream, too.

But first, she needed to get out of here!

* * *

Reflecting on that moment as she scurried across the catwalks then down now-memorized hallways and stairways, Gabriela granted herself a big smile and a tiny laugh.

She couldn't help it. No playwright would attempt such a scene for fear of being laughed out of London on grounds of unrealistic inanity, yet there she'd stood, mouthing oaths at Alfonso as he actually charmed the key to her dressing room out of the wardrobe mistress in the hall.

As the pair had fumbled with the lock, Gaby had anxiously paced—until desperation ignited inspiration. Her sights alighted on the wall behind her dressing screen—and the movable panel in the old wood there, a feature Marcus had excitedly showed her many weeks back. At the time, Gabriela had only rolled her eyes at his story that the Drury Lane "ghost" had installed the secret compartment, the spook's purpose long forgotten to some volume in the theater's history vault. Tonight, she still didn't care about the spirit's original intentions, but she'd sent a quick thanks to whatever spectral realm he called home as she stepped into the surprisingly roomy niche. She'd yanked her skirt out of the way and slid the panel home just as Alfonso pounced into the room, only to find himself short on the cue and long on perplexity.

Remembering the snake's fratch of creative cursing after that, Gaby allowed a longer giggle as she skipped up the last flight of stairs before the apartment's carved wood door. Yet despite the exertion of climbing half a dozen flights before that, her heart didn't start racing and her senses didn't start thrumming until she pushed on the slightly opened portal, and saw him again.

And felt him again.

Dark power. Deep aching. Profound love . . . for her.

"Marcus," she said on a joyous sigh. In that same surge, she swept to where he sat on folded knees in the middle of the living room floor. She dropped and molded herself to his back, reveling in the broad, muscled shape of him all over again. She buried her nose in his hair, which smelled of fog and rain and an earthier scent she couldn't identify. Then she kissed the back of his neck in greeting.

His shoulders bunched tangibly in reply. Then nothing.

Fear seized a small part of her chest.

"I . . . I'm sorry I'm late," she rushed on. "The curtain call took forever . . . the show went very well tonight . . . then . . . well, then Alfonso was waiting outside my dressing room . . ."

His shoulders constricted harder.

"It's all right, love," she soothed. "He didn't do anything. I hid in the secret closet you showed me—do you remember?" She laughed into his ear. "I wish you'd been there. It was quite funny, listening to him rant and rave about how I'd outfoxed him. But he took forever to leave. I came straight up in my costume, though I so wanted you to see me in the new gown. And oh, the dress . . . it's beautiful, Marcus. Thank you . . ." She kissed the valley behind his ear, secured her arms tighter around his chest. "Thank you."

She nestled her chin on his shoulder, awaiting at least an obligatory "you're welcome." But she prayed for something more—like a bone-melting kiss.

Marcus raised one hand and wrapped slow, but strong fingers around her forearm.

Then nothing.

Trepidation bit off a bigger piece of her heart.

"I . . . I got up here as quickly as I could," she rambled faster. "I was worried I'd kept you waiting so long. I didn't want to anger you."

That incited a reaction. "Anger me?" His voice resonated with a strange mixture of sadness, incredulity, and the traces of a dark laugh. Then, in a rough whisper, "I am not angry, Gabriela."

"Well." She underlined the word with determination. "Good."

At that, she swung herself around and into his lap, forcing him to either hold her or let her plop to the carpet. Gabriela wagered he'd no sooner let her plummet half a foot to the floor than he'd watch her fall thirty feet to the Drury stage.

If only such certain odds abounded at Ascot. The thought, along with Marcus's arms encircling her and cradling her to him once more, filled her with a warmth that brimmed into a full, uncontrollable smile. With unafraid abandon, she looked up to Marcus and gave that smile back to him. She didn't stifle a degree of her feeling, yet in case he didn't read the message in her eyes, she reached along the pathways of their invisible bond and told him so with her soul:

Nobody has ever made me this happy. I love you, Marcus. Thank you.

She knew he heard and understood by the way he traced one slow, treasuring finger over her upturned lips . . . by the way a luminous silver sheen materialized in his quiet, adoring gaze.

His silent, sad gaze. . . .

Gabriela's smile faded. As swiftly as the last rays of sunset drowned by the tide of night, her senses acknowledged him in return—and flooded with his strange, unnameable discomfort. Her heart cramped with a sorrow even her loving words hadn't penetrated.

Fear didn't just nibble at her now. Her heart became the sensation's evening feast.

"Marcus . . . what's wrong?" She played no coy entr'acte to the query. His distress penetrated too deeply for such frippery.

Yet for a long moment, he squandered time away to heavy silence. Gabriela watched the glimmer in his eyes pierce to new depths of his soul.

Finally, he swallowed deeply. Then emitted one lonely word. "I—"

"What?" she urged.

"Gabriela—"

"What?"

In the still air between them, only faint dust motes stirred.

But then, upon the taut strings of her soul, a faint chord of words strummed. The strain came so soft, Gaby almost thought she imagined it . . . as if its composer resisted every note.

I love you, too.

She snapped a wide stare at Marcus at the same moment he whipped away from her.

As if he'd deter her like *that.* Now Gabriela tumbled to the floor on her own will. She quickly rolled to sit before him, knee to knee. She grabbed for his arm and pulled, hard.

He resisted. With intensity.

When Marcus did something with intensity, Gabriela doubted even Augustus brooked him. Her fingers stung with friction burns where his copper cotton shirt, and the broad shoulder beneath, ripped from beneath her grasp.

She reached for him again, anyway.

Marcus clenched again, but didn't jerk from her.

Nor did he look at her.

"I . . ." he grated again. The syllable instigated a consuming shudder down his rigid frame.

"What?" Gabriela prodded. "Marcus . . . sweeting . . ." She couldn't help a smile when using the endearment he normally whispered to her. "Come on, grump," she continued, on the longing the tease would prompt a similar grin from him. "Of what dark and horrible dread are you thinking?"

He did not grin.

That comprised the extent of Gaby's perceptions

through the next stunning moment. All she knew was that between one blink and the next, she went from kneeling beside him to being hauled to her feet, standing face to face with him.

But before she collected herself to ask why or how, Marcus bore a stare into her of utterly smooth, fearfully dark gray pewter.

"I am thinking," he stated in an equally cold cadence, "that you should leave."

Oh, she remembered blinking *this* time. All too vividly, she experienced every aching second of the next moment, of how hard she wanted to shake her head, certain her mind sorted his words wrong and misspelled them as a different message.

Instead, her lips parted with the only word she seemed to know tonight. "What?"

Gently—dear God, so gently, it made her nauseous—he took a slow step back. "I said I think you should go now."

Again, she listened to him space the words like dominoes: evenly, carefully, gently. As if his damnable gentleness made any blasted difference. Her heart already felt toppled, crushed.

"I'm not going anywhere," she countered. "Not until you tell me what's going on." Amazing. Her delivery flowed of poise and conviction, leading diva material— when her nerves hammered like a frittering chorus girl.

"Gabriela," Marcus muttered. "Please, I am overtired."

All right, so she *did* resemble a frittering chorus girl, as she rushed to chain her hands around his neck and press every inch of her body to his. Fleetingly, Gabriela conceded she didn't care if she looked the foolish maiden. *She didn't care.*

Struggling to compress down the surge of desperation from her voice, she whispered into his ear, "If you're tired, then let's go to bed."

Her answer came straightway: more taut, airless silence.

Neither his body nor spirit twitched to meet the submission of hers. " 'Twould nay be wise," he finally emitted in a strained murmur.

"Nay." Gaby threw his archival accent back at him with a deliberate, sensual undulation. She issued a corresponding offer with the length of her body. " 'Twould be very wise, I think," she added against the side of his neck.

At that, Marcus shifted—but only to pull her hands from his nape and hold them between his chest and hers, a space growing larger by his renewed backstepping. "You do not see—"

"I *do* see."

She reclosed the gap in two urgent strides. Her second step caught on the hem of her costume. A loud rip gashed the air. The sound barely nicked Gabriela's attention, centered on Marcus's averted features and bowed, self-conscious stance . . . though she had to admit, she barely recognized the posture on the tall lines of her lover's form. Over the years, that same awkward pose had always occupied the more diminutive forms of the couple preferring to stay childless rather than adopt her.

No! Every cell in her body screamed. *No! I've been a good girl this time. You won't leave me. You* love *me. Your heart just whispered it, Marcus . . . I heard, I heard . . . you love me!*

"Marcus," she began again, commanding her tone to a level of reason, but unable to secure the shaking delivery it tightroped on. "Marcus, I know this won't be an easy situation. You're Drury's owner, and I'm just a developing actress. We'll have to be discreet. I know that. So now do you see? I understand everything, really."

His head dropped. His fingers tightened around hers. "You understand nothing."

"You're wrong." She squeezed back, despite intensifying the throb of pain beneath her fingernails. "I do."

"Nay." She'd heard milder growls from lions pacing in the zoo. "You do *not.*"

"Don't tell me what I am capable of comprehending, blast it! I know what I'm doing. Last night—"

"Was a mistake."

Now he chose to look at her. His head came up on a smooth snap. An instant later, the unfettered intent of his gaze ensued.

And lightning struck her world.

Indeed, Gabriela thought, this was what an ill-starred tree felt when heaven roiled overhead and spewed a bolt of silver fire through one's heart, soul, and roots of existence. She'd heard Marcus utter the destroying words, even heard the calmness and conviction about his dispatch, but didn't fathom to think him serious until his gaze impacted her: stark and hard, so unfeeling. . . .

So unfamiliar.

Dear God. What's happened to you, Marcus? Where have you gone away from me?

Yet in that soul's cry of question, she found the spark for her shock-filled, hard-breathing protest. "No," she blurted. "No. You don't mean it. Marcus, *you* don't mean this."

But his second snarl drowned her last word. Vibrating from some deep core of him, the eruption surpassed beastly magnitude. He thrust her hands away and wiped his palms on his cotton wool-covered thighs—as if she'd soiled him. Gabriela gulped back a tide of bile and tears, blinking to keep her vision straight.

"God's teeth," he muttered then. "You're not going to *weep*, are you? Oh, Gabriela . . ." He shook his head, gave a soft clicking of his tongue. "Gabriela." His condescending tone, another uncharted dimension of this stand-in for Marcus, only churned her gut harder.

"Last eve was wonderful," he continued with barely disguised impatience, "and pray have naught a fear that I did not . . . enjoy you. We both had a bit of nice prattle and bed sport—"

"Bed sport!" She didn't know whether to laugh or sob. The urge for both welled inside, making her sicker. "No. *No.* It wasn't just that, and you know it. You *know* it." Against her mind's dictates for rationality and self-respect, she stepped to him, arms outstretched. "Why are you doing this, Marcus? Why are you *really* doing this?"

At that, for a shining hope of an instant, a shadow shaded his gaze, muscles flinched in his legs . . . as if the very physical essence of him couldn't ignore her pain. Gabriela held back her gasp of elation, using the effort to reach out to him with spiritual arms, as well.

Go away. Get away from me, damn you!

The words struck with unearthly force; a psychic attack—a tactile blow. Gabriela reeled and fell to the floor, but his mental fingers gave chase, curling around her soul, constricting like vengeful talons. Her throat gasped for air as her soul fought for life.

But, she suddenly realized, she didn't struggle alone. Between her breaths, Marcus's labored rasps resonated in the room. She knew the precise moment he swung his stare back to her, for that silver force now hovered over her like a vast, turmoiled storm.

On her hands and knees, shaking from head to toe, Gabriela turned to face that storm—vowing, somehow, to conquer it.

She looked up, up . . . sights ascending the wide-braced set of his legs, unmoving save for those involuntary spasms in his towering thighs. From there, she looked to his hands: clenched so hard at his sides, they looked marbleized in their smoothness, bound to forearms with pulsing veins forming a strangely beautiful landscape against straining muscles. Yes, she marveled in perverse awe, even now he formed a hypnotizing sight: dark rage, fathomless wrath, flawlessly embodied.

When she looked to his face, that conclusion rang more achingly true. Gabriela couldn't restrain a shocked sob at finding her way through a tangle of sweat-soaked black hair to his glowing, glaring eyes—eyes that loathed and loved, agonized and adored with ageless, merciless intensity. A piece of her died with each moment she stared back, her soul no match for the overwhelming anger he emanated, yet she didn't move, couldn't turn away, somehow joined to him . . . loving him; hating him.

"Leave me, Gabriela." Now, his command came on shuddering breaths. "I pray you, leave me the hell alone."

Against her staunchest effort, tears scalded the corners of her eyes. Who—*what*—was this creature who'd taken possession of her beloved? For no other explanation for this torment possibly existed . . . why else couldn't he see inside of her any more? Why didn't he see how he ripped away more of her soul with each word, how he gave life to the worst pain she'd ever feared?

"Is that what you really want?" she finally managed in a quivered whisper.

"That nay matters."

"The bloody hell it doesn't." She scrambled to her feet and stalked toward him with the frustration refusing to be constrained any more. She barely held back from slapping his dark, beautiful face. "Dear God, Marcus! After all these months . . . after last night . . . don't you fathom it by now? I'm not just in love with you . . . I am *bound* to you. Your feelings"—she pressed fervent fingers to his chest— "are my feelings. I don't just sympathize with your pain. I *feel* it."

"Nay." He jerked away, pacing across the room, dragging both hands through his hair. " 'Tis not possible. 'Tis . . . not . . . possible."

"I don't care what's possible. I know what I feel. At this moment, my heart's hammering so hard it hurts, just as yours. My eyes see out that window you're glaring through . . . there's a ship on the Thames, and you're wishing you could sail away on it."

He snapped a narrowed, shocked stare at her.

Gabriela only lifted a bittersweet smile, more potent tears rolling against her lips. "Don't you see?" she repeated. "I know you better than I know myself."

"Nay." He whipped back to the window. She watched him lower shaking fists to the ledge. "Cease this absurdity, Gabriela. You nay know me at all."

"I know your strength and your pride," she persisted. "I know your patience and your love."

"You still . . . you *nay* know me."

"What else is there?" Like a tide pulled to the shore, an inexorable force moved her to him again. "Marcus"— she spread arms wide to grip his shoulders—*"what is it?"*

She felt the vibrations of his quivering breath, the quaking of his whole body, as if his mind vacillated on the edge of a terrifying precipice. Finally, he said on a husky breath, "You do not want to know."

She held him tighter. "Untrue. I want to know all of you."

"Nay . . . nay, you do not."

"I love you."

"Stop it!"

"No!"

His countering roar shook the window. His muscles bunched, then burst from beneath her as he rose up and twisted, turning on her with a glare she hadn't seen in his most enraged Hamlet.

And for the first time ever, Gabriela was afraid of him.

"Damn you!" the monster-Marcus seethed, grabbing her shoulders with clawing fingers, jerking her like a sawdust prop mannequin. "Leave me be!"

"I won't." Gabriela questioned her sanity with each rasped syllable, but also knew an execution squad couldn't have stayed her from them. "I can't. I won't leave you, Marcus . . . not until you tell me what's going on."

To her morbid surprise, he laughed then—a biting, bitter chuckle, baring locked, gleaming teeth. "So that is the game, then? You want to know 'what's going on.' "

The last, he spouted as if she'd begun a joke, but only he knew the finishing line. As he threw his head back and enjoyed the cruel jest, Marcus hauled her across the apartment, starting and stopping their journey in raging rushes of movement.

"Marcus," Gabriela winced, squirming in his increasingly constricting grip, "Marcus, you're hurting me—"

He laughed harder. "Too late for hurt now, sweeting." But when he stopped to tighten his hold on her, his mirth again descended into a beast's twisted glower. " 'Tis too goddamned late!"

They reached the opposite wall of the room, just four feet from the double doors Gabriela had entered through. Marcus stunned Gabriela again—he flung back a wide Persian drape to reveal a second door to the apartment: smaller, more narrow, strangely suspicious. . . .

Utterly eerie.

"Come, you little fool," snarled her looming, terrifying captor, as he kicked the door back into a narrow, unrelenting blackness. "Come with me to hell."

Nine

Blackness. Ugliness. A twisted, furious maze, plummeting deeper and darker toward disaster. . . .

His mind, or the dank passageway ingesting their steps into the earth's bowels?

Marcus had long ceased knowing the difference. Had long ceased knowing if such a disparity still existed.

Had long ceased to care.

So, the lovely little idiot loved him despite his relentless rejection, did she? She refused to be a normal flibbertigibbet and reward his insults with a clean slap across the face and a merciful fare-thee-well? She nay believed he could be such a heartless bastard, such a self-serving coistrel, such a repulsive beast?

Then, damn her, he would show her just what a beast she ignored.

Indeed, as he wrenched her down a flight of spiraling stairs, through the thick oak door in Drury's foundations, and finally along the dim, damp passageway so far beneath the living world, human breaths no longer escaped him—wolfish huffs and grunts echoed in his ears. An animal's pulse began to answer his heart's pound, racing harder and hotter through his veins.

He tried to care about Gabriela's breathless effort to keep up with him. He searched for concern about her pained whimpers at every harsh jerk he meted. He desperately sought anxiety for *himself,* clawing out for a vestige of horrified reason to turn him back from this stupid, potentially fatal stunt.

But when the beast possessed him this time, the beast had come to conquer.

And the conqueror seized Marcus's humanity as first prisoner of war.

They finally arrived at the fateful door. The wide oak portal, bound by hinges of menacing black iron, had never looked more a hated enemy. Unfettered by thoughts of decency or control, Marcus tore away the big lead lock and its mounting plate from the breast of his nemesis. He tossed the wreckage against the stone wall. A clatter roared through the passageway, but rapidly faded to naught but the scratchings of night creatures and the incessant ploppings of underground moisture.

"M-Marcus?" The dim awareness came of Gabriela's trembling voice at his shoulder. "Marcus, what's going on? Where are we?"

The beast answered her with a jeering laugh. The monster stole the sound from his chest with no preamble and no remorse. Immediately, Marcus's debilitated psyche felt the responding rip in Gabriela's heart. He ached with her disbelieving hurt, her shivering confusion.

Nay. Nay!

He seconded that soul's cry with a primal, echoing bellow. He'd promised to show her hell, but now he wondered how she'd see inside his mind. How she'd see this hell of hating himself so much . . .

Of hating her, for making him go through with this atrocity.

With that hate, he shoved back the door and flung Gabriela into the chamber.

She stumbled several steps ahead of him, feet tangling in her costume hem and flailing for balance—but he knew clumsiness was nay the root that finally tripped her to the ground.

She fell when she saw his open, candlelit coffin.

Yet as she crouched there, shoulders shaking with every breath, eyes wide with glimmering copper confusion and her costume bunched around her knees in a neglected disarray, she had never looked more touchable, more beautiful. Sweet God, Marcus's groin actually leapt for her. His heart raced to his throat and throbbed there.

He wanted to take her there on the packed dirt floor. Hard and fast and wild.

He could never touch her again.

The realization struck him with such agonizing finality, the wick of his soul sputtered a last great effort for life, then snuffed out. It withered and died, unable to kindle any reaction at all—no more rage, no more hate, not even more arousal—nothing remained inside but a sense of artificial propriety that he carried out from sheer habit rather than substantiating self-respect.

It was that blackened shell of himself that rested one hand on the coffin's edge, pressed the other over the cavity he had once called a chest, and dipped a bow so low and stately, it bordered on caricature. "Madam, I bid you welcome to my realm," he said with acid elegance.

He felt Gabriela's stunned stare follow every inch of his gesture. When he rose, he met that look directly, to notice dark pools of horrified comprehension at last forming in the tides of her eyes. Soon, so very soon now, he anticipated, she'd finally begin to hate him back.

Thank God.

"What is this?" Gabriela hissed at him. "What the hell is this, Marcus? Your idea of a sick joke?"

To his surprise, an indulgent grin escaped the beast's guardianship. "Is that what you think?"

And at last, he witnessed the storm explode: the raw anger twisting her features as she sprang to her feet again;

the rage unfurling with each step of her sweeping, strident advance; the wild fall of her hair from its combs and finally, the violent billow of her skirts across his boots as she skidded to a taut, seething halt but inches from him.

"I think," she said then, past quivering lips and tearshimmered eyes, "that you're afraid, Marcus Danewell. You're so terrified of what we shared—of what we still share—that now you're trying to frighten me, too." Sable ringlets whipped across her cheeks as she shook her head. "Well, guess what? I'm not scared, Marcus. I'm not scared to love you! I'm not scared of your silly coffin, or the difference in our status, or the difference in our age—"

He could not control the laugh he bellowed into her diatribe. Yet after an oddly exhilarating indulgence in the outburst, head thrown back, the self-loathing returned, flooding his gut thrice as harshly as before. Marcus survived the assault only by shoving from the coffin and pacing the length of the chamber, very aware of his resemblance to a caged beast.

"The difference in our age," he repeated through a sardonic growl. "Oh, 'tis a rich humor you spin tonight, sweet."

"Stop it!" He felt the infuriated heat of her breath with the retort, indicating how doggedly, how *stupidly* she followed him. "Speak *English*, blast it, not your poetic gibberish!"

He halted to laugh at that, too. But this time, the sound didn't echo back a note of satisfying depth. His mirth died somewhere deep in the hollow cavern of himself, as his sight fell upon the leather-bound book he kept stored in the nook next to his writing table.

As usual, a lone candle stood vigil over the niche, protecting the sole object once capable of restoring at least a dim sense of identity to his homeless soul, bringing back vague images of who he once was, what he once loved, the dreams he once aspired to. . . .

An illusion, Marcus now realized. That book was no more a stand-in for reality than the scrims, props, and costumes waiting in the wings of the theater far above.

"Poetic gibberish," he murmured, still staring at the journal. "Oh, Gabriela . . . 'When a man's verses cannot be understood, it strikes him more dead than a great reckoning . . .' "

"Very good." Her sarcastic sniff still came excruciatingly close behind. "*As You Like It*, Act Three, I believe. Now do you want to explain what's really lathering you?"

He sighed. Just once. But somewhere between the overture and final curtain of that breath, a chill of resignation finally whispered across the stage of his soul. The gust rendered the winter inside him complete. Only a flicker of heat remained because he stole it from the ignited fury of Gabriela's spirit. Gabriela's incredible, undaunted mortal spirit . . .

Marcus drew on the last ember of that flame to move to the alcove. The journal's binding let out a protesting crackle as he opened the front cover. Dry shushes filled the nook and wobbled the candle glow with each reverent turn he gave the pages.

At last finding the entry he sought, he stretched a beckoning hand to Gabriela. "Come here, my heart."

She wasted no time in meeting his request. Her fingers slipped between his, warm and slender and surprisingly strong. Why had he nay remembered how strong she was?

Perhaps because his psyche never had to use that strength just to remain standing.

With that renewed bond to her, he heard her heart begging him to look at her. Marcus kept his gaze lowered to the journal.

"How old do you believe me, Gabriela?"

As he expected, only her impatient sigh flickered the candle as reply.

" 'Tis what I thought." He curled an arm around her shoulder and guided her toward the book.

"Marcus," she grumbled, "It doesn't make a diff—"

"Read it." He pointed to the exact line he wished even as he slid his burning eyes shut.

"I can't," she retorted a moment later. "It's written in some sort of archaic script. As a matter of fact, grump, it looks much like the way *you* write."

"Look at it again."

"Marcus, where is this getting us?"

"Look at it again, and take your time."

He opened his eyes in time to catch her achingly adorable grimace, her painfully innocent huff. But she obeyed his hest, bending and focusing on the yellowed page.

After a long moment, she began to read in unpracticed, but articulate segments: "On this sixth day of June, in the year of our Lord fifteen hundred eighty five, we dost rejoice to christen our beloved son, now three months on this good earth . . . we have named him Marcus James, after his muchly-loved grandfath . . ."

Her voice trailed off, finally cut completely by a sharp gasp. She snapped wide eyes up at him, above cheeks rapidly draining of color.

Marcus released her hand and wrapped that arm around the other side of her. The muscles beneath his touch shook with consuming trembles. He prepared himself to cushion her leaden faint.

He never expected her vehement shove. Nor her nearly hysterical whirl back to the book, slamming it shut as if he'd just made her read an obituary. In a way, he supposed, he had.

"I've had enough of this, Marcus. Damn you, *enough!* What is this? What—the—hell is this?"

She emphasized her angriest syllables with furious jabs toward the journal, each movement such a perfect companion to its dialogue, Marcus marveled at her in a moment of bittersweet awe. If they exchanged these words on a stage, some Buckingham minion would be waiting in the wings at curtain to demand a private royal performance.

Only this scene was all too real. Every step she took and breath she seized pierced her deeply, painfully. Marcus didn't have to enact their bond to know it. He watched disillusion twist its cruel blade via each shudder of her chest, each quiver of her lips, every flinch and blink of her eyes.

Then came the worst observation: he held the next dagger—sited for her heart.

"What is this?" he rhetorized, forcing himself to repose against the wall as if she merely asked after the location of his bath linens. " 'Tis my family bible, sweeting. You just read the account of my christening day."

She shook her head—three short, harsh jerks. "I . . . I don't understand."

Of course she didn't. Had he really expected her to take in this bizarre spectacle, assimilate it all in her shocked mind, and pop out the most hideous conclusion she could dream of?

"Gabriela, I was born in Shropshire, on a birthing stool in my mother's bedroom, on a spring morning in 1585."

"On a *what?*"

Even through the suffocating pain, he almost emitted another laugh. The impression struck that she gaped more at the first portion of his announcement than the last.

Still, he forced himself on. "I grew up verily happy, at least as 'happy' was defined then. We were lucky . . . it was a time of great growth for the country, and my father turned a love of Oriental imports into a lucrative importing business."

He squeezed his eyes shut, feeling a grimace claim his features as he remembered Darius Danewell, hale and hearty, passionate and creative—and many years dead now. "I . . . loved him," he murmured roughly. "Therefore, when I became of age and he expressed his dream to sponsor me at court, I never thought of refusing." The grimace became a resigned shrug. "The day after my sixteenth birthday, I was off to Whitehall."

She still didn't comprehend. In the shifting shadows of her eyes, Marcus watched her wage an inner battle between the safety of logic and the insanity of believing him. She twisted unsalvagable knots to her costume's skirting while pacing the chamber at a staccato tempo.

"Whitehall," she stammered. "Whitehall *Palace?*"

"Aye," he answered softly.

She paced faster. "Ridiculous. Whitehall Palace was wiped out by fire almost two hundred years ago."

"Aye. But that was long after my years there."

"Don't!" She stopped and jerked up both arms, spreading them out as if his words formed a racing steam train instead of a sentence. "Stop saying these things. *Why* are you saying these things?"

Marcus used her expectant pause to gently ensnare her upheld wrists, slowly pull them to his chest. "Because," he said, keeping her gaze locked to his, " 'tis the truth."

"It's impossible!"

He gripped her hands tighter. "Not for a vampire."

Despite his precaution, she wrenched free. The motion flung her back several steps before she stumbled to a stop, gasped down a trio of dry breaths. Then she grated, "What?"

Like a flood, her disbelief doused his senses. With what little psychic force he could summon, Marcus argued back the validity of his assertion. Her soul nay listened. Her mind whirled in too much chaos to hear. And her heart had no room . . . it still overflowed with her anguished, aching love.

He attempted to reach her through physical contact, instead. "Gabriela . . ." He reached to her again. "Look at me, and think about it. Listen to me—"

"No." She staggered backward, fingers scraping for support, but she only found the coffin, sending her into a more frantic retreat. "You're lying. You're *lying*." Her tear-layered cheeks shimmered in the candlelight. "Why are you lying to me?"

"Sweeting—"

"Don't call me that!"

"Gabriela."

He had no choice about his next action. Every time he tried to touch her by mortal standards of movement, she bolted from his range, a maddening Puck in his midsummer night's nightmare. Instead, deliberately not hypnotizing her senses against the sight, he covered the distance across the chamber and hauled her into his grasp—a feat only accomplished by superreal ability.

He held her again—yet he also succeeded at shocking her into silence. Unprepared for *that* irregularity, he fumbled through the next moment, until his brain locked back to the last decent concern he remembered having.

She deserved the truth.

At all cost or explanation.

"Listen to me," he continued tightly, swiftly. "I thrived at Whitehall, Gabriela. I loved it there . . . I loved it too much."

Now, she didn't so much as blink a retort.

Sweet God, he hadn't wanted it to be like this. This explanation possessed all the warmth of a military briefing. But no more time existed for tactful grace or gentle lead-ins. The instant he had pulled her close and she had turned her eyes up to him, those sienna depths sparkled with such piercing grief, the ramparts of his own control began corroding. Marcus estimated only a few minutes remained before his battlements completely collapsed, sinking him into a morass of despair beyond the reach of words.

Only a few minutes left to finish breaking her heart.

"In only a matter of months, my desire to please my father turned into something more," he forced himself to continue. "The craving for success became an obsession of my own heart. Status . . . ah God, status was *everything* at Whitehall. A man either had it, or he did not. He was either somebody, or nobody."

He shook his head and let a self-deprecating snort escape. Hearing himself tell the story for the first time moved one long-abiding perception into irrevocable truth: how ridiculous a farce they'd called the Whitehall Court. All the pomp and glory, the titles and clothes and ostentation they wasted so much time on—in the end, it had all benefitted only a handful, reflected the true honor of even fewer, and, two hundred years later, was remembered by none but little London historians and their little librarian wives.

And one lonely vampire who lived in the sewers beneath Drury Lane Theatre.

"I wanted to be a somebody," Marcus proceeded, turning from her as the memories pulled him tighter into their grip. "I wanted it more than anything. Yet I nay yearned for the status of wealth or riches so much as the opportunity for the prestige, the respect. I wanted the preferred seats at Will's performances . . . I thrived on the deferring nods as I walked the court halls . . . I liked being watched and admired and listened to. I liked being much more than just a paltry merchant's son with nowhere to go, no legacy to leave."

At that, the next barrage of remembrance crashed over him—now eroding huge chunks of his fortitude. "And yet, it wasn't enough," he grated. "Can you believe it? I wanted *more.*"

He clenched his hands until they shook, hating the next words he dredged from the muck of his soul, loathing the image of hell's viperess they brought along.

"That 'more' came one night in the form of a surprise

guest to Whitehall. Her name was Raquelle de Lanya. She was exquisite . . . torturously exquisite, and mysterious, and magical . . . she stole my mortal soul in the space of one shared bransle dance." He turned slowly back to Gabriela. "By midnight of the next eve, she stole my immortal soul, as well."

For a moment, only a tearful sniff and an audible swallow gave him any indication Gabriela hadn't at last given in to a faint.

Finally, she blurted in a bitter whisper, "So you're telling me this . . . this Raquelle person just threw you to the ground, sank her teeth into your neck and didn't stop until you grew three-foot teeth and raced off in search of a sleeping virgin?"

"Nay," Marcus countered.

"Nay? Nay *what*?"

With carefully measured steps, he approached the cave's recess she'd taken refuge in—conveniently near the door. "She came nowhere near my neck," he said. "Raquelle found her feeding much more satisfying when quaffing straight from her lover's heart."

He felt her laugh bubble through her senses, disoriented and disbelieving, before she bounced it off the stones at him.

He also felt that mirth die, by horror's ruthless blade, as he ripped open his shirt and guided her fingers to the pair of puncture scars in his chest.

"I know," he answered her soul's silent perplexity. "They are not very big. Not the boon one expects when visited by the undead, aye? Yet they were not much different over two hundred and fifty years ago."

Her face reflected a dozen shadings and sensations during the two steps she jerked back from him. But her hand never lowered. She rotated her arm at the wrist and stared at her fingers, then back at him.

"Two . . . two hundred and . . ." she stammered.

"Aye. A little more than that now. Raquelle took me in 1600."

"Then why . . ." Her voice caught on a dry wince. "Why are you bleeding now?"

With a start, Marcus looked down to his chest. Just as she said, a spattering of black-red droplets littered the V where his shirt hung open.

He did not wipe the mess clean. The effort to raise his head and give her an answer yanked the last stones from his soul's foundation.

"It is not my blood, Gabriela."

She laughed again. High, hysterically. The sound mingled with her tears, a strange and vulnerable and heartbreaking music. Marcus had ceased his sojourns to Italy nearly a century ago, cursing the opera for the unendurable agony of its arias . . . he now damned himself the fool, presuming he ever knew what agony was before this moment.

"Oh . . . oh, of course," she continued in a frightened, faltering whisper. "Now you're going to tell me—"

"That I fed tonight, and chanced to get a little slovenly," he finished.

She dropped her hand. And her smile. She crossed arms across her chest and tried to conceal her head-to-toe shiver. "I don't believe you."

"I know."

But he lied. He knew she knew that, as well. Marcus said nothing else as he watched the doubt finally begin to creep over her: the uncontrollable quiver of her chin, the rise and fall of her chest on short, hard breaths . . . her refusal to look at him anymore, her wide stare raking the chamber's confines with the dread of a Gertrude just told she had swallowed poisoned wine.

"Who . . . what . . ." she stuttered. "*How* did you . . ."

"Nobody you know." Marcus strove for a reassuring tone, but ended up with a graveled apology. "Nobody *anyone* knows. I have a . . . well, a friend at St. Thomas Hospital. When there is a body with no name or identification—"

"Stop." She sagged against the wall, breathing harder. "Don't . . . don't say any more. Oh . . . oh, this isn't true," she rasped. "I cannot believe this."

"But you do."

"No!" She turned and clawed at the stones, wetting their coldness with her hot tears.

" 'Tis no use to deny me, sweeting. You said it yourself, in the apartment. We are bound. We know each other."

She whirled, actually snarling at him. "*Know* you? You monster! I don't *know* you!"

She jerked forward, as if to strike him, but at the last moment, diverted her movement toward the door. "Don't ever say that again!" she seethed. "I don't know you . . . whoever or whatever you are. I *never* knew you."

And here it was. The moment he'd worked for, furiously driven them both at for the last hour. Success, at last. The truth, finally known. The ordeal, done and over.

Then why did the torment in his heart rage beyond any pain he'd ever imagined?

Why did he stagger after Gabriela, begging her to let him explain further, instead of enjoying his neatly planned scenario of falling into bed, declaring the chit good riddance, and sleeping off the heartbreak for three days?

Why did he feel carved out alive when she bolted from him, face white with terror, hissing, "Get . . . away . . . from . . . me."

He'd never know. He'd never know anything again but the black, dark agony when she spun around, raced past the door, and slammed it behind her with a terminality unequaled anywhere but the depths of hell.

Thank God Donna wasn't home. The moment Gabriela burst into the flat, breathless with grief and horror and exhaustion, she crumbled to the floor and sobbed until she passed out. When she woke up, she retched until the tears came again. Somehow she made it into bed, calling herself every synonym she knew for fool between the heaving, racking sobs.

Well, Gaby, her mind relentlessly rebuked. *You had to start calling yourself the world's expert on pain. You had to believe you'd had your quota of lies and heartbreak for one lifetime.*

Then again, you believed Marcus Danewell a gift from heaven.

The man was a better actor than she dreamed.

Correction to the script. She hadn't been gulled by a *man.* She'd believed the grandest deception in the world by a man more than two hundred and fifty years old—

What?

"Dear God," she whispered. What kind of a beast had she made love with last night? What hellish atrocity had she welcomed into her body, her soul, rejoicing in its touch, hoping her womb nurtured life to its *baby?*

And what kind of a creature had he transformed *her* into, that her deepest woman's instinct still craved his body's heat . . . that her empty, aching soul still cried out for the union of his?

She shuddered with harder sobs. Her body convulsed with them, shaking the bed until she felt somebody weigh down the mattress behind her.

Cool, long-nailed fingers pressed her cheek. "Dove?" came a familiar voice, echoing to her down a tunnel of semiconsciousness. "Saint Genesius, you're burning up. And you're filthy. And what is this . . . Gaby, you're still in your *costume* . . . Gaby, what the bloody hell happened to you?"

A laugh surged past the dried bile in her throat. She heard the sound reverberate off her pillow, high and hysterical, intermingled with words that made no sense. As if the truth would strike Donna as any more coherent. *You see, I've been having this affair with a vampire . . . yes, that's right . . . well, I actually didn't know myself, until he just happened*

*to let it slip . . . why didn't I notice that he talked like a scholar,
dressed like a pirate, and referred to William Shakespeare like a
best friend? Because I'm a fool, Donna. An oblivious, obtuse fool.*

And then the abyss of anguish swallowed her.

She had no idea how much time passed as she traversed
that violent, cold chasm, each thought of her dissipated
consciousness more racking than the last, each movement
of her sluggish body only reaffirming her dispassion to
continue living. When sleep came, she inevitably woke up
screaming from a recurring dream: she and Marcus made
love on a downy cloud, two dark angels in a world of light,
only when she turned to kiss him, he met her with burning
eyes and gleaming teeth, grinning wickedly as he pulled
her off the cloud and toward the pit of hell.

She needed no East End Gypsy to translate the meaning
of her visions. As she cried in Donna's arms through the
next five days and nights, her heart and soul confirmed
that message in resounding unison:

She still loved him.

And hated him.

And feared him.

God help her.

Somehow, in some merciful way, the Almighty heard that
feeble appeal—and on the sixth day, in a morning already
too mucky and muggy for its own good, He sent her an
effective, if not questionable, angel.

"Up," Donna barked, throwing back the bedroom curtains, ignoring Gaby's moan at the invading flood of light.
"You have breakfast in a half hour and rehearsal at ten
o'clock."

She braved the glare to shoot a glower into Donna's
bustling form. "I have what?"

"You heard me." Her friend clunked a teapot and accompanying cup to the night stand. "You have some catching up to do. Augustus made some major revisions to Act
Two."

She rolled back into her pillow. "I don't care."

"The bloody hell you don't." The creak of her armoire door crept through her shield of blankets. "It will probably rain today. Do you want to wear your wool pinstripe or the blue walking dress?"

"I . . . don't . . . care."

"Yes," the covers suddenly flew into the air, blasting Gaby awake with a whoosh of moist air, "you do. The walking dress, I think. It'll put some color into your complexion. God knows you need it."

Gabriela crossed both arms over her torso and cast another miserable scowl up at her friend. "Donna, what are you doing?"

The woman, already impeccably coiffed and made up, tossed stockings, petticoat, and corset at her. "Saving your career, if you must know." Donna set hands to hips and pursed a lipsticked frown. "Gaby, Drury's abuzz about you, and the rumors *aren't* nice. Half the ballet's convinced you ran away with a Swedish duke, the stage crew is betting Alfonso has you tied down somewhere in Saint John's Wood, and the rest are divided between looking you up at Bedlam or writing you off to opium."

She choked on a sip of tea. "Opium!"

Donna gave a vindicated nod. *"Now* do you care?"

Gaby looked away, repeating the question to her benumbed heart. She didn't know what she cared about any more. Or who.

Or if she could ever care again.

She pronounced the only certain conclusion her contemplations delivered. "Donna . . . I can't go back there."

But as her friend stalked off to check on breakfast with a colorful curse, Gaby wrestled with the impression that she wasn't going to have much choice.

* * *

The moment Marcus awakened, he knew she had returned to Drury.

Even interred by the stretch of rock between them, he felt the instant change in the air, in the very rocks around him. He vaulted out of the coffin, senses crackling with her nearness, pulse instantly pacing itself to hers, psyche throbbing with the effort not to invade her mind anymore—but blasted with the shrill clarion of her misery despite his effort. Within one moment, he experienced it all: all the days of her mindless heartache and grief, her vain thrashings in a sea of confusion, so lost, so helpless, never knowing if she'd trust or cherish anyone again . . . hating him, loving him.

The last comprehension slammed him to a dizzy stop.

Loving him.

Loving him?

On second thought, he had better sit down. He stumbled to his desk and sank into the velvet-padded chair in front. He dragged numb fingers through his disheveled hair, not sure what to call the feelings whirling through him . . . so conclusive he had been about never feeling anything again.

And what of the unignorable need that had driven him up to the catwalks each night, shamelessly listening to the whispers of backstage gossip for a sentence, a *word* of where she had fled? What of the twisting spasms in his chest at imagining her locked in a Bedlam cell, or fleeing from him to another country—or, dear bloody Jesu, fleeing to the arms of Alfonso Renard?

What *of* those sensations?

He bolted up from the desk. Stabbed his fingers into his hair again. Stopped both hands over his ears, battling to block the clashing cries from his heart and mind and body, all raging at him at once, discordant trumpets in an ill-practiced orchestra.

But over the next torturous eon—he glared at the clock

marking the passage as only three hours—that orchestra blared its cacophonous symphony over and over. Once as he envisioned her above, being welcomed back by naught but curious stares and odd whispers, but bravely preparing for the night's performance, nonetheless . . . a second time when the audience's din signaled the curtain's opening rise; another when the lights came up for the evening's interval.

Finally, as the clock knelled nine hours and twenty minutes, the symphony played the unendurable suite one time too many. Marcus clenched himself back from stopping the torment by tearing down the chamber walls.

Instead, he wrenched back the door, ran up the stone stairway without lighting a torch, and spun right at the first landing—toward his private box.

He had to see her again. Just once. His honor be damned.

Bloody hell, his soul already was.

It was nice to be back, Gabriela admitted. Nice, but nothing more. The smoke of the stage lamps and the busy sweat of backstage slid over her senses with a musty familiarity. The motions of getting into costume—Louis somehow had her Act Three ensemble replaced without question—and of applying makeup to the rhythm of Donna's chatter were a comfortable surface salve to the gaping wound where her heart once lay.

But they were *surface* repairs. Nothing more.

Act One elapsed with pleasing alacrity. Gaby defied Donna's command to eat some apples and cheese during intermission. Merely looking at the food brought back images of a magical midnight, it seemed so long ago now, when she'd last eaten the fruit . . . and then, when Marcus had first tasted of *her* nectar. . . .

The thought induced only the impulse to throw up the little breakfast Donna had forced upon her.

Standing in the wings now, listening to the French diva emote her way through Augustus's new Act Two monologue, Gaby employed the same obdurate will to focus concentration away from the hollow in her gut and the fuzziness in her head, and onto the words being spoken. Blast it, which line was her cue again?

A terse cough from center stage snapped her head up. The diva's flaming glare declared that the cue, whatever it was, had been delivered. Twice.

Gabriela gulped. And rushed on stage.

And felt Marcus in the very air she breathed.

His gaze, unblinking, followed her every step. His pain, somehow mingled of her pain, too, enwrapped her body in tangible, uncontrollable intensity. She knew his power and presence everywhere . . . outside her, inside her.

She heard the gasp she emitted—sharp, shocked, echoing over an expectant audience to the back of the theater.

To the private boxes.

She looked there. She looked to him, her soul screaming at him, and yet, oh *yes*, her heart sobbing for him. Wanting him. Needing him. Calling for him . . .

But only darkness returned her cry. Darkness, darkness, enshrouding her, falling over her senses like a black bridal veil . . .

A moment before that nuptial knew consummation, she heard a woman's scream signal the start of audiencewide chaos:

"My God! She's fainted!"

Ten

Marcus vaulted to the ledge of his box and leapt over without stopping. Neither did he pause to care about the dozen witnesses on the ground floor who gaped as if he were a vulture of Ares come to life, this stranger in black who had plummeted into their midst from fifty feet above.

Yet for the first time in his undead days, he wished such a beastly comparison true. He yearned to take flight over the jostling throng he plunged into, all shoving back as violently as he shoved, their curses contradictory punctuation to their chuckling jibes about what force had clipped the wings of the fallen angel on stage.

Their slander, so easily inverted from praise of a week ago, fueled the terror in Marcus's veins to a protective fury he'd never experienced—a need to show them that wings or no, *this* angel was avenged by a nightmare from hell. The hair stretched taut on the arms he clawed toward the stage. His shoulders and chest heaved with the burden of breathing, of feeling, of loving.

And the snarl in his throat exploded into one tortured word, filling the theater to the rafters and beyond:

"GABRIELA!"

But the crowd only heeded him with more laughter. "Poor man," someone giggled. "Hopelessly smitten," said another. "Poor *Gabriela,*" quipped another, answered by another cloud of chuckles.

Not even Louis paused, in the middle of giving his terse assurance for refunds to all, before scooping the angel up and whisking her behind the closing curtain.

Two hours later, the indecipherable fury burned to a new degree of raging frustration. Marcus paced the cat-walks until they shook, his steps echoing in the cavern of Drury's now-empty house, peppered by his growls of every profanity that knew its vogue within the last three hundred years.

He had once likened himself addicted to her like opium. He wondered if he now endured the torment called with-drawal.

He stopped only to hearken for any sound from the greenroom or dressing rooms. Anything, *anything*—

Nothing. Aside from the brief moment he had felt her snap back to consciousness, an impenetrable barricade had slammed shut on their invisible bond.

But, the rest of his preternatural functions still intact, Marcus heard everything else: the gossiping whispers of the ballet as they prepared for their suddenly free evening, their conjectures growing more elaborate at the arrival of the company physician . . . then Louis sending a missive to Augustus, requesting a morning meeting to discuss can-didates for Miss Rozina's replacement. . . .

Then, for well on the last thirty minutes, nothing.

Marcus paced harder. His imagination took the ballet's wild stories and added terrifying embellishments. She had fallen into a coma. She was dying. She was already dead. . . .

The physician departed, shaking his head. The last of the crew left, lasciviously eyeing some of the ballet. Louis rumbled out, wearing a scowl worthy of any soliloquy in the *Hamlet* script.

Marcus stalked faster. Started to swear in different lan-

guages. Kicked a chunk out of a dusty corner in the theater's wall. Where was she? What had happened to her?
God's teeth, had they all left her in that dressing room to
die?

His dread finally forced him to a desperate crossroads.
Either go to her, or tear apart every inch of Drury's interior
with his bare hands.

He snarled one more determined oath as he hurdled
the catwalk rail and unloosed a length of scenery line.
Without stopping to reconsider the command of his heart,
he descended to the stage in a swift and effortless sweep—

And nearly collided with a wrenchingly familiar figure
wobbling from the greenroom door.

Even at his near miss, Gabriela cried out in surprise and
stumbled back. Her equilibrium still clearly fragile, she
tripped and toppled, only missing another collision with
the floorboards by a foot—and Marcus's rescuing grip.

He wasted no time in sweeping her to him. He held her
tightly, desperately, treasuring the moments before she realized the identity of her savior and cursed him a demon
anew.

Yet no sound sliced through him except—

Gabriela's sob?

Dear God, did her *tears* soak the front of his shirt? And
yet, if so, did that flood denote her joy or her agony?

"Marcus," she rasped into his neck, a plaintive, confused sound, giving him no more explanation than before.
But she locked her arms around his nape as her tears
coursed harder.

"I am sorry," he grated back, holding her tighter, con-
demning himself for the spineless sin. "I should let you
go. I *have* to let you go."

"No!"

Yet she followed the protest with a large step back, her
gaze fixed to the ground—because she forced herself, he

wondered, or because she couldn't bear to look anywhere else?

"I . . . I mean . . . yes, you're right, of course," she continued, but another sob tore her composure apart. Her shoulders heaved with the effort to remain standing. "Oh, I don't know what's wrong or right any more! I don't know! Marcus; oh, Marcus . . ."

"My heart." The words came from *his* heart, breaking for her, reaching for her again, hauling her crumbled, crying form to him as a vehement sting clouded and burned behind his own vision. "I should not have come," he stammered. "God's teeth, I have done naught but make you miserable."

At *that*, she looked up at him—and doused the silver intensity of his confusion with the copper flames of her own. Like forest fires at midnight, those gold blazes raged against dark and unreadable horizons, neither denying nor confirming his contention—perhaps burning a message of both.

"I knew naught what had happened," Marcus went on. "I went insane with the waiting. I could not sense you anymore."

"I know."

He felt his left eyebrow drop. "You do?"

Gabriela's brow now puckered into perplexity, too. She glanced away swiftly, fingers tugging at the top button of his shirt. "I . . . I tried to reach you, too. I cried out for you . . ."

"You *did*?"

He lifted a finger beneath her chin, coercing her gaze back. Bright sienna tears glimmered as she nodded. "I called to you from inside . . . from my heart. I was frightened; I've never been so disconnected with my body before . . . I didn't know who else to turn to. But the doctor gave me some medicine. It muddled me. I knew you couldn't hear." She emitted a tiny, awkward laugh. "Believe it or not, that made me more frightened."

A grimace conquered her features, conveying the remainder of her ordeal in ample detail. Gabriela added a handful of his shirt to her shaking grasp, but Marcus curled her loose, slipping her fingers into the cocoon of his, instead.

'Tis all right, he sent his soul to whisper inside hers. *'Tis all right, Gabriela. I hear you now.*

He nay lied. Again, the captivating angles of her face showed her own comprehension of that. Her lips lifted into a smile. More shining tears—this time, he clearly saw, with joyous glints in them—slipped down her cheeks, as she delivered his soul back with a precious message of her own.

Oh, Marcus . . . I cannot help it . . . I love you; I love you so much.

Ah, God. The knowledge of it and the saying of it; such a minuscule, *monumental* difference. His senses reeled with wonder. His heartbeat thudded in every nerve ending.

"Sweeting," he forced himself to whisper, "are you sure?"

Her tears softened to a misty, happy haze. "I'm sure that I have never known another man like you, nor will again."

He gave a sardonic snort. *"That* is undisputed truth."

"I am not teasing about this."

"Nor am I."

His concise, clipped tone sank into him. Nay, this was *not* a silly script turn. This was not a script at all. This was the crossroads of a real life—Gabriela's. It was time for terrifying questions, and potentially anguishing answers.

Knowing that, Marcus tilted Gabriela's sight up to him. He leveled the full force of his vampire's gaze into hers. He gripped her shoulders with all the strength—and violence—he dared unleash in his vampire's body. "So what *do* you want, Gabriela? Am I a monster or a lover? A demon or a dream?"

Against his most strident vow not to, he quivered through an ensuing pause, knowing she saw his dependence on her answer in every inch of his stone-hard face.

"I cannot be both, sweeting," he charged from barely moving lips. "You cannot curse me and kiss me at once."

For a moment, Gabriela only nodded. Slowly. Silently.

Then she pressed close to him. Very close. She molded each inch of her body to every inch of his, as both her hands lifted to cup each side of his face.

And then she kissed him.

Ah, God, *she* kissed *him*, right on his monster's mouth. She wet his monster's cheeks with her soft, salty tears; she declared her love again into both of his monster's ears.

And then came the most incredible awareness of all.

Marcus didn't feel at all a monster anymore.

As a matter of fact, his pulse started to race with very mortal alacrity . . . his blood heated in all-too-human receptiveness to Gabriela's shy, then not-so-shy caresses of his shoulders and chest. His head clouded with blissful masculine befuddlement at the intoxicating scent of her hair, her perfume . . . her desire.

He groaned, deepening the kiss. Then he growled, deep and low, when she succumbed to the slick, hot invasion of his urgent, seeking tongue. Sweet Jesu, the effect she had on him . . . conscious thought was incinerated in the unthinking madness from her touch, her kisses, the little longing mewls she emitted in her throat. She burned him so deeply, he began to wonder which one of them had truly spent the last fortnight writhing in sleepless fever.

Amazingly, the ramifications of that thought penetrated a functioning part of his brain. Marcus broke off the kiss with a determined jerk.

"We must desist," he said between hard breaths, even then unable to stop his hands from roaming the graceful contours of her back. It hadn't escaped his attention that she'd shorn all her costume save a lace-topped chemise, covered only by a frothy white dressing robe secured by one entirely too accessible sash.

"We *will* desist," Gabriela responded against his ear, pressing that damn sash directly against his erection, "after you make love to me."

Her arms slipped around his waist. Her lips found the most sensitive spot on his collarbone. By all the saints and sinners, how did she know about that spot?

"Nay," Marcus managed to grate. *"Nay.* You've been ill."

He fumbled to catch her hands and set her away. But she had the advantage. She reached through the aroused tangle of his psyche to move thirty seconds ahead of him, easily slipping away before he found her, each time finding a new place to enflame his body with her caresses.

"I'm not ill anymore," she told him in another ear-warming whisper.

Marcus shook his head. "You fainted . . ."

"If I do it again, you'll catch me."

Despite himself, he loosed a husky chuckle. "And what if *I* faint?"

She replied to that by kissing him again. Openly. Ferociously. A brand of pure possession, snapping away the crutches of his polite concern as ruthlessly as she tugged apart the robe herself and offered the treasure beneath in a knowing slide of soft curve against hard vulnerability.

His manhood shot through with lightning while his senses flooded with hot need. Instinctively, Marcus slammed his eyes shut as molten silver surged his brain. At the far edges of that blinding heat, he felt Gabriela's mouth at his jaw, her fingers at the ties of his shirt. So good . . . bloody damn, she felt so good. He only had to allow the flywheel of his control to slip one more notch, and the curtain would furl free . . . the play of passion would know its crescendo.

But crescendos backlashed into disasters if not all players knew their purpose on stage.

With heaving breaths of effort, he hauled back the drape of desire long enough to grab Gabriela. He transposed their positions in a fierce, fast sweep. She gasped in surprise, as he expected—but those ten seconds devoured a clean half of the remaining self-control in him.

The other half, he spent to tell her in a determined growl, "You know not what you're doing, Gabriela."

Her retaliation came swift and angry—and winced with pain. "The bloody *blast* I don't."

She looked straight up at him—*into* him—beholding the very depths of his condemned soul, and not cowering an inch. "How dare you," she leveled then. "How dare you say that, when you know the hell you put me through. Save that speech I see you preparing, too, Mr. Danewell. My hell is just as grim as yours, because it's the exact same ordeal. Hell, Marcus, is not who you are, what you are, where you live, or even how you live. Hell is living that existence *alone.*"

He said nothing. He could not. He stood there, bowing his head, silenced by the conviction of her words, accused by the light of her truth.

Until her beautiful hands reached up to lift his face.

And grasped his heart, as well.

"I don't want to be alone anymore, Marcus," she told him in a tear-filled whisper. At that, he looked again to her eyes . . . so shimmering, so sad . . . was *she* pleading with *him* for deliverance? Dear God, he must be dreaming this!

But she spoke again, very real, very close. "Don't you see? For the first time in my life, I know exactly what I'm doing. I know exactly where I belong . . . right here, on stage, with you. I've found my heaven." Her fingers pressed tighter as she raised her lips to tenderly take him. "*Our* heaven."

If his faculties reeled before, they capsized now. Marcus accepted her kiss with a shuddering sigh, afraid to move, to shatter whatever miracle she had wrought to give him this moment, this perfect star of an instant, where his soul exploded past the confines of this wretched world and indeed glimpsed a place of light and life.

Still, he rasped, "Heaven . . . sweeting, I nay think I know how to believe in heaven."

Like the brush of an angel's wing, her answer came gossamer soft against his lips. "I'll show you how." Her touch slid down his neck, beneath his shirt, pressing warm and strong over the increasing cadence of his heart. "Don't be afraid, Marcus. I'll show you the way. If you'll only let me—"

He interrupted her with his answer—a kiss as much surrender as command, equal part domination and submission, pleading for her guidance even as he felt her body tremoring at expert lover's touches he'd thought forgotten a century ago. She shivered and arched for him; she whimpered and sighed; she answered the strokes of his fingers and the escalating heat of his movements with a guileless sensuality he had never thought possible in a woman.

And with that purity, that wondering, awakening joy, she proved herself good to her word. She led him out of his darkness on a stairway of kisses and soft words, and at the top, she cleansed him in the nirvana of her goodness and love. Marcus's soul burst with amazement. His lungs struggled to breathe as they pumped out dry, speechless sobs. He clung to her, yearning to climb inside her for the forever of his days, so he should never hate anymore . . . so he should never hurt.

Somewhere in the silver white glory of that heaven, her lips found his again. They drank of each other greedily, passionately, tasting of the communion they'd soon become. And while their mouths and tongues intertwined in desire, her heart wound into his with a plea that stopped his breath in its fervor.

Don't make me go away again. Please don't make me go away.

Never, my love, he answered with every straining inch of his being. *Never again* . . .

She rendered him incapable of any words after that. Marcus hissed amazed breath through his teeth as Gabriela slipped an eager hand to the taut rise between his thighs. And then, dear God, when she started to knead him there . . .

He withstood the torment for thirty seconds, well nigh a phenomenon for *his* suprahuman capacity, before forcing her hand against the wall over her head. As time burned away the next minute, he slammed both her arms to that arousing position, her two wrists captive beneath his unrelenting grip, as his other hand yanked her chemise over her hips in urgent fistfuls.

When he unsheathed the vortex of her sexuality, a slide of fingers to that moist cavity elicited a moan he'd never heard from her before—a deep, primal sound that shook the core of his own male instincts. Marcus growled and replaced the caress of his hand with the swell of his need.

Gabriela responded by lifting a sleek, satiny leg around his waist.

He grabbed the curve of her thigh and pulled her harder against him. "Little wench," he accused in a hot, heavy whisper against her ear. "Naughty, lovely little wench."

And at that, he freed himself at last, giving rein to the final throbs of blood that turned his unbearable arousal into an unstoppable ache. Two instants later, he drove up inside her, far and full and complete. He dropped her hands in order to brace both of his to the wall, making her ride each lunge of his desire to its longest, hardest extent. Her cries of his name coincided with each thrust of their bodies, and soon he realized, with incredulity, she interspersed other words in her adjurations, too:

"More, Marcus. I want more. More!"

And he gave it to her. He gave her all he had. All he was.

Perhaps, all he would ever be.

Later, he sank to the floor and cradled her until she fell into a peaceful sleep—most likely, her first complete rest in days. Then, wrapping her back in the robe, he climbed back up into the catwalks and began ascending Drury's silent heights toward their apartment hideaway.

Marcus looked down at his swaddled prize many times during that climb, not hesitating to admit his sudden commiseration to the thieves of the world—for tonight, he had no less than taken a shard of light from the domain of day. How long fate would turn its back and feign ignorance on his sin, he knew not, he cared not. For now, he and Gabriela would make rainbows out of moonbeams and dewdrops out of falling stars, the night their new heaven, the dark their new discovery, and love their sweet, stolen scrap from the unfeeling claws of time.

Stolen time . . .

It was more than he had ever hoped for. More than he had ever dreamed.

He was euphoric with the precious gift. Grateful. Satisfied.

He only wondered how long Gabriela could be.

Eleven

"Gabriela, we must talk."

Gaby emitted a slow sigh into Marcus's chest. Ten minutes ago, she'd awakened here with a smile on her face and a wish that time would stand still. And for now, she chose to ignore the impossibility of such a thing. For a while longer, she'd rather believe the same clock that had ticked through nearly three hundred years to bring this man to her would halt at seven minutes after three o'clock on this dark May morning, and let her keep him next to her heart forever.

Then again, she should have remembered Marcus wouldn't stand for that. The man she loved did not consider forever a blessing.

"There are matters we must discuss before I leave," he persisted into her silence. "Important matters."

Gaby suggestively kissed her way up over his heartbeat. "Can't we just make love again?"

"Nay." Not even her ruthless attack on his collarbone altered his tone—though the involuntary twitches of his thigh muscles maintained her hope of attempting another incursion.

"Very well," she acquiesced for the moment. "My ears are yours, grump."

Marcus turned to his side and pierced her with a gaze

more somber than his tone. "I nay thought we were jesting about this."

She flashed him a pout. "And you're in the wrong act, Mr. Danewell. That was several hours ago."

Nonetheless, with the same barely tamped ferocity he'd used those hours prior, Marcus snapped a hand around the back of her neck, forcing her to accept his direct, decisive gaze. "We will have no more lies between us, Gabriela. You *must* consider the truth of our situation from now on."

He took breath to say something more, but stopped suddenly and closed his eyes, as if repenting for his outburst. His touch gentled at her nape. "You must realize," he murmured, "I am not just a . . . a grump. I am—"

"I know." Gabriela pressed two emphasizing fingers over his lips. "You're a vampire. I know."

Something flickered in his eyes, a surreal silver light—as if her words both healed him and killed him. Finally, low and tentative, "Do you? Do you really *believe* this, Gabriela? Do you *accept* it?"

She couldn't help a quick, sardonic laugh. "What do you think I've been bloody near meditating on for the last five days? What do you think occupied every moment of my waking conscious and invaded any second I managed to sleep? Marcus . . ." She slid her hand to his jaw, now making *him* meet *her* gaze—and look to the sincerity of her soul. "Believe me, I haven't been able to stop realizing what you are."

His gaze flinched again. But Gaby shook her head and smiled softly. "Hear me out," she urged. "When I walked onto the stage tonight and felt you again—and felt *alive* again—I discovered something very important. *What* you are is not as important as *who* you are . . . or what you are to me, or the magic we make when we're together."

Still, the assurance, and the lingering kiss she finished it with, didn't straighten the black V of his furrowed brows—a scowl so very redolent of an unsure Elizabethan boy. "But . . . is magic enough?"

"Oh, Marcus." She kissed him again. "It's more than enough."

At last, the frown eased a fraction. Gaby smiled and coaxed his brows back farther with tender tracings of her finger. "But now that we *are* speaking of magic . . . Marcus, I would like to know about this bond we share."

His forehead tensed beneath her touch again. But she persisted. "Please, Marcus, it . . . it overwhelms me. Sometimes it frightens me. Sometimes, I swear my heart beats in time to yours. It's not like anything I've ever felt before."

As the words solemnized her smile, they warmed a soft grin on Marcus. "Me neither, my heart." He tilted his head back to catch her finger between his lips, then suckle it in a cherishing kiss.

"Then . . . what is it?" she prodded. "It's *not* normal . . ."

"Nay." He gathered her hand against his chest as he lowered his gaze back to her. A meaningful gray mist darkened his eyes.

"Then what?" Involuntarily, Gaby's voice dropped to a whisper. She almost didn't want the significance of that dark gray stare translated—perhaps the line between the man and the mystery of him went best continued a blur— but an uncontrollable necessity drove her on, an age-old female need to know this man—*her* man—as no one knew him before.

But to do that, she'd have to plunge into his darkness, unravel his deepest mysteries. "Is . . . is this some kind of a force you can wield as a vampire?" she asked. "Sometimes it feels as if you climb right inside my mind . . ."

At that, she trailed off and glanced away. She hadn't blurted anything so ridiculous since Christmas Services 1866, when she confused her angel-heard-on-high with the Macbeth ghost she'd been practicing. The macabre

4 BESTSELLING HISTORICAL ROMANCES BY YOUR FAVORITE AUTHORS CAN BE YOURS, FREE!

Kensington Choice, our newest book club now brings you historical romances by your favorite bestselling authors including Janelle Taylor, Shannon Drake, Rosanne Bittner, Jo Beverley, and Georgina Gentry, just to name a few! Each book is filled with passion, adventure and the excitement of bygone times!

To introduce you to this great new club which is part of Zebra Home Subscription Service, we'd like to send you your first 4 bestselling historical romances, absolutely free! And once you get these 4 free books to savor at home, we'll rush you the next 4 brand-new books at the lowest prices available, as soon as they are published.

The way the club works is that after your initial FREE shipment, you will get our 4 newest bestselling historical romances delivered to your

doorstep each month at the preferred subscriber's rate of only $4.20 per book, a savings of up to $7.16 per month (since these titles sell in bookstores for $4.99-$5.99)! All books are sent on a 10-day free examination basis and there is no minimum number of books to buy. (A postage and handling charge of $1.50 is added to each shipment.) Plus as a regular subscriber, you'll receive our FREE monthly newsletter, *Zebra/Pinnacle Romance News*, which features author profiles, contests, subscriber benefits, book previews and more.

So start today by returning the FREE BOOK CERTIFICATE provided. We'll send you 4 FREE BOOKS with no further obligation: A FREE gift offering you hours of reading pleasure with no obligation...how can you lose?

KENSINGTON CHOICE
Zebra Home Subscription Service, Inc.
120 Brighton Road
P.O.Box 5214
Clifton, NJ 07015-5214

AFFIX
STAMP
HERE

heights of her imagination might prove to be the greatest advantage to their love—and the greatest frustration.

She steeled herself for his condescending chuckle.

Marcus didn't emit a sound. When Gabriela finally looked back up, his serious, sincere stare still awaited her.

She wanted to weep in happiness.

She wanted to kiss him senseless.

Reading *that* thought flitted a smile across his lips. But he answered her in low, thoughtful tones. "I cannot enter your mind, not physically," he told her. "I am afraid 'tis too tight. I *can*, however, change my own physical dimensions, to the larger or smaller, within limits."

Gaby couldn't help flicking a grin of her own now. "Such as becoming a bat at will?"

"If I fancy. But I do not often fancy." He shifted uncomfortably. If Gaby read his suddenly stiff stature as she would stage direction, she'd classify his mien as embarrassed. "Yet if I am forced to that sort of situation, I prefer to become a wolf. Or"—he shifted again—"a butterfly."

Gaby bit the inside of her cheek. Hard. And gulped back the giggle threatening to snort out her nose. She should have let the laugh come, anyway. Marcus snapped a dark glower at her, easily discerning her reaction.

"Oh, Marcus," she murmured, "My Marcus . . . I'm sorry. I . . . I don't know much about all this, except from some scenes I performed as practice from the play by Planché, *The Bride of the Isles*. And of course, what they print in the weekly serials."

His vehement grunt relayed what he thought of her sources, especially the latter. His ambiguity only incited her to push back toward her original concern. "But most works agree about the ability of a vampire to hypnotize his victims," she said. "Is that what's going on, Marcus?" She now turned to her side, as well. "Have you been hypnotizing me?"

He took a long moment to contemplate his reply. As he

did, he lifted her hand back to his lips. He looked down to her fingers, bestowing a soft nip to each knuckle.

"I tried," he finally answered. "And I was triumphant—once. On my second attempt, you found me out. *You* ended up controlling *me*, with your orders to come back and help you with your rehearsals." He shrugged, his Elizabethan boy now graduated to a cocky lad ready to take Whitehall by storm. "I'm afraid my skills lie in sensual, not supernatural, conquests."

Now Gaby's eyebrows crunched together. "But you still could be using me, and I wouldn't . . ."

"And if I am," he countered, deferring her by pushing her back to the pillows, "would you be able to see into *my* heart and soul, as well?"

Again, Gabriela sighed into his chest, now an unavoidable broadness atop her. The man—and his enticing torso—had a point. But his deduction didn't bring her any closer to understanding the awesome, sometimes fearsome, connection they shared. The enigma brought the endless layers beneath Drury's stage to mind. One successfully snapped trap door only led to encountering the closed hatch of the next. . . .

To further thicken the muddle, Marcus's voice, loving but uncompromising, came echoing in her head:

Sweeting, look at me.

Defiance should have occurred to her, if only to protest his invasion of her vulnerable mindset. But in that word, her quandary lay. Marcus didn't invade—he *belonged* inside her. He always had. He always would.

Without a second's hesitation, she obeyed his hest.

The youthful slack in his posture had tightened back to significant purpose. He no longer sent words to her mind, but a message awaited her in his eyes, telling her how completely he comprehended her confusion—telling her perhaps, together, they could spring the next trap door.

He took a deep, resolute breath. "I shall try to explain.

What you and I share is common . . . and yet not so common."

"Oh, thanks," she returned on a frustrated huff. "I understand ever so clearly now."

When he didn't fling back a similarly sharpened riposte, but dropped his forehead to the valley above her breasts and slowly, defeatedly shook his head, Gaby wished her words back into the unthinking gutter she'd thrown them from. She reached up and buried her fingers in his mussed hair, again heeding ageless instinct to comb the thick strands across his scalp, reassuring him, encouraging him to say the words when he had them.

It never struck her until now. . . . She moved about the world each day, telling dozens of people "I'm an actress," or "I live on Hay's Mews, in Mayfair." Not normal declarations by most Londoners' standards, but simple categories by the dictates of their repetition. This man had lived thousands and thousands of days—and perhaps only this moment confronted the first time he'd had to put his existence into words.

No wonder he took a good five minutes to look back up at her and begin again.

"A vampire *is* capable of sharing a mental bond with a mortal," Marcus told her softly. "Much like the link we share. The connected couple is able to share thoughts and feelings, even commune with each other over some distances." He dropped back to his side while taking in another long breath. "But the union is usually only begotten through an act called initiation."

"Initiation," she echoed. "When . . . when did we do that? What was it? Did I know you were doing it?"

" 'Tis just my meaning, true heart." He looked back to her, his gaze scanning her intently. "I have *not* initiated you." He shoved a mass of black waves off his forehead. "God only knows what would happen if I did."

Gaby felt his frustration, his taut perplexity. But that

awareness only abetted the bemused grin tugging her lips. "So you're saying we did this all by ourselves?"

Marcus's left eyebrow dropped above his darkening scowl. Yet a trace of amazed comprehension sneaked into his responding murmur. "I suppose I am."

At that, Gabriela laughed. Then caught his face on both sides of his adorable glower, and pulled him down for a long, wet kiss.

"Magic," she told him in a whisper. "Now doesn't it make perfect sense?"

And then Marcus chuckled, too. He kissed her back and filled her with the sound, a deep, rich rumble of summer thunder precluding the blossoming rainbow in her heart. They laughed and kissed and teased some more, rolling from one side of the huge bed to the other, young lovers bantering in a meadow of down and candlelight. . . .

And magic.

Several minutes later, they lay breathless and content in the hopeless tangle of sheets they'd created. When Marcus pulled Gabriela tighter, she didn't resist. He traced lazy circles on her shoulder while she traced lazy circles on his chest.

Halfway through her twelfth circle, she softly ventured, "Marcus?"

"Hmmmm?"

"What *is* initiation?"

As she anticipated, all his muscles stiffened. But he replied in a strangely calm voice, " 'Tis the act of feeding, more or less. A vampire takes blood from a mortal, but drains them not."

Gabriela nodded. She'd expected an answer like that. "So does the mortal turn into . . . half a vampire?"

A suppressed chuckle underlined his reply with warm velvet. "Nay. But the blood bond is a powerful link betwixt the pair, so the mortal often fatigues easily during the day, and is more attuned to the world of the darkness. When awakening at dusk, the vampire can summon the mortal with a mere thought."

That disclosure wove his tone from velvet to an uncomfortable burlap. "Very simply, the vampire has complete control over his . . . disciple." He growled low, and his body tensed tighter. " 'Tis not a natural or honorable authority to have. I have seen it abused on several ugly occasions."

Gabriela considered that, but nonetheless issued her own conclusion. "It sounds romantic to me."

"It is *not.*"

His unbreaching tone precluded an equal fortress of silence. Gaby respected his unspoken command, allowing a minute, then two to go by, feeling him battling back the dark and unwanted memories of those "ugly occasions." He battled hard. She came to the conclusion "ugly" only began to describe the horrors.

More than two hundred and fifty years of such nightmares . . . dear God, what kind of existence *had* this beautiful man endured? Would she ever really know? Would she ever comprehend the scope of his knowledge, the breadth of his experience . . . the depth of his loneliness?

She wanted to. With all her breath and being, she yearned to.

That unquenchable longing compelled her beyond the hesitance to phrase her next question. She had to know. . . .

"Did Raquelle initiate you?"

To her surprise, Marcus spat a harsh laugh. "Hardly. Raquelle was not the initiating sort."

But she surprised herself more. More accurately, her next words shocked the warmth straight out of her limbs. "Will you initiate me?"

Marcus's answering glare pierced far beyond shock. As he spun and bolted off the bed, he snapped, "Absolutely not."

His sudden absence stung like a gust of North Sea wind—
bringing the logic behind her request into ice-sharp focus.
What, indeed, was so staggering about wanting to be that
much closer to him? What was so wrong with yearning for
an intimacy beyond dreams, a sharing beyond belief, a soul-
mating with the one and only man she'd ever love?

As a matter of fact, the idea made perfect, beautiful
sense!

"Marcus," she leveled, gathering a sheet around her and
rising on her knees, "just think of all we could share . . ."

"We share enough already." He whipped his shirt off a
chair and shoved his way into the sleeves.

"But I love you."

"I love you, too. 'Tis why the subject is closed." Damn
it all, he slid into his breeches swifter than he'd taken them
off. As he secured the codpiece with rapid jerks, he commenced a swift search for his boots.

Gaby climbed off the bed and followed him, persistent.
"Marcus—"

She didn't know what cut off the rest of her words first:
his furious whirl back upon her, the upraised finger he
swung along with the motion, or the silver-fired stare he
backed the silent command with.

She only knew there would be no further argument tonight—just as she identified the soul-deep pain underlin-
ing his low and final words.

"The subject is *closed,* Gabriela. Mention it not again."

For once, she heeded his behest. Five and a half weeks
later, in a moment of rare, but peaceful solitude at his
writing nook, Marcus thanked the forces of nature that
had combined to effect that small miracle.

Gabriela had spoken no more of initiation, though Marcus agreed to help her learn about other aspects of what
she termed his "unique mode of living" in exchange for

her return to the stage and renewed commitment to win-
ning a visit from the Prince's Grand Theatre Troupe. No
secret lay between them about who had cinched the better
half of the deal. The next evening, the woman threw herself into a performance gleaning three roof-raising ova-
tions, as well as Louis's silence about seeking her
replacement. Every night thereafter, Gabriela pushed the
role to new and greater success, reflecting the breakthroughs of awareness and ability she achieved nearly
nightly in their after-hours sessions . . . their rehearsals begun with Shakespeare or Dryden, and inevitably ended
with passion and fulfillment.

Aye, she flowered and bloomed beneath his careful guidance, sometimes beyond what *he* envisioned, unfolding the
petals of herself as willing student, precious soulmate, in-
satiable and unbelievable lover . . . as if she had only
needed him all along. Indeed, like a flower needed the
sun.

Christ. Such an absurd notion! But had Marcus not
found himself pushing past the more than two-hundred-
and-fifty-year-old topsoil of his own loneliness to meet the
coaxing warmth of her ardent questions? Did he not
search the most disturbing realms of himself to bring back
serious answers for her sincere queries about his life, despite the constant terror that one of those responses could
send her running from him forever in repulsed horror?

But she never shrieked. She never ran. She had accepted
his answers with rapt, quiet attention, as if he explained
the secret to playing a perfect Lady Macbeth instead of
such useless morbidity as his feeding needs, sleeping
schedule, and what it felt like to hear every whisper in
Drury's house if he so cared.

The only moment he had noted revulsion in her gaze
came when he recounted the incident in Hungary with
Gertrude, his "sweet" farm girl, with her big eyes, bigger
breasts, and a big, vampire-hunting village. Gabriela had

emitted a snort of open hostility and called Gertrude a
spineless backwoods bumpkin—at which, quite suddenly
and shockingly, he found himself restraining a burst of
adoring laughter.

And hatred? Aye, Gabriela showed him hatred, too—
only once. The night she softly requested the full story of
what Raquelle had done to him, and how.

She had listened while he held nothing back, beginning
with Raquelle's tickle of a seduction in his ear, bidding
him to a tryst in a forest glade not far from London, at
midnight of the next eve. There was a cave in that glade,
one of his mates told him later, where exotic and erotic
ecstasies took place, unspeakable and unforgettable. . . .

He had barely slept that night and, of course, arrived
at the glade an hour early, yet Raquelle was already waiting,
teasing him with that throaty laugh of hers. And indeed,
she led him to that dark, warm grotto. She left a path of
her own clothes to guide him deeper into her lair, the
walls seeming to pulse around him, like the convulsions
of a climax. Before he knew what happened, Raquelle had
intoxicated him beyond thought with her laugh and her
body and some sweet alcoholic ambrosia she kept plying
to his lips.

He swallowed hard then, the words locking in his throat,
but Gabriela's touch had drawn out courage he thought
long dead. He had continued, telling her how he suddenly
found himself naked and tied down to a massive stone
slab, staring up at a ceiling of leering stars and the full,
smirking moon . . . and Raquelle's body, incredible and
unreal, riding him, milking him, before she dropped her
head to his chest and sank her teeth into his heart. . . .

And only then, the words came no more, choked by the
dry heaves he emitted over the side of the bed . . . until
Gabriela had gathered him back into her arms and held
him through the shuddering, terrifying minutes when the
memory refused to grant him mercy. Shaking, sobbing, he

relived that heinous moment of shock, of helplessness, of raging, of railing, of dying, then of living again . . . ah God, of Raquelle pressing her own breast to his mouth and forcing him to live again. . . .

He had blocked his thoughts from Gabriela after that, unable to expose even her brave soul to the two-week hell following his transformation. He could not tell her of his vow to wither away dead before taking the blood of another, only to fail his task in humiliation when Raquelle brought the irresistible corpse of a sheepherder to the grotto. He barely brought *himself* to recall his insane wanderings through the forest, arms swung over his head, pleading with God and the angels for some respite from the sudden onslaught of perception; of smelling, hearing, and seeing every sound and sight and life within fifty miles. Especially anything with blood flowing in its veins. . . .

But most of all, he would not tell Gabriela of the hope.

He nay knew why he bothered to call it such any more. He had long since given up on Raquelle's cryptic announcement of so long ago, delivered just after she cackled her way through an explanation of what she had done to him. At *that*, he had leapt up and tried to kill her, of course, but she had a hundred years and a body full of blood on him.

"Dear Marcus," she had crooned after effectively slamming him back to the cave wall, "you will get used to this. In time, I believe you might even thank me for it. *Non?* Well, in that case, I might as well tell you: I have heard a cure does, in fact, exist for milquetoasts who have been transformed against their will. Do not ask me what it is; I have never cared to find out. I have only heard them say it is not instant, nor easy, and involves a magical spell, or some such *absurdités*. If you care to waste your precious nights seeking something like this, I cannot stop you. Yet neither do I care to play party to it. So I will say *adieu,* my *chéri.*" Then she had clucked her tongue and shaken her head. "Too, too bad, Marcus. I thought you would be such fun. *Au revoir.*"

And he had never seen her again.

Nor had he found the miraculous "cure."

And he had searched for it. God, how he had searched. By the torch light and moon glow of his miserable, lonely nights, he had combed one end of the world then the next, seeking the deliverance from his wretched infirmity. He toured France with a one-eyed Gypsy woman, exhausting every hex and vile-tasting *brasseur de le vampire* in her memory. He tarred his face and crossed a jungle to have a voodoo shaman bless a dead snake around his neck. He hiked the Himalayas for ten years, inhaling every incense and praying to every spirit the *lamas* would teach to him; he spent another ten in the Orient, speared with three-foot-long acupuncture needles. He tried enchantments and spells, crystals and even simple cold cures.

But in the end, the sun always rose again. In the end, he always felt his skin crackling with the encroaching, deadly heat. . . .

In the end, before racing to the pathetic black safety of his coffin, he cursed the God who turned His back on an unsuspecting fool named Marcus Danewell.

In time, however, he lost the will to curse. That came shortly after he terminated the hope of Raquelle's "cure." A few weeks later, he returned to England, where the sky, the fog, and the cold seemed a perfect manifestation of his life's damp, gray, dismal eternity.

By then, Drury Lane was concocted, constructed, and basking in the patronage of a king madly in love with—who would have dreamed it possible—an actress. Marcus's need for extremely private living space suddenly received royal sanction—and if Charlie ever noticed the dismal creature sharing his specially forged subterranean passageways, the promise of Nell Gwyn's waiting bosom obviously relegated the matter to a secondary concern.

While thankful for his soveriegn's mindless mooning, Marcus had observed that whole affair with disturbed perplexion. A few times, he considered coming forward; just jumping from the darkness, seizing the man's shoulders and shouting, *You are acting a moron! She is only a woman; a viperess disguised in soft skin and perfume! You are the bloody king of England, and she shall ruin you!*

Now, Marcus was glad he had kept to the shadows—though now he also realized his actions would nay have daunted Charlie half a step. For now, he understood what kind of a power drove a man to burrow beneath city streets, woo the wrath of an entire court, and defy the expectations of an entire matrimony-minded country.

Now, he understood the power of a thing called love.

That thought welled up into a soft chuckle, echoing in the twilight stillness of the subterranean chamber, effectively ushering him back to the present. *Now look at the peagoose who is mindlessly mooning,* came a good-natured chide from a pleasant niche in his heart—a place still surprising in his discovery and exploration of it, filled with newness and wonder, exhilaration and, aye, a touch of terror at the fact that nearly three hundred years of existence had not turned up *this* sensation before: such childlike uncertainty, yet such a man's heady thrum of triumph; such a primal need to possess, yet such shameless prostration at the altar of his beloved. Such confusion. Such contradiction.

Such bliss.

He laughed again, and even allowed a content sigh to escape and flicker the candle flames over his writing table.

The deep nasal incredulity of a countering chuckle shook the flames harder. Startlement jerked Marcus's senses out of their reverie—the feather pen, out of his hand. As the source of the snicker moved closer, he snatched the quill up from the pool of blue ink it deposited on the fragile rag paper beneath—a sheet pirated from the back of the Danewell family bible.

"Well, damn me," came Joseph's amiable drawl, "there *is* a first time fer everything. Do believe if I were a snake, ye'd be dead by now, guvnah."

Marcus pivoted with the beginnings of a scowl tightening his temples—but found his inner peace immune even to Joseph's crudities. Instead, he curled up one side of his mouth and replied, "Not bloody likely, my friend."

Joseph's smile dropped. Flickered to life again. Fell again. On suddenly shifting feet, the pudgy man grumbled, "Well, what the blemmin' hell do ye want? I almost thought yer note was a mistake. I just brought a fresh piece fer ye last night; I don't think I can pull a stroke like it two nights in a row without anybody noticin'. What're ye doin' anyway, guv? Sharin' the spoils with a friend?"

Marcus turned back to see what he could salvage of the paper. "I nay said I needed another . . . 'piece.' "

Even a mortal could have sensed the disconcertation—perhaps even the fear—knelling through Joseph's rapidly muttered reply. "Ye've . . . ye've just never asked fer anythin' else before."

Fear. Oh aye, poor Joseph definitely stood there quaking in fear. And Marcus cursed himself for the responding impulse to emit a good-natured chuckle at the awareness. But his reminiscences of Gabriela and the happiness they had gifted to his senses as a result, made even Joseph's self-dignity a prime commodity.

Painstakingly shielding his mirth, Marcus looked up and gave the man an agreeable nod. "I admit I have simple needs."

A slobbery snort retaliated. "I wouldn't call 'em *simple.*"

"Nevertheless, I think you shall find this eve's request easier to fulfill than usual. And my gratitude," he added, leveling an impenetrable stare into wary eyes, "twice as substantial."

At that, between what Joseph perceived as one moment and the next, Marcus flipped open a "stone" in the wall, clicked access to the wall safe beneath and flourished a handful of solid gold sovereign pounds, each still bearing a perfectly pounded likeness of Queen Bess.

Joseph glared at him naught through slits any more. "Jesus, guv." His stubbled jaw lifted with a chuckle of renewed insolence. "Now that ye talk with *those* words, I think we can do business."

Marcus slipped the coins into a cloth pouch. "Good."

"And I know just the place to get ye the goods. Little place over in Belgravia, believe it or no. Finest in London, I hear 'em say."

Marcus found it his turn to narrow a perplexed stare. "Finest in . . . ?" He shook his head. "You know not what I need yet."

"The hell I don't." The man laughed more enthusiastically while cuffing a hearty slap to Marcus's shoulder. "Aw, there's no need fer airs around me, guv. I'm even proud o' ye, now that I tinker on it."

Marcus's scowl plummeted lower. Joseph only deemed a few of life's subjects worth "tinkering" over. He nay knew if he wanted to guess which vice he had indulged hard enough to sufficiently arouse the man's faculties.

"Oh, c'mon," Joseph prodded. "There's only one thing this kinda quid gets rolled fer: women. And *this* kinda quid'll get ye . . ."

"A dozen raspberry tarts with fresh cream," Marcus cut him off. He slammed the payment into Joseph's hand and turned before any connotation but the obvious be gleaned.

Nonetheless, like the tangible gust after the passage of a speeding coach, he felt the mortal's confusion swirl the chamber's air. He sensed Joseph peering down at the pouch, assessing the small fortune encompassed there, his puny brain actually wondering if he had missed a vital section of the conversation telling him what the bundle *really* stood for.

Marcus didn't prolong his assistant's dilemma. "You need but pick up and render payment for the pastries," he confirmed. "I already ordered them."

And he had—a clear week ago, after Gabriela brought half a dozen of the little pies up to the apartment and devoured the lot in a half hour. As Marcus watched her lick the bright pink filling off her thumbs in near-carnal ecstasy, he had instantly started planning tonight's surprise: a candlelit homage to his love, beginning with the tarts and a bottle of 1598 chablis. The evening's second course would consist of fruit, cheese, and bread, which she would devour while giving him an act-by-act detailing of the night's performance. Course three: a new silk gown and matching peignoir set, leading swiftly into course four, begun by her girlish sighs of delight and thanks . . . and finished with his lesson in how delicious raspberry filling could taste on places other than thumbs. . . .

God's bodkin. He could hardly wait.

"You shall go here," Marcus charged, scribbling the street and number of old Gertha's cottage on the edge of town. "She is a friend who takes special orders for me, so do not look for a baker's shingle." Gertha had reluctantly taken down her sign in 1817, after "neighborly" gossipings mutated into dangerous suspicions about the pastry woman who never appeared after the 5 A.M. bread rush, who created beautiful birthday cakes for everyone but herself, and for that matter, who never had a birthday.

Joseph looked at the address, jerked a gruff shrug. "Seems like a terrific fartin' falderal, just fer a dozen bleedin' tarts."

"*Raspberry* tarts."

Marcus did not deliver the correction as a jest. Still, Joseph cocked a knowing grin as his eyes alighted with a new gleam of mischief.

"All right, guv," the little man finally quipped. "Who is she?"

Marcus swallowed. And promptly wanted to slit his own throat for the all-telling gesture. "She?" he managed to retort with convincing indignance.

"Ohhh, aye." The croon floated across the room on underlines of certainty only attempted by witless mortals. "Blemmin' hell, but I must be losin' it. I really shoulda called yer horse the second I walked in. Here ye are frit-terin' about like a rangy school lad, wearin' fancy velvet clothes I never knew ye possessed, sittin' in such a lovesick moon that I bloody well could have snuck up and—"

"Joseph—"

"And quite the testy lad, too." The mortal rocked back on his heels and hooked his thumbs through dirty sus-penders. "Like I said, this kinda quid is only thrown about fer one thing."

"Joseph."

"Awww, c'mon," Joseph pressed—an attempt, much to Marcus's incredulity, at a fatherly prod. "Just a hint," the man persisted. "Ye . . . ye really care about the chit, eh?"

To his further shock, Marcus rose, turned, and contem-plated the query with a heel-rocking stance of his own. "Aye," he actually heard himself say. "Aye, I love her."

And then, Marcus actually smiled at the man. A slow, sublime, utterly carefree smile, filled with only the purity of the words he had just spoken.

So this was what they meant by catharsis. *This* caused those matrons in box seven to soak three handkerchiefs each during the crypt scene in *Romeo and Juliet*. This was the great dramatic device touted by scholars and actors, that Will himself swore by. . . .

Marcus had never understood the fanfare, until now. Until, for the first time since he breathed air on this earth, he confessed not only a feeling of his heart, but a com-mitment of his soul.

And he stepped from chains he never knew he wore.

"Well, bleedin' hell," came another chuckle from Joseph. "Of all the . . . er, people, who I never thought it possible . . . well, that *is* wonderful, guv. Wonderful."

Oddly, the mortal's second shoulder slap provided a comforting anchor in the sea of Marcus's newfound freedom.

The man's ensuing leer was another matter. "So," Joseph continued in a suggestive mutter, "how soon 'till ye got 'er on the back and full-in-the-belly?"

Marcus sighed again as he spun back toward his writing table. While renewed disgust prevented him from matching Joseph's quip, an equally potent sentiment held him back from venting raw fury on the man . . . a deep and disturbing twist to his inner core at the vision Joseph's statement exploded to mind. . . .

The impression of Gabriela, round and ripe with his child.

Impossible.

But vampiric offspring *had* been known to happen . . . rarely. Mostly when vampires coupled with Gypsy women, or were Gypsies as mortals themselves. Still, there were the odd incidents throughout the centuries. . . .

Terribly, highly impossible.

He heard the results varied from disastrous to joyous. . . .

Unthinkable.

A dream never to come true. A reality never to happen. A life he'd never have.

Life, he resolutely reminded himself, only existed of tonight. All it *could* exist of. Perhaps, in a few hours, a hope of tomorrow night might start to glimmer as realistic possibility, but beyond that, the future belonged to the darkness of the unknown. Weeks ago, cradling Gabriela's precious, slumbering form in his arms, he had vowed the mercurial miracle of their temporary heaven would be enough.

He repledged himself to that promise now. He would transform the next hours and minutes into diamonds and sapphires, and adorn the queen of his world with every sparkling second of them. Tonight, past would meld with present, and future only extended as far as the next kiss. And perhaps, maybe, if he paid worthy homage to his sovereign, if he loved her hard enough and strong enough, that future would battle time for him, fighting to stay locked in the sweet ecstasy of this magical eve.

Now, he only had to make everything perfect.

After shooing Joseph away to attend the detail of the tarts, Marcus sprinted up to the apartment one more time. On his way, he honed one ear toward Drury's stage—everything was running on schedule; Gabriela had just made her Act Two entrance—bringing him a satisfied smile when he reached the upper rooms.

He lit the last of the candles around the sitting room, dozens of the tapers glowing from ornate candelabra he had interspersed between towering urns full of dark red roses. He ran a critical glance over each of the bouquets, each bloom hand-selected and arranged by him.

He had pulled petals from another dozen roses and strewn them in a path leading to the bedroom. The trail ended at the foot of the bed, where the ivory lace gown and peignor lay glowing in dark amber radiance against the coverlet. Now, as an additional inspiration, Marcus gathered some petals and scattered them across the bed pillows, as well. Gabriela's hair would smell even sweeter with the hint of rose in its silken bouquet.

Gabriela's hair . . . God, how he loved to bury his face in the thick, fragrant stuff when he made love to her. How he loved it even more when she wrapped the tresses around his body, as well, stroking his spine with the wavy strands, teasing the backs of his thighs with the soft, scented tendrils. . . .

Dear *God*, he could nay wait.

Yet, he waited. He made one more critique of the room, rearranging her new clothes across the bed three times, checking the temperature of the champagne four times, and cursing his exile from mirrors five times as he ran anxious hands over his face, his hair, his never-worn-before clothes. He had found the black velvet doublet and soft leather whole hose in mother's cedar chest three days after she had died, eighteen years after she had presumed him dead.

Marcus instantly knew why she had kept the finery, anyway. The pieces were to comprise his wedding attire.

My Lady Danewell, came the fervent, fleeting prayer, *if you could only see your fidgeting groom of a son now.*

"Christ's foot," he gritted as he rushed back down to meet Joseph. They only now dropped the curtain on Act Two. As he carried the warm tray of tarts to the apartment, sugary scent filling his nostrils and even sweeter thoughts swirling his mind, Marcus decided "anticipation" was an entirely overrated concept.

Still, he waited.

At last, the nightly thunder storm of applause surged up through the building to him, signaling final curtain, marking another mob of Londoners befallen to Gabriela's spell of beauty, magnetism, and talent.

And he waited.

Thirty minutes.

An hour.

The tarts cooled, then hardened. The champagne now rested in a tepid puddle instead of sparkling ice.

She was waylaid backstage, he nervously, silently affirmed himself. No doubt one of Augustus's sniveling but eminent friends had "popped" by, slavering her wrists with kisses and boring her to tears with Parliament's latest meaningless drama. He rose and reached out his thoughts to her undoubtedly listless and receptive mind, calling in the most seductive of tones: *I am waiting for you. I want you. I want you now. Gabriela, come to me . . .*

He received no response.

But Gabriela's unawareness didn't ring an ominous knell in his mind, as in those harrowing hours after her onstage collapse. Unlike then, he still felt her presence in the building . . . mayhap even a smile on her lips, a bloom of happiness in her heart. . . .

She just chose not to share the feelings with him.

And Marcus chose not to believe that for an instant.

He held on to that conviction with shaking rigidity. He confined a knot of dread to his gut with clenched jaw, coiled fists and locked knees, though that hideous herald of logic came rising from a place even deeper than that gut, intoning its own ruthless conclusion at his brittle composure:

You knew this was coming, Danewell. You knew this would be the bridge to cross in the end. You told yourself to be ready, told yourself not to dream of holding her forever—

"She is coming back, damn it," he retorted in a lock-lipped growl. "She is coming back."

He paced away more interminable seconds. Acid ate its way across his stomach through more eternities of minutes. He stopped keeping track of how many when he crushed the clock with one quaking fist.

And still, he waited.

And still, Gabriela didn't appear in his thoughts . . . or his doorway.

Twelve

Gabriela paused, breathless, in the apartment's doorway. She'd sprinted all the way up from the catwalks, not an easy feat in the emerald silk and cream lace production of a gown she'd hastened into.

But her first sight of Marcus made the extra twenty pounds of corset, petticoat, and heeled shoes well worth the ordeal. Gaby leaned against the door frame for a long moment, simply absorbing the candlelit glory of him. Shamelessly, she took advantage of his rare unawareness of her, thanks to his closed eyes, half-reposed position on the couch, and the mental partition she'd deliberately erected between them for the last two hours.

Two hours . . . it felt like two lifetimes. Her heart caught and her knees puddled as if gazing upon his broad-torsoed, lean-legged beauty for the first time. Her black-clad angel, such an important part of why tonight's incredible events had happened at all . . .

And how many times during those proceedings had she yearned to envision that strong jaw, those defined lips, the noble nose, and wisdom-lined eyes of that incredible face, summoning him to life in her mind, feeling his smile join the growing triumph and joy in her heart?

But through all one hundred twenty of those minutes, she'd staunchly resisted that urge. She'd called upon every ounce of willpower, despite the pull of Marcus's repeated and emphatic calls, telling herself this moment would be worth the wait—this moment, when she'd watch his explosion of jubilation with her own eyes, feel the burst of his elation with her physical as well as spiritual senses.

She could no longer endure the anticipation. Gratefully, she let the bonds on her senses slip free—and promptly, stumbled back a few steps. Dear God, even after two hours, the renewed flow of his presence hit her like a tidal wave.

Then his eyes snapped open.

And lightning joined the tidal wave.

"Marcus." She rushed toward him as she emitted the joyous whisper. But she stopped short, clutching her bodice, when another inundation of feeling struck her. Pain. A chasm of it, black and nearly bottomless, knowing its end only in a dark, deep pool of loneliness.

She knew this sensation. She'd experienced it before, the night they'd first encountered each other, when he spun and damned her for making him feel it. Now she didn't begrudge him one instant of the action.

But his grief possessed a distinct difference this time. Months ago, Marcus had whirled on her like a wounded beast, raging against his injury, fighting it. Yet this creature before her . . . his aching, bloodshot, defeated stare told her everything.

He hadn't thought she was coming back.

Part of him didn't believe she was real *now.*

And part of him—a very large part—was prepared to lie on that couch past dawn because of that conclusion.

"Marcus." Now her lips barely forced out the word. Gabriela dropped to the floor at his side, lifting her hands to his taut face and sweat-tipped hair. "Oh, Marcus . . . Marcus, sweeting, I'm here."

His eyes slid shut then squeezed hard, as if her touch brought both dream and nightmare. Gabriela burrowed her fingers deeper into his hair and angled his face for her soft, lingering kiss.

He froze. Held his breath. His hands rose slowly, curving around her shoulders, at first barely touching her, then gripping fiercely. "Gabriela? *Gabriela?*"

"Silly grump," she whispered against his lips. "Did you truly think I wasn't coming back?"

"Gabriela." This time, the sound reverberated through him, then her, a low growl of gratitude, of possession. He drew the rest of her unresisting body atop him, but not prior to tearing free the ties and buttons of her petticoat, then dragging the stiff framework from beneath her skirts and flinging it across the room.

He clutched her to him for long, unspeaking minutes—yet Gabriela needed no words to understand the convulsions of his muscles and the chaos of his mind. Her heart listened to his soul's outcry, wrapped assuring warmth around the frightened core of his spirit—though each advent brought an inundation of deepening amazement to her own senses.

It couldn't possibly be. . . .

This man had lived hundreds of years. He'd danced with a queen and shared an underground abyss with a king. He'd traveled the world dozens of times over. He had even shown Gaby the handful of treasures he'd saved from his favorite places: a jade elephant from the Orient, a fist-sized sea shell playing a Caribbean ocean song, a beaded friendship bracelet from a Sioux Indian boy on the western American plains.

Undoubtedly, he'd known women in those strange and beautiful lands. Exotic women. Erotic women, well-versed in the language of pleasure, all too eager to teach their special tongue to a silver-eyed stranger with the touch of an angel and the body of a god.

Therefore, it couldn't possibly be that a man like him contemplated suicide because of an insecure, inconsequential twit like her.

She presented him a pleasant diversion, perhaps. A di-

version he loved; but a fleeting season in his life, nonetheless. A worthy cause in which to dedicate himself for the
next twenty-five or thirty years, until she collapsed again,
age and fatigue finally overtaking her, and a younger, pret-
tier face convinced him he'd done his duty by this love;
time to start anew with the next.

It couldn't possibly be that he felt the same bone-aching,
heart-tearing, life-and-death-in-one completion that she
knew every time she gazed upon his face.

Could it?

For a suspended, marvelous minute, she allowed herself
to believe the answer yes—the minute Marcus urged her
head up by sliding his hands up her nape and into her
hair, his guttural purr betraying his tactile gratification in
the act. Ohhh, and then the hooded intensity of his gaze
as he traced his fingertips over her temples, her eyelids,
down the bridge of her nose, over her slightly parted lips;
exploring her, learning her.

Oh, God. Yes. In this minute, she believed even the impossible true.

It made her greedy for more. *Please, God, just one more
minute of this joy. Just one more heartbeat of this wonder. Just
one more moment for this odd little Italian girl to finally feel
cherished . . .*

To finally feel needed.

She laughed in soft delight when heaven seemed to not
only hear her hest, but give its instant compliance in Marcus's suddenly needful caress. His hands descended to the
V of her bodice and dipped urgently beneath, cupping
her with broad, bold strokes. Her nipples budded between
his questing fingers; a sheen of mesmerizing silver mist
swirled in his eyes.

"Sweet Jesu," he grated. "How I've missed you."

"Marcus . . ."

But her adoring sigh caught into a rapturous gasp when
his hips rose beneath her, urging her to straddle the evi-

dence of how *much* he'd missed her. As she formed the hollow of her body to the hardening ridge of his, Marcus's fierce hiss joined her breathless song. Only the thin cambric of her drawers and the pliable leather of his breeches held the completion of their opus at excruciatingly sweet bay.

The concerto climbed a gradual scale of passion, the loving strings of their hearts melding with the bestirred horns of their bodies. Each measure played inexorably into the next, following the beautiful tumble of notes and beats and trebles. Gabriela sank into Marcus again and they kissed, hard. Then they kissed, soft. Then their mouths simply fused, tongues tasting, desires swelling, pulses pounding.

"My love," Gabriela finally said against his lips, "I missed you, too."

She expected a responding smile. Instead, Marcus's mouth tightened; she opened her eyes to meet the probing query in his darkened gaze.

"But . . . I tried to reach you." He raised a hand to cup her face. His remembered pain again threaded its sharp needle through her heart. "So many times, in my mind, I called for you, and—"

"I know" She emphasized the assurance with a long, savoring kiss, pressing her body tighter to his, yearning to close out all the fears and uncertainties, hers *and* his, until nothing existed but the exquisite oneness and blessed surety of *we*.

"I—" he began again, but halted on a perplexed grunt. "But why did you not answer?"

At that, Gaby conducted the concerto into a new movement, sending him a smile as slow and elusive as the undulations she inaugurated with his lower body. "Sometimes a girl has to have her secrets, Mr. Danewell."

Marcus gulped. His eyes slid shut. His head fell back over the couch's arm, displaying the labored oscillation of his Adam's apple one more time before he uttered, "S-Se-crets?"

"Oh, yes." She said it with pouting lip and demure eyes, even as she trailed her hands down the ebony velvet encasing his broad chest. Such a heavenly incongruency . . . plush softness against hard definition; the color of midnight swathing a vista as stark, pale, and magnificent as the moon. Lower; she raked fingers lower over that wonderful, muscular surface until she alighted on the codpiece of the historical breeches that fit him so blessedly well. With two deft tugs, she opened the restraints between his thighs. . . .

"Oh, *yes.*" She slipped a hand into the juncture, sighing in reverent awe at the growing hardness she stroked there. "You see?" she teased at him in a meaning-filled whisper. "Secrets can be splendid when you finally get to share them."

Marcus precluded his reply with a bestial growl, corresponding to the pawlike grip he clenched to both sides of her waist. "I am afraid . . . you have unearthed every shred of my secrets tonight, wicked lady." His eyes dragged open, piercing Gabriela through with a shaft of pure silver brilliance. "I lie quite . . . bare to your mercies."

"Oh, no, my love," Gaby countered. "It is *I* who lie open to *your* benevolence." She punctuated the declaration in a vindicating gasp, her words given immediate validation when his erection found the slit in her drawers and insinuated its heat against her womanly curls.

"Ohhh, aye . . . I remember." He both breathed and rumbled the words, creating a new instrument for their composition, magical woodwind crossed with majestic bass. "We were speaking of your naughty secrets."

She laughed, husky and soft; the laugh of a woman deliciously, daringly in love. "Not naughty. Just . . . secret."

"Nay," he murmured. "Very naughty." As if to emphasize, he pushed up harder against the nub of her arousal, rubbing her with his velvet-smooth head, back and forth, but slowly, sinuously . . . sheer torture, unequalled heaven.

"*Marcus* . . ."

"Confess it to me," he ordered in a rasp. "Tell me what roguery kept you from my arms, from my heart . . ." Then, his voice broke just enough that Gaby looked down at him, really looked, to the suddenly harsh compression of his brow and the terse line of his mouth. "Tell me what kept your light from my soul."

Oh, such providence that she didn't carry *England's* imperial secrets. The country's security would have seen doom in the moment she locked eyes with this man, his soul indeed pouring through his molten silver gaze, entrapping her—and instantly pulling the words he demanded from her.

"Louis called me to his office after the performance tonight . . ." She trailed off into a gasp. Sweet mercy. Such sweet, surrendering bliss, as Marcus wrested the conductor's baton completely away from her, leading their orchestra closer toward crescendo with his teasing, tantalizing little thrusts. . . .

"And?" Marcus's tone dipped lower and sexier with his newfound authority, while shivering desire arrested *any* sound from escaping Gaby's dry throat. When he reiterated the prompt and she still didn't respond, he slowed his pace and eased a fraction away.

"No!" she finally managed in a choked whimper. "Oh Marcus, please—"

"Louis called you into his office," he reminded, even lower, so infuriatingly controlled. He could taunt her with his beautiful arousal all night, and they both knew it. She hated him. She wanted him.

"There . . . there were two men waiting there . . . oh Marcus, *yes*, don't stop—"

"Two men?"

Even in her delirious state, Gaby smiled at the distinctly

jealous growl undercutting his query. "Two men," she clarified, "from the Prince's Grand Theatre Troupe."

At *that,* he halted completely. Then he drove a gleaming steel sword of a stare up at her, double-edged with glints of apprehension and anticipation. His hands tightened on her waist, gripping with sudden, potent tension. His large thumbs dug into the bottoms of her ribs.

But Gabriela rejoiced in that pressing pain. Perhaps he did care so desperately for her! Even if only for tonight, she prayed. Yes, if only for tonight, perhaps her fate was his fate, too. Her joys, his joys.

And her triumph, his for the sharing. The taking.

And oh, how she longed to be taken.

"The troupe producers want to see me," she told him, softly—at first. Her tone quickly ascended the scale of happiness. "They're coming to the *Hamlet* opening night next week, and they want to talk to me after the show."

But Marcus's reaction swiftly diminished her mien. Two moments of unmoving silence. Three. For a moment, Gaby didn't know if she'd caused some kind of a superreal seizure beneath that gloriously carved chest, and had just killed the only man she'd ever love.

But then, Marcus James Danewell smiled back at her.

Not just any smile. Not his scampish lad's smile or his sultry lover's smile. Not even his approving mentor's smile, which Gaby greatly expected, even in their current positions. . . .

No, his lips parted on the biggest, whitest, most powerful, yet most poignant smile she'd ever seen on a man's features. As if every dream he'd ever dreamed had just come true. As if every falling star he'd ever seen or lucky shilling he'd tossed in a fountain had heard him wish for this moment, shared with her, yes, *her,* their hearts joined in exultation.

As if he'd cry for her.

If he could.

Instead, Gabriela shed the tears for them both. The first
sob came with his sudden and spectacular upthrust, coupled with the urgent pull he gave her hips, at last joining
their bodies in a bonfire of triumph. The circle of their
connected souls swiftly surrounded the beautiful blaze,
taking up the chorus of their passion song, uniting with
their orchestra in a rising, racing, pulsing production, carrying their bodies and minds toward the shattering cym-
bals and crashing drums of climax.

And when that culmination came, Marcus ripping open
the couch cushion as he pumped his searing flood into
her, Gabriela joined his name to the collected tears on her
lips. Absolute emotion claimed her senses as absolute ecstasy claimed her body.

Dear God, she yearned, that they could claim this moment as their forever: Marcus, so taut and dark and magnificent beneath her, black-waved head arched back,
sharing the same white-hot wonder claiming *her* body and
soul . . . their thundering union of the physical, signifying
their ineffable fusion of the spiritual.

The feelings of two, shed in the tears of one.

Tears of gratitude for this nirvana they had.

Tears of longing for what could never be.

He insisted on celebrating. Gaby's pleas to remain right
where they were, even coupled with a valiant nuzzle to
his collarbone, didn't falter his determination an iota.
Neither did her blatant attempt at seducing him into the
rose-petaled paradise of a bed *he'd* created. Marcus merely
hauled her out of the sheets, smacked her half-draped
breasts with brisk kisses, and ordered her into the lace
dream of a gown he seemed to produce from nowhere.
"And be ready in ten minutes," he decreed, as well. "We
have *much* celebration to attend."

The man, as usual, stood by his command to the letter.

Ten minutes and five seconds later, he whisked her out into the sparkling London night, the air kissed by enough of summer's approaching warmth to imbue their nocturnal adventure with a special caress of magic. With his cocky rogue's grin firmly in place again, he proffered one hand to her, carrying a beautifully packed picnic basket in the other.

And then he gave her a more staggering gift than his dazzling smile.

As they walked down the deserted, moonlit city streets, Marcus sang to her. Softly, really lifting just a whisper of volume . . . yet his soul-deep breaths of bass, soaring into heart-held prayers of tenor, opened a world of awareness Gabriela had never known. A world where knights still fought for the favors of princesses, where explorers crossed half the globe for their queen, and lovers defied the world for each other. A world where honor was more than a word and love was a treasure, not a toy. . . .

"Like lovers do their love," he continued to tell her in song, "so joy I in you seeing. Let nothing me remove . . . from always with you being."

Let nothing me remove, Gabriela echoed with a silent harmony of her heart. *Nothing, my love.*

The rest of the courtly ballad took them down St. Martin's Lane, across Trafalgar Square and into the besilvered beauty of St. James's Park. Marcus continued to hum the simple melody as they followed a winding path along the park's largest lake, the breeze-rippled water and the gently blowing tree leaves comprising his accompaniment against a backdrop of starlit stillness.

But he severed the song on an abrupt step as they emerged from a bower of willows—and beheld the stately silhouette of Whitehall along the opposite bank of the water.

Instantly, Gabriela felt the confines of Marcus's soul heed the lead of his rigidifying body. His thoughts coiled away from her as his fists curled at his sides. But he couldn't cache away all his revelations. No, he couldn't cut down the curtain fast enough on the maelstrom of feelings assaulting the stage of his senses: she experienced his battle between yearning memories of a life long past, glorious and joyous, and the lust to destroy what the fire of 1698 hadn't, to make cinders of the site where Raquelle had pulled him the first step toward damnation.

"I . . . I am sorry," he finally said through the tension to her. He dropped his head away from the sight and his tone into a rough cough. "I . . . I walk past here all the time," he tried to explain. "The bloody place never affects me so anymore."

But never two hours after a nervy mortal has all but ripped your insides asunder, Gabriela's logic finished all too swiftly—and effortlessly—for him. *Never after you've been drained of so many defenses, or stripped of so many barriers.*

You are not crazy, Marcus. I know how it feels. I know how you feel . . .

But while she sent the awkward, almost apologetic thought out so clearly over the psychic path between them, Marcus didn't hear, let alone respond. His physical withdrawal perfectly mirrored his mental retreat. And Gaby could only stand there and witness both in helpless silence.

Then determined courage gave her the perfect cue.

Gently, she disengaged the basket from Marcus's opposite hand, set it on the knoll behind them, and replaced her fingers in his damp, tight grip. Now grasping both his hands, she stood before him, Whitehall behind her.

"Marcus," she whispered up to him, "I know it hurts sometimes. I . . . I hurt sometimes, too." She leaned and pressed a soft, soothing kiss to the underside of his clamped jaw. "But I don't let the hurt win. I summon up all the *good* memories . . . and you must, too. Remember all the beauty and happiness you found at Whitehall . . . remember the *good.*"

Then she held her breath for an eternal pause.

Then he expelled his, slowly, softly.

Then together, they smiled.

"Aye," he finally replied, his breath warming her temple as he gathered her close. "You are right, my love." He laughed gruffly. "I nay think Good Bess would fondle kindly to the remainder of her good halls being torched to the ground."

Gaby pulled back enough to look in his eyes while sliding her hands up around his neck. "You really knew Queen Elizabeth that well?"

To her slight surprise, Marcus chuckled harder. "Everybody knew her that well. She was a beloved and respected sovereign; generous with her wit as well as her rage."

Gaby tilted her head, scrutinizing the reminiscent haze of his eyes more closely. "Please tell me more."

To her exhilaration, Marcus smiled wider. He drew her near again, seductively drawling into her ear, "So ye want to know of Elizabeth's fine court, do ye?"

But then he broke the contact, spinning her out into a courtly pirouette while dipping a gallant bow himself. Gabriela couldn't help a maidenly giggle as he bent his lips to her hand and brushed her knuckles with the most regally proper of kisses.

But her laughter stuck in her throat when he lifted his head back up to her.

The teasing glints in his eyes now ignited into a hypnotizing eddy of silver swirls, flowing into her and over her, heating her with a blatantly incongruous message to the mannered chevalier who'd just occupied his space.

Gaby stopped breathing. More tendrils of that exquisite heat spiraled down her arms and legs, into her breasts . . . then filling her most secret core. Her arrested laugh turned into a defenseless sigh as Marcus pulled her back again with sudden and potent force.

"Court's unwritten rule number one," he told her in a

thick, meaningful murmur, "the more chaste the kisses, the more lecherous the man."

Then the whirlpool of his stare darkened and deepened—pulling her directly into the vortex of his soul, his desire. And Gabriela went there willingly, eagerly, letting him slide her yet tighter to his proud, powerful courtier's stance.

Yet when just a whisper of night separated them, he spun her around again—an action she'd have taken as a snap of anger, if not for the increasing need she caught in his starfired stare. Then he hauled her shoulders back against his chest, her head into the crook of his neck . . . her bottom against his arousal.

And then . . . oh then, he began to rock, back and forth, dragging her pliant form with him into swaying, sinuous, but inherently intense slides of motion. He surrounded her, hard and irresistible. He possessed her, in body and mind. He was passion barely reined. Animal barely tamed. Darkness barely dimmed.

A fantasy come to life.

Finally, his voice came at her ear, low and seductive, yet as mesmerizing and melodic as his minstrel's song. Oh, such rapture, to hear him speak like this all night. . . .

"The days of Elizabeth's court were a wondrous time," he began, already introducing her imagination to scenes filled with bold courtiers and demure gentlewomen. "Later, many called our court one of the centers of the Renaissance . . . the rebirth."

"I wonder why," Gaby slipped in on a sardonic breath. Dear God, she felt a newborn herself in this spellbound moment, her body so clumsy, flopping and weak against the fluid force of his.

" 'Twas much to learn." He punctuated the assertion with a suggestive nip at the back hollow of her neck. "Aye, we all felt as babes each new day, discovering new beauty and knowledge about the world, then sharing it in song or poetry, or perhaps by paintbrush or sculptor's spatula."

Gabriela reacted to that with a pretended pout. "And was that *all* you did, sir?"

Marcus's grip tightened around her waist, as if to scold her for that thinly disguised innuendo—until his other hand descended along the front of her abdomen. His fingers, so long, so magical, splayed across the top bone of her thigh, then pressed the flat of flesh just below . . . inducing her tighter back against him, harder against the heat and power of him.

"Nay," he growled, his voice vibrating into her nape. " 'Twas not all, my curious maid. 'Twas not all by far."

Gaby's eyes slid shut. His voice drugged her, spun an intoxicating spell over her. "Go on," she pleaded.

"Well . . ." His tone gained the wistful warmth of remembrance. "The evening's revelries always began with the feast. Dear God, the endless feast . . . but I always did enjoy the toasts more than the food." She felt him indulge a small smile. "Jesu, how we all vied to come up more grand and eloquent ways to salute Bess. One eve, Sir Walter—"

"Raleigh?"

"The one," he confirmed, as if merely telling her the name of his cat. "Now, Sir Walter delivered this toast"—he gave an annoyed grunt—"by the time he finished, the bloody wine had become another vintage."

Now Gabriela heard herself emit a soft laugh. How clearly she envisioned what his mind did, as memories grew clearer; their mental link, stronger. She smiled as she really saw that magnificent hall, candlelight casting rich and romantic light on silks and satins, velvets and furs, pearl-draped breasts and hose-encased thighs. Thighs like Marcus's . . . so solid, so powerful, in full and distinct view all night, endlessly enticing a woman, forcing her thoughts down sinful and wicked paths. . . .

"And after the feast?" she responded on that wave of thought, wondering if he heard the dragging tension in her tone . . . or knew its prompting heat, pulsing stronger in her blood by the minute.

"Ahhhh," he intoned, so richly—and yes, so knowingly. "Ah, the after. My *very* favorite part . . ."

But he made her wait for his conclusion through a long, tormented moment, shifting his lips against the inner curve of her ear, sending frissons of vibrating heat down through her breasts, through her senses.

Finally, he told her, "In the after, my fair lady, came the *dance.*"

And then, more clearly than the visions behind her eyes, the music began in her head. A beautifully dulcet blend of recorder and dulcimer, drum and tambourine, to which her feet moved without thinking, without caring. She didn't know the name of the dance and she didn't care; she only accepted Marcus's mental tutorial with deepening, loving gratitude. She'd longed to know of the world that had created him . . . never expecting to become part of it. She wondered if he realized how precious a gift he gave this eve.

They moved perfectly together there in the moonlight, stepping, dipping, and circling in time to the silent song flowing between them, exchanging occasional smiles . . . and thickening glances. Amazing. As the courtly choreography dictated, they only touched at the hands, but each brush of Marcus's fingers or clasp of his strong palm stoked a growing warmth in Gabriela's center . . . a very odd and almost frightening heat, similar to nothing she'd experienced before. The sensation was blistering and yet liquid, like watching a bonfire through mullioned glass. She didn't know whether to welcome it or run from it. To surrender, or to fight. . . .

They danced on. Prismic dew drops sprayed off her sweeping skirts. Deepening night urged the wind higher, lifting Marcus's black waves off his face, redefining his jaw into even more formidable angles. Soon, Gaby couldn't pull her stare from the sight of him. Glances became a fusion of gazes. Fleeting touches became lingering hand clasps . . . then daring caresses to waists, to faces . . . to eyes and cheeks and lips. . . .

When the music faded to a stop, Marcus took the single step remaining between them. Instinct dictated them another mysterious stage direction: his arms fell to his sides; Gabriela's arms followed. They stood, only breaths and gazes mingling now, yet their sweet, sensual expectancy tautening to a new, nearly intolerable tension.

Tension? No, Gabriela corrected, this was *torment*. She wanted to touch this beautiful man; she wanted to touch him everywhere. She longed to push that soft velvet over his hard shoulders, to slide those sinful breeches down his long, muscled legs, then run her hands over every defined inch of him . . . especially the parts that made him moan and tighten in pleasure. . . .

But that yearning also formed the shackles of fear binding her arms. What if she broke those bonds and showed this man how much she needed him now more than ever? What if she curled against him as she longed to, whispering that the exhilaration of tonight had only introduced her to an entirely new script called petrified insecurity? What if she confessed she was scared, so terribly scared that she'd come so far only to fail now . . . only to fail *him*?

What would Marcus say if she gave in to such fooleries? What would he do?

She couldn't bear to ponder the possible answers.

Instead, she forced her lips around a safer query. "And . . . and what did the court do when they finished dancing?"

For a long moment, the whoo of an owl and the whir of a cicada formed her only response. With calculated stealth, that gnawing insecurity used the time to claw back into her spirit, the invasion worsened by the very strange, very strong, and very unreadable stare Marcus washed over her.

The apprehension grew into dread. Gabriela struggled back tears.

She knew it. He could read every weak and stupid nuance of her feelings while she, so small and insecure and *mortal*, couldn't swim far enough past the morass of her confusion to sense a single of his thoughts, let alone whole feelings.

Mortal, *mortal*.

She wasn't good enough for this incredible man. She never would be.

But then, Marcus Danewell, dark and magnificent holder of her heart, smiled at her. That perfect, powerful smile, shined into her soul, burned into even the loneliest and most frightening corners of her.

Yet before Gabriela could recover from her stunned joy to smile back, his smirk slanted a decidedly risqué angle as he at last replied, "Who says we are finished dancing?"

And *then*, Gabriela smiled. Just before she wound her arms around him and crushed her lips to his damnably sexy mouth.

But Marcus was ready for her. Dear God, more than ready. He answered her riposte with a bold plunge of tongue and teeth, swiftly showing her who still led this dance, despite their new positioning of the "steps" to the grassy bed below them. They fell upon the dark softness together, gasping and kissing, bodies twining and heating through the sweetly torturous confines of their clothes.

The earth embraced her from below. The sky careened overhead, an endless vortex of stars and wind and moon—and Marcus. Oh, Marcus, sliding his weight against her, over her, molding his lips to hers as they rocked together in heated imitation of the union they craved.

She sighed. He moaned. They writhed harder and faster,

night dew and night wind whirling around them, through them. Gabriela slid her hands around Marcus's thighs to urge him tighter against her, closer to the aching, yearning crux of her. But at her first insistent touch, he broke his mouth away on a guttural groan. The sound echoed endlessly into her, eliciting a strange combination of intrigue . . . and terror.

"Marcus?" she murmured, reflecting confusion at her discrepant reaction.

"*Stop,*" came his swift and desperate retort. "God, *God*, Gabriela, take your hands from me—just for a moment, love . . . please."

But in that instant, in the raw and deep and needing tremble of his voice, an innate feminine resolve overrode her apprehension. Gabriela didn't move her hands an inch. And that same womanly instinct told her Marcus didn't truly want her to, either—no matter how harshly his lips growled against her neck or how violently his body shook beneath her hands.

"Gabriela," he rumbled, "*please.*"

She stopped him with a wet, seeking kiss. "Why? Oh, Marcus . . . I need to touch you, Marcus."

And at that, she squeezed harder, forming soft leather around the lean firmness of his buttocks. He sucked in sharp air through his teeth, shuddering against her. "*Nay.* I pray you, sweeting. I will lose control—"

She smiled, slid a seductive kiss along his neck. "But I want you to lose control."

"Nay!"

"Yes," Gabriela persisted, now not only skidding her hands over his torso, but jerking free the ornate ties of his shirt along the way. "Yes, my love."

"You . . . you know not what you ask."

But she knew exactly what she asked. Oh, yes; she knew exactly the wild, unthinking response she sought from him—the unlocking of this man in his entire, passionate, supernatural glory.

Of course, she didn't know exactly what that goal entailed. And, yes, her spine absorbed a frisson of fear at the unknown valley she approached. . . .

But the rest of her body, especially her heart, compelled her forward as uncontrollably as her head rose and her mouth pressed to the hard flesh of his muscled torso.

"I want to give you pleasure, Marcus," she said into the hollow of his neck. "*Complete* pleasure."

"Nay," he croaked. "Oh nay, you little vixen. Look . . . look what you're doing . . . my doublet is falling apart . . ."

"Good."

"Gabriela, please . . . oh, bloody damn, your lips feel so good there . . . Gabriela, *nay.*"

"Give it to me, Marcus." She enticed him relentlessly, rounding his shoulder with moist nips, grazing his neck with her top teeth. "I want you, darling. I want *all* of you this time."

"You . . . you cannot have . . . everything you want." He threw his head back, swallowing heavily, attempting to escape her merciless sucklings, but only straining the ties across his chest tighter . . . widening the gap to his chest for her questing lips.

Gabriela didn't let the opportunity go unclaimed. And claim this man she did, feeling the moment he let his sanity slip, and using the instant to lift her legs around him, locking his body against hers.

"Sweet Jesu," he rasped, grabbing for her chemise and drawers, but finding only the curves of her moist, naked flesh. "You really are a vixen."

Gabriela didn't deliver her prepared comeback. His big hands, with those long, poetry-filled fingers, began to stroke magic into her skin and her senses, robbing her thoughts, stealing her lucidity.

"Touch me, Marcus," she finally pleaded. "Don't stop touching me."

He repeated several earthy oaths, some Elizabethan-accented phrases she didn't understand, before breathing, "You're so wet, love. You're so wet and ready for me."

"Take me. Please Marcus, take me . . ."

His responding growl had to be the most beautiful music he'd produced tonight. Savage and masculine, the sound punctuated his urgent tugs to open his breeches, at last freeing his clamoring arousal.

And in another instant, he was inside her. Gabriela welcomed him home with high, breathy, utterly shameless sighs, even though she strained to remember her goal—longed to keep her wits as they made love this one special time, in order to watch his face in all its otherworldly power as he found his ultimate release.

But the intent faded farther away as quicksilver light engulfed more of her body . . . as molten silver droplets replaced her blood and tears . . . as the world became the silver-hot scream and silver-soft sibilance of Marcus, Marcus, Marcus. Marcus's hardness, buried in the core of her. Marcus's arms, twining around her, lifting her off the ground to hold her yet tighter. Marcus's torso, so taut with exertion yet not sweating a drop, lungs and heart pumping their wild timpani madness against her own.

But, sweet fate forgive her, it all only made her want more of him. Oh yes, she felt him, every hard muscle straining against her, every breath resounding through her, but she didn't *feel* him; not the way he'd made her *feel* his courtly world just minutes past. She wanted to experience every degree of the magnificent heat that gave his eyes the magic of lightning and his limbs the strength of thunder. She longed to touch, smell, and hear the world with *his* fingers, nose, and ears.

Most of all, she yearned to know how her body felt

around him, tight and wet and welcoming, drawing out the deepest, most precious heat from him. . . .

The scrape of the matter was, she knew she could. That exquisite knowledge could so easily be hers, just a prick of her skin away. She wanted that oneness . . . dear God, how she longed to be truly one with this man, to share his deepest dreams, his darkest nights, his despairing loneliness, and his star-filled fantasies. And she'd complete the circle by making him part of her . . . the biggest, brightest part. When he woke, he'd see the sunset through her eyes, and she'd give him the dawn to dream of as he slipped off to sleep. The Thames in sunrise, the Strand in twilight. Their hearts inside each other, their lives irrevocably entwined.

Even as the dream swelled and filled her mind, Marcus's body swelled and filled her. He expanded into the center of her, driving passionately toward his zenith. With each thrust, he shuddered and growled, losing more of his logic, surrendering more of his will. His heartbeat raged against her breasts. His guttural groan filled her head.

And his mouth panted hot and fast at her neck.

His teeth just inches from her jugular.

Gabriela swallowed just once. Then came to her heart-pounding decision.

She clutched the back of his head. Then pressed his lips to the throbbing vein in her neck.

"Do it now, Marcus," she implored, praying the hot salt of her tears would only seduce his hunger into unbearable voracity. "Do it, please do it. Initiate me, my love. Make me yours . . . for the rest of my life."

Thirteen

Oh, aye; aye! Marcus's senses screamed in instant unanimity. *Take her now. Just one sip. Just one taste. Ah God, she shall taste so good . . .*

The torment intensified when he sipped the ambrosia of her tears. A needing, hungering whine clawed up his throat and resounded in his senses, making way for the beast in him, slashing farther into him. He licked the salty honey from her skin as he pounded harder into her body, lapping at her from cheek to chin to delicious, quivering breasts.

Then he dipped his mouth to the pulse in her neck again. Eagerly laved the succulent tastes there. Shuddered through another soul-deep groan as the beast ravaged his control, drowning him in silver savagery. *Aye, aye! Take her. Take her. So close, so hot. You can taste the rich wine of her already . . .*

"Yes," came her strident whisper in his ear, chorusing with the beast, luring him closer to the edge of insanity's sweet abyss. "Yes, Marcus, please!"

Nay.

Nay, something suddenly made no sense at all. What was this? What was going on? Gabriela, his luminous and fearless Gabriela, now an *ally* with the monster she had vowed to help him fight? Pleading with him to initiate her into a world so opposite her courage and life?

So easily betraying herself—so easily betraying *him?*

With a disgusted roar, he catapulted away from her.

Through the long moments that his outcry echoed through the trees and across the water, he could not move from his hands and knees. He let his head sag as his lungs heaved the pungence of the grass and dirt his fingers clawed up. Behind him, he heard Gabriela's similar struggle for air.

Her rough breaths gave way to a shaking gulp. Then, in a barely audible rasp, "Marcus . . ."

"Shut up," he snarled, jerking his breeches closed again. "Just shut up and set your clothes aright, Gabriela."

"No." She lunged for him. Like a night beetle caught in sudden light, he scrambled from her. But he should have known it took nay less than a crate of explosives to stop the woman. "No," Gabriela persisted dauntlessly "not until you listen—"

"Listen!" He found the explosives. They now detonated a raging blast in his gut, shooting him to his feet once more. "*Listen* to more lies from your fleeceful mouth?"

She did warrant credit for her mettle, however stupid or misplaced it might be. She bolted to a stance as rigidly furious as his, clinging grass clumps turning her hair into a wild kind of forest, fingers working more creases into her skewed gown.

She looked a mess.

She also looked more beautiful than he ever remembered.

Goddamn her.

"You think I *lied* to you?" she finally whispered from those barely parted and well-kissed lips.

In answer, Marcus away spun from her. Spun away from the sudden, fierce sheen of her stare; that light as bright as fire-tempered copper—razing his chest with equally devastating heat.

Another deception, he forced himself to acknowledge

Copper trying to pass itself off as gold. Another empty seduction.

"Little thinking had to be done," he returned with the blistering resentment ignited by that mental breakfire. "You made your ultimate ambition a little more than clear, sweet."

He heard her sharp skip of breath. Then nothing. Then nothing *but* her breaths, coming harder and faster as she paced to him. Hard and fast—the only way she could stay the hot, confused tears. He knew because he felt every stinging drop of them. God. *God.* She made sure no mental walls stood between them *now.*

In other words, she took advantage of every manipulating trick in the book.

Well, almost every trick. She stopped three steps away from him—perhaps four on her beautiful mortal legs—yet nay attempted to touch him.

Then she spoke. Again, hard and fast, between her shaking attempts for breath. "And what the bloody hell is that supposed to mean?"

A chuckle emanated from God-knew-where inside the turmoil of his gut. Strangely, the sound tricked Marcus into thinking he could face her again.

But as soon as he completed his cocksure pivot, he nay knew copper from gold again. He could not discern her pain and upheaval from his own. He could not tell. . . .

Her pain? *Her* upheaval?

God's teeth, the chit had become a better actress than he thought. The desperate pumping of her chest, the wobbling tears at the corners of her eyes, the goosebumped waver of her chin—all so convincing, so *real.* She had developed a good act, all right. A bloody good act.

The thought rekindled enough reflexive fury for him to close the gap between them himself. When standing but a breath away, Marcus snapped up the trembling tip of her chin between his thumb and forefinger.

When he spoke, he lilted his voice to emulate her own breathy pitch of a few minutes ago. " 'I want to bring you complete pleasure, Marcus. Give it to me, Marcus.' " But he dropped his tone as he dropped his hand. "Bravissima, sweeting," he drawled. "Your performance was worthy of a commission from Will himself."

At that, he half expected the brunt of her slapping hand. Or mayhap a wide-eyed gape of missish indignation, followed by a burst of such feigned tears, he would nay help but laugh himself deeper into his shelter of wrath. Anything to distract him from acknowledging that anger had nothing to do with this acidic ache between his ribs.

Marcus did *not* expect her to keep standing there, only inches from him, clearly fighting for the strength to step back, but wrestling against unseen chains of fear and fury. . . .

Clearly enduring an acidic ache between her ribs.

In a small, but astoundingly steady voice, she finally said "I meant every syllable of those things."

"I do not doubt it," he returned—after a vehement in ner reminder that the woman made a living jerking at peo ple's hearts and guts. "Nay," he concluded, "I do no doubt it at all, as long as those sweet syllables reaped you ultimate aspiration."

At least this time, she gave him the wide-eyed glare— only the predictability of her reaction stopped there Where Marcus had expected—hoped for?—overdrama tized outrage and underhanded tears, this woman onc more somersaulted his world with the intensity of her dr clear stare: like the gleam of polished chestnut, renderin him speechless with her burnished, unmarred beauty.

Unmarred by everything except one inescapable stai of emotion.

Pain.

"Aspiration?" she finally echoed him—and now, h voice began to shed its meek volume, as well, emergir with a glaring ferocity. "Aspiration? Is that what you think, Marcus? That the only reason I went along with your little dead-of-night picnic and rambling, archaic memories is because I *planned* to ask you for initiation tonight? That I had it in mind all along?"

Damn and demons take her. Marcus could say or do nothing but slam his arms across his chest, hands clenching at opposite shoulders, wondering why *he* suddenly felt on trial—worse, ruminating why his treasonous body hardened so fast for the woman when *her* only goal looked to be his slow and tortured death.

"If that had been my intent," she finally, softly added, "why didn't you feel it in my heart, or read it in my mind?"

At last she posed an interrogation easily answered. "You forget, sweeting, that earlier this eve, you rather adequately blocked me from your mind for two hours."

"So that deems me guilty of it now?"

Marcus did not waver his scrutiny. "It lends integrity to the plaintiff."

"Oh, please!" Gabriela moved from *him* then, snapping back on a sharp stomp. She paraded toward the lake, aiming her escalating outrage and upshooting hands at a hapless gaggle of half-awake brown ducks. "Can you believe this?" she fired at them. Then she slashed one arm back at him. "Tell this man the moon has robbed him of his sanity!"

Marcus did not plan on favoring her antics by following them. But patience be damned. She huffed at him like a wife merely caught with her hand in the emergency money jar—and by sweet Bess's grave, if the situation were only so simple. If only they could spend all night battling about things like the children, the house, her cooking, his table manners . . . anything, dear God, but things like her self-control, her self-will. . . .

The fate of her soul.

"Damn it," he growled, catching up and yanking her

back by the elbow. "We are not children pretending at a fantasy here, Gabriela. 'Tis a very real playing board you move on now, with very real forces of spirit at work!"

She said nothing to that. Just stood there and breathed hard at him.

Even so, as their gazes locked again, as the frustration in her stare smacked him like the back of a triple-veneered contrabass, Marcus locked a grip to her other arm. "I love you," he said through locked teeth. "Do you nay know that by now? Do you nay understand? Can you not comprehend 'tis why I ordered you not to speak of initiation again?"

"But it's a ridiculous order!" Her tearless veneer went up in a glare of dark copper wrath. *"No,"* Gabriela emphasized, clamping a hold to both his elbows in return. "No, I do *not* understand." She advanced her chin an inch higher. "And I do not wish to, either."

At that, beyond Marcus's volition, his fingers screwed tighter into her flesh, squeezing her, bruising her. He fought against the action—Jesu, how he fought against wielding his superworldly strength in such a terrifying manner upon her—but in the end, her reckless stupidity, so casually spat upon the words he proclaimed from his deepest heart, proved the ultimate breach upon his restraint.

"Oh, sweet," he leveled at her from a throat convulsing on low, broken thunder, "you had better understand. You had better *start* to understand."

"Why?"

It was one simple word, so barely uttered from her trembling lips—yet in the space of that simple, soft syllable, the woman worked another of her damnable, inconceivable miracles. For in the space of that sole question, Gabriela completely switched the keys of their embrace. Though she still comprehended it not, *she* now became *his* jailer. Her grasp softened against his arms, yet chained him with thrice the force of iron shackles . . . as she slid that magical touch up his arms and then to either side of his face, she effectively locked his sensory world to her. Then came her love-filled gaze and her upturned jaw, binding chains of conviction and bravery around the snarling felon of his nearly three-hundred-year-old cynicism.

"Oh, Marcus. My Marcus." She slowly shook her head. "I'm sorry. I'm *sorry.* I simply cannot understand nor accept the ugliness you speak of. If initiation is half the miracle you say it is, then I can think of no sweeter gift you can grant me."

"Miracle?" he finally interjected, punctuating with an incredulous snort. "Gabriela—"

"Ssshhh." Two silencing fingers trailed to his lips. "Marcus, I want to fuse my soul with yours. I want to bind my heart to yours, to make my thoughts become yours, so we'll never truly be apart again." She splayed her fingers against his jaw again, worked her soul-touching caress along the taut and aching edge. "What is so wrong about that? What is so horrid?"

"Stop." Even after waging such intense battle against his super-real self, he was amazed to hear the uneven tenor of his voice—astounded at how urgently *he'd* started to snatch at the lure of her ridiculous fantasy. He grasped her hands into the big grotto of his own, holding them between the rapid beatings of both their hearts. "Stop it, Gabriela. You know not of what you speak."

Her reply came after a moment of weighted contemplation. "Perhaps," she conceded. "Perhaps I don't know of it all." She lifted her gaze again to his. "But I know I'm not afraid."

Marcus dropped her hands and swung away. "You should be," he growled. "Damn you, you should be."

Persistently, she followed half a step behind. "And I know I want to give you as much as you'll give me."

A cynical chuckle rolled from his lips. "Now you truly know not of what you speak."

"The bloody hell I don't." And before he could enact an evasive move, she darted in front of him again, stopping him with her whole body, arms around his neck, entrancing curves pressed to every inch of him. She burrowed her lips against his neck as she murmured, "I want to give you sustenance, Marcus. *My* sustenance."

Ah, dear God.

"Gabriela," he warned, "nay."

"My blood, flowing in your veins—"

"Stop it!" He forced her away with shuddering arms. *Stop it ere I give in to your heinous seduction, you muddled, magnificent girl.*

"Stop," he grated again. "Just stop."

"Why?"

That word again. Damn her, that soft, beautiful word again.

And she knew it, Marcus thought dismally. She knew just how deep a casualty she rendered with the combined forces of her body and her words. Her voice strengthened with that advantage as she repeated the soft query, approaching him again, steadily, assuredly.

But a wound did not a war decide.

And, whatever forces of heaven or hell help him, he must win *this* war.

"Why, Marcus?" came her ever-nearing murmur—damn her, damn her, as if she looked straight through the chaos of his thoughts and realized how perfectly she embodied his Venus and Aphrodite, his Beatrice, his Eve, his dreams and hopes . . . his weakness and downfall.

"Why stop," she pressed, "when it's what we both want? What we both need?"

He wheeled on her then. Turned and bore down on her with the full demon's height of his body and hell' power of his eyes. "Because you will give me more than your blood, you little fool!" He held no seething note of his voice in check, either. "Look at me, Gabriela! *Look!* I am not man. I am monster. You will be a mental slave to a monster!"

Damn her again. He could have told her the year-to-date rainfall for Yorkshire and inspired a more troubled reper- cussion. Head held high, indeed with all the serenity of Aphrodite, she countered, "That's my decision to make, not yours."

He spun from her again. Jammed fingers through his hair to avoid throwing her over his knee and showing just where she could put that disgusting, demure little come- back. "God's bodkin it is," he finally snapped.

The rush of her frustrated sigh should have come as a relief. Instead, the defeated downfall of her heart jerked on his own like a seven-ton anchor, landing them both in a sea of angry silence.

"Damn you, Danewell," she finally rasped, tears heavy in her voice. "I'm not asking you to infect me with the plague."

Not turning, and very wearily, Marcus replied, "Nay, sweeting. You are asking much worse."

Gabriela noticed the change the moment she stepped through the stage door the next afternoon. The little things told her: a compliment on her hat from a passing stagehand, the way the ballet girls now nodded to her in- stead of giggling at her, even Louis's gentled manner in giving her a blocking switch for Act Three due to a mal- functioning scenery pulley.

Yes, word traveled swiftly down Drury's backstage halls. In the space of one postperformance meeting last night, she'd finally been relieved from the role of cast cuckoo.

Over the following days, more "little things" added up to assist the tutelage of her new role. "A symbol of our

dreams," said a card accompanying two dozen yellow roses
from the orchestra. "A survivor, even of our merciless teasing," came the ballet's note, as adorably awkward in apology as they were strikingly graceful on stage. But the fly
crews came up with her favorite affection: their catcalls of,
"Go win those blokes over, champ!" echoed ceaselessly
through Drury's rafters—and her heart.

And yet, the victory rang hollow. The applause, at last
begun, fell on her deafened ears.

Marcus had departed her soul.

Oh, she still saw him, even felt him—physically. Every
night, an hour after final curtain to the minute, he materialized from the stage right shadows, leather-bound copy
of *Hamlet* in one big hand, immediately and tersely re-
minding her where they'd broken rehearsal the previous
eve. He answered no questions and responded to no comments save those related to the dramatic labors of the evening. In all their preceding rehearsals combined, Gaby had
never seen him more committed in body or dedicated in
mind.

She'd also never reached her senses so far into his, and
encountered nothing but deadbolted doors.

Of course, the first time he'd appeared to her like that,
the night after their clash in St. James's, he'd nearly sent
her flying into the catwalks without a ladder. Will Shakespeare himself would have been a less startling, and certainly less silent, visitor.

She had stopped in her place for a very long moment
that night, indeed wondering if she merely imagined the
sight of him, so complete an incarnation of her fantasies
he was . . . strength of shadow and desire of darkness, as
commanding as midnight—yet in his eyes, always in his
ageless and yet guileless eyes, the unguarded longing of
silver-tipped morning mist. . . .

"How now, Ophelia?"

The perfect inflection of the words, even upon such a

simple phrase, prompted Gaby back to the present. Still, as she turned to the table where Marcus leaned in wait for her response to his cue, she fumbled frantically through her memory—dreading having to admit she'd been oblivious to his first reminder.

Dreading to admit she'd been occupied with visions of him.

Finally, her pause extended too long for dramatic impact—or Marcus's ever-shortening patience.

"Act Four, Scene Five." He bit the syllables to shreds almost before they left his lips. "Nearly your last scene in the play. Is it too much to ask that we get through this tonight, as you open in this tomorrow eve?"

Her memory easily found the line now. But the breath she took to commence the words came out a frustrated sigh, instead.

She looked to Marcus. He had already dropped his head back over his script, nose buried between the pages with an intensity having nothing to do with the excitement of the reading matter.

And in that moment, she knew she wouldn't utter another word of that bloody play tonight.

She'd gained three determined steps toward him when he glanced back up, puzzled by her silence. She took two more as his left eyebrow fell, his hand tautened against the script's aged binding. One more as his lips parted a fraction enough to lend him the look of a suddenly cornered panther.

"Gabriela . . ." he warned—as she expected. Seeking strength in his anger.

His snarling didn't slow her an inch. She used the last vestiges of his puzzlement to lean over and yank the script from his hold.

"Gabriela."

"I know, I know." She gave the book a soft, but sizable toss into the stage left wings. "I open tomorrow night."

Allowing no time for his protest, she lowered her hand directly into his, forcing his fingers around hers as she trapped his stunned panther's gaze with the unyielding shackles of her own. "I'd like to know just one thing, Marcus," she said with an equal fusion of whisper and demand. "Are you going to be here to see me?"

He didn't try to release her hold. Instead, he escaped her scrutiny via a perturbed scowl into the wings, as if to join his script by the sheer force of his look. "What the hell are you talking about?"

"Just answer the question." She issued the rebuttal with no mercy. . . .

And finally elicited the reaction she strove for.

She made Marcus Danewell squirm.

The man, of course, took to the experience as well as a flash singer thrown into an Italian opera. "Damn it, woman."

"Never mind." Gaby ended his torment herself on a shove inspired by an unseen, unexpected wave of pain. "I know your answer now, Mr. Danewell." His name came out a sharp, stinging rush of syllables, which drove her agitation deeper.

"I don't believe it," she suddenly emitted on a bitter laugh, shaking her head. "Even more than two hundred and fifty years of existence hasn't taught your mule-stubborn brain a thing."

He stopped squirming then. Jerked his head back toward her, eyes glinting like a new-sharpened dagger. "And what the hell is that riddle about?"

"No riddles, Marcus." Gaby hardened her stare, but gentled her voice. "Just the truth."

He aligned his own glare then; A floorboard creaked in the stage right wings, straining in the density of their unmoving confrontation.

"You're still trying to make up for it, aren't you?" she finally, softly asked.

A leaden sigh rumbled up his throat. His dark head rolled back in weary frustration. "Gabriela, what the—"

"Your only sin . . . falling prey to Raquelle's game. You're trying to earn atonement for it, even now. You're still aching to prove yourself a worthy proxy of the Danewell name."

She whirled and laughed again, this time at herself. "Saint Genesius, why didn't *I* see it before? The court has changed, but the rules are the same. Instead of marking your mettle in the chambers of Whitehall, you've taken on the noble cause of a poor little actress with stars in her eyes."

She turned back then, bringing her hands together in slow, sad claps. She wished stars indeed filled her eyes, instead of the hot, constricting onslaught of tears. "Congratulations, sir," she told him in a wet rasp. "Father would be very proud of your success, Marcus."

She didn't know why the swift jerk he gained to his feet came as such a surprise. Nevertheless, Gaby found herself scrambling back in rhythm to his rapid, angry advance.

But just as abruptly, Marcus slammed to a stop several feet from her. His tension-racked muscles filled the confines of the Elizabethan tunic and hose he'd taken to wearing. He loomed furious and huge and yet glorious and dark, like a fathomless fantasy god.

"My *father,*" he leveled tightly, "has nothing to do with *us.*"

"Marcus," Gaby countered in a whisper, "he has everything to do with us."

Compelled by a force she no more understood than controlled, she recovered the distance between them herself. But once accomplished of the trek, she didn't touch him. Just stood a half breath away, swaying in the power of his presence, the power he'd never stop having over her, the power of her own mayhemmed emotions, finally surging past the dams of her composure and pushing rivulets of silent tears onto her cheeks.

"Don't you see?" she entreated him then. "He has everything to do with *anything* you do." She trailed her gaze downward, taking in the formidable height of him— truly *looking* at him, and, for the first time, realizing just how many years that beautiful, lean body had roamed the earth.

Gaby shook her head. "It amazes me that you've lived this long, Marcus. Truly astounding, that the guilt hasn't eaten you alive by now. It devours every step you take, every action you make."

"*Stop.*" His rough growl vibrated through to her toes. "You nay have the right—"

"I have *every* right. I have every bloody right in the world, damn you."

She reached to him then, only with a jerking, pummel- ing fist, beating at his shoulders and chest with every other word exploding from her gut, her heart. "*Damn* you!" she cried. "Damn you for letting me love you, for letting me care about you, then for shutting me out with less regard than given a leper." She raised the other fist in proportion to the anguish burning its way through her. "Why did you even come back, you bastard? *Why?* I hate you, Marcus. Damn you, damn you, I love you!"

How long the world went away after that, she didn't com- prehend. She only knew the raging cadence of her fists against the hardness of his chest; the outpouring, at last, of the hurt and tension and unbearable anticipation of the last fortnight.

Finally, his voice came seeping in through her tear-laden fog. He murmured her name as his hands curled around her shoulders, fingers pressing stiff lace against her trem- bling muscles in imitation of the rough threads in his voice.

"Gabriela," he repeated, "sweeting, I pray you to understand. 'Tis not a matter of your guilt or mine. For once, simply, you asked too much of me."

She wanted to react by wresting out of his abysmal, wonderful hold. And for the first time in days, she watched Marcus as he probed her mind, deciphering that fact.

She should have thanked fate for *that* miracle. But then, even more incredibly, his grip tightened around her in instant correlation to his finding.

And with that, damn him, the man managed to render her helpless once more. On the battlefront of her senses, the homecoming of his embrace far outweighed the enticement of continued hostility. As tearful as Gaby's next words came, she delivered them as her hands curled around his neck, as her body slid full against the breadth of his chest and the length of his legs.

"I only asked to be closer to you," she whispered.

"In a manner I cannot grant." His hand reached up and encompassed the back of her head. His fingers gently combed through her rioting curls. "I am sorry, Gabriela. I cannot."

"Marcus . . ." At that, she leaned up and layered soft but fervent kisses along the crest of his defined cheekbone. "Marcus, there can be nothing wrong about initiation, if two people both want it."

He sucked in an unsteady breath. Gulped it down slowly. "There is our plight, then. Both of us do not want it."

"Look at me and say that."

"Gabriela . . ."

"You can't, can you?"

"Gabriela . . ."

"You can't because you like this. Because you want more of this, just as I do."

"Gabriela!"

He meant the harsh exclamation to terrify her. A swift and surreptitious trip into his mind verified that. But her poor, flustered love didn't know he'd just aided the opposite effect in Gaby's heart—and body. Her own pent-up fury and frustration smoldered dangerously close to the embers of desire, of need, of want. At but a prod, the two flickers showed threat of erupting into one uncontrolled inferno.

His outburst was that prod.

And as the inferno ignited through her blood, through her body, Gabriela clutched his face with both hands and crushed her lips to his.

She felt the stunned tremoring of his body. The instinctual clench of his arms around her, hands pressing wondrous heat into her flesh: tentative but urgent strokes born of their torturous absence from each other. She felt his lips part for her, his moaning mouth welcome her. And she felt the silver-hot heat course through him, jolting into his manhood, nearly searing through their clothes in its unfettered, unworldly intensity.

And in that blazing rapture of a moment, Gabriela knew the perfect joy of one very startling conclusion:

This was enough.

Oh, dear wonders of heaven and earth combined, who needed some silly initiation when she had the completion of this man's embrace, the marvel of his touch, the power of his love? She had more than what most women dared to dream of: a love created by the force of fantasy itself, a lover who held the ages in his eyes, who held magic in his heart.

Marcus insisted on terming his existence a curse.

In this moment, Gabriela thanked fate for the miracle of him.

She reached that thought out to his own heart, retwining the cords of their silent bond as she went, vowing nothing would fray those connections ever again.

Until, with a suddenly ferocious growl, he shoved her away with a shaking arm. With the other, he reached up and dragged his shirtsleeve across his lips.

Gabriela's jaw snapped wide. Her brain rushed a frantic search for words. But when Marcus jerked his arm back and raised his gaze to her, lightning-hard silver glaring out from black spikes of hair fallen into his eyes, dread drowned the words, and her jaw struggled just to choke down air.

Only then did she notice his lips quirking into a very sinister and very humorless half-smile.

"It seems I now return your congratulations, lady," he broke the silence in a low grate. "That performance was your best yet." Then, the smile suddenly disappearing, "Not even Raquelle could better it."

She went dead inside. All the warmth she grappled to hold for the man, all the joy and all the hope, were killed in one slice of his caustic words, spilling a million drops of her heart's blood.

And yet, amazingly, that heart continued to throb throughout every fiber of her being as she paced two noiseless steps to the beast who still fixed his unblinking glare on her.

Then that heart stopped. Just for a moment. As she slapped his face with all the strength left in her body.

Somehow, she found the stamina to turn and leave him, too, for her next cognizant perception came of her dressing room door, offering some semblance of haven from his physical presence, if not the inescapable demon of pain he'd loosed upon her spirit. Gabriela wrenched open the door and stumbled inside, gasping in huge but shuddering breaths, wondering why she couldn't cry, but thanking God she didn't.

She backed against the door to close and lock it. The smell of satin and feathers, old dust and new rice powder washed over her with as much comforting force as the mother's perfume she barely remembered, the cozy home kitchen she never had—and now, for the first time in her life, could write that deficiency off as no great loss.

How, indeed, had she wasted so many years pining for a family, dreaming of somebody to love, when love only brought this shattering defeat to endure, this crushing weight of hurt and heartache? What a damnable farce! If they named love a play, it would close on opening night beneath a barrage of rotten apples!

Well, she'd buy no more tickets to *this* show, Gaby vowed. From now on, the stages of the world would be her home; every new audience, her family. Pain would exist only in scripts, experienced only through the safe distance of the characters she played.

And she'd never, never let herself love again.

Arriving at the resolution gave her new fortitude already. On a strengthened sigh, she pushed from the door with shoulders newly squared and head held high.

She yanked her breath back in on a sharp gasp—as an imposing figure slid completely from the shadows and into her path.

"Alfonso," she stammered, unable to suppress her perplexed scowl, though the man's patrician features didn't alter an iota from their even, probing mien.

"Good evening, Gabriela," he said with equal, sure smoothness.

Too much smoothness.

Trying to ignore the strange, cold frisson skittering up her spine, Gaby bustled across the room with businesslike haste. "What . . . what are you doing here at this hour?"

She almost reached her chair before the mirror. Almost. Alfonso's hand shot around her elbow with speed she'd only seen once before: in a lizard's tongue at the zoo. He jerked her back to him so vehemently, she wondered if her shoulder remained in its socket.

But he still spoke with chilling, low calm. "Oh, I think the more interesting question is what *you're* doing here at this hour."

With the last words, his grip curled painfully into her

arm. Strangely, Gaby knew the sudden urge to laugh at that tactic. Maybe once the action would have instigated a shudder down to her toes, a serious requestioning of her self-esteem. Now, she didn't lower her head the width of a pin, meeting Alfonso's stare with equally pointed acuity. Equally undeviating determination. Equally tempered confidence.

As much as she loathed to admit it, Marcus's love had given her that sole legacy.

"I have told you a thousand times," she leveled lowly, "I stay here at night to rehearse. Now, *sir*, please take your hand—"

His bark of laughter cut her short. "Rehearse? Is that what they're calling it these days? That *is* new on me." Yet as Alfonso hauled her to face him fully, latching his other hand into her opposite arm, a glare of twisted fury turned his mirth into a monster's visage—a living and suddenly very real version of a penny dreadful cover.

"Rehearsing," he repeated on a sneer, dipping his lips just inches from hers—lips reeking of heavy vodka and cheap brandy. "Hmmm. Tell me, Gabriela, what do you call it when you screw him? Act One? And when he comes inside you . . . that's curtain call, is that it?"

The skitter down her spine burst into a siege of fear. "Wh-what are you talking about?" she blurted before she knew it—though a deep and chilling dread already predicted his answer.

"*Don't* play witless with me, Gabriela!" Her head snapped back as he jerked her again, his hands now kneading restlessly at her shoulders. "I saw you—you and your beautiful black-haired lover. Shoving your tongue down his throat, writhing all over him like the slut you really are."

"Alfonso," she managed with surprising composure, "stop this. This . . . this isn't you."

"You're right," he drawled. "It isn't. But maybe it should

have been all along." He threw his head back on another high, maniacal laugh. "And I just tried to *buy* you! God, God, what a fool. I brought you flowers and furs, when all you wanted was a little rough play. Is that it, Gabriela? To be shoved around a bit? Does that turn you on?"

He released her then. With a push that sent her flying across the room, across her dressing table—into her dressing table mirror.

And any composure she still possessed shattered along with the glass biting into her face and arms.

"Alfonso," she pleaded as he grabbed her again, dragging her across her broken makeup jars, "Alfonso, no!"

"I can do it just like he does, Gabriela. Just watch me. Just *feel* me."

"No . . . please—"

"Shut up. Shut up, you ungrateful little bitch!"

"Alfonso! Alfonso!"

But somewhere between the fifth and sixth times his fists pounded into her, her lips formed around another name, praying to God he'd hear her desperate rasps . . . praying to God for her life.

"Marcus . . . *Marcus* . . ."

Fourteen

The torment continued into eternity. And he didn't hear. He'd never hear her again, Gabriela thought dimly, finally enduring the barrage of slicing pain and grunting expletives in semiconscious silence. Only her heart kept calling out in soundless contrition, in unspeakable despair. . . .

Marcus. I'm sorry. I never stopped loving you. I never will.

She retreated within herself as Alfonso threw her to the floor, thrust up her skirts and shoved her legs apart. She ran to the secret place inside, far away and numb, that she hadn't been since the day Lord and Lady Rothschild took Fiona Warfield home instead of her. But this time she ran to that haven with Marcus, and as they ran, he sang to her again, and they laughed together one last time.

And she almost forgot Alfonso Renard ripping at his trousers as he fell ruthlessly upon her. She almost pretended she didn't hear his slurred, stale-breathed, "Here you are, slut," as he readied his body to invade her.

She almost shut out the scream surrounding her senses after that.

Funny, though, next came a bizarre and disoriented thought—why didn't she recognize her own scream? Even more queer: why did her teeth still press against the back of her clamped, shut lips?

She forced her eyes open and her head up.

And came to the certain conclusion she'd started to hallucinate.

Through a sticky mist of blood flowing anew from her forehead, she focused on Alfonso's contorted features, as he screamed again and cowered before the biggest wolf she'd ever seen. The animal shook its back haunches free of splinters from the door it just pounced through. Alfonso's left trouser leg hung in tatters from the knee down. The wolf spat the material away, then peeled back jowls in a snarl of echoing, otherworldly fury, exposing very white, very sharp teeth.

Very white, very sharp, and very perfect teeth.

Gabriela's entire body jerked with a burst of astonishment. She scrambled to her knees, wiping the blood and hair from her face as she raked a wide gape over the rest of the beast.

Those teeth gleamed even more prominently against the wolf's dark, waving fur—thick as a midnight forest, black as a midnight sky. But that snarl paled in comparison to the glow of the beast's ageless, fearless silver eyes.

When I am, however, forced into that situation, I prefer becoming a wolf . . .

A wolf or a butterfly . . .

"Oh, my God," Gabriela choked. "Oh, my God!"

She had barely gotten the words past the shock and fea clogging her throat, but Marcus heard. Ah God, how h heard. In wolf's form, he heard, smelled, saw, and fel everything with even more awareness than his normal su perreal abilities.

But the feeling part—aye, that was the worst. After firs hearing her silent scream as he had stood on Drury's de serted stage, he actually flinched as Renard's next blo drove into her. And when the bastard had pushed her the floor, when that maggot readied Gabriela for his body

violation, Marcus had thrown his head back into a roar
that shattered six stage lamps.

Then, swiftly and methodically, he'd cleared his mind
of everything but one purpose:

To kill Alfonso Renard in the most terrifying and painful
manner possible.

Now, that intent swelled through every erect hackle and
tensed haunch of his being, riding the growing surge of
rage, the same feral bloodlust escalated in the moment
between his first crash into the room and Renard's
astonished glance up at him.

The moment he had seen that gutter snake kneeling
between Gabriela's legs.

That image carried Marcus across the floor now, stalking
steadily, barely holding his fury in check, but enjoying
every second of Renard's eye-bulging, lip-trembling panic.
A pleasureful growl echoed all the way up from his massive
paws. The maggot's last minutes of life would also be his
most horrifying, and the intensified instincts of this animal
form made Marcus's conquest all the more delicious. Aye,
Renard's blood would be the sweetest nectar to ever flow
down his throat. . . .

"What the hell!" He watched more than heard Renard
blurt the words, the sounds garbled against the chaos of
anger, instinct, and primal canine awareness swimming in
his head. He snarled again, the tang of the pursuit filling
his mouth. Then he advanced farther, backing Renard into
the corner behind Gabriela's dressing table. She would
already have to listen to him kill the man; he would save
her the atrocity of watching the deed, as well.

"What . . . bloody hell . . . is this?" Renard shouted; this
time, Marcus saw, over his head and across the room.
"Gabriela . . . call . . . bloody pet off me!"

Marcus coiled his muscles and snapped his jaws, three
seconds away from showing the whoreson just who he
would brand "pet," when another voice made its way

through the din in his senses—this time, echoing *inside* his senses. . . .

Marcus . . . Marcus, please, if you can hear me, don't do this. Don't do this!

He wanted to tell her to shut up. He wanted to tell her how much he loved her. Ah God, he wanted to say so much—but his brain grappled and grunted to form the few elemental words it could.

Beat—you, he forced back at her. *Raped—you.*

No. No, he didn't rape me. You got here in time.

Still—deserves—die.

No! No, Marcus, please. He's not a faceless beggar from the hospital! They'll search for his killer. They'll search for you!

But if the truth of her words caused him to reconsider her plea at all, Renard stole that choice from him in the next moment. A broad grin suddenly replaced the man's dreading gape of sixty seconds prior. Against the sweaty sheen of aquiline features, the leer turned the man into something bordering on a cackling demon.

A demon that advanced casually, yet possessively back toward Gabriela.

"Nice poochie," Renard growled on his way "Poochie . . . right? Ah, Gabriela . . . nice try . . . almos had me gulled." As he passed Marcus, the bastard rake a brutally dismissing hand across his head, nearly rippin one ear off with the motion. "Run along, mutt. Miss Roz ina . . . me . . . unfinished business to attend."

Even after that humiliation, the spawn of a sow migh have warranted himself a shred of mercy—if he ha dropped his hand. Bloody hell, if he had put that han anywhere except around Gabriela's breast, squeezing s hard, a sharp cry escaped her lips. If only he did not rai that hand to silence her with such a powerful backhan blow, her head snapped back and her body sagged dizzi

If only he had not done that.

The maggot might have saved himself a sliver of lig

in Marcus's storm of rage. Mayhap a moment of contemplated control before the enfuried frenzy blazed through every inch of wolf muscle and every wolf instinct. Maybe a minuscule chance to escape the howling, slavering wolf now flying through the air and into bone and flesh, tearing at everything, stopping at nothing, savoring the scent of fear and the climax of victory.

But most of all, reveling in the taste of blood.

Marcus took his first sample just after Renard's terrified wail—when he discovered the man's thumb and forefinger between his teeth. He remembered nothing about how the things got there, except the annihilating need to ensure the bastard's hand never hurt Gabriéla again. He had fallen well short of the mark, but even his disappointment nay overpowered his thirst, the driest and deepest he had ever known, driven by a fusion of real need, rage's desire, his wolf's raw nature, and his man's raw wrath.

And he counted his earlier fancying now as prophecy. Renard's blood, stirred liberally with the honey of revenge, was the most delectable ambrosia he'd tasted.

It made him want more.

He spat the fingers out and spun toward the quarry once more. Renard now plummeted to his knees. He let out a hoarse shriek for every horrified gasp as he gaped at his bleeding hand, like he lived a nightmare that would disappear if he blinked hard enough.

Haven't—begun—know nightmare, bastard, came the delicious morsels of thought through the soup of Marcus's brain. He took his time about his renewed offensive, relishing his role as blood hunter for the first time in his existence.

But he should have known she'd be watching. And listening. And coming after him with her damnable, inescapable chains of love and concern. *No! Marcus, please, no!*

Go—away, he fired back in a mental snarl.

"What . . . hell is this?" Renard's incredulous sob inter-

rupted them both. "What . . . hell? My—my hand . . . my
hand! That—*thing* bit off . . . hand! Kill you . . . this! I'll
kill you . . . goddamn monster!"

"Alfonso!" a harsh rasp cut him off—and for a moment,
Marcus wondered who else had happened upon their
scene. Surely, dear Jesu, that weak and wincing sound had
not come from his stubborn, strong Gabriela . . .

But she spoke again. And filled his senses with sick certainty.

"Please, Alfonso," he heard her beg across the thick,
sweaty air. "Don't . . . another word. Don't . . . another
muscle!"

Renard threw his head back into the ear-pinning laugh
again, his temerity explained by his shock-sheened gaze.
"Or . . . hound of hell . . . finish job?" He lowered his
features with a glazed, contemptuous sneer. "Don't
threaten . . . again, Gabriela. Not your style."

The whoreson, Marcus decided, had lived much too
long.

With that his last resolved thought, he sprang forward
again. This time, a full bark slashed up the length of his
spine and out his bared teeth, a primitive, possessive ser-
ration of sound. *Show you—her style,* his instincts roared as
he increased speed. His sights narrowed to the top button
of the man's bloodied waistcoat. Vengeful victory rushed
nearer. After ripping through those dandy's clothes, he'd
easily find the man's heart. . . .

He leapt. Descended hard, with Renard beneath him.
Let the scent of the prey's terror, sweat, and blood infil-
trate his nostrils. Velvet waistcoat and fine lawn shirt came
away with one bite. A scream resounded through his head.
Good, he answered in savage satisfaction. *Scream—for life—
bastard.*

"Marcus—Marcus, no! Listen to me! *Listen* to me!"

He froze. Breaths still frothing through his teeth, senses
still swimming with fury and fire, he watched the white of

Renard's eyes disappear as the man dropped into a limp faint.

Nay. *Nay! You—not—be here!* he seethed at her. Only the bastard and him, only the kill and the blood and exhausted retribution at last. Compensation for what this gutter worm had done . . . ah God, for what he had done! The things he had called her. The way he had touched her. . . .

Touched? Marcus vented a sardonic snarl. This moron nay knew how to *touch* anyone or anything. The pitiful bastard never realized that true power did not come from the shine of a shilling or the threat of a fist.

Power—oh, *power,* dear bells of heaven, was the echo of Gabriela's voice in his mind, sweeping in and conquering his concentration with the battle ax of her gentleness and the claymore of her soft, shaking whisper. *Touch* was the urgent clutch of her arms despite her dwindling strength, burrowing through blood and fur to pull him back with every ounce of mettle she still possessed.

"Marcus . . . please . . . if murder him . . . have to run." Her whisper spread tear-filled warmth over the hairs inside his ear. An involuntary shiver coursed over him. "Marcus . . . need you. Need . . . now. Please . . . don't run. Please . . . I . . . need . . ."

That shiver became full, freezing fear—as her arms went limp, her voice died away.

Gabriela!

"Gabriela!"

The sound of his human bellow rang through buzzing senses. He looked down once more to his crouching arms, his bent knees, his blood-spattered chest.

He was naked. He nay cared. His sights and senses filled with Gabriela. A dark crimson gash ran the length of her forehead. More blood trickled from deep cuts down her neck and arms, and splotched the gown now stuck to her thighs and legs. Her wet eyelashes closed on clammy skin, one cheek swelled twice the size of the other with a fist-sized bruise marbled of purple, blue, and black. Her ripped gown revealed more bruises fanned across her breasts, in the distinct pattern of spread fingers.

"God," he choked. "God." He yearned to touch her. He pulled back his hand. He was terrified to touch her. "Gabriela. Gabriela." His voice still sounded like another creature. Lost. Tortured. Alone. So alone without her.

Nay.

"Nay!" he shouted, scrambling off Renard and hauling her close to him. Cold. *She was so cold.* A raw, raging outcry overflowed the room the next moment; he barely felt the force of the sound ripping up his throat. He crushed her closer as he leapt to his feet, pressing her to his heart as he sprinted down the hall and up into the catwalks, holding her next to his soul as he took the stairs to their apartment five at a time.

Damn you, Gabriela, that soul roared the whole way. *Damn you, damn you; hold on, hold on!*

He kicked the double doors in and sped with her to the bedroom. When he laid her on the white coverlet, he didn't know whether to laugh or cry.

A chill no longer claimed her.

But the first glistening beads of fever did.

Dread and rage clashed, turning him into a helpless, motionless beast who only sat there and blurted her name over and over again—until realizing her lips moved with *his* name as she shifted restlessly on the mattress, writhing her head side to side against the fiery approach of infection.

"Marcus. *Marcus* . . ."

"I'm here, love." He captured her flailing wrists, kissed her burning knuckles. *What do you want to hear, love? What do you want me to do, to say? I shall say it. I shall do it. Just tell me, Gabriela. Just hang on. Please, just hang on!*

But the bonfire in her body already scorched through the awareness of her mind. "Hot," she whimpered, oblivi-

ous to his heart's beseechings. "Marcus, I'm so . . ." She
wriggled a hand from him and pulled at her tattered gown,
sobbing when the material nay yielded to her feeble tug-
gings. "Marcus . . . oh, Marcus, help me . . ."

"Aye. Aye," he muttered, ridding her of the ruined
clothes in the same two seconds. Of course. *Of course,* he
berated himself; he should have done so upon identifying
the fever. He should have done so many things. He should
not have let her leave the stage in the first place. He should
have apologized. He should not have been such an inflex-
ible ass!

That self-turned wrath propelled him up, into the washroom and back with a basin of water, a clean cloth and a
bottle of alcohol he had only used once—gargled the stuff,
after Joseph confessed he had accidentally brought a chol-
era victim for dinner. *That* memory effectively sealed the
resolve not to drag her anywhere near the hospital.

Marcus repeated that journey countless times during the
next hours, pouring dark pink floods down the sink every
time he returned—the dark pink of the blood and sweat
he blotted from her body. But endlessly, no matter how
many compresses he applied or bandages he wrapped, the
wounds kept draining from her . . . draining her strength,
draining her life.

Yet he did not stop. He could not. He ceased thinking,
conserving his energy only for the steeled fortitude it took
to emerge from that washroom, to look at her lying there
so broken and bloody, then go to her again, soothing her
with soft songs while he tortured her with the wound-
cleansing ministrations of the cloth and the skin-searing
sting of the alcohol.

Until, close to the hundredth time he settled to the mattress next to her, she flailed out her arm, sending the basin
shattering to the floor.

"No," she rasped. "No more." Her eyes slid shut, her
tongue swiped at sweat collected on her lips. With

astonishing strength, she clasped his hand and pressed it between her breasts. The grip of death, Marcus thought in racing, raging agony.

"Lie beside me," she pleaded in a whisper. "Just come lie beside me, Marcus."

He hesitated one half a moment. Then blew out the candle on the night stand.

And then there, in the deep abyss of that night, in the darkness so emulating the oppressive weight of his heart and soul, Marcus lowered himself next to her. He lay upon a coverlet puddled with blood, and did not fight a single breath of thirst or pang of hunger. Grief annihilated any sensation in his body. Fear seized every stronghold in his brain.

"No," Gabriela sighed into the thick blackness. "No, Marcus, don't be afraid."

He jerked to one elbow, bolstered by hope, squeezing her fingers with his other hand. "You . . . you can hear me inside of you again?"

He felt her force down a dry swallow. "Not in words. But in feeling—" She interrupted herself with a soft sniff. "Oh, my love, I'll always know what you're feeling. You're here, in my heart now . . . don't you know that? You'll always be here. Even after—"

"*Stop.*" He barely forced the word past the boulder of bile in his gut. "Stop it, Gabriela. Stop speaking that way, damn you."

He would have gladly faced hell that moment for one jaw-jarring slap from her in reply. Instead, Gabriela swallowed several more times . . . long, convulsing, sobbing swallows, as she tangled her fingers in his hair and pulled him against her sweat-drenched body.

"Marcus," she whimpered. "Marcus, Marcus, I'm sorry. I'm sorry I did this to you. And I'm so sorry I was impossible all those times."

"Nay." He smoothed the hair off her battered, beautiful

face. "I was such an ass. Ah, God, I wasted so much time on anger."

He kissed her then, gently, vowing to rectify that mistake beginning at once. He felt her smile against his lips and in his heart.

"It doesn't matter now," she told him on a strange, peaceful lilt. Then her head fell back to the pillow—as if merely drifting off for a nap. "Doesn't . . . matter."

"Gabriela!" Ice-sharp shards shot up his arms. He grabbed her, jerked her back to him. "Gabriela, damn you, it *does* matter!"

"It's all right, Marcus." Her head lolled over his arm, her fingers alighting as soft as mice steps on his chest. "I love you. It's all right."

'Tis not all right, his soul raved on silent, straining screams. *'Tis not all right at all!*

He repeated that decree to the heaven that no longer listened to him, but he nay cared. He no longer believed in a heaven that floated uncaring over a world where angels like this were allowed to die by the hand of beasts like Alfonso Renard. Where the gifts of this woman's life and light were spat back in her face before she had the chance to share them with the world, dying in a pool of her own blood, in the arms of an undead monster who had received more life than he ever earned.

God, *God*, that he could trade one hundred years of his misbegotten life for one more of hers. He would give up two hundred breaths for a sigh, a smile. Surrender the very beat of his preternatural heart and strength of his superreal limbs, that she would walk and live and love again. . . .

Dear Jesu.

As the impact of his sudden realization set in, Marcus did not breathe for a full minute. Then, slowly brushing his hand down the side of Gabriela's battered body, he damned himself for not comprehending the one certain

way to save his love, here and now, beyond the relief of
any compresses, the miracles of any doctors, the force of
any prayers.

His strength. *His* heartbeat. *His* life.

He almost laughed. Almost. The little vixen was to get
her way with him, after all. No other choice remained.

No other choice but to let her die.

Marcus slid his arm from beneath Gabriela, laying her
back to the wet counterpane despite her kitten-like cry of
discomfort. "I know, sweeting," he murmured into her
ear, stretching out fully beside her again, attempting to
reassure her with his size and strength. "It will nay hurt
much longer, I promise."

She only sighed, softly and seemingly happy once more,
as he traced silver-soft kisses over her lips, along her jaw,
behind her ear . . . back to the smooth skin protecting the
main artery in her neck.

Her heart began beating faster. He knew from the increasing pulse beneath his nose and lips. *Damn*, Marcus
gasped inside. Bloody damn . . . she smelled so sweet,
tasted so good. *Damn, Gabriela. Oh, damn.*

Must nay take too much, another voice ordered from the
region of his head. *Remember—just enough!*

But what was enough? He had never done this before!
He hesitated like a lad fumbling through a first tumble
with the milk maid. Ah God, now she attempted to caress
him back, so weak and clumsy and beautiful, sighing
louder. He wanted her so badly, he burned . . . but how
much was too much?

Gabriela stole the luxury of deliberation from him the
next moment. While turning and capturing his lips in a
long, lingering kiss, she flung limp, weighted arms around
his neck, arching languorously against the length of him.
Every inch of their bodies now fitted flawlessly, heating his
senses mercilessly. Her heartbeat echoed through his

nerve endings. And her blood coursed warm and close, so very close, beneath his lips.

Marcus let the feel and the scent of her wash over him, through him. Anticipation flooded him in a wave he had never known so completely, with an ecstasy he never imagined. Pure silver sensation throbbed in his toenails, out his fingertips . . . along his quivering tongue and throat. He coiled one arm back around Gabriela, returning her embrace with savage intensity. With the other hand, he shoved her hair from her neck, angling her beneath him just so . . . just perfectly.

He lowered his head and scraped her silken skin with one fast-stretching eye tooth.

Aye. Aye, dear God, I cannot wait any longer!

"Marcus," came her bewildered gasp, halting him but a hair's width from descending into her. "Marcus, what's happening? What are you—"

"Hush." He licked the skin to keep it moist, warm, ready. "Everything *is* all right . . . I am making it all right."

"Wh-what? What do you mean?"

"Gabriela," he moaned, now shaking with frustration, expectation. "Oh Gabriela, I love you so much. Love me, too. Trust me. Surrender to me. . . ."

And in a moment, my heart, you will truly be mine.

Fifteen

You will truly be mine.

Gabriela gasped. At least she thought she did. But her dry and fevered throat convulsed on breath that no longer seemed available—breath that wasn't important, anyway; not after the joyous rush of Marcus's words in her head again.

And, most incredibly, from realizing what they meant.

"Marcus," she whispered in joy and amazement and, yes, a little awed fear. Oh, that he'd do this for her, that he'd trust her with this darkest secret of his—this ultimate revelation of his death, that she might live. And as he repeated silent words of love to her, readying her for the consummation of their souls, she listened and knew, truly knew how much he meant every syllable.

"Marcus," she whispered in return, trying so hard to tell him, too, but battling her waning strength, battling to live just one more moment for him. "Marcus . . . I love . . . you . . . too . . . I . . ."

The sound soared into a high, halting gasp—then floated away on space and time as his mouth parted for his long, guttural groan . . . and his sinking, suckling teeth.

They both froze as he pierced her deep, hard. They both moaned as he drank deep, full.

Then lightning flooded her world.

Lightning, full of life. Of strength. Of Marcus—oh, Marcus, *Marcus*, everywhere inside and outside of her. . . . *Marcus*, she was a little boy running in a Shropshire meadow with a pinwheel. . . . *Marcus*, she was a terrified new vampire wandering alone and cold through a black forest. . . . *Marcus*, she was a vampire, over two hundred and fifty years old, gazing from the Drury Lane catwalks at a dreamy-eyed actress named Gabriela Rozina, and falling immediately, hopelessly in love. . . .

Marcus.
I never knew it would be like this.
Marcus . . . Marcus . . .
You're beautiful!

He had told her he nay believed in miracles.
But then she told him he was beautiful.
Him! Marcus reeled in wonder at the memory even now, hours later, as he lay back against the satin of his coffin in satiated bliss—and continuing amazement. Not even dawn's increasing approach fatigued him from shaking his head at the wonder of the thought.
Beautiful.
She had said *that* to *him,* the monster who lay there draining the very life from her, so drunk with the taste of her, he barely forced himself to stop. Out of his mind with her. Out of control with her. Utterly consumed by the life and love and brilliance of her.
Gabriela, Gabriela!
Gabriela, he was a five year-old girl dropping tear-stained daisies on her mother's grave. . . . *Gabriela,* he was an unsure actress, hoping the director could not hear the growl of her stomach over the lines of her audition. . . . *Gabriela,* he was a heartbroken woman, looking up from where she had collapsed weeping on her dressing room floor, up into

the silver eyes of a stranger, and thinking him the most beautiful creature she'd ever seen. . . .

Beautiful.

Gabriela.

How did I earn the gift of you?

Her soft chuckle came now as answer to that, betraying her eavesdropping on his thoughts, but she gained herself pardon with a warm, long kiss across his collarbone. Marcus had to admit their fit in his "bed" a tight situation at best, but when he had finally forced himself away from her, petrified with the certainty he had taken enough blood to kill her, Gabriela had hauled him back with a vigor nearing *his* in alacrity and intensity. Then, with a shockingly healthy dose of volume, she had all but ordered him not to move two inches from her.

Aye; in the sinew of her muscle and the cells of her blood, initiation had already begun its secret wonders.

But in the sea of her thoughts and emotions, Marcus had stirred a hurricane beyond compare. A hurricane he might have managed, had he not found himself sucked in to that vexing vortex, as well.

As usual, his ingenuous little angel expressed the sensation best for both of them. *I never knew it would be like this.* If he had not lain there trembling with the near-narcotic effects of their unnatural union, a resounding "Amen" might have spilled from his lips.

By heaven's own truth, he had *no* idea it would be like this. He envisioned himself the strong one after their bonding, patiently helping her with the onslaught of perception, guiding her through the labyrinth of her supernatural awakening with as much ease as he navigated her across a Shakespearean plot.

Nobody told him immortals got initiated, too.

Nobody told him about the infinite, unbelievable completion of his own body and soul, the total loss of self, the devastating flood of feeling. The soaring joy. The shatter ing sorrow. The lifetime of memories, comprised of so many extraordinary thoughts and marveling discoveries. Jesu, he never knew women saw the world like *this*. He had wanted to stay inside her forever, knowing her world, living her life.

Little wonder struck, then, that when the sun slipped its first sleepy fingers over the city—and him—and when Gabriela wrapped herself around him with a cry of protest bordering on a mourning moan, Marcus did not hesitate to merely pick her up and take her with him.

But while she let him lead their descent through the inky underground with silent contentment, barely glancing up from the shoulder she reclined against, Marcus wondered how much her "guide" he truly remained—how radically their roles in this plot had been skewed forever, and whether the reformation had just dealt their production the seal of doom. For tonight, they embarked on a passage down mazes far more tangled and dangerous than the London underground.

Tonight, they began to travel each other's lives. Paths of memories and dreams, heartaches and hopes, triumphs and losses. The loneliness of the past. The vulnerability of the present.

And what of the future?

He did not know.

And it had been a very long time since he looked into the face of the unknown.

The last time, he had crouched against the wall of a forest cave as Raquelle De Lanya's laughter echoed in his ears.

With that meditation, fear suddenly gripped Marcus. Very hard. Very painfully.

He knew just how painfully by Gabriela's sharp, comprehending convulsion against him. She jerked up her head, inundating him with a stare sparked of dark gold alarm.

Yet a moment later, those sparks softened to embers of

understanding. "Marcus," she whispered, spanning his jaw
with her fingertips, "it's all right now. *You're* all right.
Raquelle . . . she was a lifetime ago. *Several* lifetimes."

And then, as she melded her lips with his, she fused the
words of her heart to his: *Let* me *be your lifetime now. Please,
Marcus, say I can stay with you. Say I can stay always.*

He could not hide his answer from her—no matter how
desperately he still wished such a delusion possible. No
matter how now more than ever, he still scrambled
through his senses for just one last wall to throw up against
her; one last indulgent lover's smile to fulfill her fancies
of a happy-ever-after with a beast like him. Just one last
time. One last shred of reality to save them both.

But his search yielded no such asylum. Within the moment, Gabriela easily heard his heart's acceptance of her
plea; she clearly saw the disgraceful gamut of his soul's
deepest fantasies: impossible dreams of sunshine, futile
fantasies of forever, and always, *always,* endless visions of
her. Making love to her in a dawn-bright meadow. Helping
her give birth to their sixth, maybe their seventh, child.
Getting sick with her. Growing old with her. Living and
loving and dying with her.

The hopeless hopes of a monster. The unreachable
heaven to a creature of hell.

And Gabriela saw them all.

And Marcus jerked his sights away, ashamed, embarrassed.

Until she slid her fingers up against his skull, and forced
his head back toward her. Forced him to see her brilliant,
tear-brimmed eyes, and her watery, dopey smile. Forced
him to hear the chorusing words of her heart, peeling in
his sense's like church bells on a royal wedding day:

*Don't you know me by now, you wonderful, stubborn ape? Mar-
cus, Marcus . . . I don't care what you are! I love who you are.
I love you!*

And suddenly, he laughed. And she laughed. And they kissed. Deeply. Passionately.

And suddenly, for the first time ever, this dim, dank cavern transformed into a magical, magnificent palace. Marcus's army of candelabras no longer waged a glistening battle against the dark, but served the higher purpose of romance's glow. The plops and swishes of subterranean moisture and wind were no longer a dirge marking his cursed days, but a harmony of texture and sound, an enchanted lullaby, pulling them both toward the welcoming arms of slumber.

Gabriela succumbed to the hypnotizing song first, her breaths evening to a soft cadence against Marcus's chest. In the last moments before his own drugged senses followed her, he stole the time to again swallow down the gargantuan weight of his astonishment at this woman.

She had accomplished it yet again. Transformed his world. Transformed *him*. When viewed through her magical eyes, cobwebs and clay floors formed into a castle. A coffin turned into a luxurious feather bed.

And a beast became the prince of her heart.

Oh, my love, his own heart joined on a breeze smelling of warm candle wax and cool subterranean ferns, *oh, that I could have you here with me forever.*

That same instant, he ordered the thought forgotten. He also banished the other thoughts connected to it— those forbidden musings lying so close, *too* close to the surface of his conscience. Ready to *annihilate* his conscience.

Ready to tell him that at a word from Gabriela, he would nay stop at initiation next time. At a mere pull at their intensified bond, all he had to do was surrender to the temptation, truly making her his for the next millennia and beyond.

And that terrified him more than anything.

Because for one irresistible, carnal fantasy of a moment, forever nay seemed such a dreadful place any more.

Forever.

Gabriela wanted to scream as the word resounded in her head for the five hundredth time. But as she sat for the *Times* and the *Chronicle*'s sketch artists during the private press session Augustus had invited "a select few" journalists to take advantage of, her heart winced the word three more times. As she made polite excuses to the fawning reporters, citing the orchestra's first meandering notes as her cue for last-minute preparations, the dooming syllables coincided with every violin scale and every testing trumpet bleat echoing through the reaches of Drury.

As she rushed back down the hall to her dressing room, she let her mind finally cry it out to the uppermost rafters over her head—and beyond.

Forever. It's been forever, Marcus. I don't care what you say. It's been forever.

Sweeting, came his maddeningly calm response, *look at your clock. We only parted an hour and thirty ago.*

See? What did I tell you? It's been forever!

His chuckle swirled through her nerve endings as if he only followed a pace behind her, admiring how the sapphire blue silk of her maiden's costume flowed around her hips as she walked.

In reply to *that*, Gabriela stomped into her dressing room on the most furious steps she could manage. She slammed the door then dropped back against it, glaring at her reflection in the tabletop mirror on her dressing table. Louis had helped her clean the room's mess from last night without a question, even when she adamantly refused to have a new full-sized mirror ordered. He'd produced the smaller version a few minutes later, taking in the nearly healed gash across her forehead with the same frowning, but quiet mien of understanding—to which Gabriela could only smile her profuse thanks.

Since then, her emotions had ridden the same runaway cart of confusion. Up and down. Side to side. Desperation, then elation. Galloping farther from her control every minute.

And the only being able to help her find the reins now sat somewhere on high, laughing at her.

She decided she hated him.

You do not hate me, came that damnably spellbinding mix of baritone and tenor, strength and gentleness.

"Yes, I do." Gaby fired off the retort before his words could work their way into her system, robbing her anger. "Go away."

But she'd forgotten the man read her mind better than he knew her body. *Gabriela,* his voice came inside of her the next moment, his plea almost a prayer in its whispering intensity—yet impacting her with the thoroughness of a well-placed battle assault. *Gabriela . . .*

Gaby's knees gave way to the attack first. She slid to the floor, crouching into a helpless ball, desperately wondering—yet strangely, almost hoping—if she'd forever be like this without Marcus by her side, against her heart, crushing every inch of her body to his hardness, his strength. Yes, she admitted, the very strength her own body had borrowed to heal with miraculous speed as they'd slept through the day . . . the strength her blood cells used to multiply again, her muscles gleaned to bond and repair themselves. The very strength which had saved her life.

The strength Marcus had insisted she utilize to leave him "an hour and thirty" ago, despite the agony of taking one step from him. At the time, she thought he comprehended her grief at merely thinking of the action; she'd even caught the flash of very real pain across his features when he'd flinched while helping her into her wrap.

But he'd made her go, anyway. He'd made her go with

the same words he now reached across the heights of
Drury to command at her again:

*This night is part of why you clung to life for me last eve. 'Tis
what we have waited for, worked for, dreamed for. I will not let—*

"*We* have waited for," Gaby retaliated, snapping her
sights toward the ceiling. "*We* have worked for; *we* have
dreamed for. Notice a common thread of scripting here,
Mr. Danewell?"

His long sigh echoed in her head. He emitted it past
those locked, beautiful teeth of his; she knew simply by
the guttural resonance of the sound. And he probably followed by crossing his arms, dropping his head and pacing
the floor like an obstinate, adorable mule.

Gabriela . . . sweeting . . . this is your night—

"*Our* night."

Damn it, I will not let you throw away this chance!

"This chance means nothing without you."

He retaliated with that extended, exasperated sigh
again. *But I am with you.*

"Ohhhh, no." Gaby jerked to her feet with a knowing
smile, a shaking head. She paced the room once, then sat
again with an angry plummet. "You can't use that line on
me, sir. I originated the part, remember?"

No "line," Gabriela. No "parts." Just you . . . and me.

She didn't sling back anything to that. As a matter of
fact, she watched her hand reach for her hairbrush—then
also watched her fingers go still around the chipped
enamel handle; numb, indecisive.

That tone, *his* tone, rose as an altered entity inside
her . . . transformed from his refined, safe, musical into-
nations to a low, primal thunder. Very serious, very commanding thunder.

Followed by a velvet rainstorm of tone, of voice . . . of
magic.

I am here, Gabriela. Right now, right here. Beside you, inside you . . . forever, for always. You have only to look for me. To take my love, to use my strength.

"Marcus—"

Hush.

"Marcus!"

But another person breathed the word. Another someone still capable of thought, someone who didn't suddenly sag in that chair from the cascade of sensation washing over her, into her. No . . . more than sensation. A whole presence filling her, taking over her body, her mind, her muscles and blood, nerve endings and fingertips, hair follicles and spinal cord and kneecaps . . . her collarbone even grew by three inches, now possessing an excruciatingly sensitive spot, and her thighs shifted at the awareness of a heavy length between them, growing bigger and harder with the stimulation of two bodies fused into one. Dear God. Dear *God.*

But also, as Marcus promised, she knew strength. *Strength?* She discounted that, too, as vast understatement. Power consumed her as she'd never fathomed, supernatural and superreal, convulsing her so violently, she heard the hairbrush snap between her fingers and saw her foot punch a well-sized chunk out of her dressing screen. So strange, so odd—why did her leg look the same, too skinny at the ankle and too curved at the calf, foot still encased in dainty pale blue slippers, when she'd so obviously become this other looming, lusting, demanding creature?

This desperate, aching, magnificent creature . . . so fervently wanting just to love and be loved. . . .

Oh, Marcus . . .

I love you, too.

She returned to reality by slow, blinking increments. First, she perceived her own body again. Then she took in sections of the room and impressions of the outer world, all as if awakening from a long and restful nap. . . .

Despite Louis's wall-shaking bang at her door. "Gaby!"

His bellow added the ceiling beams to the quake. "Five minute call to curtain. You're on in twenty. You bloody well better be ready, missy!"

Gabriela didn't answer at first. She only smiled. Then stood.

Then wrapped her arms around herself and spun a dizzy, delirious circle in the middle of the room—all the while, envisioning a black-haired, sinfully handsome someone suddenly jerked to his own feet on the apartment's Persian carpet, and forced to follow her.

Her smile inched higher as the back of her brain echoed with Marcus's winded mutter:

Crafty wench.

Not my fault, she countered. *You made me feel too good, Mr. Danewell.*

A determined snort. *We shall see who feels too bloody good by the end of this eve.*

Is that a promise?

'Tis a fact. Especially if my instinct proves correct.

Instinct of what?

Of Davis Webber himself leading your standing ovation.

Gabriela laughed and yanked him through one more whirling spin.

Now she was ready.

And as she shouted that back to Louis in a high, strong voice, she knew she'd never meant anything more in her life.

Or felt more alive.

So this is what it felt like to be alive.

Marcus contemplated that conclusion as he hurried along the final stretch of the private hall to his box, the velvet of mum's handmade finery rustling in time to the echoing pounds of his polished boots. So this was what it all meant . . . this was real emotion, manifested in real physical reactions.

Spiraling into other, very real sensations he had absolutely no control over.

His steps corresponded to Gabriela's own as she moved through the stage wings to await her cue. Every pace dipped him into alternating vats of hot and cold anticipation. His chest resonated with the escalating pound of her heartbeat—and strengthened his certainty that the entire house heard the trouncing of his own. His sights and his attention followed the narrowing focus of hers: toward the scene the stagehands now pumped over with a fine "Denmark mist" as the curtain rose, the audience stilled, and another Drury Lane production began its opening performance.

And a swift blade of anxiety sliced off the air from his lungs to his throat.

Aye, this was it. His Christmas Day, his World Exhibition. The state of being alive. The experience he'd waited several lifetimes to know again.

Not surprisingly, Marcus found himself seriously questioning the worth of that wait.

Yet he had just slipped into his box and dropped gratefully into the back seat when her tiny, but joyous whisper wafted through his head: *Marcus . . . oh Marcus, isn't this exciting?*

Exciting. If one considered the transformation of their gut into a wad heavy as a coal lump and appetizing as the pit it came from . . . oh aye, then, definitely exciting.

He made a quick mental note to avoid all future contact with "exciting."

He adhered to that contract, as well—for a whole quarter of an hour. He adhered all the way up until the moment Gabriela appeared on stage.

Then lightning struck his world.

Her performance transcended their expectations. She

knew it, as well. He felt her exhilaration grow as the scene progressed, felt her drawing on the memory of the special union he had given her in the dressing room before the show. He also felt her seeking the remembrances he had shared their eve in St. James's Park, using the images to transport herself back to courts replete with Hamlets, Horatios, Claudiuses, Gertrudes . . . and ethereal, entrancing, tragic young heroines named Ophelia.

Entrancing. Indeed, he selected the ideal term there, if the audience's assessment bore at all on the issue. When Gabriela exited from her sole scene in the first act, seeming to float through her steps as she did, a rare wave of spirited applause broke out to follow her.

Marcus did not watch the act after that. He leaned back in his seat, closed his eyes and let a wide smile spread as he raced back to her dressing room with her, accepted the accolades along the way with her, pressed amazed hands to joy-flushed cheeks with her.

And let his heart fill with the breathless, beautiful words from her: *Thank you, my love. Thank you.*

Her lengthy scene in Act Two elicited the same crowd response, resulting in an intermission full of more backstage cheers and adulation.

"You're so beautiful!" three ballet chits chorused.

"You're so *good,*" Donna seethed good-naturedly.

"Will Shakespeare himself couldn't have played it better," Louis stuck his head in to murmur with pride.

Yet all ended their tributes with the same bewildered tilt of head and intent phrasing of question:

How in the world did you do it?

To which Marcus and Gabriela only shared a soft, secret smile in answer.

A crowd-hypnotizing version of that smile accompanied her entrance into Act Three—but beneath her poised angle of chin and flowing ease of expression, an artist's unsure psyche still reached out for him, pleaded to him for the ongoing surety of his presence. Here marked what many deemed the true start of an Ophelia's test of mettle. This scene not only followed the famous "to be or not to be" sequence, but revolved solely around Hamlet, Ophelia and a bordello's worth of double meanings. Subtlety was essential; timing, critical.

Yet Gabriela had no stage full of other performers to render meaningful reactions or offer forgotten lines. No dramatic shouts, drawn swords, or moving scenery were written in to dilute the audience's scrutiny, either. She had to trust only her instinct, her talent and her heart—and, God willing, the equal portions of each in the Hamlet across the stage.

But Marcus had no worry of that. He had bloody near commanded Augustus to award the production's lead to Sean Smithton, a young actor he had accidentally happened over while brooding along the south bank in January. Marcus had hardly dressed against the cold that night, hoping to clear both body and mind of a sable-haired angel who, at the time, had no idea he existed. Upon ducking into the Vic music house for a respite of warmth, he found poor Sean playing a highly forgettable role to a highly unappreciative mob—with a dedication and passion Marcus recognized as highly *un*forgettable. He would be, Marcus, determined then, their perfect Hamlet, whether an unknown or not.

He would also compliment Gabriela like fine velvet beneath a silken rose.

Marcus smiled while deeming himself resoundingly right on both counts. Then he leaned forward, hands braced to knees and sights riveted to the stage, to absorb every moment of Gabriela's conclusive victory over tonight's crowd.

She stepped to her place center stage as Sean temporarily disappeared into the wings—another "renovation" to Will's original script, Marcus noted dryly. According to

Augustus, the new blocking moves maintained longer audience interest by keeping the action on stage constant, and also allowed Sean to add a black poncho cape to his costume, guaranteed to make him the chief subject of tea salon swoons by tomorrow afternoon. Marcus had to confess, a sliver of his anticipation owed itself to finally seeing this renowned cape.

But even after a notable pause, neither Sean nor the cape reappeared.

A puzzled murmur rippled through the crowd.

A small furrow cut between Gabriela's brows. She smoothed it over just as quickly. So there *was* a backstage snag . . . yet Marcus discerned naught a flutter of panic from her. She merely turned a page in the "poetry book" she held, acted out an amused laugh at something she "read," and executed a winsome pirouette, enough to show the women her grace and the men, her legs.

The audience murmured again—in approval.

Sean still did not reenter.

A deeper furrow twitched her brows.

A heavy thunk sounded from the wings.

The audience jumped.

Gabriela did, too. She pressed an instinctive hand to her chest, darted a surreptitious glance toward his box. *Marcus,* came her mind's urgent whisper, *this isn't right.*

Ssshhh, he soothed her. *I am here. And you have been through worse than this. It is likely Sean fumbling with that bloody cape.*

I know, but—

Keep moving. Keep thinking.

But in that instant, she ceased to move. She ceased to think. As her gaze turned back to the wings, her mind snapped off from him like one of the winter morning icicles that fell from Drury's eaves.

Marcus lurched forward, physically shadowing his mental lunge to jerk her back, but he indeed might as well have tried for an icicle. Everywhere he tried to enter her senses, only bone-chilling cold met his effort. Only one sound echoed in his ears: the pound of her heart, as overwhelming as a glacier, as merciless as a hail storm.

And then, it gripped him, too—this feeling turning her into a pale, swaying ice sculpture before his eyes.

She was consumed with terror.

Gabriela, Talk to me. What is it, sweeting? What the hell is it?

In response, the frozen shell of a woman on stage only shivered once. From head to toe. Very hard. Very violently.

Just before Alfonso Renard emerged into the gaslight, dressed in Sean's costume.

Sixteen

The book slipped from Gabriela's hand. Crashed to the stage. The impact resounded in her head as if she'd dropped a block of iron, instead.

But the collision never neared the slab of shock Alfonso wielded. The echo following the drop, a swift and sharp sound across the blackened house, barely registered against the clank of the shackles he clapped around her heart, her mind, her limbs. In two seconds, he rendered her a motionless prisoner where she stood, chained by the lead-black malice in his eyes and the steel-stiff menace in his stance.

Locking everything from her mind but the certainty he'd come back to Drury for only one thing.

And the surety that this time, he didn't plan to let his prize go.

As one fist coiled harder at his side—the fist consisting of soiled bandages and only three quaking fingers—Gabriela wondered if he planned to let his prize *live*.

"Oh, God," she heard her parched lips rasp. "Oh, God. God help me."

And someone else. She should be calling for someone else, too . . . someone who helped God . . . one of his angels? Yes, yes, her guardian angel . . . but oh God, what was his name? God help her, what was his name?

Her brain clawed at the wall of amnesia in vain. Alfonso

choked her memory tighter with his ever-darkening gaze.
He murdered her last lucid thoughts with the force of his
grimace, his stubbled jaw spasming around a scowl of
sweaty lips and seething teeth. He took slow, measured
wheezes of breaths from nostrils distended far past their
aquiline familiarity.

This had to be a nightmare. Please God, this was only
a nightmare, and she'd awake in a moment, safely ensconced in that place where night protected all and she
slept in the strong, sure arms of an angel. . . .

What was his name?

She didn't remember. And she didn't wake up. She knew
that fact because then, the nightmare truly began.

Alfonso stepped toward her.

Gabriela didn't move.

Couldn't move.

Couldn't speak. Couldn't cry out. Couldn't breathe.

And in half a minute, he'd loom over her again. He'd
yank at his trousers again, call her those vile names again,
and the whole world would play witness to her degrada-
tion. Then the lamps would turn back up and the world
would rise, murmuring things like, "Thought she had such
a future," and "Who'd have guessed; a whore behind that
sincere face?" before they moved on to more pleasant subjects over their soufflés at the Berkeley.

*No. No! You won't do this to me! Please . . . please, Alfonso,
you can't do this to me!*

But her heart's scream and her crumbling composure
only garnered a grin on Alfonso's contorted features. The
sneer started at his lower left lip, edged upward in tiny
twitches until it prompted him to continue his cocksure
advance, suede-booted feet thudding the floorboards, glit-
tering coal stare taking in her body in increasingly savage
sweeps.

Until some unseen entity suddenly snapped that stare
wide. Then commanded him to lower those unblinking

sights to the floorboards. A second force slammed him to such a hard stop, he stumbled and nearly fell over his feet; a move she hadn't seen since the age of twelve, when Parson Reeves caught Billy Babcock in the girl's dormitory in nothing but his underdrawers. Also following Billy's lead, Alfonso's smirking lips plummeted into whispers of something between the Lord's Prayer and an order at himself to wake up from this aberration of a dream.

Through the ensuing pause, thick and taut, Gabriela just concentrated on maintaining her own stance. Gratitude razed her like lightning through a tree, tempting her to topple like a sundered limb, as well. *Thank you, God. And thank you, thank you, my nameless, fearless angel.*

Only after Alfonso began to back toward the wings again, as flimsy and powerless as a play puppet on a string, did she realize the lightning had nothing to do with gratitude.

The lightning. . . .

The lightning.

Marcus!

Here, inside her mind and her heart and her being once more.

Marcus!

She raced stunned sights toward the depths of the wings. Blinked past the mist of her tears and the flood of her joy. Her senses reached out for him. Her heart ached in its need for him.

And then she found him. She barely managed a shaking breath at the sight of him, a manifestation of the shadows themselves, towering and assured, dark and intent, one hand raised toward Alfonso with fingers extended in balletic perfection.

Watching him, Gabriela now discerned the pull of his hypnotic command over Alfonso, but that dim awareness comprised the limit of her own vulnerability to the force.

She still didn't move, marveling at Marcus's force of will, narrowing his power to only one mortal in this small space.

Especially the mortal he hadn't initiated. The mortal who didn't know the extent of the molten fury sluicing his veins and teeming through his sights. The mortal who didn't see past that rage, into his heart, and have to force back sobs at encountering the magnitude of his love for the trembling woman across the stage. The mortal who didn't have to relive the moment he'd watched, senses screaming with an outrage more violent than he'd ever known, as the embodiment of her nightmares advanced across the stage at her, before he'd confronted a terror of his own, dissolving himself into a mist for the first time, then streaking wild and wrath-filled toward a backstage corner where he materialized again, Sean Smithton's unconscious form his only witness. . . .

The mortal who'd never know the Herculean effort it took not to give London's elite a real murder on their playbill tonight.

Even now, Gabriela felt Marcus struggle against the sweet temptation of the deed. *You would naught even have to touch him,* she overheard his brain murmur to his heart. *Just one neat, neck-snapping flick of your wrist, Danewell . . . one flick, and the whoreson is done.*

At that, she saw his hand quaver, battling against the desire to finally, at last, use his dark curse to do the world some good. She saw a flash of savoring satisfaction in the stormy silver of his stare; that eruption corresponded to the spasm jerking through Alfonso, who indeed appeared, with wide white eyes and terrified grimace, like a man backing toward the gallows emblazoned with his name.

Even as Marcus pulled him the last two steps into the shadows, Gabriela fought for her own pleasureful glint of gaze, her own inner *hurrah* for justice finally befalling the true monster. She searched for her own gratified indifference to the snuffing of a very useless life.

But she only found the overwhelming urge to throw up. When she looked away, the floorboards spun a crazy tilt beneath her. Without the reservoir of Marcus's strength and belief, she was still as weak as a curbside lace girl. And thrice as helpless on this stage.

She stumbled and grabbed for a support, *any* support— her first movement in God knew how many minutes, though she supposed Davis Webber or any of his entourage in the first row could tell her the precise count. Lord, they murmured enough to each other about *something* in that blackness just beyond the stage's edge. A something, she concluded as she fell dizzily to the couch on center stage, definitely *not* related to her further consideration for the Prince's Grand Theatre Troupe ensemble.

"Damn," she whispered, licking tears off her lips as she bowed her head and waited for Louis to render the notice for a dropped curtain—and a ruined production. Fleetingly, she wondered if Sean might put in a word for her at that music hall on the south bank. . . .

"Damn," she rasped again. "Bloody, bloody damn."

"The fair Ophelia. Nymph, in thy orisons be all my sins remembered."

Gaby's breath caught along with the audience's. But she didn't look up. She didn't have to. Every inch of her tingled with the same summer storm magic as the first time Marcus had delivered her that line.

And, as the tingles dissipated out the ends of her enlivened toe and fingertips, one polished black boot shifted into her view, cocking its heel on the arm of the couch. Gaby tracked her gaze up an attached shin, then a powerful knee, where two magnificent forearms crossed with roguish ease. The limbs led to straight, epauleted shoulders, which blended to a high, velvet-doubleted chest, which was brushed by the feather curling out and down from a black, broad-rimmed hat. . . .

Which framed the night-hewn features of her own perfect, proud Hamlet.

The audience, it seemed, immediately agreed with that assessment. Approving murmurs rippled across the main floor and up through the boxes. As the sound swelled into a wave of warmth around them, Gabriela at last looked into his eyes—glowing, mesmeric eyes that washed her anew in his transcendent strength, his angel's love.

Marcus, she whispered to him from within. *You didn't kill him, did you?*

He only cocked his head with a scoundrel's infinite insolence and an actor's flawless timing—igniting a gust of female sighs across the audience. All that before he bestowed *her* with a private, affirming smile.

Marcus. God, how she wanted to touch him, right there along the carved, half-smirking edge of his jaw; how she wanted to kiss him, hold him, show him this constituted the greatest gift he'd ever given her. *Marcus, thank you.*

Madam, came his rejoinder at last, albeit in an irked mutter, *I know not who this 'Marcus' be. Prithee call me my Christian appellative, Hamlet of Denmark, if thee are to call me at all.*

He signed the statement with a flourish of movement, pushing from the couch and strutting downstage left with, indeed, all the self-conviction of a Danish prince. Of *any* prince.

No, Gabriela amended that perception as she ducked her head to hide a captivated smile, of *her* prince.

That same prince who now pointedly cleared his throat, pivoted back toward her with the grace of Taglioni yet the potency of Pitt, and delivered her cue line one more time. *The* last *time,* his over-enunciated tone commanded. *Ophelia, I refuse to further play with naught but myself before our company.*

She yearned to look back up to him and tilt her eyebrows

in a wordless expression of, *Danewell, you've gone truly bedlam this time.*

Instead, Gabriela raised her head—and heard her lips issue the line he awaited.

At least she thought so. The words seemed the syllables and inflections she'd relentlessly rehearsed the last six weeks—yet in an incredible, inexplicable way, they weren't. The sounds didn't erupt from her memory, but from her mind and her heart, impromptu words tripping off her tongue with fervency gained only from the sense she'd never spoken them before. As if she and this rogue didn't perform a scene, but simply carried forth a conversation with several hundred witnesses.

As if she were, indeed, an infatuated court maid called Ophelia.

The fantastical catch being, through the next superreal minutes, she *was*.

She knew she didn't imagine the phenomenon as she finished her sentence with a graceful rise from the couch—far more graceful than she'd proved capable even before last night's waltz with the mirror. Immediately, Gabriela snapped an amazed stare to the man across the stage. At first, her gaze took in the same outward vision as the audience: a Hamlet eyeing her like a demoness incarnate. But in her heart, her soul, her spirit . . .

He filled her. Surrounded her. Possessed her as none could or ever would, wrapping her in a big, velvet cloak of confidence and courage until nothing else existed but this, the world where only they lived, a prince and a maiden, yet also just a woman and a man, playing out shades of truth and conflicts of meaning as timeless as the Cheviots, as universal as the Proverbs.

And beyond. The magic went beyond even that exquisite fusion, connecting their very breaths and bodies, their thoughts, their actions. . . .

They'd never run any scene in the play together like

this, unstopping, combining both lines and actions, but no rehearsal took the place of the bond they knew, the completeness they shared. She saw every move of this man's body before he commenced it. As she delivered her lines, she already heard the inflection of his reply just by looking into his eyes.

Perfect balance. Sublime harmony. Symphony of words, ballet of souls. A strange, sweet duet, felt as one, played by two.

She only knew the beautiful enchantment had ended when his presence departed her in a sudden rush. From where she stood in the darkened wings, Gabriela let out a gasping protest, but his voice cut her short, echoing a loving whisper in her head. . . .

Later. Come to me upstairs. Later. We shall celebrate. I love you . . .

"Marcus!"

But she reached at thin air with the desperate whisper. *Marcus?* She lifted her sights—and the silent plea—to the rafters. *Marcus,* she beseeched, *celebrate what?*

He didn't respond. As a matter of fact, she sensed him stepping back, now completely pulling his cloak from her again. . . .

And allowing the lights of the next hour to shine and show her that answer, instead. The light of the house lamps turned up as she took her curtain call, their warmth only surpassed by the swell of applause and the audience's surge to its feet. Then the lights on the police wagon, their stark yellow glare completing the transformation of Alfonso into a full, snarling monster as a now-conscious Sean officially identified him, and they took him away.

At last, yet brighter than all that luminescence combined, there was the light from the crowd of smiles waiting in her dressing room—headed by a beaming Louis and a proud, even if a few degrees short of smiling himself, Augustus Harris.

"Ahhhh!" Augustus boomed to the satin and silk-clad contingent. "Here's our lovely little star now!"

Gaby stopped a step short from the threshold. Had someone knocked down a wall somewhere when she hadn't looked? Or had her box of a dressing room magically stretched to accommodate, technically, this small mob of strangers?

"Now don't be shy, Gabriela." Her producer urged. "Come in, come in."

Augustus bounded forward and curled her hand around his proffered arm. He wiggled his big brows in the same rhythm he used before informing casts he'd added a horse stampede to Act Three, or deleted a program interval to make room for a "simple" forty-person chorus number.

"I believe there's somebody here you've been waiting to meet," he pronounced mischievously.

Funny, Gaby pondered faintly, that she'd contemplated horse stampedes. Surely a thousand thoroughbreds galloped down her throat, across her heart, and through her belly as Augustus swept her into the midst of the throng—to a gentleman she somehow needed no introduction to. Like the waters making way for Moses, the crowd clearly deferred to this figure in fashionable cutaway evening coat, well-fitted trousers, and dashing white neck scarf, topped by the confident, chiseled features of a well-practiced ladies' man—and a well-respected leader of men.

Augustus cleared his throat with calculated drama before proclaiming, "Miss Rozina, it is my honor to present you to—"

"Davis Webber," Gaby blurted in a reverent rush. As the crowd reacted in a spatter of amused chuckles, she bit the inside of her cheek in embarrassment. "I . . . I mean, the honor is all mine, sir," she hurried on, wishing the room's secret wall panel had a companion in the floor to oblige her swift disappearance.

The guest of honor didn't seem to share the group's

mirth. For a long moment, Webber said nothing, as well. Then he held up just one finger.

The crowd fell silent.

As they did, Davis Webber cracked a very full, very white smile at her.

The intake of female breaths created a tangible vacuum in the room. Even Gaby found herself suddenly seeking some air. The man, and his perfect grin, were indeed a potent mix of command and charisma.

At last, he withdrew his upraised finger. The next moment, he lowered that hand directly to hers. In one eloquent move, he lifted her quavering knuckles to his sure lips. But his keen hazel eyes never left her face.

"Sir?" he finally said, his brow crunching into a bemused half-scowl. The effect should have looked odd, but instead, inspired another round of feminine suspirations. "Miss Rozina," he at last continued, "if we are to be working together for the next year, I suggest you start calling me Davis."

Then, Davis Webber winked at her.

And Gabriela's thread-thin nerves snapped into an enchanted smile.

The crowd broke into approving applause.

Augustus gave a whoop worthy of Cody's Wild West Show. Then, her producer actually swung her off the floor in an ecstatic embrace. Several dizzying spins later, Augustus plopped her back down while inviting the whole room to the Savoy for champagne, on him.

But Gabriela didn't want champagne. She didn't *need* champagne. Her head fizzed with joyous bubbles already; the world swam in a haze of delirious disbelief as she and Mr. Webber——*Davis,* he reminded her with a mock scowl—— agreed to an appointment for her first read-through and costume fitting, six weeks hence, when *Hamlet* finished its run and she'd be officially free to sign with the Prince's Grand Theatre Troupe.

The Prince's Grand Theatre Troupe . . .

She whispered the words several times over, slowly and disbelievingly, after the colorful contingent left her alone to change. The Prince's Grand Theatre Troupe . . . **The** Prince's Grand Theatre Troupe . . .

"I'm dreaming," she decided in a murmur, hugging her dressing robe beneath her chin. "I must, oh I *must* be dreaming."

But when she dropped into her chair and gazed into the tabletop mirror, the reflection in the glass gaped back with eyes of real enough sienna shock, flecked with real gold incredulity. When she pressed tremoring palms to both of her flushed cheeks, her skin emanated an inferno of real exhilaration.

And when she glanced to her dressing table again, a solitary calling card still answered her stare, in real, gilt-trimmed lettering:

> *Davis Webber*
> *Creative Director, Co-Producer,*
> *Prince's Grand Theatre Troupe*
> *Headquarters: West End*

No, she wasn't dreaming.

Just drunk.

Drunk with happiness. Intoxicated with triumph. Inebriated with victory.

She did *not* need champagne.

She only needed Marcus.

Augustus would just have to understand. *So sorry, Mr. Harris, but the headache came on so suddenly. You understand; the strain of the performance and the pressure of the situation . . . a doctor? . . . oh, no, just a good night's sleep and I'll be fine . . . yes, thank you; thank you for your consideration. . . .*

Then a short climb, and she'd reunite with her love.

Together, basking in their glory. Together, knowing their triumph.

Together . . . simply together.

Was it possible they could banish hell with the sweetness of such a heaven?

She couldn't wait to find out.

She couldn't wait to get out of here.

Marcus couldn't wait to get out of there.

He didn't bother to light any candles other than the single taper he carried, moving across the underground chamber in a tiny circle of flickering light. He required naught else to collect the pail of dirt from beneath his coffin, then be gone. . . .

For when his next sleep came, he vowed, he would welcome it upon white perfumed sheets, draped around the woman he loved. The soil, a necessity dictated by too much folklore to disregard, was the last element he needed. Long ago, he had assured the apartment's wood shutters served more than decorative fancy, in case any unforseen accident led him to sunrise a near half-mile away from his usual resting place: aye, the coffin, presented to him by a rather penitent Raquelle (as penitent as the woman would ever be) on the first anniversary of his transformation.

Marcus had kept and slept in the monstrosity for self-punishment more than comfort. Raquelle had *not* been amused. She never came back to see him. It seemed all clouds had their silver linings, after all.

But from tonight forward, coffins had no place in his life. He no longer wallowed in darkness or cowered in subterranean seclusion. To do so would sentence Gabriela to the same lot, for asking her not to follow him down here would prove useless as exiling Juliet from her balcony, as ordering the Lady of the Lake to simply toss forth Excalibur. And claim as she did to love this cavern, *his* lady deserved more than stone walls for inspiration and water beetles for company—over and above the countless infections waiting to seize her from the chamber's cold, moist air.

Marcus crouched to the ground, but paused before scooping the pail into the dirt. A self-deprecating grin touched his lips. So the unbelievable had come to pass. Oh aye, despite the vehement campaign he had waged otherwise, despite his furious fears and his most terrifying apprehensions, the remarkable little wench had finally gotten her way. Gabriela Angelica Rozina, damn and bless her beautiful hide at once, had bound herself to him, irrevocably worked herself inside of him. Conquered his mind, consumed his heart.

Become the center of his life.

Their life.

Their life . . . In strength, in weakness. In happiness, in sorrow. In sickness, in health . . .

Until death do them part.

Marcus lurched back to his feet.

His labored swallow took on a supernatural echo in his head, muffling the sharp *ding* of his boot against the pail, the *dong dong dong* of the container tumbling across the hard dirt and finally against a black-shrouded wall.

A blackness as impenetrable as death.

Nay.

He willed his brain to repeat the command as he grabbed the candle and, at an impatient pace, pursued the bucket. Death had *no* reserved solo on tonight's program—and the bastard would have to wait a while for a slot, as well. Another fifty or sixty years, to calculate it precisely.

Until then, Marcus vowed, he would make Gabriela Rozina the happiest, most well-loved woman on—

"Marcus? Marcus, is that you?"

The slow, rasping voice came from everywhere, yet nowhere—insinuating itself through his limbs with the same pervading, terrifying intimacy. The sound seized him so swiftly, Marcus froze where he was. His right foot hung in midair, three-inches from the stride he had yet to complete.

Yet faced with the option of maintaining that excruciating pose, or acknowledging that voice—dear God, that voice, why was it so hauntingly, harrowingly familiar?—he would learn to live with the pain of being a breathing statue until dawn.

The voice, to his expectation, to his dread, had other plans. "Marcus . . ." Again, the sound whispered all around him. Again, a cold presence slithered inside his mind. Desperate as grief. Cold as the grave.

"Marcus . . . over here."

And like a horse forced to follow its tether, he wheeled to the left, toward the alcove where Joseph left off his deliveries. Oddly, Marcus's racing gaze welcomed the candle's irradiation of the carved wood beams surrounding the space, the damp gray walls, even the massive stone slab, with its stains of old and new blood. An expected sight; nothing unusual. Everything in its place.

Nothing that had *spoken* to him before.

A delusion, he decided. After all, tonight had measured far from a normal eve, *and* it was far from over. His senses still reeled with the newness of initiation, not to mention his first-time expedition in mist form. Three minutes after rematerializing, he'd had to hypnotize Renard in front of a sold-out house, *then* perform the last three acts of *Hamlet* from memory. . . .

Phantom whispers, he concluded, were the *simplest* challenge this nightfall had hurled at him so far.

Marcus eased out a long, even breath. Then turned to hunt down his bucket once more.

Just as a small, ghostly white figure shuffled into the corner of his sights.

He swung back around—and recoiled just as swiftly. But
the decaying, decrepit . . . *thing* advanced another step toward him; another. Then the specter reached to him with
bony white arms that poked from limp drapes of what used
to be, as far as he could fathom, an ornate crimson ball
gown. With each of those slow slides forward, slivers of
that unreal skin peeled loose, swirling to the ground like
snowflakes in a child's winter fantasy globe.

Only when *these* flurries met the ground, they melted
not to slush.

They dissolved into ash.

For an unblinking minute, Marcus only stared at the
mounting pile of soot at the thing's feet, likening himself
to every pathetic killcow who stopped to watch the
wounded taken from carriage accident sites. Revolted, yet
riveted, he searched for lucid thoughts, but found only
paralyzed shock—scrambled for the strength to glance
away, but realized he could not feel his body beyond his
neck.

Still, he heard his feet grind the ground in a desperate
bid for escape from the agonizingly familiar wraith.

The wraith only laughed.

A dark, deep, throaty laugh.

And in that moment, halting his retreat, freezing his
blood, comprehension invaded. Catapulted him more
than two hundred and fifty years into the past. Threw him
upon a cold stone slab and lashed him there, helpless,
lifeless—only one savage word slicing past his clenched jaw
and hate-twisted lips.

"Raquelle."

Seventeen

Something inside Marcus still prayed imagination had merely bested him. Surely he'd identified the wrong vampire. Nay, better yet, nothing truly stood there before him—a blink, and the apparition would disappear. . . .

She shattered that hope with an ironically serene lift of her head. A pair of eyes glowed out at him: pupils drenched of pure blood red, upon fields of gray no more alive than graveyard fog.

But between those two realms, a third, thin ring of color entrapped Marcus's stare—and gored his soul with sick, sure recognition. The color was violet. The most fathomless, unforgettable shade he had known. The violet of royal velvet. Of wizard's crystals.

Of fatal seduction.

"Marcus," she said once more—a valiant attempt at the purr that had once turned him hard as stone in seconds. She also tried to smile, but the brown, broken-toothed result never neared the look that captivated him across a Whitehall ballroom, so long ago. "Darling, dearest Marcus. How are you, love?"

With a flood of relief, he found himself capable of movement again. He dropped the candle, spun to the coffin and braced both hands to the lowered lid. "I am *not* your love," he seethed.

A torturously familiar cluck of tongue came softly behind him. "Well," she returned breezily. "Whatever you wish, crabapple."

Finally, fiercely, he managed to force out, "What the hell do you want, Raquelle?"

Even at their present stances, he damn near saw the sultry pout she affected then. That perception almost induced him to an ironic laugh. Some things never did change. Especially court harlots.

"What the hell do you want?" she answered by way of mimicking his growl. "Oh, Marcus. Tsk, tsk, tsk. After all this time, I have bothered to come see you; after all these years, I have taken this time, and the only amenity you afford me is 'what the hell do you want?' "

This time, he *did* indulge the laugh—a harsh, humorless grunt. "Sorry," he snarled, kneading the black-lacquered wood in order to camouflage the shaking of his hands. "The butler has the night off."

Raquelle actually began an obligatory chuckle—which swiftly deteriorated into a hacking choke. She did not stop for several minutes. And Marcus did not move. He shut his eyes and battled to cut off his senses from the pathetic sounds—strained to tell himself the sight of her, the decaying reek of her, the wheezing weakness of her meant nothing to him. Not a shred of concern or a twinge of pity. And certainly did not terrify every bone and muscle in his body.

His body, so like hers.

His mind rebelled at the thought with a silent scream. His soul recoiled with less restraint, its hiss exploding past his compressed lips.

Then his body ran with every supernatural drop of strength it possessed.

He clawed around the coffin's edge and used its weight to slingshot himself across the chamber, toward the door. Toward Gabriela. Toward sweet forgetfulness of this night mare, of this demoness who had haunted him so long, *too long*—

But the demoness had saved her own stores of immortal strength. As Marcus lunged for the door, a hand of five fingers suddenly whipped into his way—nay, talons more than fingers—and snagged his doublet in a quivering death grip.

A death grip. He had another hysterical urge to laugh. And weep.

But when Raquelle spoke again, she shocked him from doing either.

"Marcus." Jesu. He had never heard the woman plead before, much less in this suddenly desperate rasp. The word came in two jagged breaths set in time to her frantic scrabblings over his chest, struggling for purchase as her depleted limbs refused to hold her aright much longer. "Marcus . . . please help me, Marcus . . . I need you!"

Still, sympathy remained a distant stranger. "Nonsense, darling." He avenged her earlier taunt by drawling the words with classic Raquelle sensuality. "You have needed naught a thing since the eve we met."

"Please," she persisted. "Marcus . . . Marcus, I have not fed in two weeks—"

"Truly? I nay noticed."

"Marcus . . . Marcus, damn you, *look* at me! Please . . . help me!"

Despite every protesting cell in his being, he did look. Perhaps *because* of those rioting voices. Perhaps because he *was* a pathetic killcow.

Perhaps because he had secretly yearned for this moment for more than two hundred and fifty years.

But as his gaze met the desperate red stare as he took in the strands of mossy hair drooping over the once-proud forehead, the viscid skin hanging upon the once-carved cheekbones, the unmitigated fear in features once stamped with naught but knowing sensuality, Marcus

basked in no flood of righteous triumph. He received no
jolt of joyous revenge. He felt no elation, nor hate, nor
even pity.

He felt nothing.

"Damn you," Raquelle croaked, actually attempting an
ecclesiastical tone of her own for the cause now. "Damn
you, you have no right to stand there in Peter's judgment
upon me!"

Correction: he felt *one* thing. Disgust, perhaps tinted with
a hue of disbelief, as he pried her loose, shoved her against
the coffin and wiped his hands down his thighs as he backed
away, ridding his skin of her scales and her stench.

"I have no right?" he repeated with slow, almost surprising softness. "Darling, that line is more creamy rich than
the thighs you once spread for half of England."

"Bastard!" she screeched. "Our accounts are nay settled, Marcus. You are *mine*. Damn you, damn you, I made
you what you are!"

His fingers curled at his sides. His pulse throbbed an
agonizing tattoo in his jaw. "Worry none, lady," he returned in a pitch as black, bleak, and depthless as the labyrinth of grottoes around them. "I have not forgotten."

Raquelle only slumped against the coffin and rolled her
eyes. "Oh, spare me your noble martyr trattle, Sir Danewell. And take that high priest's glower with it."

A dark, damp silence fell. They both said nothing, until
Raquelle decided her line merited an ironic giggle. Despite the effort it clearly took her to *breathe*, she succumbed
to the outburst—and the resulting attack of wheezes.

Then, once more lifting her head with enough regality
to turn Good Bess blonde with envy: "I have a little piece
of news for you, darling. You were a pitifully easy duck that
eve. Dearest Marcus, you craved immortality more than all
the other dullards in Whitehall put together. 'Twas written
on your face, more blatant than a *baudstrot*'s smirk."

Now she cocked that head a fraction to the right, her

smile inching a calculated degree higher. "You saw the dream without even knowing you saw it, Marcus. You simply required a little . . . guidance to aid your perceptions."

For another extended moment, Marcus nay answered her—this time, not for lack of wanting. His voice engaged in mortal battle against the bayonets of bitterness stabbing his throat.

"Guidance," he finally managed, again with shocking, deceiving calm. "So that is how you phrased it." He adopted a steeled version of her head-tilted pose. "Such a fascinating way of saying you murdered me."

He should have expected the witch's reaction. Should have known Raquelle would find his tragedy the best entertainment she had known in years, judging from the delighted scream of laughter she threw back her head to send echoing into the night.

He should have expected it—but he had not. And that threw him into a deeper morass of enfuried vexation. And *that* rendered him impotent of much else but standing there, senses roiling, fists quivering, while this creature, even three steps from collapsing with starvation, finished degrading him once again.

Finally, Raquelle's thinning lungs reduced her mirth to a handful of titters, then a spatter of giggles . . . then a collection of labored, perhaps even frightened, breaths.

Then she inclined her gaze to him again.

And true confusion assaulted him. Marcus didn't know what to feel or how to react to the startling sobriety now infiltrating those rings of violet still confirming her humanity. Rings growing thinner by the minute—yet drawing him more powerfully than they ever had beneath Whitehall's chandeliers.

"Murder, my love," Raquelle began in an equally unsettling rasp, frail as chandelier glass, thin as gaslamp smoke, "would have been to leave you in that cave after I had finished, rotting to your death. Lud only knew *you* were not jumping to help yourself."

She tried to shake her head—or perhaps nod it. Marcus could nay tell. Her body began a grand effort to keep up with her quivering voice. "I . . . I cared for you, Marcus," she confessed in an even softer sibilance. "Whether you believe me or nay, I thought I gave you what you truly desired."

Marcus only inhaled an unsteady breath of his own. She was right. He did not believe her. Oh, her performance was exemplary—but her performance was precisely that. An exterior display, as easily donned as costume and makeup, as effortlessly shed.

And yet, unignorable truth also spoke through her monologue. Raquelle had, indeed, kept him alive through those first horrifying weeks. Another perverse twist of nature, he remembered thinking with black revulsion as she would saunter back into the cave every other night, proudly dragging her kill, laying the pitiful heap before his hunger-racked body with a queen-of-the-beasts smile.

Queen of how many beasts, just like him?

But he had long stopped caring about the answer to that. At this moment, only one resolution made any sense about his interminable existence.

He had lived to know Gabriela. To know the light of her smiles, the healing of her touch, the brief, blissful sanity of her love.

And for that miracle, his gut forced him to concede one more veracity to Raquelle.

Their accounts truly had not been settled.

The winch in his gut stretched into his chest. Still, he willed himself to turn, find the candle where it still flickered on the ground, then carry it with him to the alcove housing his desk. Subterranean wind heeded the night's heightening call, throwing the flame glow into wild white and yellow patterns across the paper which accepted his

hastily-scrawled missive. Without waiting for the ink to fully
dry, he folded the note in thirds, scrawled the words,
"Joseph Berger, St. Thomas's Hospital Morgue" across
one side, then sealed the flap with a wax seal imprinted
with a single, distinct "D."

"Get into the coffin and rest yourself, Raquelle," he said
wearily as he released the weight to slide open Joseph's
delivery door. "You shall feel yourself again soon." *God
help us all.*

He thought she actually wept in thanks. He'd never be
certain, for he barely heard her overacted soliloquy of
gratitude beyond, "Oh, Marcus; Marcus, you *angel!*"

From there, his mind surrendered to a thickening, buzzing roar, eclipsing all else as he sank back into the chair
at the desk. He dropped his head into the clawed cradle
of his hands, and fed the echoes of her adoration to that
roar—not surprised when the mixture exploded past his
lips into something between a lunatic sob . . . and a self-
contemptuous snarl.

Angel. *Angel.* How long had he dreamed to hear himself
called that, just one time, only to experience his triumph
in the ravings of a half-dead demon? Strange, he thought
on another hard snort, that someone had nay thought to
endow dear old Will with this supernatural permanence.
Marcus envisioned the playwright wielding his quill in glee
at the exquisite poetic irony of this eve.

As his heart swallowed that hemlock of comprehension
in bitter gulps, his fingers dug harder and harder against
his skull—longing to rip out the nerves and blood and
tissues of the brain now agonizingly capable of such sensation . . . of such pain.

The pain you knew damn well to expect, Danewell, came that
relentlessly cold voice from those same twisting depths.
*The price you readily agreed upon when you returned that first
beautiful kiss, when you knew Gabriela's first sweet embrace. The*

contract you signed the moment you reached for the gold . . . for the joy.

The joy. *Aye, aye,* he fought back, *remember the joy. Remember the brief, blissful madness of touching mortality again; remember the fear, the fulfillment . . .*

And the deep, secret seed of hope . . .

Oh Jesu, the hope.

The hope of one day gazing into Gabriela's eyes, and seeing the reflection of an angel.

His throat vibrated with another long, tortured growl. *Who the hell are you gulling, Danewell? You are no angel. You will not ever be.*

He was the same kind of monster he watched spring from the coffin the moment Joseph arrived with the new delivery. The same kind of beast that raced to the stone slab with an intensity he had nay witnessed but once: in a tiger in India, on a feeding frenzy. Ah, God, he was the same kind of creature that feverishly ripped open the dingy sack Joseph had dumped there; in the same sweep of movement, sinking her teeth into the corpse's chest with a mindless sob of satisfaction.

He was a being doomed to continue his life by draining it from others. Unnatural. Unholy. Undead.

Undead.

He lurched to his feet and spun from the alcove, where the candle shadows cavorted a taunting heathen dance in time to that word, resounding and unrelenting, inside his head. *Undead . . . undead . . .* But the action only beat the phrase into louder refrain as Marcus discovered himself three steps from the alcove where a head rose, no longer covered with haggish strands, but a queen's thick ebony mane. *Undead . . . undead . . .*

And the persecution continued, stronger, faster, as Raquelle raised sights to him once again, her satiated smile dripping one crimson drop, which she dabbed away with a long-nailed finger. Refilled and renewed, she now stood barely covered by the ravages of the ruby gown, abundant breasts and sleek-rounded hips snagging the material in places to bring Jim Naylor himself to a gawking halt.

But Marcus only saw a monster.

A monster he had helped recreate.

And all he heard, dimly breaking through the tormenting chorus in his senses, was that cold and wretched inner voice, whispering a piercingly grotesque truth:

It was easy, aye, Danewell? So pathetically, mindlessly easy . . .

He ground his teeth and clenched his hands until they ached, resisting the words he felt coming next—the conclusion he did not, would not, hear. . . .

And consider what fortunate practice this has given you. If it was so easy to help the witch you loathe with all the bile in your gut, how much easier will it be to transform Gabriela?

His fists began to shake. His throat filled with cold lead. His head filled with seething silver.

Why, 'twill be naught effort at all. 'Twill be nothing to grant her passionate pleas for eternity . . . mayhap tonight, while you are making love to her. One simple act, and it will be done. One painless bite, and she'll be your own little vampiress, forever.

You see, Danewell, you are *capable of being a good monster.*

At that, his monster's roar conceded no longer to the shackles of his chest. The sound ripped up his throat and across the chamber, screaming its raw, unearthly torment into every crack and corner as he wheeled from Raquelle, dizzy and desperate . . .

And damned.

Damned to do what he should have that first moment Gabriela looked upon him, even then, beginning to love him—and with her watery smile, instantly sealing his love for her . . .

Their love . . . the greatest and only gift life had allowed him to unwrap.

Their love . . . just the memories of the precious joy trumpeted his senses in songs of heaven's own choir.

Their love . . . the only light he would carry back with him to damnation's depthless abyss.

Alone. Again. Forever.

Eighteen

Gabriela wondered why Marcus started when she sneaked up to the doorway of the apartment's bedroom and greeted him a quiet, "Hello, my prince." But the thought went quickly canceled by the awareness she'd never seen the man jump like that—another unexpected glimpse of a daydreaming Elizabethan lad.

The effect, she decided, was adorable. Unable to resist any longer, she slid up behind where he stood next to the bed, circling arms around his lean waist, reveling in the rich feel of embroidered velvet beneath her fingers. He didn't return her caress, but his indrawn breath and tightening muscles bespoke his reaction clearer than a Samuel Phelps monologue.

"I'm sorry I took a while," she said softly, readily acceding to the tranquillity between them—a sweet calm after the pellmell storm of tonight's events. "I tried to sneak away after changing, but Louis found out my game before I reached the greenroom door."

She smiled then, and flattened her hands against his stomach. An image of the muscled ridges beneath slid easily, sensually into her mind. "I told him I had an imperative assignation to keep with his boss," she continued, the smile now sneaking into her voice, "but he didn't believe a word. So I talked *them* into a compromise: one glass of champagne in Louis's office."

Now that she pondered it, the libation *had* been nice. The bubbles still tingled up her spine, danced through her limbs—and emboldened her fingers to explore lower as she ventured on a lingering murmur, "Did you miss me?"

She felt Marcus's deep swallow. Heard him attempt a measured breath—which emerged more a faltering sigh—before answering lowly, "I shall always miss you when you are nay near."

"Mmmmm," she returned, snuggling her cheek against the firm plane between his shoulder blades. "That's good." A fraction of a frown interrupted her reverie. "For a moment, I thought you were . . . well . . . afraid to see me."

"Nay," he countered with odd, incongruous speed—almost with eager haste—as he shifted to reach for something on the bed. "Nay, just busy."

"With what?" Gabriela popped up on tiptoes, trying to see over his shoulder. She gave herself a giggling beratement at that impossibility; her brow barely cleared his nape. Instead, she decided to swing around him, deciding he should make himself "busy" with *her*.

She caught herself inches short of joining the tumble of articles stuffed inside a large leather satchel lying on the counterpane. First, she noted several books, including his beloved leatherbound *Hamlet* and the volume of Middleton comedies he'd reenacted for her at least three times—in the nude. Peeking from beneath those was a ribbon-tied stack of letters from her, as well as several pieces of official-looking correspondence. And after that . . .

She frowned. The bottom of the heap looked a twist of every shirt, waistcoat, or other piece of fashion history he'd accidentally left behind up here. She knew the articles because she'd been lovingly compiling them in the bureau's upper left drawer . . . which, she now observed, lay open and empty.

And then, stuffed against the side of the satchel, she saw the picture.

It was a framed likeness of *her*, sketched by the Drury artist countless months ago . . . months before Marcus had even come to her. Augustus had commissioned the small portrait to be part of the publicity posters for the city squares and the theater lobby, demanding she be made to look like "Galatea herself come back to life." Gaby never knew if the result, indeed an eye-capturing swirl of mountain greens and autumn coppers to match her wood nymph's costume and her rather exaggerated fall of hair, fulfilled the man's requirements—but she did remember Augustus's tantrum when Alfonso offered an exorbitant price for the painting, and the objet d'art turned up missing.

She also remembered raising her eyes and thanking heaven for the anonymous culprit.

Now, she raised her eyes and directed a puzzled stare at that culprit.

As she pulled the portrait out, she swallowed against an oddly forbidding cramp in her stomach. She had to force steady modulation over the syllables of her soft question. "Marcus . . . what is this?"

He shrugged at her. *Shrugged,* as loose-limbed as a dandy on the town—but thereby exposing his growing tension clearer than any locked jaw or stiffened spine he'd ever cast at her. Gabriela didn't know what in the world to fathom of the gesture. She didn't know what to fathom of *all* his sudden idiosyncrasies.

"You find me guilty as charged, madam," he at last answered, shrugging again. "I took the portrait the day after I saw your first dress rehearsal. I could nay stomach the thought of Renard possessing—"

"I don't *care* about the portrait." She leveled the assertion at the same moment she comprehended it. She shook her head, hoping the action yielded more such clarities of thought, but instead found herself floundering through a murk of confusion as she stuffed the painting back into the satchel.

"Take the portrait," Gaby told him softly. "I'm *glad* you have the portrait. But . . ." her fingers traced the embroidered black fleur-de-lis centered on a cravat showing yellowed signs of its one hundred years, "but all of your things . . . why are you taking all of your things . . . Marcus?" She shook her head again, trying to discern why her heart suddenly thudded in her throat. "Marcus?" she asked again, looking to him. . . .

To find his gaze rapidly averted. *Purposely* averted.

He shoved the portrait deeper into the satchel. Then, after a deep and measured breath, "I . . . I must go away for a while, Gabriela."

"Away?" She sounded like a bad soprano with laryngitis. She sounded lost, little, and desperate. She sounded . . .

The way she prayed she'd never sound.

"What do you mean, away?" And jealous. She sounded jealous, and afraid, and stupid. But she couldn't stop, struggling to reconcile the words heard by her brain with the promise he'd given her heart . . . the words of just an hour ago . . . hadn't he said? . . .

"But you said to meet you here. You said we'd celebrate. You said it inside my mind, Marcus . . ." *Inside my heart.*

At that, a surge of renewed hope rushed the channels of her senses. *Of course—in my heart. In my heart . . .*

She reached the words out to him, throwing back the shutters on her spirit to prepare for the blinding flood of his. Surely once their souls reinitiated to each other, he'd cease this terrifying talk of just leaving, just like that. Because, well, he just couldn't do that. They were bonded. They were one. *It's my turn now to belong, Parson Reeves . . . it's my turn to be loved. I've been a good girl, and my angel at last has come, and you can't take him from me. I won't let you take him from me!*

Marcus . . . Angel . . . can't you hear me?
Her heart's outcry only disappeared into blackness.
No, not even blackness.
His psyche answered hers with absolutely nothing.
To her spirit's outstretched arms: empty, inexplicable silence. To her fervent, searching stare, Marcus didn't turn once. As a matter of fact, he only moved to shift from foot to foot as he turned a longing look at the door.

"Gabriela," he finally stated, conjuring more conceptions of Parson Reeves with that tone, such a terrifying mix of pity and patience—only used when she'd been called to the orphanage office to be told she just wasn't the little girl the Fairchilds or the Hardwicks or the Rhynes had in mind. "Gabriela, I'll only be gone a little while."

"No, you won't."

Her voice shed the laryngitis—for a more frightening alternative. Now, only mortally calm certainty underlined the truth she somehow saw in him, like a sliver of February morning light streaming through a sudden crack in his soul's wall.

"Gabriela, it . . . it is business. I cannot simply—"

"You're lying." So simple. But so agonizingly positive. So bloody certain, as the fissure inside him widened, and, no matter how vehemently her heart now yearned to turn back from the comprehension, she experienced the coiled ache of his gut, the burning weight across his chest—the whole torture chamber his body had become with the burden of betraying her.

"Why, Marcus?" Her hands fell to the drapes of her *tablier* and began kneading the material into miniature lambrequins, instead. "Why are you lying to me? Why are you doing this to me again?" she started to pace in time to her kneadings. "Is this what you're really about, Mr. Danewell? Seducing little pigeons like me, training them to fly in your private little show, and then, when they need you most, breaking their hearts and waiting for their wings to follow?"

He surprised her then. For the first time since she'd entered, he emerged from the shelter of his hunched shoulders, slowly raising his head, deliberately meeting her gaze.

And sucked out half her breath with the bleak, gray misery of his eyes . . . of his soul.

And robbed her of the other half with the low, sad grate of his voice . . . of his spirit.

"You nay need me anymore, Gabriela."

"The bloody *hell* I don't!" She hated the quiver in her retort, the growing heat behind her eyes. She hated *him* for making her stand here once more, her spine aching with the effort of holding her chin aloft while specters of long-ago days and visions of a long-ago Gabriela rose from the painfully packed graves in her heart. . . .

Now child, do not be so sad; the Fairchilds just had someone more like Elizabeth in mind. . . .

Now Gabriela, ye mustn't cry; the Rhynes liked you, they really did. . . .

Next week, Gabriela, more folks will come next week. . . .

Someone will love you someday, Gabriela. Someday, Gabriela.

"Gabriela."

She flinched, struggling to discern his voice between the cold echoes of memory and the freezing truth of the present—for a boggled, disabled moment, fearing the two inextricably meshed.

Then he touched her. Just there; just there at the top of her shoulder; a penetrating cool, a haunting warmth. Flourishing from nowhere, filling her everywhere. And, oh God, so real. So beautifully, horribly real . . .

"Gabriela, listen to me. You grew those wings with your own heart, your own purpose. And now . . . oh, now, sweeting, you shall fly on them with the same. You shall fly to the ends of the earth, and show them the beauty of all your Ophelias and Juliets and Cleopatras . . ."

"N-no!" The word emerged more a sob than a sound. The same unthinking agony shot down her arms, helping thrust him away before propelling her out into the sitting room again. Gabriela felt him follow her, felt the cruelly continuing power of his presence, the unnatural, addictable, ruthlessly desirable pull of him.

She felt everything but his own addictions and desires. As if she'd never known *anything* about him.

As if they'd never known each other the way they had last night.

Which turned his gentle behest into a heartless mockery. "Gabriela—"

"No." She kept him at bay with an outstretched hand, fingers spread and white and aching. "They all lied to me," she grated, "and now you are lying, too!"

The world keeled as she shook her head, senses searching for an answer to the question she didn't want to ask, clamoring its hideous vulnerability just beneath her dry lips. But the next moment, the effort didn't matter. "What is it, Marcus?" Those lips forsook her with a rasp that burned her throat and turned her stomach. "What did I do wrong? I . . . I've been a good girl, haven't I? Marcus . . . haven't I?"

And she awaited his response in shivering, dreading silence.

And for a long moment, it seemed her torture went for naught. Marcus only continued to look upon her, immobile, unreadable; a distant stranger.

Then . . . a shaking shadow crossed his face. The invisible mask lifted from his eyes, and his soul glowed out from them: silver pain, miseried gloss of rain, the tearless tears of a frightened boy locked inside an accursed man.

Then he took a heavy step toward her. Another. Gabriela snapped her hand higher, extending a finger in warning.

But Marcus didn't hesitate over a reaction this time. He reached up himself, to press her quavering knuckle back into her fist, so gently, so intently. Then he encircled the trembling mass of her hand with his own, one long, magical finger at a time.

Only then, as he dragged her into the consuming crush of his embrace, did he let one phrase escape, guttural and grating and knelling. A verbal Golgotha bell . . . a funereal goodbye.

"My heart."

And then, Gabriela saw all the way into his mind.

Shock ripped through her senses. A cry tore past her lips. She scratched away from him like a cat about to be tossed into the Thames—not certain she'd prefer such an ordeal to this drowning torment.

"Oh, God," she gasped, fingers coiling into the lace pleats at her neck. "God; God, Marcus, it's her, isn't it?"

Again, fathomless silence. But a royal decree's worth of confirmation ignited in his eyes before he slammed them shut and wheeled away, stammering an entirely unbelievable, "What the hell are you talking about?"

"Stop it!" Gabriela lashed. "Damn you, just stop it! I saw her, Marcus. I saw!"

"You saw the bloody hell *what?*"

"In your mind! Stop pretending such penny novel innocence! I saw her. I saw that woman—"

Another explosion of comprehension blasted her so hard, she bent over to gain breath. "Raquelle," she heard her lips choke—and her heart scream. "Oh, my God. It's Raquelle. *She's* Raquelle."

She didn't even bother to phrase it a question to him. The certainty flooded her soul more completely than the nausea surging her stomach. She folded to the floor as the image assaulted her again, her accusation unleashing every detail of the creature out of Marcus's mind and into hers. Hair of mesmerizing midnight satin. Lips of knowing carnal mystery. A body promising sleek, alabaster pleasures.

And velvet, violet eyes of blatant, bold possession.

You are mine, Marcus, those eyes commanded in a sure, sensual purr. *I made you what you are. You are mine forever.*

A sound escaped Gabriela as nothing she'd emitted before. Beyond a sob. More annihilating than a scream. A deep, quivering, aching sound, betokening the removal of her heart from her being, one shredded scrap at a time.

Yet through that unending, unthinking misery, she felt Marcus's continuing stare, a tangible presence around her . . . though never inside her. As if he willed the beams of his gaze to reach like the arms of his embrace, only to be held back by invisible prison bars.

Oh, yes, her soul agreed with bitter lucidity. *He's in prison, all right. The "prison" of Raquelle's caresses. No wonder you found him packing in such a hurry.*

"It was so easy for her," Gabriela uttered then, softly, searchingly, "wasn't it? It was so easy for her to simply strut back into your life, curl her little finger, and watch you heel at her feet again . . . wasn't it?"

An acrid laugh spilled from her trembling lips. Saint Genesius, she longed to cry. She longed to cry for days. But he'd raped the tears from her many, many minutes ago . . . an agony-filled world ago.

"And look at what a good puppy you are, Marcus," she said with the rough remnants of that laugh. "It was easy for you, too, wasn't it? So easy to forget your sorry little mortal slut when the great Raquelle bid you to her bed again."

But Marcus didn't render even a blink of reaction to that. He barely moved, save for one shallow wave of a swallow, rippling down the cords of his neck and into his beautifully broad, unearthly inert chest.

"Is that what you think?" he finally asked, again so level, again so still.

"Is that what I—" Gabriela jerked once more to her

feet. "For God's sake, Marcus, tell me what else I'm supposed to think!"

She lunged at him, reaching out white-fingered arms, curling her grip into his shirt, then his shoulders. "Damn you!" she charged. "Damn you, damn you; deny me, Marcus. Tell me I'm wrong! Tell me I'm more lunatic than Marx, then kiss me senseless to prove it!"

She didn't know how her grip traveled to his doublet front, nor did she care—nor did she allow herself to ponder the slashes in the thick material; slashes the distinct width of feminine fingernails. "Marcus," she implored, pressing her forehead to his chest, "just tell me, and I'll believe you. I swear I'll believe you!"

And then, she waited. Holding her breath. But feeling him suck in hard, heavy air, hearing his lungs push out a long, fragmented sigh. Gabriela strained to sense him yet further, listened through her throbbing heart for the corresponding beat of his own—please God, just one last thread left secured between them. Just *that* last thread . . .

But she heard nothing. And felt less.

Except the renewed twist in her chest when a low, leaden voice said against her hair: "I have naught to tell you, Gabriela."

Her arms clenched with the lust to beat him. Instead, that passion erupted into her quaking fingers, fastening her grip tighter to him. *"No."* The word resounded from the depths of her belly. "No. You're lying. You're lying again! Why are you doing this, Marcus? Why are you doing this *now?*"

His own grasp slipped around her shoulders, an excruciating, almost mocking caress of movement. "I am going, Gabriela. I *must* go."

He moved to set her away. She didn't let him. "You mean you're leaving." His hold compressed tighter. She resisted harder. "Well, I won't let you. I'm not going to let you. If she wants you, she'll have to fight for you."

"Gabriela." He sighed the word, as if wearied with a disobedient child. But his grip coiled with the strength of a dozen well-rested—and well-angered—men.

Gaby didn't care. She continued the fight not only against him, but her own body, drained by outrage, exhausted by dread, sapped by the struggle of refusing to accept his effortless duplicity as truth, his marble-statued mien as reality.

"Tell her!" she ordered. "If you can envision her, you can call her. Summon that witch and tell her *I'm* willing to die for you. She can even do the deed herself." Another caustic laugh burned up her throat. "I'll bet she'd like that. Ask her, Marcus. Damn you, ask her!"

But her sharp gasp came as a surprise stand-in for the gauntlet of a stare she'd planned next. Despite her resistance, Marcus pushed her back with a head-snapping thrust and the broadsword of his furious gaze.

"Damn *you*," he countered, jerking her again, hard. "Damn you, Gabriela, desist making this such an agony for me!"

And then and there, as he sliced his whole countenance at her again, as he stared *through* her, Gabriela stopped struggling. She stood shocked by this creature clutching her—who *was* this creature clutching her? Who, or what, was this being not only paralyzing her body, but her mind with his glare of such raging, wild-fired wrath, entwined with a grimace of such helpless, fathomless pain?

The answer to that stunned her with its swiftness, swooping into her mind like a crystal dove, perfect and clear—and the only explanation for this atrocity. But a triumphant smile only formed halfway upon Gabriela's lips when the dove plummeted, engulfed by a fog of confusion . . . a haze emanating from outside as well as inside her . . . a befuddling mist she'd felt just once before: in the depths of another night, when Marcus had also told her he had to leave. . . .

"Go to the couch, Gabriela," his voice came through the fog, seemingly *part* of the fog . . . again just like that night, again unfaltering in his command. "Go to the couch," he repeated, "and sit down." He turned her that direction with one swift, silent hand—though he never touched her. "I pray you . . . just sit down."

Yes, it was all just like that faraway night—with a single harrowing exception. *This* eve, Gabriela discovered herself without a cell of self-will to ward off his extrahuman spell. Her feet scuffled in protest to his invisible push. Her arms trembled with the effort to spin herself back around. She tossed her head back and forth against his mind's deepening foray, viciously fighting his siege of her thoughts, his assault of her movements, his piracy of her volition.

But she slid an inch closer to the couch with every passing, raging heartbeat.

The initiation, her heart mourned through that torturous cacophany. *It was the initiation. He said you'd surrender him all . . . and he was right. He said you could—possibly would— regret it. And he was right.*

"N . . . n . . . nooo!" she protested in a high, hurting moan. She damned the tears *now* choosing to make their entrance, damned the force keeping her from lifting even a finger to wipe them away. "No . . . no . . . Marcus, please stop this. Please don't!"

"I must." With that same mesmeric, maddening wand of a hand, he directed her knees to bend around the couch's cushions, then her body, the battlefield of their warring pysches, to follow in a convulsing descent. "Forgive me," came his haunting, consuming whisper. "Forgive me, my heart, I must."

Desperately, she wielded her only weapon against him now: her tear-streaked glare. Marcus's hand faltered a fraction, pivoting inward atop his wrist. Then nothing.

"I hate you for this," she spat.

"I know," he replied, low and aching.

And, in that gaping, grieving darkness of a moment between them, she knew he did.

The recognition imbued her with one last flash of defiance—one last burst of strength she used to try and break through his all-powerful hold.

Gabriela coiled determined fists into her skirts, planted her feet, and stood.

Two seconds later, she plummeted to the floor, beaten down by a blow of overwhelming mental force.

Though she only fell to her hands and knees, they instantly buckled beneath her. She didn't care. The Persian carpet dampened beneath her drenched cheeks. Her lungs heaved against the unyielding boards beneath the rug. She wished he'd physically struck her. Mortal pain could not surpass the wounds her soul bore now.

"I . . . am sorry," Marcus stammered, a hard inhalation breaking apart his words. "Gabriela . . . I am so sorry. But you nay understand. You do not *want* to understand."

She had thought her fury spent. Her heart proved her sanity wrong. An enraged inferno blazed through her senses, gusted into her reascending sights. "I—understand—perfectly," she seethed.

"You—understand—naught!"

His roaring return sent a Chinese vase to the floor—and Gabriela into a stunned jolt. Marcus didn't notice either. With that same glare mixed of such anguish and outrage, he spun upon her. On his way, he seized a couch cushion in each hand. He hurled the pads at, and then through, the Rubens originals on the wall, detonating a maelstrom of canvas, paint, velvet, and stuffing. As that demented storm rained around him, he raised his hands into fists; Gabriela heard the echoes of the soundless, savage curses he hurled at a heaven, which listened no further than this chaos, beneath this ceiling.

And then, in a sudden and strange silence, they both watched the storm expend itself. Raindrops of pigment

and flurries of feathers first whirled like flotsam in a de-
moniac blizzard, only to stop, turn, and float back to earth
like angel's tears.

Demon's fears.

Angel's tears.

A North Sea gale could not have reflected its creator's
soul more powerfully.

"In time," he at last whispered, his voice dropping to
that odd, after-storm kind of hush, "in a very short time,
sweeting, you shall forgive me. And then, I promise . . .
you will forget me."

His own, earlier words haunted her as the pitifully perfect comeback. "Is that what you think?" Gaby returned
through her tears.

A sharp sigh broke through his reverie. "Gabriela—"

"Damn you, Marcus." She couldn't—and wouldn't—
wait to interject. *"Damn* you. Do you truly think my heart
will glue back together like that vase? Do you truly think
I'll *forget* you?"

"Gabriela, please—"

"I *love* you!"

"Gabriela, *cease!*"

"No."

She knew he wouldn't let her stand, at least not while
he remained, but Gaby shoved to her knees with all the
dignity and determination left in her shaking muscles. "I
shall *never* cease," she leveled through her exertion, past
gritted teeth. "You convey that to lovely Mistress Raquelle
as well. You tell her to get prepared, Marcus—because she
might have taken the battle tonight, but we'll see who takes
the bloody Waterloo.

"You tell her I shall surrender the breath in my body
before I cease loving you."

* * *

Damn her. Sweet Jesu, damn her; the woman truly meant her little declaration of war.

Little? Marcus clawed through the exhausted mire of his mind to amend his inaccuracy—a decidedly more successful endeavor than his body's effort to crawl from the subterranean crevice he had used for a bed the last three days.

Three days . . . with a certainty, he decided, he owed himself a correction for that, too. Could it have been only that fraction of a fortnight ago that he had rewarded Gabriela's beautiful, brave declaration with his coward's pathetic treachery? Could only three moons have set, then risen since the white and weeping orb that watched him flee after casting her into sleep's abyss rather than endure another second of her penetrating stare—or a moment of her beautiful love?

But most unbelievable: could it have been only three nights since she had awakened from that sleep, only to find her stubborn, *stupid,* way to the London underground?

The London underground . . . ah, God, this wretched tomb of an underground, which damned him further by carrying her voice higher and sweeter than Drury's sorry rafters ever could; which echoed her soggy, searching steps down passages *he'd* barely navigated for want of light or sanity.

Which began to reverberate with the sound and presence of her again this eve.

Marcus froze, listening, then confirming her distant calls. His knees went to rubble. He plummeted to the cold earth with a deep, desolate moan, curled in on himself like the writhing sewer scum he had become. But then, true sewer scum could thrive in blissful nescience of the voice calling down the twisting tunnels to him. Holy Mary, so full of life. Bloody *hell,* so full of pain.

"Marcus! Marcus, blast you, answer me! I know you're

down here, you half-nerved, back-biting bastard! Damn
you, you *beautiful* bastard . . .

"Oh Marcus, I can *feel* you here. I can feel you trying
to hide, but don't you know you can't? Your walls aren't
high enough, Marcus. They never will be. Marcus . . .
don't you know how much I love you?"

With a guttural growl, he clamped both hands over his
ears. *Why?* raged the pounding, tormented brain beneath.
Why did he still know when each of her *toes* touched down
to slime-covered rock; why did he still feel each of her
unsteady breaths dissipate into the darkness? . . .

And *why* did he hear each note of her terrified cry as a
slipped step sent her plunging into the waist-high currents
of London's combined rain water, bath water, and toilet
water?

And why, damn her, did he still feel her loving him as
she clamored back to the quay and continued to walk on?

His unmerciful little nemesis had the perfectly soul-
piercing answer for that, too.

"I told you I wouldn't stop, Mr. Danewell. I told you I'd
never stop loving you. And I won't. I'll tear these walls
apart, Marcus. You can't hide behind them all!"

Something between a laugh and a sob fluttered across
his lips. The nervy little hellion. He held no doubt she
planned to hold fast by her claims, as well, syllable by syllable and stone by stone—utilizing the very tenacity he
had nourished in her.

Damn her. *Damn* her, anyway!

At that, the sob cascaded into a full seizure, throwing
his muscles and bones into contortions that brought
memories of voodoo ceremonies and demonic posses-
sions. So long ago . . . those rain forest days seemed so
long ago, yet just a day. Back then, Marcus had turned a
skeptical glower on those savages' assemblies, maintaining
no mortal's ability to truly comprehend the supernatu-

ral—and certainly, not to affect it in return with their meaningless simpkin sacrifices.

Now, as he fought the shudders that intensified at each step of one maddeningly persistent mortal, he cursed *himself* the idiot. The blind, self-bloated idiot. How had he ever thought it such a great mystery that he had so stupidly walked into this hell for all eternity?

Eternity. *Eternity.*

Do you hear that, Gabriela? I am a creature of hell for forever, *Gabriela. We cannot change it. You cannot change it.*

Redemption, Gabriela, is a heaven I cannot ever know.

But beyond the chamber walls, she trod obliviously on—oblivious, he guaranteed, to even the anguished moan his throat finished to his soul's excommunication. Marcus trembled harder with the effort of sustaining that rampart against her, hurrying to erect another layer of mental brick and mortar as he felt her follow an "intuition" down a narrower passage leading closer to his cavern. *Closer . . . nay, nay, please don't come any closer!*

The extra exertion meant he would probably have to feed again tonight—an act drained of its small and evanescent pleasure by the exhibition Raquelle had so graciously favored him with . . . and the echoes of Gabriela's voice in every crack and cranny around him. An act, he had begun to ponder with a terrifying increase of occurrence, only endurable *because* of Gabriela. Because, grand threats to dismantle the London sewer system or not, she could not ever find him again. She *would* not.

He would not let Raquelle know the ultimate triumph of a continuing legacy. Especially *not* through Gabriela.

No matter how vehemently the vexing chit attempted otherwise.

"Marcus!" came her shout with renewed, reverberating strength—in the most horrifying literal sense of the words. He felt the warmth of her breath permeating the bricks in front of her—the same bricks at his suddenly motionless feet.

Any strength Marcus had preserved went the way of stale flour in the flood of her life, her intensity, her love. The resulting paste of his body slithered a desperate path back to his crevice, while he nay dared even a glance back at that wall. The slightest slip of composure would instantly betray his awareness of her every movement, his desire of her tiniest fiber, the excruciating bliss he stole from her every aching, wonderful, horrible syllable. . . .

"Oh, Marcus . . . Marcus, why do I feel you so near? Marcus, why don't you answer me? Marcus . . . please . . . I love you."

Nay! the deepest part of his soul gnarled, hating its new position: on his sleeve. Hating *her.* But most of all, hating himself. *Stop! Stop loving me, damn you! Stop tormenting me, curse you!*

"Marcus . . . please . . ."

GO AWAY!

And, unbelievably, with exigent thanks to whatever force of the universe still listening to him, she did.

Her steps dissipated slowly at first, punctuated by one dry, slicing sob that echoed exactly a dozen times through the chamber's stones. He knew the count because each repercussion carved out another chunk of his spirit.

And then, finally, came the reprieve and relief of penetrating silence.

Or so Marcus rather proficiently convinced himself for the next week. Then the next, and the next. Fiercely, firmly telling himself that eternity would not always seem so . . . eternal. That mere fortnights would not always seem a century; that minutes would not always tick by like hours. . . .

That he would not always wander the nights in search of a name for his missing half other than *Gabriela.*

"Gabriela."

He uttered it now—indulging the single instance per

eve he gave himself to say the word aloud—sending it as
a worshiping whisper into the gathering mists off the
Thames. But so swiftly, *too* swiftly, the moment was over,
his pronunciation swirling into the gray fog-forest like the
tails of terrified foxes merging with the scenery before the
hounds converged.

So it occurred every night. But this time, Marcus
amended a new turn to the rite. Slowly but steadily, he
lifted his arm from the rail of Blackfriars Bridge, stretching
a taut hand into that murky void in search of his lost
world—in search of the heat, hope, and happiness so un-
fairly spent in four fleeting syllables.

Into the similar fog bank between his ribs, his mind
delved a concurring journey, peering for the heart where
he always thought his nightly declaration ended. There,
the sound would transform into strength; hopefully,
strength that would one day fill just a small canyon in the
chasm of his existence.

But he suddenly realized he had nay seen his heart in
three weeks. Had nay *looked* for it.

Had nay wanted to.

His hand returned from the mist with naught but con-
densed mist.

His mind returned from his soul with naught but memories of a choking, echoing sob.

And at that, he knew he must see her again.

Just once. *Just once*, he swore to himself before even leaving the bridge. And just briefly . . . just a moment enough
to garner the memory of her golden smile again, to assure
she now restricted her dramatic sojourns to the confines
of stage boards and footlights. The little dreamer needed
to concentrate, after all—did she not begin rehearsals with
Webber and the Prince's Troupe next week? God's codpiece, Marcus suddenly wondered, what day *was* it? More
questions arrowed at him after that, which his mind dis-

patched with an alertness and aliveness he had not known since. . . .

Since he'd played Hamlet to the most beautiful Ophelia on earth.

Jesu, he couldn't wait to look upon her again.

He noted the time, gonged across the city by Big Ben: 3:00 A.M. If fate still smiled a little on him, and if he hurried, mayhap he'd find her just finishing one of her after-hours sessions. No doubt she would be lost in thought in the middle of the stage, flipping some script passage over and over in the mind behind her furrowed, adorable brow. Or mayhap, fate's fortune be with him just once more, she would be in her dressing room, nodding off in the middle of making a journal entry, curled in her chair in much the same way he had first approached her.

Ah, she had been so beautiful then; so damnably, deliriously beautiful. And she would be more so this eve, her eyes deepened with the alloy of self-confidence, her stature heightened with self-knowledge, her steps sure and steady toward the gleaming horizon of her life. A life waiting with promise and passions, triumphs and travels, daylight and dreams. A life she would never have known with him.

He would wish her a swift, silent Godspeed into that life, and then return to the abyss of his.

Ten minutes later, he entered Drury by way of the private street entrance to his box. He could have completed the trip in a thrice fraction of that time, but he forced his movements to mirror the mortal confines he held in place on his mind. True, he had nay felt the seeking tendrils of Gabriela's thoughts or emotions for well past a fortnight now, but he nay dared the slightest slip on his own control now. Not when a stray thought could lead her straight to him. Not when his protecting stone walls lay a near half mile below.

His heart throbbed like thunder as he inched into his box and looked toward the stage.

But no impassioned sable-haired figure paced the dim floorboards there.

Marcus smiled. So fortune still favored him a bit, after all. She was in her dressing room. . . .

He hastened his pace along the stage right catwalk. Then bloody near ran down the passage over the stage and the greenroom—and then jerked to a stunned stop.

For another heart-halted moment, he sucked in breath for his death scream. The sudden blaze of so much lamp light, especially after the shadows of the house and stage areas, struck him as no less than a burst of sunlight.

But after his eyes adjusted and his gut somersaulted back to normal, he confirmed he'd never seen the greenroom so illuminated—or so crowded. Every current Drury Lane cast and crew member, as well as a few who'd moved on to other theaters and productions, stood or sat together in the meager room, pressing at the walls and doors like raspberries about to spill from one of Gertha's overstuffed tarts. Even Louis joined the throng, one beefy leg propped atop a section of "wall" from the "Castle of Denmark." Alfonso Renard, face as taut and white as the bandage around his hand, stood next to him.

And everyone held either a lamp or a candle.

And all of them stared at those straining walls and doors as if someone had died.

All except Gabriela . . . who was nowhere to be seen.

"Are . . . are you certain that's what the doctors said, Mr. Harris?" a dark-haired waif from the ballet rasped across the room. "They said 'no hope'; that's what they really said?"

Marcus snapped an amazed look the same direction as the waif. Jesu, it was true. He had not noticed Augustus before, the man's lumbering form turned toward the fireplace and buried beneath his overcoat. Now, as his partner pivoted back to the group with very aged slowness and very red eyes, a leaden claw of dread began to clench Marcus's chest . . . a pervading, paralyzing knowingness cutting the breath from his throat, the blood from his veins.

Sweet God, nay. Nay, God, nay.

"I came directly from St. Thomas's, Trina," Augustus said, his tone actually underscored with tenderness. "We spoke for an hour. The physicians told me exactly what I have told you all. Gabriela was found a fortnight ago by a city plumber, wandering in a drainage corridor beneath St. Martin's Lane. She was damn near dead then, and her condition has only worsened. The fluid in her lungs will not drain, and she has no strength to cough it up anymore. But that's because the damn little fool refuses to eat. That, of course, is no help to the fever, or those unexplainable spasms . . ."

The man stopped himself there with a frustrated oath. Finally, he continued on a bare croak of a voice and a helpless jerk of a shrug. "She has simply lost the will to live. That's all they will say to explain it, my friends. She just . . . does not want to live."

At that, the group released a collective sigh. . . .

Effectively muffling the hard thud of Marcus's collapse.

Finally, breaking into the ensuing, disbelieving silence, someone whispered, "Why?"

"She had so much," another qualified. "So much to do, so much she'd dreamed . . ."

"Yes," someone else said. "Why?"

At first, Augustus just looked away again. Away and up, his newly ancient eyes probing the ceiling, long and unwavering and unblinking, but not with the same fervent confusion blanketing the others' faces.

Nay, Marcus determined with pounding certainty, Augustus knew precisely what he looked for in these rafters. And precisely *who*.

That certitude gained a thunderous cadence as the man, with his gaze still lifted, answered the group's question in a fatally calm—and shrewdly convicting—tone.

"We know nothing save that any time Gabriela *has* roused, she has only said one thing . . . one word . . . a name."

As one, the crowd snapped stares to Renard.

Renard didn't blink so much of an eye in return. Except the seething flush that crept up from the dandy's neck—betraying his own seething, instinctual foreknowledge of the information about to spill from Augustus's lips.

"Gabriela keeps calling for someone named *Marcus.*"

Nineteen

He doubled over and let out a moan so violent and tortured and consuming, the mortal ears below never discerned a note of its unearthly anguish. The sound resonated with the same pain burning its searing, scathing path through every cell in Marcus's body. And *her* body. Jesu and Mary, aye, in her body, too—the awareness flogged him with full, furious force now that he ripped away the walls on his mind and flew to her on desperately beating psychic wings.

He should have known she would do this. He *could* have known, had he not been so senseless, so blind . . . so *stupid.* So eager to confirm his pathetically skewed nobility, to prove his nonexistent honor, to create his own warped little Camelot where self-sacrifice equaled tragic perfection . . . and, mayhap, heavenly redemption.

Ah, *God,* how far off the mark he had landed! And how damnably, despicably right Raquelle had been. Heaven did not give monsters like him a sanction for self-sacrifice. His pitiful grasps at morality only became, in the bitch's agonizingly accurate summation, a rendition of martyrdom fit for naught but a two shilling minstrel hall.

Gabriela . . . Gabriela, I am so sorry. I am so wrong. Gabriela, Gabriela please tell me I am not a murderer, too!

But only a fog, thicker and darker than any Thames River mist, swirled in and answered his heart's plea. On a shell of semiconsciousness loomed where he had once been able to feel her heart beating, her desires burning, her thoughts and dreams growing.

Oh aye, she still existed.

But did she still live?

The need to know that answer, to feel her, to see her, ate at him like a three-pound parasite: in gulping, raging chunks. As teeth, the monster used serrated blades of memory from the far and near past:

I love you, Marcus. Don't you know I'll always love you?

Blazes, guv. Sounds like ya truly love this chit.

Don't ever leave me, Marcus . . . please, don't ever leave me.

They said there's no hope. Her condition has only worsened. . . .

I shall surrender the breath in my body before I stop loving you.

The breath in my body . . .

His throat convulsed on a shuddering sigh. His body shivered anew as her words echoed along the stones of his soul, the acoustics there more harrowing and haunting than the longest arteries of the London underground. *The breath in my body . . .*

And that, his heart echoed back with but one answer.

The hell you will, Gabriela.

And I am going to make assured of it.

And at *that*, Marcus lifted his head. The movement came slowly, steadily, as a very new, very inundating sensation took the place of the usual fire behind his eyes. Ice . . . silver ice. A solid, unbreakable sheet of it, frozen of every tear he never shed and every dream he never lived, now congealed into a block of resolved conviction, a decision of unfaltering surety.

The only choice he had left to make.

The one dream he could still make right.

With that realization, the ice deluged the rest of his body.

The frozen flood sluiced through his legs and rendered his feet numb as he rose to his feet. As he made his way back along the inky paths of the catwalks, the icewater raced down veins and through nerve endings; as he exited Drury again, it gripped certain, frosty fingers around his heart, lungs, and stomach.

Yet he did not resist the invasion. As a matter of point, the cold conqueror became a best friend, his body's aide-de-camp as he turned south down Bow Street without a break in determined stride. The ice lent fortitude to muscles already turning sluggish, dripped cool drops into a bloodstream already beginning to simmer as Big Ben sent four gongs across the city's rooftops. The tolls resounded into a sky full of naught but dwindling stars and awakening morning birds. . . .

So odd, he pondered then . . . so odd. When had the sun ever risen on this city in such a sky, without a wisp of fog or a tendril of coal smoke?

The next moment, he emitted a derisive grunt at his musing. As if he were so qualified to know how London sunrises behaved!

Still, it all seemed *odd*. The fresh-doughy warmth of a baker's shop he passed. . . .

Surreal.

The morning dew, which clung to the daisies he purchased from a wide-eyed flower girl. . . .

Unreal.

The echo of his steps against the whistle of the early Brighton train . . .

Unnatural.

And suddenly, at that conclusion, it seemed a very fitting dawn, indeed.

A very fitting end.

They had her in a room at the end of a dim hall, on the fourth floor of the hospital, which still smelled of age and death despite the nurses' delusions that bleach an turpentine wielded the same mortal might as claymore and crossbow . . . or mayhap, wooden stake and silver bullet.

Following the instinct behind that thought, Marcus avoided the piercing temptation to simply race the nearly empty hallways to Gabriela's room. Instead, on swift but noiseless steps, he rounded to the building's back door and reluctantly diverted a piece of his psyche from Gabriela in order to hypnotize the two orderlies slouched there. Then he launched himself against the bricks over the door frame. One careful, suctioning hand grip at a time, he pulled himself up that cold wall, across a cold window ledge and into the even colder corridor at the dim end of Floor Four.

The feat did not come without its price. His strength drained from him rapidly enough without the unconventional climb. Marcus managed no more than two steps down the hall before grappling for the inside wall, sliding down the rough surface, and dropping his head between his knees to wait out a surge of vertigo, nausea—and terror.

Only when he fought back the final acrid remnants of that incursion did he realize his biggest obstacle had yet to be assailed.

He looked past the dust, scuffs, and nicks on his boots—to the ebony-sharp shine of fresh patent leather oxfords. A shine he remembered verily too well—from when he had lunged his hating wolf's jaws at it.

With purposeful, disdainful leisure, Marcus raised his gaze past those patent-perfect shoes, up the length of tailored black trousers, over a tailored gray waistcoat, around a tailored black jacket, and finally, to the bastard's tailored, vacuous face.

"Renard," he said out the side of his sneering lips. "How nice of you to issue a personal greeting. Good morrow to you, sir." The last word, he dragged long and low enough to drive home his true, mocking meaning.

The rake's nostrils flared over a disgustingly perfect twist of both lips. Marcus wondered whether Renard had patterned the look after Kean's Richard III or Beerbohm-Tree's Macbeth. Either way, the killcow had pitifully miscast himself.

"How do you know who I am?" As the bastard intoned it, he took the bearing of yet another role he so erroneously fancied himself: Grand High Spanish Inquisitor.

The incongruity of the analogy was too hilarious to be ignored. Before Marcus could tamp it, a barbed chuckle erupted. "I trow we both know the answer to that," he drawled derisively.

The lips contorted harder. Aquiline brows fell, forming an upper facial bowl for a forehead suddenly brimming with furrows. Renard pounded closer, but halted several steps short of placing himself within Marcus's reach, clearly battling equal measures of fury and fear. "Who . . . *what* . . . the hell are you?"

On an exasperated sigh, Marcus turned, gripped the wall again, and began the torture of pulling up to his feet. "I trow you know the answer to that as well." He pushed away after accomplishing a hunch-backed semblance of a stance—not turning even a glance back. "Just as I trow you shall not try to stop me now."

But the bastard's reckless rage blinded him as thoroughly as it flooded Marcus's senses.

"Well, you trow wrong!" Renard snarled on the beginnings of a double-fisted lunge—a move Marcus also anticipated half a dozen seconds earlier. A countering gnarl exploded from the depths of his gut as he shot up, whirled, and met the offensive with a crushing grip to Renard's left wrist. That hold provided the necessary ballast to hurl the man into a more than satisfactory heap against the footboards Marcus had just come from.

But the triumph brought sheer hell. While wildfire ravaged his bloodstream, his lungs pumped like blistering bellows in search of air. Still, his body could choose naught

but to heed the command of his spirit, leading forth into
a raging charge of his own. He nay halted until he hung
mere feet over Renard's gaping, tremoring features—an
unworldly silver glow reflecting off the bastard's waxen
complexion.

"Do not *think* of getting up, you blackhearted son of a
whore," he seethed. "Just as you will not think of stopping
me from seeing her. Just as *you* will not think of seeing
her, even after this night; even after she leaves here—for
she *will* leave here."

Then Marcus lowered his head two inches, forcing
Renard to jerk his own in weak acknowledgment. "Aye,"
he continued, dipping another register lower in his gut,
"you had best agree, for this contract is not up for haggle.
And if you ever deem it to be, I swear by all of heaven and
hell that I shall find you, no matter where or whatever I
am." He watched Renard's skin gain an even more intense
sheen of silver. He allowed the trace of a savoring smile
to touch his lips. "I shall find you," he promised the bastard again, "and I shall make you pay with more than a
few fingers."

And before the whoreson's jaw hit his chest or his eyes
finished flashing in shock, Marcus advanced to Gabriela's
door, and swiftly slid inside.

He closed the portal with his back—then simply stood
there for an eternity of moments. Then an eternity more,
as he quaked with the presence of her . . . as he rejoiced
in the nearness of her.

Hating himself for the sight of her.

Ah, God . . . hating himself with such a vehement violence, such a shuddering savagery, he now realized he had
only played at being a monster for the last century and a
half.

But you have arrived now, aye, Danewell? his soul interjected on a merciless sneer. *Much felicitations, man. You have
proven your malevolence well. Just behold the proof, lying so clear,*

so pale, so small in that hell of a hospital bed. Behold her there, with eye sockets turned such an ideally emaciated black and lips made up in a perfect, gravely white. And that skin, such a flawless match for her tombstone already, bettered only by the utterly dead way she's breathing . . .

Oh, aye. You have done well, Danewell. 'Tis a befitting way for a demon to leave the world, aye? By taking an angel with him?

He roared.

Not in his throat. In his spirit.

He roared from the dark, dead agony of his dark, dead spirit, an outcry so hateful, so despairing and so grieving that his knees sagged into primitive, paralytic angles and his hands curled into spidery, beastly claws. Those claws groped desperately for the bed, pulled his shaking, afflicted body closer to the motionless seraph ensconced in the sheets.

Closer . . .

Oh, so close to her . . .

Oh, the sweet, soft heaven of her . . .

Please, oh mighty God, just let me see her once again. Just let me know her one last time.

And God, for once, heard his prayer. Marcus crumpled to the mattress next to her, every inch of him throbbing, thrumming and heaving with the nearness of her. He reached trembling knuckles to brush a dark hair from her ashen cheek, but yanked back at the last moment; what if he infected her face with his sudden deformity just as he'd ruined her heart with his soul's distortion?

So he sat there—a helpless freak; an impotent fiend; a dying demon. So much to say . . . nothing to say at all. So much to feel that feeling went transcended. So much; he wanted to tell her so much, to give her so much. . . .

So little time.

So little time.

The thought struck at the same moment a distinct peach

glow warmed the rooftops beyond the window. Sharply, fearfully, Marcus gasped. Reflexively, desperately, he grabbed for Gabriela's hand. Damning himself for betraying his own mandate, he pulled the small, skeletal fingers hard against his chest.

"Gabriela," he whispered against her paper-thin skin, "Oh, Gabriela, sweeting, I am so sorry."

Only a hand . . . but it was all he had, and he worshiped it, kissing each of her fingers, kissing each of the dry creases between them, kissing each weak wafer of a fingernail. "And oh, Gabriela Angelica Rozina," he breathed, "I am so in love with you."

Then he looked back to her face, so unmoving, so still. He delved into her mind, so silent, so sepulchral. "Do you hear me?" he grated. "Oh, Gabriela, somewhere in that darkness of yours, please hear me. Please hear me say I love you. I love you, I love you . . . I love the life you forced on me, the world you opened for me, the light you gave to me. And from the ashes of my body, from the damnation of my spirit, from wherever I am going, I shall still love you with all my being . . . I shall love you with all my wretched, unredeemable soul."

Then slowly, reluctantly, he turned her hand over. Pressed his lips to the faint, faraway pulse beneath the skin of her inner wrist. "Throughout time," he told her, between aching, broken gulps. "Throughout eternity."

Then he waited.

The sky turned from peach to amber.

She did not move.

Marcus roared again.

This time, he poured the sound into *her:* burying his face below her breasts as he clutched her like a last piece of driftwood to a drowning, dying seaman.

A *sinking* piece of driftwood . . .

"*Nay!* Nay, damn you!" Spawned from the depths of the roar, the curse ripped through him along with the memory of the *first* time he had pounded her with the malediction, in the hall outside her dressing room. She had been so beautiful, so persistent, so alive—ah God, so *alive!*

"Damn you! Damn you, Gabriela! You shall live! You . . . shall . . . live!"

The command streamed from him a litanous command, over and over, as he held her tighter with each moment, harder with each minute, trothing the last breaths and heartbeats of his existence to the sole quest of renewing hers. Every thought of his mind, power of his spirit and passion of his soul united in the besiegement, desperately squeezing the last drops from the night . . . the last seconds from his life.

"You—shall—live. *You—shall—live!*"

He roared it. He raged it. He cried it.

He *cried* it, as sunlight streamed into the room, bright and brilliant and blazing.

And lightning struck his world.

First, the heat blasted through his mind. That struck him as odd, because he still felt the rest of his body going up in flames, white-hot and all-consuming, a conflagration that rendered him aware of everything and nothing at once. Every blood cell and muscle ligament, all the marrow in every bone and all the follicles of every hair; Marcus knew them, felt them, *heard* them, a frenzied, fiery orchestra of nerves and instincts and feelings; *oh, so many feelings;* and yet. . . .

No feelings at all.

Nay, he amended to that a moment later; not an utter absence of feeling, but a considerably diminished realm of the stuff. Like a swift assault of Thames fog was glopping atop his senses as he felt his head rising . . . his eyes opening. . . .

Opening to look at his trembling, upraised hands.

His hands. Still very whole. And both very wet . . . but wet with what? That could nay be the shine of his *tears!*

More baffling yet, why were his fingers so dark? He nay remembered them being so dark since—well, since that fateful day he had gone to the forest to meet Raquelle. . . .

"Sweet Jesu," he heard himself blurt. "Sweet, merciful, incredible Jesu."

Through the haze of Gabriela's awareness, his voice came; strong as an Italian concerto, yet melodic as a French love ballad. And stirring her ten times as forcefully as much as either. Oh dear God, tormenting her. Calling her again; coaxing her away from her body's safe cocoon of blackness, then *ordering* her out; and then crying to her . . . oh yes, dear Lord, she heard Marcus *crying* for her. . . .

A dream. *A dream,* she rebuked herself. So impossible. So beautiful, but so impossible.

Gabriela . . . oh, Gabriela, sweeting wake up.

No. Not this again. Not this violation of her mind, her senses; not this appeal to the deepest, most vulnerable core of her. He wouldn't hurt this part of her again!

She had to forget. She had to *forget.*

She had to return to the blackness. Wonderful, numbing blackness . . .

"Gabriela."

She answered with a moan. The effort of it hurt, grating up her parched throat like wind across a graveled desert, echoing through her head like thunder through a lonely forest.

But he called again. "Gabriela. My love. Gabriela."

"Mmmmphh. No. *No.*"

Yet he persisted. Damn him, even in the realm of her imagination, he pressed on with tenacity unequaled since the days of the queen who'd taught him the trait.

First, he leveled the attack of his touch. He slid his smooth fingers over her brow, along her nose, over the

crook of her neck, down between her breasts. He waged
his next campaign with a repeat volley of his voice: softly
singing that tender **ballad from** the night they'd walked
in the wind and **wonder of a** London midnight. The
memories of that **journey formed** the arrows of the third
assault: her mind seeing **him** as if he walked next to her
again, gazing at her, smiling at her, so proud of her, so in
love with her. . . .

But she could endure the barrage no longer.

With a weak, anguished cry, Gaby opened her eyes.

At least she thought she opened them. But several bewildered blinks later, she wondered why the dream man
of her mind wouldn't fade away from the field of her consciousness. She still must be very ill, she concluded, for
her sights indeed took in the hospital walls, the hospital
trays, the hospital window, and the hospital ledge beyond,
awash in the rare, clear light of a late summer morning.

It was just that Marcus wouldn't disappear from the
scene.

Her imagination refused to give him up—but she didn't
hold one doubt why. He sat there so breathtaking, so incredibly handsome. A streak of sunshine fell over his newly
swarthy features. His darker skin served a magnificent con-
trast to the dancing blue-silver lights in his eyes and the
perfection of his ear-to-ear grin.

He made her heart swell.

He made her heart break.

"Marcus," she whispered. Oh, she longed to reach to
him, to touch him, to feel him just once more—but fear
stayed her. Fear of shattering this exquisite dream, this
beautiful image, this flawless, fleeting mirage of a moment.

"Marcus," she breathed again, voice wavering with her
grief. "Marcus, why can't I let you go?"

"Because I will never let you."

Now she *knew* she still raged with fever. Healthy people
didn't let the voices of fantasies send quicksilver light down

to their toes. Lucid people didn't feel their own hearts
batting at the walls of their chest, begging to fly to those
nonexistent voices.

But bloody, damnable hell. If this was insanity, let her
never know reason again!

Her heart lifting on that rebellious cry, Gabriela reached
for him.

She reached—then she touched.

Dear God.

Then she *touched*.

Then she sobbed. And she grabbed. And she held him.
She held him so tight; oh, she couldn't hold tight *enough*;
fingers digging into his flesh, hands wrapping around his
muscles; muscles so hard and warm. . . .

And real?

"Marcus? Marcus . . . *Marcus!*"

He laughed as she bolted up in the bed, curling incredulous hands into his shirtfront, running furtive fingers over
his eyes, his nose, his lips and jaw. Then he returned her
ministrations, finishing by tunneling a hand into her hair,
pulling her close against him, and kissing her as he never
had before. A searing, possessing, utterly physical, utterly
mortal kiss. Inundated with joy, consumed by wonder and
filled with a new, ravenous passion, Gabriela reveled in his
assault—until she couldn't silence her slew of questions
any longer.

"How?" she fired, lips not working fast enough—lips
not working at *all*. "Why? Where . . . who . . . what . . .
what happened?"

"Sssshh," he chuckled, ravishing her mouth with more
tender intent this time. "Sssshh . . . you need to get your
rest." Then, in a rough whisper as he laid her back against
the pillows, extending his own graceful, magnificent
length next to her, "There will be time for your answers
later. Ah, sweeting . . . there will be time for everything.
A lifetime's worth of everything."

But Gabriela, as usual, couldn't obey him at the expense of her love. Through surreptitiously parted lashes, she peeked at him once more, hardly daring to believe he lay here, *here*, next to her, beside her, never to leave again.

But then a morning breeze wafted aside the room's curtains, sprinkling ambered petals of sunlight across the room, across the commanding face and broad form of her dark angel. . . .

And she did dare to believe.

Just as she knew Marcus had dared—at the risk of everything he was or ever would be.

Dared to believe in the power of love.

Dared to believe in its beautiful, magical redemption.

Epilogue

" 'Tis the most beautiful yet."

Marcus's murmur mingled with the sea wind in Gabriela's ear. "You say that about every sunrise," she laughed in return, snuggling tighter into the shelter of his embrace, "but today, I may have to agree with you."

And she did. Today, the entire world seemed to have come to life, even the ancient Cornwall cliff they stood upon, and the newer—but not by much—watchman's house they'd just left. Inside, they'd shared a predawn breakfast of raspberry tarts, hot coffee (one of Marcus's new mortal passions), and blissfully exhausting lovemaking.

The cliff overlooked a spanse of endless, restless waters, the foamy crests reflecting the same changing hues of the sky: blindingly vivid expanses of aqua and orange played hide-and-seek with the shifting silvers and sapphires of the approaching October storm.

Oh, yes it all made one feel deliciously, delightedly alive. Deliciously, delightedly *mortal.*

Marcus's lips again nudged at her ear before he softly said, "Aye. I agree."

She smiled. He chuckled. But the next moment, her features crunched into a perplexed scowl. She tilted that look up at him. "Marcus . . . I don't understand something."

"What?"

"How can you still do that? How can you still see into my mind, even after you've become . . . well . . ."

"Normal?" he supplied, tender grin growing.

"Yes. How can you do that, even though you're normal again? All your other supernatural abilities and powers have disappeared, but you can still read *me* like a Palladium showbill."

Somewhat to her disconcertation, he laughed again. "But I was nay supposed to understand you so clearly to begin with, remember?" He pressed a gentle kiss to each corner of her mouth, urging those downset curves back up into an expression assuredly making her appear a bad version of Ellen Terry's Lady Macbeth crossed with Sarah Bernhardt's Juliet. "Which actually eliminates all but one answer," he continued—so breezily succinct, he'd apparently shared the answer with all the world but her.

Gabriela curled exasperated fists into the shirt folds between his shoulder blades. *"What?"*

Marcus taunted her with a slow, mysterious grin. Then rewarded her with a lingering, adoring kiss. "Magic," he revealed in an intimate sibilance. "The simple magic of me and thee, my sweet."

"Mmmmm," she purred, *"Now* I'll agree with you . . ."

And oh, she did. She returned his affection with langorous seduction, reveling in feeling him shake with the new force of mortal desire, even at her tiny titillations . . . yet also, at discovering parts of the ageless Marcus still intact—such as the shudder she sent through him by simply dipping her mouth to the end of his collarbone.

"Magic," she repeated softly when they finally, reluctantly pulled apart. "Magic," she said once more—but now, underlined the word with another question. "And . . . magic . . . Marcus, is *that* what happened in my hospital room last month?"

At that moment, a thick pewter cloud skudded across the sun—as if the man in her arms had indeed retained

specific superhuman powers, and summoned the haze
with his fluctuating thoughts. But Gaby couldn't determine as such for certain. The moss on the rocks suddenly
gained the full force of Marcus's gaze.

Audacious man. As if he thought *she'd* concede to such
paltry evasive maneuvers.

"Marcus," she persisted, moving her determined hold
from the back of his shoulders to the front, "You . . . you
were not expecting to survive that sunrise, were you?"

By small, jerking increments, he shook his head.

"But you came to the hospital to see me, anyway."

With the same taut difficulty, he nodded.

"Why?"

At that, with resigned reluctance, he lifted his gaze to
hers once more. And like heaven's cleansing tears pressing
at the confines of the clouds above, a beautiful silver sheen
glimmered from the consuming, mesmerizing depths
which hungrily took in every inch of her features.

"Because . . ." he at last answered her in his gentle, beautiful tenor, "because I love you more than I do my own life."

The desire to kiss the man surpassed any such urge
Gabriela had known so far. But before she acted on the
yearning, Marcus emitted a short chuckle. "To think the
answer was as simple as that," he murmured, "yet I never
saw it." He shook his head again; this time, with a bewildered slant. "Nay," he amended then, "I was not *meant* to
see it. Not until now . . ." He slipped a smooth, warm hand
into hers, "Not until you."

Gaby took no pain to disguise the extent of her confusion *now.* "What on earth are you talking about?" she fired.
Then, invoking a favorite private quip they'd adopted during the last few weeks of intensive rehearsals, "Excuse me,
Mr. Webber, I think I missed a line." She appended the
jest in a grumble, "perhaps a whole scene."

Marcus squeezed her hand again. "Prompter's fault,"
he apologized. He took a deep breath before adding, "And

Mr. Danewell's turn to explain." He tugged her toward
the cliff's winding footpath. "Walk with me. There is a
story I must share with you."

But when they reached the trail, Gabriela stopped and
decided to take a chance on a knowing glance of her own.
"Does this story, by any chance, begin with, 'once upon a
time, Raquelle turned Marcus into a vampire'?"

His left eyebrow plummeted—serving her statement ample confirmation. But following the same sixth instinct that
inspired her assumption, Gabriela didn't indulge a victory
grin or a gloating strut. She waited in the ensuing, taut
silence; waited for Marcus to clasp her hand tighter, then
lead her farther down that path between the ocean and
sky.

"There's . . . much more to that story than I have told
you," he finally said.

"I know." Gaby felt his startled stare arrow down at her,
but didn't return the look. Something told her to garner
all the fortitude she still had, for his following words would
be much more than just a story.

They were.

Marcus held true to his promise and began the tale from
the moment Raquelle forced him into immortality. But
from there, the narrative took on so many new details,
Gabriela finally discarded the hope of matching any par-
allels to the account he'd first shared with her in their
Drury apartment.

This time, she heard of the horror—the true, tormenting extent of it. He told her of the sickness—the actual
chemical shock of suddenly finding one's body prey to a
hunger so vile it churned the stomach, yet so consuming
dream landscapes turned one color: blood red.

But she also heard of the hope.

Oh, yes. The hope. That fleeting, flippant comment
from Raquelle on that first harrowing night, tossed like
no more than a rotted bone to a begging mongrel, but

which, in Marcus's desperate grasp, became a nugget more precious than gold, a purpose higher than a priestly calling, and his obsession for the first half century of his vampiric existence.

"And . . . what did you find out?" Gabriela interjected, not able to dilute the amazed urgency from her own voice. "A cure . . . she said there was a cure, but nothing more? Not a hint of where to start? An idea of what to do?"

The path ended at a wide, flat boulder which overlooked the Channel on a sweeping, sunswept vista. Marcus guided her to the ledge and waited until they both sat to issue his answer—a response he'd clearly pondered before.

"Nay," he stated. "She gave me nothing more than that. *But,*" he swiftly justified to Gabriela's darkening glower, "I should nay have expected such. Remember, vampirism *was* Raquelle's cure. She sought no other remedy for her unhappiness, nor did she care to. So how could I expect her to be my expert tome on the subject of a solution?"

He concluded the deliberation with a short shrug, again the all-believing, ever-understanding Elizabethan lad—again, swelling Gabriela's heart until her love overflowed into a wonder-filled smile.

"So what happened when *you* went exploring?" she gently asked.

As she expected, a shadow befell his features at that. "Well," he returned on a heavy sigh, "very obviously, absolutely nothing. Oh, I had a rather grand tour of the earth without having to hurry about it . . . but after almost fifty years, I stood atop a mountain in the Himalayas and decided I had cursed heaven for the last time. I returned to England the next week, settled into the catacombs under Drury and prepared myself to be perfectly, but peacefully miserable for the rest of eternity."

At that, he slanted one potent eye of a look at her. "Until I accidentally stumbled over the greenroom while you rehearsed one eve, and in the space of a heartbeat, saw my plans muddled to all hell."

Gabriela returned his good-natured grumble with a saucy slant of her own brows—and a short, but sensual kiss. She used the gesture to press a hand to his cheek, directing his gaze into hers as she queried, "Why didn't you tell me all this before? Why didn't you share it when you first told me this story?"

She watched the cast of his features as he contemplated a number of assuredly sardonic comebacks involving her traipsing about the world on her own vampire-curing quest. Readily, Gaby admitted any of the explanations would have been true.

Still, not a trace of sarcasm entered the final murmur of his reply. "I didn't tell you because I had ceased believing in a cure myself," Marcus confessed. "I had finally discarded the concept as the capping triumph of Raquelle's little 'prank' upon me." A bemused, throat-deep laugh escaped him. "Even after the night I first told you the whole story . . . even after all the magic we shared after . . . I nay fathomed the impossible 'cure' lay right next to me."

Gabriela's forehead pursed. "What do you mean?"

"What I mean"—he pulled her closer and pressed a quick kiss to the crease over her left eye—"is love. *You* were my cure, sweetheart. I had to love another so much that I would face a sunrise for them, hand over my life to them." His chin, resting against the top of her head, turned back toward the sun as he took in a chest-consuming inhalation. "My God," he uttered. "It all sounds so unfathomable."

Gabriela smiled against his chest. "No, it doesn't."

Another husky chuckle. "Aye, my heart, you are right. It does not." He curled a finger under her chin, lifting her lips for another lingering, longing kiss. "And," he whispered as he continued ministering to her mouth i tiny, tingling circles, "I think I shall start thanking you for that right now . . ."

At that, he began a trail of tickling nibbles over her jaw, down her throat . . . down the bodice of her hastily donned walking gown. "Ah . . . we have a train to catch, Mr. Danewell," she managed, only to cut herself short with a gasping giggle as his questing tongue slid beneath fabric and across her expectant flesh. "R-remember?" she prompted. "The tour begins in one week . . . Paris . . ."

"God's bloody bodkin," Marcus grumbled, dragging himself back. "I remember."

Gabriela only laughed again, softly, and cradled his face again, tenderly. His jaw, now liberally tanned by three days' worth of mornings along the cliffs and afternoons on the beach, countered an arousing beard stubble to her lingering caress.

"You have the rest of your life to thank me," she reminded him in a gentle murmur. "The rest of *our* life to love me."

And at that, he gave her a blinding smile . . . a long, deep, consuming kiss. "Ahhh, Gabriela," he ruminated when they'd pulled apart—much, *much* later, "now I wish I *did* have eternity at my disposal."

Dear Friend,

My thanks to you for letting me share Marcus and Gabriela's story with you. This book came from the deepest part of my soul, and still haunts me with magical memories of its creation.

This was the first book I wrote in which the hero was born in my imagination first. Marcus began as but a dream when I first got hooked on vampire romances myself, yet was given full life nearly three months later, when I saw Andrew Lloyd Webber's *Phantom of the Opera* for the first time. There, in the candelabra glow of an ornate Victorian theater, I knew Marcus's story would be set. His mate would be a beauty much like the Phantom's Christine, only *this* time, the story would have a happy ending!

I plunged into this project as I had no other. Delighting in the research as much as the story, I surrounded myself—and ergo, these two characters—in all the romance, grandeur, color and drama of the Victorian theater world. From the gleam of the footlights to the tassels on the curtains to the lavish costumes and lush music, no wonder Marcus and Gaby had no trouble falling so passionately in love. They "gave" me their story to write, and for that, I am eternally grateful (pardon the pun).

I am currently exploring the idea of writing Donna's story, as well. And for *her* mate? Why, a 400-year-old *virgin* vampire, of course! I'd love to hear your comments or suggestions . . . please feel free to write me at:

P.O. Box 10059, #338
Newport Beach, CA 92658

Looking forward to hearing from you! Until then, I wish you all the magic and splendor of the night . . .

Annee Cartier